HELIODORUS

An Ethiopian Romance

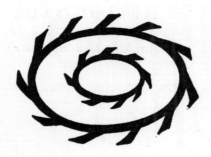

THE UNIVERSITY OF MICHIGAN PRESS — ANN ARBOR

An Ethiopian Romance

HELIO-
DORUS

TRANSLATED WITH AN INTRODUCTION

BY *Moses Hadas*

888.9
A36e

Introduction

THE GREEK NOVEL has been swallowed by its progeny. Its influence upon posterity may have been as great, in a lesser key, as that of the towering giants of classical literature, but whereas Greek tragedy and philosophy have themselves survived as permanently valid treasures in the world's store of wisdom and beauty, the novel has been supplanted rather than supplemented and has become an object of antiquarian curiosity rather than an item of normal literary consumption. Paradoxically, it is the very modernity of the Greek novel which has caused its neglect. In epic and drama the peculiar form and atmosphere of the ancient books assure them special consideration. But to moderns the novel is the most familiar of all literary forms, and the ancient examples are enough like their successors to be judged by the same gauge. The stunning beginning of the *Ethiopica*, for example, is as effective as any modern could make it, and interest in the adventures of hero and heroine is maintained until the equally stunning end; but, except for the common aim of providing literary entertainment, which the *Ethiopica*'s plot illustrates, the gauge is unfair because the design of ancient and modern novels is not the same.

The thing that distinguishes the Greek novel is the thing that distinguishes all Greek literature—a devotion to strict form which makes no concession to realism or naturalism and seeks to create no illusion. No real dialogue has ever been conducted by exchanges of single iambic lines, and no group of fifteen elders ever expressed its spontaneous emotions in elaborate songs rendered in unison. Men as different as Aeschylus, Sophocles, and Euripides follow a virtually identical form, as all Doric temples conform to a single artistic pattern; the artist's contribution is in subtle refinements of detail.

The genre of Greek literature which comes nearest to modern notions of realism is the mime. In the Alexandrian age writers of mimes were significantly called "biologists," or students of life, and the conversations between commonplace types in the mimes of Herondas do provide revealing insights into the bourgeois life of the time. But even Herondas feels constrained to use a "literary" meter and archaic words. Greek critics from Plato on use "imitation" in a particular sense: it is artistic creation in a special idiom, not reflection of reality. The Greek novelist, a conscious artist in words, fills his conventional frame with a repertoire of rhetorical embellishments—psychological soliloquies, tirades against the paradoxes of fortune, formal descriptions of works of art or zoological specimens, learned digressions on religion or science—whose only relevance to his story is to vary its color or artfully retard its progress.

For the modern reader such embellishments may be only a distraction, but the principle which dictated their inclusion is of paramount importance: the concept of the novel as a conscious art form. This is the most important legacy of the ancient romances, from which the Elizabethans learned many things—melodramatic plots, for example, which may easily be identified in such dramas as *King Lear* or *The Winter's Tale,* and the artificial view of morality which we shall glance at presently. But their most effective and enduring contribution, partly through the French romance of the seventeenth century and partly through Sidney's *Arcadia,* is the gift of complex and sustained form. In construction and in a hundred details Sidney patently follows Heliodorus, and the *Arcadia* was the principal model for Sidney's successors.

More pervasive if less tangible than the legacy of form is the influence of an artificial set of moral premises, which has long governed modern fiction and still survives in conventional moving pictures. Vice is never made attractive and virtue is always rewarded. Hero and heroine are superlatively gallant and beautiful and virtuous. Their chastity is never lost sight of; incessant but futile assaults upon it only make it the more conspicuous. The lesser characters are not so immaculate a white or undiluted a crimson, but then most of the reader's attention and all his sympathy are pre-empted by hero and heroine. The characters of Cnemon and Thisbe in the subplot of the *Ethiopica* show what Theagenes and Charicleia might be if they were not so sublimely noble and impregnably virtuous. These characters are not types to be apprehended intellectually, like the persons of an Attic drama; they demand emotional identification of the reader, who is to agonize over their perils and exult in the sudden improvement of their fortune. Always the tendency is toward the melodramatic. These moral premises had no more actual validity in the Hellenistic world than they have today, and it is not too remote to suppose that one set of artificialities indirectly influenced the other. Other suggestive affinities with moving pictures —rapidly shifting scenes and interest in the spectacular, such as shipwrecks or intimate glimpses of royalty—may be a natural development in the new medium.

But in the Greek novel the implausibilities are not due wholly to the artistic exigencies of form: they reflect an

actual view of life. Our own serious novels, like Attic
tragedy, seek to establish or illustrate universal laws of
humanity or to propose new social attitudes. In the Hellenistic world the links of causality seemed to have been
broken and man abandoned to the caprices of fortune.
When events are no longer calculable interest in them
comes to lie in their very uncertainty. And if events in
the outer world follow no discernible pattern, in the moral
world choices are undeliberated, even unmotivated. With
no vital interaction between the outer and inner worlds,
there is no necessary connection between character and
event. Emotion is reduced to sentimentality, which is fin-
gered, probed, savored, for its own sake. In this view of
life the triumph of virtue, with which the Greek authors
regularly conclude their novels, takes on the significance of
a moral preachment. Though common experience of the
world shows moral anarchy, there *are* divinities who shape
the ends of their special charges.

In view of the classical Greek concept of the poet as
teacher it would be odd if even so late-blown a form as
the novel did not have some doctrine to communicate. In
origin at least, it seems clear that the novel, too, was utili-
tarian. The form was developed by descendants of proud
peoples on the periphery of the Greek world whom the conquests of Alexander the Great had reduced to helotry. To
promote at least the cultural survival of their people, As-
syrians, Egyptians, Phrygians, Babylonians, and Jews wrote
fanciful tales involving their legendary heroes and usually
including a love story. Most of these are known only from
citations, but of the *Ninus Romance,* which dealt with the
legendary founder of Babylonia, considerable portions have
been discovered in the present century. This contains glorification of ancient tradition but also makes much of sexual
love, and so marks a neat transition to the completely ex-
tant Greek novels, in which the "historical" element recedes

from one specimen to the next while the erotic element becomes central.

Even in the late novels the motive of cultural survival does persist, and not least in the *Ethiopica*, though Heliodorus' artistry conceals his "message." In effect the book is a glorification of a dark-skinned race and an obscure sect. It is easy to believe that the author was a colored man; it is clear that he was attached to the gymnosophist cult. The gymnosophist priest Calasiris is a consistent model of sagacity and saintly benevolence. Gymnosophists are always represented in favorable postures, and in the end their faith is brilliantly vindicated and they introduce a significant moral reform. The Ethiopian king is a model of wisdom and righteousness, and his people are highly cultivated. The author's concern for these matters goes far beyond romantic requirements, and the episode at Delphi takes on special significance in this connection. Here Calasiris is accepted on terms of equality by the dignitaries of the cult of Delphi, and a descendant of Achilles himself falls in love with an Ethiopian girl who is shown to be fully his social equal. Recognition in the most ancient and highly regarded sanctuary of Greece is a sufficient victory; minorities wish only equality, not superiority. There is a close parallel in *Aristeas to Philocrates* (which gives the legend of the translation of the Septuagint), where the seventy-two Jewish sages are respectfully entertained by Ptolemy Philadelphus. To demonstrate the equality implied in recognition by that wise and famous monarch—so different from the attitude of rulers in the author's own day—is one of the main objects of the book.

Of Heliodorus himself we know nothing. In his concluding sentence he tells us that he was descended from the Sun; that and the tone of the whole work should be sufficient proof that he was not a Christian. Socrates' *Ecclesiastical History*, however, says (5.2) that both Heliodorus

and Achilles Tatius, author of *Leucippe and Clitophon,*
were bishops. It is not unlikely that the episcopal title was
attached to their names in order to make their books re-
spectable reading for Byzantine monks, who were exceedingly fond of novels and had many more to read than the
few which have survived. There is nothing to establish
Heliodorus' date, but probability points to the second or
third century A.D. The fictive date of the story is the fifth
century B.C.

The *Ethiopica* was translated into French by Amyot (the
brilliant translator of Plutarch and of *Daphnis and Chloe*)
in 1547, and into Latin by the Polish humanist Warsche-
wiczki in 1551. The Latin version rather than the Greek
original was the basis for Thomas Underdowne's widely
read and frequently printed English translation, which was
first published in 1587. Underdowne is picturesque, but
his understanding of even the Latin is frequently faulty.
The only modern English version is that of the Reverend
Rowland Smith (1855), which has all of Underdowne's
failings and few of his merits. Because there is no faithful
version in English the present translator has resolutely resisted temptation to take liberties with the Greek—especially by way of compression—for the sake of the English.
Contemporary taste runs to what the ancients would call
Attic rather than Asiatic style, and the elaborate formalism
of Heliodorus' Asianism is likely to seem precious. But to
eliminate the fullness is to betray Heliodorus, and the translator can only hope that the reader will not dismiss spacious-
ness as verbosity.

1

DAY HAD BEGUN TO SMILE and the sun was shining upon the hilltops when a band of armed pirates scaled the mountain which extends to the mouth of the Nile called the Heracleot, where it empties into the sea. They halted for a little to survey the waters which stretched before them. Out at sea, where they first directed their attention, not a sail was stirring to whet the pirates' appetite for plunder; but when they turned to look at the coastline nearby their eyes encountered a strange spectacle.

A merchant ship lay moored by its hawsers, bare of crew but heavily loaded, as was easy to conjecture, for its weight pressed the ship down until the water reached its third loading line. The beach was strewn with fresh carnage; some of the victims were dead, of others the limbs were still quivering; obviously the battle had been recent. But it was not simply of a battle that the scene gave evidence, for intermingled with the carnage were the wretched remains of a feast whose conclusion had been so fatal. Tables were still loaded with victuals; some of the tables had been seized by the combatants as weapons against a surprise attack and lay overturned; others men had crouched under in vain hope of finding shelter. Overturned goblets slipped from hands that held them, some to drink from, others to hurl in place of stones. The suddenness of the mischief had improvised this novel use and taught men to make missiles of their cups. Here lay a man cloven by an ax; there one struck by a sea shell from the beach; another was crushed by a beam; another scorched by a brand. Diverse as were their wounds, the greater number had been inflicted by darts and arrows. On this single small spot fate exhibited a spectacle compacted of a myriad of forms; wine was imbrued with blood, war conjoined with banqueting, drinks were intermingled with death, toasts with slaughter. It was this spectacle that met the eyes of the pirates; and as if it were a contrived scene they stood and gazed upon it, puzzled to divine its meaning. There lay the vanquished, but victors were nowhere to be seen; an indubitable victory, but the spoils lay unplundered; a ship denuded of men, but otherwise untouched, as if secured by a numerous guard and peacefully riding at anchor. Though baffled by the situation, the pirates still had regard for gain and, appointing themselves victors, proceeded to their booty.

They had advanced to within a short distance of the ship and the slaughter when they were struck by a spectacle more puzzling than the first. Upon a rock sat a maiden of such inexpressible beauty as to be supposed divine. Grieved by her surroundings, she yet breathed an air of noble courage. Her head was crowned with laurel, a quiver hung at her shoulder, to her left arm a bow was attached, and the other hung negligently down. She rested her left elbow on her right knee, her cheek leaning against her open hand. Her head inclined forward without moving, for she was looking fixedly at a young man who lay at her feet. The young man was disfigured with wounds, but seemed to rouse himself a little as from a deep sleep, almost of death itself. Even so he showed the bloom of manly beauty, and the flowing blood made his white cheek shine the more brilliant. Pain had clenched his eyes, but the sight of the maiden drew them toward her; they must needs see because they saw her. He collected his breath, heaved a deep sigh, and murmured faintly. "My sweet," said he, "are you truly safe, or are you too a casualty of the war? Could you not endure separation from me even in death and does your ghostly phantom hover over my fortunes?" "My preservation or the reverse," said the girl, "depends upon you. This (pointing to a dagger on her knee) has not penetrated only because your breathing has restrained it."

When she had said this she sprang from the rock. The pirates on the hill were struck with surprise and wonder as by a lightning bolt, and severally rushed for cover in the bushes. Taller and more divine did she seem to them when she rose upright; the shafts in her quiver clashed together with her motion, her gold-wrought garments glittered in the sun, and her hair, waving like a bacchant's under her tiara, flowed down over her back. These things terrified the pirates, who were more affected by what they saw because they were ignorant of what had gone before. Some declared she was a goddess, either Artemis or the native Isis; others held she was a priestess whose divine frenzy had worked the carnage they saw. Such were the opinions they ventured; the facts they did not know.

She now flew to the young man, enveloped him in her embrace, wept, kissed him, wiped off the blood, sighed deeply, could not believe she held him. At this conduct the Egyptians' impressions altered. "Is this the behavior of a goddess?" they said. "Would a deity kiss a corpse so passionately?" They encouraged one another and advanced closer to find out the truth, and then, recovering their spirits, they ran down and came up to the girl as she was busying herself with the young man's wounds. When they came up behind her they halted, not daring to say or do anything. At the noise that sounded around her and the shadows that fell across her eyes, the girl looked up, and when she had seen them, she leaned to her work again, no whit dismayed by their strange complexion and piratical bearing, but intent only on tending the wounded man. To such a degree do ardent affection and sincere love disregard all externals, painful or agreeable, and force the lover to look only at the beloved and upon him bestow all attention.

But when the robbers moved to face her and seemed on the point of aggression, the girl again looked up and observed their dusky color and savage aspect. "If you are the phantoms of the slain," said she, "you have no right to trouble me. Most of you were killed by your fellows' hands; those that fell by mine I killed in self-defense and in repelling outrage to my chastity. But if you are living men, you must be robbers, and your coming is opportune: release me from the sorrows that enmesh me, ring the curtain of death over the tragedy of my life." So she spoke in theatrical strain, but they could understand nothing of her meaning. Her and her companion they left, considering their helplessness a sufficient guard, and themselves made for the ship and unloaded its freight. Of the abundant and varied goods they neglected objects of lesser value but brought out as much gold, silver, precious stones, and silk as they could carry. When they thought they had enough —and the quantity satiated even a pirate's greed—they placed their plunder on the shore and divided it into portions; distribution was not made according to the value of the goods but by weight. The question of the girl and the young man they would settle afterward.

In the meanwhile another robber band appeared, with two horsemen in command. At sight of the newcomers the former robbers fled without raising a hand; to obviate pursuit, they ran off without taking any of the plunder. They were but ten, and observed that the newcomers were thrice their number. The girl and her companion, not yet actually captured, were now for the second time on the point of being taken. Though the robbers were eager for their prey, they were a little checked by amazement at what they saw and by ignorance of the circumstances. The fallen, they conjectured, had been slain by the former robbers, but when they saw the girl, strangely dressed in a magnificent robe, oblivious of the terrors which surrounded her, intent only upon the wounds of the young man, and affected by his pain as if it were her own, they admired her noble spirit no less than her beauty. They were astonished too at the wounded young man. His form and stature were impressive, as he lay outstretched, and now that he was gradually recovering, his countenance resumed its customary aspect.

After long hesitation the brigand chief approached, laid his hand upon the girl, and ordered her to arise and follow him. She did not understand his words, but she comprehended his meaning, so she drew Theagenes along with her (nor did he let her go) and, pointing a dagger at her bosom, threatened to slay herself unless they were carried off together. Her gesture even more than her words made her meaning clear to the brigand, who thought the young man would make a fine comrade for his most ambitious projects if he could be saved. He and his lieutenant therefore dismounted and placed the captives upon the horses; the others he ordered to pack the plunder and follow, while he himself ran beside the horses on foot and lent a hand if the rider seemed to be slipping. His conduct was not without nobility: the commander seemed to be the slave, the captor choosing to minister to the captives. Such is the power of native dignity and manifest beauty to subdue a piratical nature and to govern savage hearts.

For about two furlongs they proceeded along the shore, then turned directly toward the mountains, keeping the sea on their right. When they had, with some difficulty, crossed the heights, they came to a marsh which extended along the other side of the mountain. The nature of the region was as follows. The whole tract, called by the Egyptians The Pasturage, is a sunken valley in which an influx from the overflow of the Nile forms a lake. The middle of this lake is of unfathomable depth; around the edges it shoals into a marsh. What shores are to the sea, marshes are to lakes. Here the brigands of Egypt maintain their existence. One lives on a bit of land that rises above the water, where he builds a hut; another spends his life aboard his boat, which serves at once as transportation and living quarters. On the boat the women work their wool and bear their babies. After the babies are weaned from their mother's milk they are fed on fish from the lake which are roasted in the sun. When the baby shows signs of creeping, they tie a thong to his ankle which permits him to go the length of the boat or of the hut. The string on his ankle is a novel kind of tutor. The Pasturage folk (or buccaneers) are born on the lake, feed from it, and consider it a sufficient fatherland, for it affords a safe stronghold for brigandage. For that reason men who follow such a life stream into it; water serves as their wall, and the rank reeds as their entrenchment. Through these they cut oblique channels with many windings, making the ways easy for those who know them but impassable for others. This great safeguard they contrived to thwart any invasion.

Here, about sunset, the brigand chief and his party arrived. The young people they made dismount, and the plunder they placed in boats. A large crowd of robbers who had remained at home appeared, one dodging out of one part of the marsh and another out of another, and ran up to meet and greet the chief, receiving him as if he were royalty. When they saw the wealth of plunder and observed that the appearance of the girl possessed a certain holy beauty, they supposed that their fellow craftsmen had plundered some temple or rich shrine and had abducted the priestess or carried off the breathing image of the deity, believing, in their simple credulity, that the maiden was such. They heaped praises upon the chief for his prowess and escorted him to his own dwelling. This was a little island apart from the rest, appointed as the lodging for the chief and a few attendants. When he arrived there he dismissed the others, enjoining them all to come to him the next day. Left alone with his few companions he partook of a short repast with them. The two prisoners he delivered to a young Greek who had been made captive a short time before; because he served as interpreter, the chief had assigned him a hut near his own. He ordered him to show the young man every care and to protect the girl from all insult. He himself was fatigued by the exertions of his journey and distracted by thoughts on his present situation, and so retired to sleep.

When the marsh was wrapped in silence and the night had advanced to the first watch, the girl took advantage of the solitude and freedom from interlopers to indulge in lamentation. It was the night, I imagine, that stirred her emotions, since there was no sight or sound to distract her, and she could give herself freely to her grief. She lay apart, as had been ordered, on a low pallet, and she moaned to herself and shed many tears. "O Apollo," she said, "how much severer are your punishments than my sins! Are not my past afflictions sufficient? Deprived of family, captured by pirates, exposed to a thousand dangers at sea, and now on land again a captive, must I await experiences yet more bitter? Where will you call halt? Death without outrage would be a sweet end; but if some man is to know me shamefully, as even Theagenes has never done, I will forestall outrage with the noose. I shall keep myself pure, as

I have kept myself pure, even to death; my chastity will ennoble my funeral. There can be no judge more severe than you, Apollo."

Even as she was speaking Theagenes restrained her, saying, "Stop, Charicleia, dear heart and soul of mine. Your plaints are plausible, but you exacerbate the deity—not reproaches but petitions are wanted. By prayers are the powers propitiated, not by expostulations." "You say well," said she, "but tell me how you are?" "Easier," said he, "and better than last evening. This young man's therapy has lightened the burning of my wounds." "It will be still more lightened in the morning," said the young man who was charged to guard them. "I will procure an herb which will close the wounds in three days. I know because I have tried it. Ever since they brought me here captive, if any of the subjects of this chief came back wounded from an engagement, a few days was enough to cure him if I used this herb. You need not wonder that I am concerned for you, for you seem to share the same lot with me, and being a Greek I naturally pity Greeks." "A Greek! Ye gods!" the newcomers delightedly cried out in unison. "Verily a Greek, in race and tongue; perhaps that may alleviate your distress." "But what shall we call you?" asked Theagenes. "Cnemon," said he. "May we know your city?" "Athens." "And what has been your fortune?" "Stop," said Cnemon. "Why do you finger and pry into that subject? It is one for tragedies, and this is no time to pile my afflictions onto an act of *your* tragedy. Besides, not enough of the night is left for my tale, and you need rest from all your hardships."

They would not let him off, but begged him by all means to speak, urging that the recital of his afflictions would be the greatest solace for their own. Cnemon then began: "My father was Aristippus, a member of the Superior Council and possessed of a moderate fortune. When my mother died he was inclined to a second marriage, fearing that an only son, myself, might be an unsure basis for his hopes. He brought home a woman who was polished but an arch-mischiefmaker; her name was Demainete. As soon as she came into the family she put my father under total sub-jection and prevailed upon him to do whatever she liked. She charmed the old man by her beauty and pretty atten-tions, for she was clever, if ever woman was, in making men mad for her and past mistress in the art of seduction. When my father stepped out she sighed, and when he re-turned she ran to meet him and reproached his tardiness and seemed ready to expire if he were a little late, and would embrace him and heap every word with tears and kisses. Entangled in these wiles, my father breathed only for her, had eyes only for her. At first she pretended to regard me as a son, playing up to my father. Sometimes she would come and kiss me, and she was always wanting to enjoy my company. At first I consented, having no suspicion of the facts, though I did wonder a little at her maternal attitude. But when her advances grew more wan-ton and her kisses hotter than proper and her glances be-yond what chastity admits, I began to be suspicious and avoided her and rebuffed her when she approached me. I need not trouble you with a tedious account of the rest—the artifices she used, the promises she made. Now she called me her darling, her sweetheart, again she named me her sole affinity, and after a bit her very soul; with these fair titles she mingled blandishments and watched how I might be most affected. In graver matters she pretended to be the mother, but she plainly revealed herself the mis-tress in her unseasonable pastimes.

"This is what finally happened. At the celebration of the Panathenaic festival when the Athenians send Athena a ship by land, I, being then a cadet, had chanted the cus-tomary paean to the goddess and had participated in the procession, and then, just as I was dressed, in festal robe and crowns, returned to my own house. As soon as she saw me she fell into a transport and could no longer dissemble her passion but ran up to me with naked desire and called me her young Hippolytus, her Theseus. How do you think I felt then when I blush to tell of it even now? In the evening my father dined at the Council House, and, it being a great festival with public banqueting, was expected to spend the night there. During the night Demainete approached me and tried to satisfy her impious desires. When I resisted by every means and fought off blandishments and promises and threats, she heaved a deep and heavy sigh and departed. But that wicked woman waited only that night before putting her machinations into play against me. First of all, she failed to rise from her bed, and when my father came home and asked the reason, she pretended to be indisposed and at first made no further answer. But when my father insisted and repeatedly asked what ailed her, she said: 'That fine young man, your son and mine, whom (the gods be my witness) I loved more than you, found by certain signs that I was pregnant; I had kept it from you until I should know for certain. He waited for you to be from home, and while I was giving him my customary admonitions and advising him to be temperate and not run after harlots and drink (I knew what his behavior was, but would not tell you, lest I be suspected of talking like a stepmother), while we were talking thus privately in order to spare him embarrassment—the outrageous things he said about you and about me I am ashamed to repeat— he did jump at me and kick me in the belly, and he put me in the state you now see.'

"When my father heard this he said nothing, asked no questions, afforded no opportunity for defense, but believed that a woman so affectionately disposed to me could never lie about me. As soon as he came upon me, who was wholly ignorant of what had passed, in a part of the house, he struck me with his fist and ordered the slaves to scourge me, without showing me the common courtesy of saying why I was beaten. When his fury was satisfied, I said, 'Now at least, father, I have a right to know the occasion of these blows.' But this only increased his anger. 'Ah, the dissembler,' said he; 'his unholy deeds he wishes to learn from me!' Then he turned about and hurried to Demainete. But she was not yet satisfied, and devised a second plot against me. She had a young maid named Thisbe, who was clever at playing the harp and not bad looking. Her she loosed against me, with orders to 'fall in love' with me. Thisbe immediately complied. Though she had frequently rebuffed overtures of mine, she now drew me on with glances, nods, and gestures. Fool that I was, I thought I had suddenly become attractive, and when she eventually came to my bed at night I received her. She came again and again, and then visited me regularly. I admonished her to be very careful that her mistress should not find out, and she said: 'Cnemon, you are very naïve indeed if you think it a serious matter for a housemaid like me, bought with money, to be caught consorting with you. What do you think should be the punishment for a woman who boasts of her good birth, has a lawful husband, knows that death is the penalty of transgression, and yet commits adultery?' 'Stop,' said I, 'I cannot believe you.' 'Yet if you like,' said she, 'I can show you the adulterer in the act.' 'If you wish,' said I. 'I do wish,' she answered, 'both on your account, who have been so abused by her, and no less on my own, for day by day I suffer the extreme of torment from her jealous temper. Be a man and act promptly.'

"I promised to do so and she departed. Two nights later she roused me from sleep and told me that the adulterer was inside. She said that my father had been called to the country on some sudden emergency and that by previous

arrangement with her the man had slipped in to Demainete.
I must prepare to vindicate myself, she said, and dash in
with sword in hand to prevent the scoundrel from escaping. And so I did. I took a dagger, and with Thisbe leading
and lighting my way with a torch, I went to my mother's
bedchamber. A beam of lamplight issued from the room
when I got there; bursting with passion I smashed the
closed doors open and dashed in, shouting, 'Where is that
blackguard, that elegant lover of this paragon of virtue?'
With these words I advanced to transfix them both, when
my father—good heavens!—rolled out of the bed, fell at
my knees, and said, 'Stop a moment, son, pity your begetter. I have mistreated you, but not so far as to deserve
death. Do not surrender so wholly to passion, do not pollute your hands with parricide.' To these he added other
pitiful prayers. I stood stock-still as if struck by lightning,
stupefied and petrified. I looked about for Thisbe, but she
had spirited herself away. I stared at the bed and looked
about the room, impotent to speak, helpless to act. The
sword fell from my hand. Demainete ran up and quickly
seized it, and my father, now free from danger, laid hands
upon me and ordered me to be tied up, while Demainete
goaded him on. 'Did I not warn you,' she cried, 'that this
young fellow needed watching, that he would seize an occasion to attack? I saw his look, I understood his designs.'
'You did warn me,' he said, 'but I could not believe it.' He
kept me tied up and when I wanted to speak gave me no
chance to explain the truth of the matter.

"In the morning he took me and brought me, bound as
I was, to the assembly, and then spread dust on his head
and said: 'Not with such hopes as this, men of Athens, did
I bring this fellow up; I thought he would be a staff for
my old age. From his birth I gave him a liberal education,
I had him taught literature, I introduced him to his fra-
ternity and clan, I enrolled him as a cadet, I established his

legal status as citizen. My whole life I centered upon him. But all of this he has forgotten. First he was insolent to me and assaulted my lawful wife. Finally, he broke in upon me at night with a drawn sword and was only prevented from committing parricide by fortune, which ordained that the sword should fall from his hand in consternation. I take recourse to you and formally arraign him before you. Though the law permits me to execute him with my own hand I do not wish to do so. I leave the whole matter in your hands because I think it better to punish my son by law than by shedding blood.' Thereupon he wept, and Demainete too wailed and pretended to be grieved for my sake. She called me an unhappy man, whose death, though untimely, would be just, for my evil genius had incited me against my parents. She did not so much grieve as use grief to condemn me; her lamentations were meant to confirm the truth of the charge. When I asked that I too be permitted to speak, the clerk came forward and put the bare question whether I had burst in on my father, sword in hand. When I said, 'I did, but hear how and why,' they all shouted their judgment that I must not be allowed to make a defense. Some thought I should be stoned, others maintained I should be delivered to the public executioner to be flung into the pit. In all the tumult, while they were voting on my punishment, I kept crying, 'Ah, a stepmother! Because of a stepmother am I being killed! It is a stepmother who is destroying me without judgment!' Many in the assembly noticed those cries and conceived a suspicion of the truth. But not even then could I obtain a hearing, for the people were distracted by the incessant din.

"When the ballots were counted those condemning me to death amounted to seventeen hundred, some favoring stoning, others flinging into the pit. The remainder, a thousand in number, allowing for suspicion of the stepmother, would make the penalty perpetual banishment.

The latter prevailed, for though they were in the minority, the majority was divided, so the thousand became the largest party. And so I was driven from my ancestral hearth and my native land. But the execrable Demainete did not get off with impunity. The manner of her punishment you will hear another time; the present is a time for sleep, for the night is far advanced and you have great need of rest." "No," said Theagenes, "you will wear us down even more if your story leaves that wicked Demainete unpunished."

"Well then," said Cnemon, "if you will have it so, listen. After the trial I went down to the Piraeus, and finding a ship about to sail, I made the voyage to Aegina, for I had heard that I had cousins there on my mother's side. When I landed I found the people I sought, and my first days with them were quite agreeable. On the twentieth day, in the course of my usual walk I went down to the harbor. A felucca was standing in, and I waited a little to see whence she came and whom she carried. The gangplank was not yet well down when a passenger leapt ashore, ran up to me, and embraced me. It was my classmate Charias, and he said, 'Cnemon, I bring you good tidings! You are revenged on your enemy: Demainete is dead.' 'Bless you, Charias,' said I, 'but why do you skimp your news as if it was disagreeable? Tell me how she died. I am terribly afraid her death was the ordinary kind, and that she escaped the end she deserved.' 'Justice has not altogether forsaken earth, as Hesiod says, and though she sometimes winks at crime and defers its punishment, she yet looks upon the impious with a severe eye—and that is what has happened to wicked Demainete. I know all that was done and said, for Thisbe, with whom, as you know, I am on intimate terms, told me the whole story.'

" 'When that unjust sentence drove you to exile, your poor father repented of what he had done and retired to a

remote farm, "eating his heart out," as Homer says. But
her the Furies lashed, and she was even more madly in
love with you in your absence. She never ceased lamenting, ostensibly for you but actually for herself. Night and
day she would cry out "Cnemon," or "sweetest boy," and
she called you her own soul. The women who paid her
friendly visits were surprised at a stepmother showing such
strong maternal affection, and they tried to console and
encourage her. But she said that her trouble was beyond
consolation and that they could not know what a sting
rankled at her heart.'

" 'Whenever she collected herself she would find much
fault with Thisbe for serving her need so ill. "Prompt was
she in terrible measures," she would say, "but my love she
did not assist. To deprive me of my darling she proved
quicker than speech, and she gave me no time to change
my mind." It was obvious that she was planning some mischief against Thisbe. When Thisbe saw her furious temper,
her complete distraction, her readiness for mischief, and
most of all her paroxysms of hate and love, she determined
to forestall her and to procure her own safety by ensnaring
her mistress. She approached her then and said, "Why, mistress, do you unfairly hold your servant to blame? I have
always obeyed your wishes, and do so now. If my plan has
miscarried, we must charge the loss to fortune. Now I am
ready, if you so bid me, to devise a remedy for the present
situation." "My dear," said Demainete, "what remedy can
be found? He who could relieve me is now far away; the
unexpected charity of the jury has ruined me. If he had
been stoned to death, if he were killed, my agony would
have died with him. When its gratification is hopeless a
passion is extinguished; despair makes the afflicted callous.
But now I imagine that I see him, and I am ashamed when
he reproaches me for the unjust plot I hatched against him.
Sometimes I suppose that he will return and I will enjoy

him, sometimes that I myself will go to him, wherever he may be. Such thoughts set me afire, such thoughts drive me mad. But my sufferings, heavens above, are just. Why, instead of talking him over, did I plot against him? Why, instead of supplicating him, did I persecute him? He rejected my overtures. But that was natural; he was ashamed to visit a strange bed, and particularly his father's. Perhaps he might have been molded by time and persuasion and have yielded. But I was savage and cruel, not a mistress but a tyrant, and I considered his disobedience and his disdain of Demainete an enormity—when his beauty so far surpassed hers. But, sweet Thisbe, what is this remedy you call easy?" "Mistress," said Thisbe, "for most people Cnemon has left the city and Attica in obedience to the sentence, but I have discovered (I spare no diligence in your interest) that he is lurking in a spot outside the city. You must have heard of Arsinoe the flute girl; he is intimate with her. After his misfortune the girl received him and promised to travel abroad with him; she is keeping him in hiding at her house until she is ready to go." "Happy Arsinoe," said Demainete, "first for having Cnemon her lover, and now for the foreign sojourn she plans with him! But how can this affect me?" "Greatly, mistress," said Thisbe. "I shall pretend to be in love with Cnemon and shall ask Arsinoe, who is an old professional acquaintance of mine, to allow me to take her place with him one night. If this succeeds, it will be your part to play Arsinoe and to come to his bed in her place. I shall see to it that he is a little drunk when he goes to bed. If you obtain your desire it is quite likely that your love will be assuaged, for passion is frequently extinguished by its first gratification. Love is satisfied by the consummation of the act. But if your passion persists, as we hope it may not, we shall try another tack, as the saying goes, and other plans. Meanwhile let us take care of the present." '

" 'Demainete approved the suggestion and begged her to put it into execution at once. Thisbe asked her mistress for a day to arrange her plan properly, and then went to Arsinoe. "You know Teledemus?" she asked, and when Arsinoe said she did, she continued, "Take us into your house. I have promised to sleep with him. He will come first, and I will join him when I have put my mistress to bed." Then she hurried out to Aristippus in the country and said to him: "Master, I have come to accuse myself; use me as you will. I am partly responsible for your loss of your son. I did not wish to injure him, but was an accomplice. When I perceived that my mistress led a dissolute life and was outraging your bed, I was afraid that some harm might come to me if the thing should be discovered by anyone else, and moreover I was distressed by the sorry requital of your affection by your wife. I hesitated to communicate with you but told my young master. So that none might know, I came to him by night and told him that an adulterer was sleeping with my mistress. As you know, Cnemon had previously been aggrieved by her. He thought I said the adulterer was in her room *then;* filled with ungovernable fury, he seized a dagger and rushed madly to her bedroom. I tried hard to hold him back and said that nothing of the kind was going on at that moment, but he paid little attention or thought I had changed my mind. The rest you know. If you wish, there is now an opportunity for you to clear the character of your son, though he is himself in exile, and to punish the woman who has wronged you both. Today I will show you Demainete lying with her paramour, and at that in another's house, outside the city." "If you show me that," said Aristippus, "you shall be rewarded with your freedom, and I may be able to live again when I have avenged myself on my enemy. For a long time I have been tormented by suspicions of the truth, but I kept my peace because I had no proof. But what must I do now?" "You know the garden where the Epicureans' monument stands?" said she. "Go there and wait till evening."

" 'So saying she hurried off and came to Demainete. "Prink yourself out," she said. "You ought to go dressed in all your finery. All that I promised is ready." Demainete embraced her and did as she was bidden, and when evening came Thisbe took her to the place of assignation. When they were near it, Thisbe asked her to wait a moment, and hurried ahead to ask Arsinoe to retire to another apartment and give her full privacy. Her young man, she said, was but newly initiated into the mysteries of Aphrodite, and still shy. Arsinoe obliged, and Thisbe went back to pick Demainete up, brought her in, put her to bed, and took the lamp away on the pretext that you (who were in Aegina all the while) should not recognize her. She told her to gratify her desire in silence, and added, "I am now going to bring the young man. He is drinking with some neighbors." Thisbe went out, found Aristippus at the place agreed, and urged him to go and tie the adulterer up. He followed her, and when they reached the house he burst in, found the bed with some difficulty because of the scant moonlight, and said, "I've got you, execrable creature." As soon as he said this Thisbe banged on the doors as hard as she could and shouted, "Too bad! The adulterer has got away from us. But take care, master, not to make another mistake." "Courage," said he, "I have the vile creature I most wanted to take." He seized her then, and dragged her towards the city. She, as was natural, brooded over her situation—the disappointment of her expectations, the disgrace of her condition, the punishment the laws would inflict. She was vexed at being caught and angry at being deceived. And so when they came to the pit in the Academy—you know the place where the generals offer the customary sacrifices to our heroes—she suddenly wrenched herself loose

from the old man's hands and flung herself down head
first. A wretched death the wretched woman died. Aristippus remarked that she had only anticipated the punishment
which the law would exact. On the next day he communicated the whole matter to the people and could barely obtain forgiveness. Then he canvassed friends and relatives
to arrange some legal device for procuring your recall.
Whether they have succeeded I cannot say, for I hurried
here, as you see, on some private business of my own. But
I think you have ground to expect that the assembly will
consent to your recall and that your father will come to
find you; that is what he promised.'

"Such were Charias' tidings to me. What follows, how
I came here, what my fortunes have been, would require
a longer tale and longer time." At this Cnemon burst into
tears, and the newcomers wept also, seemingly for his afflictions but actually each for the memory of his own. Nor, in
the luxury of their grief, would they have given over their
lamentations had not sleep put an end to their tears. And so
they slept.

Thyamis, for such was the robber chief's name, had enjoyed tranquil sleep most of the night but afterward was
disturbed by incoherent dreams. Being at a loss for their
solution he shook sleep off and his perplexity kept him
awake. At the time the cocks crow—whether natural in-
tuition apprises them of the return of the sun and moves
them, as they say, to salute him as a deity, or whether because of heat and the quickened appetite for movement and
food they arouse the household to their labors with their
clarion call—at that time Thyamis was visited by a supernatural vision. He seemed to be in Memphis, his own city.
He entered the temple of Isis, which was all illuminated
with torches. The altars and hearths were filled and overflowing with the blood of many sorts of animals. The entry
hall and colonnades were filled with people and resounded

with mingled and confused noises. When he came into the
inner sanctuary, the goddess came to meet him, placed
Charicleia in his hands, and said: "Thyamis, I deliver this
maiden to you. You shall have her but not have her. You
shall be cruel and kill this foreign girl, but she shall not be
killed." This vision left him baffled, though he turned it
over in his mind this way and that to find its meaning.
Finally, he desisted and conformed an interpretation to his
own wishes: "You shall have her but not have her"—as a
wife, not as a maiden; "kill"—her maidenhead, by which
killing Charicleia would not die. So he interpreted the
dream, his desires governing his exegesis.

When day broke he ordered his principal followers to
come and bade them bring forward the spoils of war—
giving a more dignified title to the plunder. He summoned
Cnemon and enjoined him to bring his charges also. As
they were being brought they cried, "What fortune awaits
us?" and implored Cnemon to help them if he could. He
promised, and urged them to take heart. He assured them
that the chief was not altogether barbarous in character,
that there was gentleness in his disposition, that he belonged
to a distinguished family and had embraced his present way
of life under duress. When they were brought forward
and the others were gathered in a crowd, Thyamis took a
seat upon an eminence and declared that the island was
now in meeting assembled. He instructed Cnemon to trans-
late his remarks to the captives, for Cnemon had learned
Egyptian, whereas Thyamis had little Greek. "Fellow soldiers," he said, "you know what my sentiments have always been toward you. As you know, I am son of the high
priest in Memphis. After my father retired I failed to obtain the priesthood, for my brother seized it. I took refuge
with you so that I might revenge the injury and recover
my office. You have yourselves deemed me worthy to be
your leader, and until this day I have lived with you with-

out arrogating special privileges to myself. If there was a
distribution of money, I was content with an equal share;
if captives were sold I deposited their price in the common
coffer. I have always thought it the part of a good leader
to take the largest share of toil but only an equal share of
profits. As for the prisoners we took, men whose physical
vigor was likely to make them serviceable I enrolled in your
number, and the weaker I sold. Women I never outraged.
Those of good birth I released for ransom or simply because I pitied their lot. Those of inferior position, whom
not captivity but their own condition made slaves, I distributed to you as servants. But in the present case I do
ask of you one part of the booty—the foreign girl here.
Though it is possible for me to assign her to myself, I think
it better to receive her by common consent: to take the girl
perforce, to appear to act contrary to the desires of one's
friends, is folly. Even so I do not ask her of you as a gra-
tuitous favor; in recompense I shall resign all share in the
remaining spoils. Since the priestly race contemns Aphrodite the Earthy, it is not for the satisfaction of pleasure
that I intend to make this woman mine but to propagate
my seed.

"My reasons for this choice I wish to set before you. In
the first place I think her nobly born. I base my conviction on the wealth that was found about her and the fact
that she was not crushed by misfortune but from the beginning bore adversity with high spirit. Next, I conjecture
that she possesses a good and chaste character. If she sur-
passes all womankind in beauty and yet by the modesty of
her glance awes all beholders into respect, how can she not
establish a high opinion of herself? But the most effective
of my arguments is that she appears to be a priestess of
some god. Even in her misfortune she deems it a grave impiety to lay aside her sacred robe and fillets. What marriage
could be more suitable, my comrades, than for a priest to

cover the dignity of the high priesthood. So our marriage would be celebrated with better cheer, being associated with victory, and consummated under the general auspices of success and satisfaction. But I leave the matter in your decision if you think it should be done sooner. Only let my ancestral rites be performed first. I know that you will consent, for, as you say, you have been devoted to sacred matters since childhood and have pious and holy regard for what concerns the gods."

When she finished her speech she began to weep. All present approved her request, urged that it be carried out, and shouted their readiness to help. Thyamis also consented, willingly in part but unwillingly too, for his desire for Charicleia made him think even the present hour an infinitely long postponement. But he was enchanted by her speech as by a siren song, and was constrained to heed her. Furthermore, he saw his dream as an allusion to the marriage, and was convinced it would be celebrated in Memphis. Then he dismissed the assembly, having first made a distribution of the spoils, himself receiving many choice objects which the men pressed upon him of their own accord.

Thyamis ordered his men to make ready for a march to Memphis in ten days. To the Greeks he assigned the same tent they had had. Cnemon too had orders to bivouac with them, no longer as a guard, however, but now appointed to be their companion. Thyamis provided better diet than he himself enjoyed, and out of consideration for Theagenes' sister assigned him the same fare. Thyamis resolved to see Charicleia seldom, so that his burning desire for her should not be inflamed and compel him to do something contrary to what they had agreed upon and promised. Thereafter, he abstained from the sight of the girl, believing that he could not at once see her and control himself. As soon as the men had dispersed to various parts of the lake, Cnemon

went off to some distance to search for the herb which he
had promised Theagenes on the previous day.

Theagenes took advantage of this opportunity to weep
and lament, not addressing himself to Charicleia at all, but
incessantly invoking the gods. When she inquired whether
his lamentations were for their common and now commonplace tribulations or whether he had some novel affliction,
Theagenes answered, "What could be more novel or what
more sinful than transgressions of oaths and pledges, than
Charicleia's forgetting me and consenting to marry another?" "Heaven forbid," cried the girl, "do not add such
a weight to my calamities. You have enough evidence in
my past conduct not to be suspicious of words accommodated to immediate exigencies. On the contrary, you
yourself will sooner change than find me charged. That I
am unfortunate I shall not deny; but there is no force
which could induce me to be unchaste. In one thing only
do I confess lack of temperance—in the whole course of
my love for you, but that is a lawful love. Not out of complaisance to a lover, but in betrothal to a husband did I
first promise myself to you, and to this day I have kept
myself pure, avoiding intimacies and frequently resisting
your solicitations. I have looked forward to the legitimate
wedlock, if ever it may come, which we agreed upon and
pledged ourselves to by all things sacred. Foolish indeed
must you be to believe I should prefer a barbarian to a
Hellene, a robber to my beloved." "What then was the
meaning of that fine harangue of yours?" said Theagenes.
"To call me your brother was a fine trick, calculated to
prevent Thyamis' jealousy and to enable us to be together
without apprehension. I understand too that the fiction
about Ionia and straying from Delos was calculated to veil
the truth and conceal our situation from the audience. But
to consent so readily to the marriage and to fix a precise
date for its consummation, that I have neither the ability

nor the desire to explain. I would pray to sink into the ground rather than see such an ending to my hardships and hopes."

Charicleia embraced Theagenes, showered a thousand kisses upon him, and moistened him with her tears. "How sweet to me are your fears," said she. "They prove that tribulations have not shaken your love. But you must know, Theagenes, if I had not made those promises, we should not now be talking together. Resistance, as you must know, only intensifies the force of a violent passion; seeming compliance checks the impulse at its birth, and the allurement of promises lulls the sharp-set appetite. Savage lovers, I imagine, take a promise for an initial victory; they suppose that the engagement has given them the upper hand and, on the basis of their expectations, are more docile in their conduct. This is what I foresaw when I gave myself to him in words; what is to follow I entrust to the gods and to the deity appointed to preside over our love from its beginning. Many times a respite of a day or two has afforded salvation; fortune has provided safety which a thousand human expedients could never procure. That is why I contrived to postpone the crisis, countering the certainty of the present by the uncertainty of the future. We must be cautious with this ruse, my sweet; as in a wrestling match, we must keep it secret not only from the others but even from Cnemon. He is charitably disposed to us, and a Greek, yet he is a captive and likely to ingratiate himself with his master if chance dictates. Neither long friendship nor the bond of kinship gives complete assurance of his fidelity to us. If he senses something suspicious in our relationship, therefore, we must deny it from the start. A lie too can be noble if it helps those who tell it and does not harm those who hear it."

While Charicleia was making these and similar excellent suggestions, Cnemon came running up in great haste, his

face betraying the utmost agitation. "Theagenes," said he,
"I bring you that plant; apply it and cure your wounds.
But we must be prepared for other wounds and similar
slaughter." When Theagenes asked him to express his meaning more plainly, he said, "Now is no time to hear, for
there is danger that deeds will come before words. Follow
me quickly, and let Chariclea come too." He took them to
Thyamis, whom he found polishing his helmet and whet-
ting his spear. "In good time are you busy with your arms,"
said he. "Put them on, and bid the others do likewise. There
is a larger force of the enemy than ever before, and they
are so near that I could see them crossing the next hill. I
came running to tell you, and on the way warned as many
as I could to get ready without slackening my speed."

At this Thyamis sprang up and asked, "Where is Charicleia?" as if he were more apprehensive for her than for
himself. When Cnemon pointed to her cringing near the
threshold, Thyamis said to him privately, "You take her
and bring her to the cave where our treasures are safe-
guarded, and then, my friend, when you have placed her
there and have replaced the stone on the mouth of the cave
as usual, come back to me as quickly as you can. I shall address myself to the war." He ordered his squire to bring a
victim so that he might offer sacrifice to the gods of the
country before beginning battle. Cnemon carried out his
orders. Chariclea, who was lamenting and repeatedly turning toward Theagenes, he led away to the cave.

This was not a work of nature, as are many hollow places
in or beneath the earth, but was fashioned by the robbers
in imitation of nature, by laboriously and skillfully hollow-
ing out a depository for their spoils. Its construction was
somewhat as follows. Its narrow dark mouth lay beneath
the doors of a hidden chamber, whose threshold, so fitted
that it could be lifted and lowered with ease, served as an
entry. From this, irregular winding corridors diverged. The

corridors and passages which led to the inmost parts wound their separate ways with great art and a multitude of ramifications, and eventually joined and debouched at a single open space at the bottom, which received a dim light from an aperture at the surface of the marsh.

Cnemon lowered Charicleia and guided her expertly to the remotest part of the cave. He encouraged her and promised that he would return with Theagenes in the evening; he would not allow him to engage with the enemy but would withdraw him from the battle. Charicleia could utter no word; her predicament left her in a deathlike stupor, as if her soul had been separated from her with Theagenes. Cnemon left her speechless and breathless, emerged from the cave, and replaced the threshold. As he did so he shed a tear for his constraint and her fortune: he had all but buried her alive and had delivered to night and darkness the brightest bloom of humanity. He ran to Thyamis and found him boiling for the fight and, with him, Theagenes, splendidly armed. His men who had congregated about him he was rousing to frenzied enthusiasm. Standing in their midst he said: "Fellow soldiers, I see no need of encouraging you with many words; war you have always regarded as life, and you want no admonition. Furthermore, the unexpected onset of our adversaries cuts away prolixity. If we did not speedily repulse the enemy by the same means which they employ, we should be altogether derelict to our obligations. You know that it is not a matter of defending your women and children, which is generally a sufficient incitement to fight bravely; these are of lesser moment, as are other perquisites of the victorious. But our very being, our very lives, are at stake. No pirate war is ever concluded on terms or interrupted by a truce. Either we win and survive or are defeated and die. With bodies and souls keen whetted let us fall upon our hated enemies."

So saying Thyamis looked about for his squire Thermouthis and called him by name. When he was nowhere to be seen he pronounced dire threats against him and ran to the passage. Fighting had already broken out, and from the distance it could be seen that those who lived at the entrances in the remoter parts of the marsh were already defeated. The boats and huts of those who fell or fled the invaders set on fire, and the flames spread wild over the adjoining marshes. When the masses of reeds caught fire a brilliant blaze struck their eyes and a loud crackling their ears. Sight and sound showed war in all forms. The natives resisted with zeal and energy, but their numbers and the element of surprise gave the aggressors the upper hand. Some they slew on land, others they submerged in the lake with their boats and houses. From all this a confused din rose to the air, the sound of fighting by land and by water, of men slaying and men slain. The lake was incarnadined with gore, fire and water were intermingled. These sights and sounds recalled to Thyamis the dream in which he had seen Isis and all her temple filled with torches and sacrificial victims, and he identified it with the present scene. Now he interpreted the dream in a sense opposite to what he had previously given it. "He would have Charicleia and not have her"—because he would lose her in this war; "he would kill her and not wound her"—by the sword, not Aphrodite's law. He heaped reproaches upon the goddess for her trickery and thought it intolerable that another should possess Charicleia. He ordered those with him to halt for a little, and if they were obliged to fight where they stood, they should surreptitiously take positions around the island and make secret sallies from the surrounding marsh; even so it would be hard to offer adequate resistance to an enemy who so far outnumbered them. Thyamis himself pretended he was going to find Thermouthis and offer prayer to his household gods; he suffered no one to follow him, and turned toward his hut in great agitation.

Such is the barbarian character that its impulses are hard to check or deflect. When he despairs of his own safety he is wont to destroy whatever he loves, whether under the delusion that it will accompany him after death, or to save it from the insults of the enemy. So then Thyamis, oblivious of the task in hand, though he was encircled by the toils of the enemy, instigated by love, jealousy, and rage, proceeded to the cave at a run, leaped down, and shouted loud and long in Egyptian. Near the entrance he encountered a woman who addressed him in Greek, and by her voice was guided to her whereabouts. With his left hand he seized her hair, and with his right plunged his sword through her breast. She uttered a last pitiful cry and lay, a sorry sight. Thyamis hurried out, replaced the threshold, heaped up a little mound, and, shedding tears, said, "This is my bridal gift to you." Returned to the boats, he found that the others were already planning flight, for the enemy could be seen near at hand, and that Thermouthis had come and was busy with a sacrifice. He rebuked him, saying he had already offered the finest of all sacrifices, and then with Thermouthis and a rower he embarked in a boat. The marsh boats cannot carry more, for they are but rudely hollowed out of a single thick tree trunk. Theagenes with Cnemon got into another, others in other boats, and so eventually all. When they had gone a little distance from the island they sailed around it rather than away from it, and then shipped oars and drew their boats up in a line to receive the enemy face on. But when the enemy approached they could not even endure the splash of their oars, but fled on sight, terrified by their war shouts. Theagenes and Cnemon also gave ground, but fear was not their prime motive. Only Thyamis stood his ground; partly out of shame, but probably because he could not endure to survive Charicleia he flung himself against the enemy.

When the melée was hand to hand someone shouted,

"That man is Thyamis: Everyone look sharp!" Immediately they turned their boats to form a circle around him. He defended himself vigorously, and with his sword wounded some and killed others. But what happened next was remarkable. Not a man of them drew sword or cast a dart or brandished a weapon, but each did his utmost to take Thyamis alive. He resisted manfully until the simultaneous charge of a number of his adversaries deprived him of his spear. He also lost his squire, who had seconded him nobly. Having received what he thought was a mortal wound, the squire dived into the lake in despair; his practiced skill carried him beyond the range of the enemy, where he emerged and with difficulty swam to the marshland. No one offered to pursue him, for now they had taken Thyamis, and they regarded the capture of this single man as a complete victory. And though they had lost so many friends, their joy in having surrounded their executioners was greater than their grief for their fallen kin. To robbers money is more precious than their own lives, and the limits of friendship and kinship are defined by profit. So it was with these men, who, as it happened, were the very men who had run away from Thyamis and his company at the Heracleot mouth of the Nile. They were indignant because they had been deprived of what was not theirs; the loss of booty vexed them no less than if it had been their own property. They had collected their fellows who had been left at home and had also mustered men from surrounding villages by the promise of equal shares in whatever they would capture; they themselves had acted as leaders and guides.

Their reason for taking Thyamis alive was the following. In Memphis Thyamis had a brother named Petosiris. By intrigue Petosiris had deprived Thyamis of the high priesthood and himself held it—illegally, for he was the younger. When he heard that his elder brother commanded a robber band, he was afraid that Thyamis might find an opportunity to attack him, or that his own plot would one day be discovered. At the same time he sensed a general suspicion that he had done away with Thyamis, who was nowhere to be seen. By proclamations sent to all the robber villages, therefore, he offered large rewards of money and cattle to any who would bring Thyamis in alive. This was the robbers' inducement, and not even in the heat of battle did they lose sight of profits; when Thyamis was recognized they took him alive at the cost of many deaths. Assigning half their company to guard him, they sent him to the mainland in chains; all the while he rebuked them for their seeming charity and was more irritated by his fetters than by death. The remainder turned to the island to find the treasures and spoils which they sought. They rummaged through the whole island and ransacked every cranny, but could find only such trifles as had not been hidden away in the underground cave. They set fire to the huts, and when the approach of evening deterred them from remaining on the island for fear of being ambushed by the fugitives they departed to their own homes.

2

THE ISLAND, then, was afire; but as long as the sun was above the horizon Theagenes and Cnemon were not aware of it, for by day the flare of fire is dimmed by the divine luster of the sun's rays. But when the sun sank and brought the night, the now unrivaled blaze could be seen clearly at a distance. Trusting to the night, the two in the marsh raised themselves—and saw the island enveloped in bright flames. Theagenes smote his head and tore his hair and cried, "Perish life this day! Everything is ended, undone—fears, friends, anxieties, hopes, love. Charicleia has died: Theagenes has perished. In vain, wretch that I am, did I turn coward and take to unmanly flight, saving myself, my sweet, for you. But I shall not survive you, my darling. You died not by the common law of nature nor (and this is the hardest) did you yield up your life in the arms you most desired. It was by fire, alas, that you were consumed, kindled by fate instead of marriage torches. The perfection of human beauty is utterly dissipated; not even does a corpse remain as a relic of that perfect loveliness. Ah cruelty, ah unspeakable malignity of fate! Even a last embrace has been denied me. My last lifeless kisses are thwarted."

As he said this he fumbled for his sword, but Cnemon quickly pushed his hand back and said, "Why do you mourn the living? Charicleia is safe and sound. Take heart." "A tale for fools or children, Cnemon," said Theagenes, "you kill me by not letting me die so sweet a death." Cnemon swore it was true and told the whole story—Thyamis' orders, the cavern, how he himself had brought her there, and the nature of the cave; he declared that there was no danger of the fire reaching the depths, for it would be cut off by the innumerable windings. At this Theagenes drew new breath and hurried to the island. The girl he saw in his fancy as present before him, and he imagined the cave as his bridal chamber—little knowing the anguish that cave held for him. And so they bustled forward eagerly, themselves plying the oars, for their boatman had shot into the water like a projectile at the sound of the first attack. Because of their inexperience they could not keep stroke and so veered this way and that; the wind, furthermore, was adverse. Awkwardness was nevertheless vanquished by zeal.

With difficulty, then, and bathed in sweat, they reached the island, and immediately ran to the huts. These they found already gutted, and only the site was recognizable. But the stone threshold which was the cover of the cave stood out plainly. The fire had been fanned by a stiff breeze, and all the huts in its path, made of wattled reeds—and thin marsh reeds at that—had burned to the ground. All that the quick burning left was a fine ash, and this, too, the gusts carried off, leaving the ground bare and cool enough to tread on. They found some half-burnt torches and a few remaining reeds, opened the cave, and descended into it, Cnemon leading the way. When they had gone a little distance Cnemon suddenly cried out, "Zeus! What

is this? We are ruined. Charicleia is dead." He flung his
torch to the ground and extinguished it, put his hands
to his eyes, and fell weeping to his knees. Theagenes fell
upon the outstretched body as if he had been struck by
some outside force; he twined himself tightly about the
body and long lay clinging to it. Perceiving that he was
wholly maddened by his calamity and anguish, Cnemon
feared that he might do himself some mischief and so secretly removed the sword from the sheath which hung at
his side; he then left him alone and ran out to light the
torch.

In the meanwhile Theagenes broke into tragic and
mournful ejaculations: "Oh, anguish intolerable! Oh catas-
trophe heaven-sent! What insatiable Fury revels in my
afflictions? Exile from my country has she inflicted upon
me, to robbers has she repeatedly delivered me, of my
possessions has she stripped me. One sole recompense was
left, and now that is taken away. Charicleia lies dead, my
darling is a victim of war. Plainly, she was defending her
virtue, and it was for me, doubtless, that she preserved herself. She lies dead nevertheless; no profit had she of her
beauty, nor did it avail me aught. But oh, my sweet, speak
to me the last words of the dying, utter your behests if
yet you breathe a little. Alas, you are silent. Those prophetic and inspired lips are mute; darkness holds the torch-
bearer, chaos has seized the priestess of the gods. Extinguished are those bright orbs whose brilliant beauty dazzled the world; the murderer can never have seen them,
I know it well. And now what shall I name you? Bride?
But you were never married. Spouse? But you never experienced wedlock. What then shall I call you, how invoke you in the future? By the sweetest of all titles—
Charicleia. Have faith, Charicleia; your lover is loyal and
soon you will recover him. My own slaughter will I bring
you for your funerary offering; I will make libation with

the blood you held so dear. This cave will serve as a crude tomb for us both. We shall be together after death, as fate has not suffered us to be in life."

So saying he reached down to draw his sword, and when he found it gone he cried, "Ah, Cnemon, you have ruined me. Charicleia too have you wronged, again depriving her of the companionship so sweet to her." As he was going on in this fashion, the reverberation of a voice calling "Theagenes" resounded from the depths of the cave. He hearkened, no whit alarmed, and said, "I come, darling soul. Plainly you still hover about the earth, partly because you cannot bear to be separated from this body, from which you were so violently wrenched, and partly because your lack of sepulture keeps you from the nether shades." Cnemon, meanwhile, arrived with lighted torches, and again the voice was heard calling "Theagenes." "Ye gods," cried Cnemon, "is not that the voice of Charicleia? I believe she is safe, Theagenes. That voice comes from the deepest part of the cave, where I am positive I left her." "Will you never stop deceiving me?" said Theagenes. "I am deceiving you and myself, too," said Cnemon, "if we find this corpse is Charicleia." So saying he turned the corpse to his view, and when he had examined it, burst out, "Ye wonder-working deities, what is this? That is Thisbe's face!" He stepped back and stood trembling and speechless.

Theagenes, on the other hand, was newly animated and became hopeful again. He restored Cnemon from his swoon and begged him lead the way to Charicleia at once. After a little, Cnemon recovered and again examined the corpse. It was really Thisbe, and he also recognized from its hilt the sword which had fallen at her side: in his haste and fury Thyamis had left it in the wound. He also picked up a tablet which showed at Thisbe's bosom and tried to read what was written on it. But Theagenes would not let him and insisted urgently, "Let us find my darling first, if it is not some demon still deluding us; you can read the tablet afterward." Cnemon obeyed and taking the tablet and the sword they hastened towards Charicleia. On hands and feet she was creeping toward the light, and then she ran up to Theagenes and hung on his neck. Repeatedly they exclaimed, "Is it you I hold, Theagenes?" "Are you alive, my Charicleia?" Finally, they sank to the ground together and clung to one another speechless, as if welded together, and all but died in rapture. Excessive joy frequently passes into pain, and immoderate delight of itself begets distress. So these two, saved beyond hope, were in critical danger until Cnemon, grubbing down to find moisture and collecting a trickle of water in his cupped hands, sprinkled their faces with it, rubbed it over their nostrils, and so brought them to their senses.

Finding themselves lying together in an odd posture they quickly arose and blushed (especially Charicleia) before Cnemon, who had been a witness, and begged his pardon. Cnemon smiled and tried to relax them to a brighter mood. "Praiseworthy rather is that conduct," said he, "in my judgment and in that of anyone who has wrestled with love, suffered a sweet defeat, and prudently acknowledged that his opponent is irresistible. But one thing I cannot praise, and indeed was embarrassed to see—when you ignobly embraced and bewailed a strange woman who was no connection of yours, though I kept insisting that your darling was safe and sound." "Stop slandering me to Charicleia, Cnemon," said Theagenes. "It was her I bewailed in the other's body, thinking it was Charicleia who lay there. But since some benevolent deity has revealed our error, it is time to recall your own great fortitude. First you joined in my lamentations, but when you unexpectedly recognized the corpse, you ran like an actor pursued by stage Furies. Fully armed and sword in hand you dreaded a woman, and a dead one at that—our brave Attic warrior!"

This drew a laugh, but short and forced and not without tears, for their calamities introduced a larger ingredient of woe. After a little Charicleia scratched her cheek and said, "I congratulate the woman who, as Cnemon says, was bewailed and kissed by Theagenes, whoever she may be. But if you will not suspect that love makes me jealous, who was that happy woman, deemed worthy of Theagenes' tears, and how were you deceived into caressing an unknown instead of me? I should like to know if you can tell me." "You will be amazed," said Theagenes. "Cnemon here says it was Thisbe, that Athenian fiddler-girl who plotted against him and against Demainete." Charicleia showed her astonishment and said, "But Cnemon, how can she have been wafted from the middle of Greece to remotest Egypt, like a *deus ex machina*? How can we have missed her when we came down here?" "That I cannot explain," Cnemon answered her, "but this is what I know about her. After Demainete had been tricked and had flung herself into the pit, my father recounted the whole affair to the people and at that time obtained their pardon. He busied himself with procuring my recall by enactment and with traveling in search of me. My father's preoccupation gave Thisbe leisure, and this she employed in selling her art and herself for entertainments. Now she came to be favored above Arsinoe, whose fluting had become negligent; she plucked her strings with a quicker rhythm and sang gracefully in accompaniment. She was not aware that she had aroused a courtesan's envy and had provoked her hatred. Arsinoe's hatred was aggravated when Thisbe received the embraces of a rich merchant of Naucratis named Nausicles, whom Arsinoe had known first. He had come to dislike Arsinoe when he observed that her exertions in playing her instrument puffed her cheeks out, dilated her nostrils disagreeably, and reddened her eyes and thrust them forward out of their sockets.

"Swollen with anger and burning with jealousy Arsinoe went to Demainete's kinsmen and informed them of Thisbe's plot against their relative. Part she suspected herself, and the rest Thisbe had told her when they were friends. Demainete's relatives then conspired against my father and engaged the most redoubtable lawyers for large fees to press the charge that my father had put Demainete to death without trial and without proof. They insisted that he had used a charge of adultery to cover murder and bade him produce the adulterer alive or dead or at least cite his name. Finally, they demanded that Thisbe give evidence under torture. My father agreed to produce her but could not, for she had foreseen what was to come and had taken flight with the merchant—by previous agreement with him—while the investigation was still in progress. The people were angry. They did not adjudge my father a murderer, for he had fully explained the circumstances, but they did condemn him as an accomplice in the plot against Demainete and as the cause of my unjust exile, and they punished him by banishment from the city and confiscation of his property. Such profit did he obtain from his second marriage. It was thus that the vile Thisbe, whom my own eyes have just now seen punished, departed from Athens. All that I know about her is what I heard at Aegina from Anticles, and with him I sailed a second time to Egypt to look for Thisbe at Naucratis and, by bringing her back to Athens, to dispel the suspicions and charges against my father and exact vengeance for her plots against all of us. Now I find myself with you. The reasons for my being here and my fortunes in the interval you shall hear another time. But how Thisbe came to be felled in this cavern and by whom it will need some god to explain.

"Nevertheless, if you agree, let us examine the tablet which I found in her bosom. Perhaps we can learn something further from it." They agreed, and Cnemon opened the tablet and began to read. The contents were as follows: "To Cnemon her master, from Thisbe, his enemy and vindicator: First I give you glad tidings of Demainete's death, brought about by me, for your sake; the means I will relate in person if you admit me. Next I tell you that I have been on the island nine days. I was captured by one of the brigands here who boasts that he is a squire to the chief. He keeps me locked up, never so much as allowing me to look out-of-doors. He inflicts this punishment upon me, he says, out of love, but I suppose it is out of fear that someone will take me from him. Some god vouchsafed me to see you, master, as you passed and to recognize you. I have sent this clandestine tablet to you by an old woman who lives with me, whom I instructed to deliver it to the handsome Greek who is a friend of the chief. Take me from the robber's hands and receive me as your maidservant. Save me if you will, knowing that the wrongs I seemed to do were under constraint, but that what I did to punish your enemy was of my own volition. If your wrath is inexorable, exercise it upon me as you will; but let me be yours even if I must die. Better to be killed by your hands and obtain a Greek funeral than to endure a life more grievous than death and the love of a barbarian more odious than the hatred of a Greek."

So Thisbe and her tablet declared. Said Cnemon: "Admirable is your death and your account of your own misfortune, delivered to us out of your own slaughter. An avenging Fury, it seems, has pursued you over the whole earth and has not stayed its avenging scourge before it brought you to Egypt and made me, the party injured, a spectator of your punishment. But what is the plot you have been so long contriving against me? What machinations, set in train by this writing, did your punishment cut off? I suspect you even in death; I fear greatly that the death of Demainete is a fiction, that those who brought me tidings of it have deceived me, and that you have come across the sea to stage another Attic tragedy against me even in Egypt." "Will you not put an end to your courageous display," said Theagenes, "to your shrewd precautions against phantoms and shadows? You cannot say that my vision, too, is bewitched, for I have had no part in your drama. This body is truly dead and there is no reason for you to fear it, Cnemon. But the identity of the benefactor who killed her, and how she came here, and when, leave me completely baffled." "The other puzzles I cannot solve," said Cnemon, "but the man who killed her must be Thyamis, to judge by the sword which was found with her corpse. I know it is his by the ivory hilt carved in the shape of an eagle." "But could you say how, when, and why he committed the murder?" asked Theagenes. "How should I know that?" answered Cnemon. "This cave has not bestowed on me the gift of prophecy, as those of Delphi and Trophonius are said to inspire those who penetrate them." Theagenes and Chariclea broke into sudden sighs, and sorrowfully cried, "O Pytho, O Delphi!" Cnemon was puzzled and could not conjecture why the name of Pytho should affect them.

Such was their situation. But while they were in the cave, Thermouthis, Thyamis' squire who had been wounded, swam to the mainland. When night fell he embarked on a boat from the wreckage which he found floating near the marsh and hurried to the island and Thisbe. A few days before he had ambushed the merchant Nausicles, who was leading her through a narrow mountain pass, and had abducted her. In the tumult of the enemy attack, when Thyamis had sent him to bring a sacrificial victim, he had wished to put her beyond the range of the fighting and

preserve her for himself, and so he had secretly lowered
her into the cave, but in his haste and confusion he had
left her near the entry. Fear of surrounding dangers and
ignorance of the paths which led to the depths of the cave
had kept her where she had been left, and thus Thyamis
had mistaken her for Charicleia and had killed her. It was
to Thisbe that Thermouthis hurried, happy at having escaped the perils of war, and when he reached the island he
ran to the tents as quickly as he could. Of these nothing
but ashes was left, but he found the stone entry with some
difficulty, lighted some straggling reeds, and dashed down
with all speed. He called Thisbe's name, which was all the
Greek he knew. When he saw her lying dead, he stood
dumbfounded for a while. Finally, he sensed a murmuring
sound issuing from the hollows of the cave, for Theagenes
and Cnemon were still conversing. He conjectured that
these were the murderers of Thisbe but was at a loss what
to do. Piratical temper, barbarian passion, and, even more,
disappointment in love impelled him to advance against
those he considered responsible; but want of arms and a
sword checked him to unwilling self-control.

He decided that it was best not to approach them at
first as an enemy, and then if some means should turn up,
to attack them. So resolved, he advanced on Theagenes
and his company with a wild and savage look, his eyes
divulging the secret desires of his soul. At the sudden ap-
parition of a man, naked, wounded, with blood-stained face,
Charicleia shrank back to the recesses of the cave, partly
out of caution, but more out of shame before the man's
nudity and indecency. Cnemon also quietly retired; he
recognized Thermouthis, but his unexpected appearance
made him apprehensive of some wild attempt. But Theagenes was annoyed rather than frightened at the spectacle. He drew his sword, ready to repel any hostile move
and said, "Halt or I strike. I have refrained because I

recognize you a little and am yet uncertain of your intentions." Thermouthis kneeled and begged mercy, need rather than his character making him a suppliant. He called on Cnemon to help him, saying that he deserved to be saved by him, that he had never outraged him, that they had been friends to that day, and that it was as a friend that he came.

Cnemon was moved by this appeal. He approached Thermouthis and raised him from the knees of Theagenes, which he had embraced, and immediately asked him where Thyamis was. Thermouthis told him all—how Thyamis had burst upon the enemy, how he had spared neither them nor himself in the midst of the fighting, how he had killed all that came in his way while he was himself protected by the proclamation that Thyamis must be spared. What finally happened to Thyamis he could not say; he himself had been wounded and had swum to the mainland. Now he had come to the cave to find Thisbe. They asked what concern he had with Thisbe and how he had come by her. This too Thermouthis explained, telling how he had taken her from the merchant, how he had fallen madly in love with her and kept her concealed for a time, and how at the enemy attack he had placed her in the cave where he now found her slain. Who had slain her he did not know, but he would be pleased to learn their identity and their motives. Cnemon very hastily said, "Thyamis is the slayer"; he was eager to absolve himself of suspicion and exhibited the sword which had been found by the corpse as evidence. Thermouthis saw the steel still dripping blood and still exuding heat from its recent slaughter, and recognized it as Thyamis'. In his perplexity he heaved a deep and heavy sigh and was subdued in gloom and silence. He returned to the mouth of the cave and when he came to the dead body he put his head on its bosom and repeatedly murmured "O Thisbe." Gradually, his articulation of the name grew less clear and finally stopped, and Thermouthis unconsciously glided into sleep.

Theagenes, Charicleia, and also Cnemon were oppressed by thoughts of their condition. They wished to form some plan of action, but the multitude of their past tribulations, the helplessness of their present state, and the uncertainty of the future clouded their reasoning faculties. For a long while they stood staring, each waiting for the other to say something. When nothing came they turned their eyes to the ground, looked up again, sighed, and by sighing relieved the burden. Finally, Cnemon reclined on the ground, Theagenes leaned against a rock, and Charicleia let herself fall against him. Desiring to fix upon some plan they resisted the inroads of sleep for a long while; but they were exhausted by fatigue and hardship and despite themselves yielded to the law of nature. The very excess of their sorrow lulled them with a sweet and deep sleep. So even the intellectual part of the soul is constrained to accommodate itself to the physical state.

They had only begun to taste sleep, and their eyelids were barely smoothed when Charicleia, lying by Theagenes, was visited by a dream. A man with long and unkempt hair, bloody in look and hand, drew a sword and thrust out her right eye. She cried out at once and called to Theagenes that her eye was being put out. At the cry he awoke at once and was distressed by the event as if he too had felt it in a dream. Charicleia put her hand to her face and felt about in search of the member she dreamed she had lost. When she realized it was a dream she said, "It was a dream, I have my eye. Take heart, Theagenes." Theagenes breathed again and said, "It is a fine thing that those lovely sunbeams are safe. But what happened to you? What brought on that fright?" "A savage and violent man," said she, "who was not afraid even of your irresistible strength, leaped upon me, sword in hand, as I lay at

your knees, and, as I imagined, put out my right eye.
Would that the vision were true and not a dream." When
Theagenes bade her keep her speech auspicious and asked
her why she said such a thing, she answered, "Because it
is better for me to lose one of my eyes than to be anxious
for you. I am terribly afraid that the dream may refer to
you, whom I reckon my eye and my soul and my all."
"Stop," said Cnemon—he had awakened at Charicleia's
first cry and had overheard all—"it appears to me that
the dream has a different significance. Tell me, are your
parents alive?" She said that to the best of her knowledge
they were, and Cnemon continued, "Then you must believe that your father is dead. The basis of my conjecture is
this. We know that our begetters are responsible for our
entry into this life and our enjoyment of the light. It is
quite likely then that dreams allude to father and mother
through the symbolism of eyes, through whose agency we
perceive light and all things visible." "That too would be
a heavy blow," said Charicleia, "but be that, rather than
mine, the true interpretation. Let your oracular gift take
precedence over mine, and let me be proved a false proph-
etess." "So it shall be and so must we believe," said Cnemon,
"but we are behaving like true dreamers, scrutinizing fan-
cies and phantoms instead of paying attention to our own
problems. We now have an opportunity, while the Egyptian
(he meant Thermouthis) is gone to brood over and lament
his dead love."

Theagenes interposed and said, "Since some deity,
Cnemon, has joined you to us and made you our companion
in misfortune, make the first suggestion. You are familiar
with the country and its language, and besides, we are
so overwhelmed with affliction as to be incapable of proper
perception." Cnemon hesitated a little and then said,
"Which of us is richer in affliction is doubtful; for me, too,
has fortune ungrudgingly loaded with calamity. But I am

the elder and will speak of our situation as you bid me.
The island, as you see, is empty; there is no one besides
ourselves. There is gold, silver, and clothing in abundance,
for Thyamis and his crew have deposited in the cave much
plunder that they took from you and from others; but
of grain and other necessities of life there is not a trace.
If we remain here we must perish of hunger or be destroyed
by an incursion, either of the enemy, who may return, or
of our own party, if they should reassemble and come to
fetch the treasures which they know are here. We could
not escape destruction or, at the most charitable, exposure
to their insults. The buccaneer kind is always unreliable,
and particularly now when they have lost the chief who
controlled and checked them. We must abandon the island, therefore, and escape from it as if it were a snare or
a prison. We should first send Thermouthis out, on the
pretext of making inquiries and learning what he can
about Thyamis. It will be easier for us to deliberate and
take measures by ourselves, and in any case it is well to
be rid of a man whose character is vacillating, piratical,
and quarrelsome, and who, moreover, is suspicious of us on
Thisbe's account and would not hesitate to do us mischief
if opportunity offered."

This advice they approved and resolved to follow. They
knew that day had risen, and moved to the mouth of the
cave where they aroused Thermouthis, who was sunk in
sleep. They explained as much of their plan as was proper,
and easily won the fickle man over. The body of Thisbe
they put in a hollow place and covered it with ashes from
the tents. The customary religious rites they performed as
well as circumstances permitted, and they dedicated tears
and lamentations instead of the usual offerings. Then they
sent Thermouthis on the mission they had agreed upon.
He went a little distance but returned and said he would
not go alone; he would not incur the great danger of scout-

ing unless Cnemon were willing to share the mission. Theagenes noticed that Cnemon was very timorous, for his
agitation was easy to see when he translated the Egyptian's
remarks. Theagenes therefore said to him, "You were stal-
wart in giving counsel but your spirit is weak; I have noticed it on other occasions and more plainly now. But whet
your temper keen, rouse your mood to forthright manliness. For the present it is essential to consent; he must not
suspect that we plan to escape. Accompany him for a
time: an armed man, sword in hand, need not fear to
go with one unarmed. You will find some opportunity to
elude and leave him, and rejoin us at some place on which
we may agree. Let us agree on some nearby village, if you
know any where the inhabitants are civilized." This seemed
reasonable to Cnemon and he mentioned a village named
Chemmis. This was a rich and populous place on the
banks of the Nile, situated on a hill for protection from
the buccaneers. Its distance, after traversing the marsh,
was not much less than a hundred furlongs, and its direction was due south.

"That is a hard journey," said Theagenes, "especially for
Charicleia, who is not used to walking so far; but we
shall get there, nevertheless. We will disguise ourselves as
mendicant jugglers." "By Zeus," said Cnemon, "your looks
are deformed enough, and especially Charicleia's, who
lately had her eye knocked out; you seem to me fitter to
ask for 'women and cauldrons' than broken crusts." This
sally was met by a brief and forced smile which did not
go beyond the lips. They pledged each other's faith to what
they had agreed, called the gods to witness that they would
never willingly forsake one another, and then proceeded to
carry out their plan.

At daybreak Cnemon and Thermouthis crossed the lake
and made their way through a thick and deep forest which
was almost impassable. Thermouthis led the way, at the

express desire of Cnemon, who alleged that Thermouthis' experience of the difficult region made it appropriate for him to act as guide; actually Cnemon was consulting his own safety and preparing an occasion for running away. As they went forward they came upon a flock whose shepherds ran away to hide in the densest part of the forest. They slaughtered a ram who was a leader of the flock, roasted it in the fire which the shepherds had got ready, and devoured the flesh without even waiting for it to be properly cooked. They were hurried on by their starving bellies. Like wolves or jackals they gulped down the pieces as soon as they were cut off and a little blackened in the fire. The half-done lumps dripped blood on their chins as they ate. When they were stuffed full they drank milk and resumed their journey. About the hour when the ox is unhitched they ascended a hill at the foot of which, Thermouthis said, was the village where he imagined that Thyamis was either held prisoner or had been slain. Here Cnemon complained of great pain in his stomach caused by his gormandizing and of violent diarrhea caused by the milk. He urged Thermouthis to go forward and said he would soon overtake him. By doing this once and again and a third time, he appeared to confirm that what he said was true, and each time he complained of difficulty in keeping up with the Egyptian.

The Egyptian had grown accustomed to these delays, and once when he was far ahead Cnemon ran as fast as he could downhill through rough ground to a very thick forest. When Thermouthis reached the summit of the hill he rested on a rock, waiting for the evening and darkness, when it had been agreed they would enter the village to make inquiries about Thyamis. He was waiting, too, for the coming of Cnemon, against whom he was devising some sinister plan, for he had never given up the suspicion that Cnemon had killed Thisbe. He was thinking, in his madness, how he might put Cnemon out of the way, and then how he would attack Theagenes and Charicleia. But when Cnemon nowhere appeared and night fell betimes, Thermouthis turned to sleep. A brazen sleep it was, the last of his life, for an asp bit him, perhaps by design of the fates, and ended his life as beseemed his character.

After he left Thermouthis, Cnemon did not pause in his flight before the darkness of night arrested his course. He hid himself where he stopped and heaped the greatest possible quantity of leaves over himself. Lying under this heap he passed a wretched and for the most part sleepless night; every noise, every gust of wind or stirring of a leaf he thought was Thermouthis. If ever he succumbed to sleep for a moment he dreamed he was still fleeing and turned around to look back for a pursuer who was not pursuing. He wished to sleep but resisted his wish, for his dreams were worse than reality. He seemed angry with the night, which he imagined was longer than any other. He was happy to see daylight, and his first step, in order not to appear terrifying or suspicious to any who met him, was to cut short his long hair, which he had let grow in the pirate fashion when he was among the buccaneers. Among other means they employ to make themselves seem formidable, the buccaneers grow their hair down over their eyebrows and allow it to sweep down over their shoulders, well aware that long hair makes lovers blithe and robbers terrible.

When Cnemon had cut his hair to look more like a dandy than a brigand, he hastened toward Chemmis, the village where he had engaged to meet Theagenes. He was already near the Nile and preparing to cross over to Chemmis when he saw an old man wandering on its banks. He was striding up and down by the side of the stream and seemed to be communicating some of his thoughts to the river. His hair was long, in the priestly manner, and com-

pletely white; his beard was thick and venerable; his cape
and other garments followed the Greek fashion. Cnemon
paused a while, but when the old man repeatedly passed
him without seeming to notice his presence (so intent was
he on his thoughts and so absorbed in his meditations)
Cnemon confronted and greeted him, "Fare well!" The
old man said he could not, for his fortune did not allow it.
"Are you a Greek," said Cnemon in surprise, "or a foreigner? Whence are you?" "Neither Greek nor foreigner,"
said he, "but an Egyptian of Egypt." "Why is your dress
Greek?" "My misfortunes," said he, "have changed me
into this elegant attire." Cnemon, wondering how misfortunes could improve a man's appearance, asked an explanation. "You ask an Odyssey," replied the old man,
"you stir up a swarm of troubles and will bring upon
yourself an endless buzzing. But where are you going,
young man, and from where? How do you speak Greek
in Egypt?" "A droll thing," said Cnemon, "you tell me
nothing about yourself, though I asked you first, and yet
you wish to know about my affairs." "Well then," said he,
"since you seem to be a Greek and some fortune has transformed you and you are very eager to hear my story—I
myself am bursting to tell it, and if I had not met you
would probably have told it to the reeds here, like the man
in the story—let us leave the Nile and its banks. A place
scorched by the noonday sun is no fit spot to listen to a
long tale. Let us go to yonder village which you see opposite, if you have no more pressing business. I will enter-
tain you, not in my own house but in that of a good man
who received me as a suppliant. There you may learn my
story, if you will, and tell me yours in turn." "Let us go,"
said Cnemon, "my journey is to that same village, where
I have engaged to wait for certain connections of mine."

They embarked on one of the many boats bobbing up
and down along the bank available to passengers for a

fee, crossed over to the village, and arrived at the house
where the old man lodged. The master of the house was
not at home, but they were welcomed most heartily by the
host's daughter, a girl of marriageable age, and all the
servants in the house treated their guest as if he were their
father—probably on their master's orders. One washed his
feet and wiped the dust from his shins, another prepared
his bed and spread it with soft cushions, another brought
a pitcher and kindled a fire, still another brought a table
loaded with wheaten bread and a variety of fruits. Cnemon
expressed his astonishment: "We have come, it seems, to
the court of Zeus of Guests, father, so extraordinary is
the attention and so manifest the good will." "Not the
house of Zeus," said the elder, "but of a scrupulous devotee
of Zeus of Guests and Suppliants. His life too is a wanderer's; he is a merchant, and he has had experience of
many cities and of the manners and minds of many people.
Likely he has shared his roof with many a wandering
stranger, as he did with me a few days since." "And why
this wandering you speak of, father?" "My children have
been carried away by brigands," said he. "I know the
malefactors but cannot contend with them, and so I flit
about the spot and give vent to my suffering in lamentations. I am like some bird, I suppose, whose nest a snake
has ravaged. Before her eyes he devours her young, and
she is afraid to advance and cannot bear to flee; yearning
and grief struggle within her; screaming she hovers over
the carnage, and pours her futile supplication and her
maternal dirge into savage ears which nature has not taught
mercy." "Would you not wish," said Cnemon, "to tell how
and when you encountered this heavy war?" "Later," said
he, "now it is time to tend to our bellies. That is why
Homer makes everything secondary to the belly and calls
it 'greatly accursed.' But first let us pour libation to the
gods, as the law requires of Egyptian sages. Nothing will

induce me to transgress this law, nor can sorrow grow so strong as to make me forget religious obligations."

So saying he poured pure water (his habitual drink) from a flask and said, "Let us make libation to the gods, native and Greek, to Pythian Apollo himself, and also to Theagenes and Charicleia, the beautiful and the good, for them too I remember with the gods." Then he wept as if he would make another libation of his tears. Cnemon was astounded at hearing the names. He looked the old man up and down and said, "How do you say? Are Theagenes and Charicleia really your children?" "My children, stranger," said he, "born to me without a mother. Through fortune the gods designated them mine, and the travail of my soul brought them to birth. My affection for them was accounted a natural tie, and for this reason did they consider me and name me father. But tell me, how did you come to know them?" "Not only do I know them," said Cnemon, "but I assure you that they are safe." "Apollo and ye gods," he cried, "show me where they are. I shall call you savior and peer of the gods." "But what will my reward be?" said he. "For the present," the old man said, "gratitude, the finest present, I think, for a man of sense. I know that many men have laid it up in their souls as a treasure. But when we reach our own country—and the gods signify to me that this will be in no long while—your utmost desires will be satisfied." "You make vague and remote promises," said Cnemon, "when you have the wherewithal to requite me now." "Tell me what you see that I possess," said the old man. "I am ready to give up any part of my body." "There is no need to mutilate you," said Cnemon. "I shall consider myself paid in full if you are willing to tell me whence the young people derive, who their parents are, how they have come here, and what their fortune has been." "You shall have a magnificent reward, beyond all other, even if you asked all human wealth.

But for the present let us take a little food, for the story will take a long time for you to hear and me to tell." They then ate heartily of nuts, figs, fresh dates, and similar food on which the old man customarily dined: he would take no life for the sake of victuals. Then they drank, the old man water, and Cnemon wine. After a bit Cnemon said, "You know, father, how Dionysus takes pleasure in myths and loves comedies. Now Dionysus has settled in me; he invites me to listen and impels me to demand the reward you promised. It is now time for you to raise your curtain on the play, as the saying goes." "You shall hear it," said he, "but I wish that the good Nausicles were here present with us. He has often urged me to give the première of my tale, but I have put him off for one reason or another."

"Where is he now?" asked Cnemon when he heard Nausicles' name. "He's gone hunting," said the old man. And when Cnemon asked what he was hunting the old man said, "The wildest of beasts. They are called men and cowherds, but their trade is brigandage and they are difficult to catch, for instead of dens and holes they have a marsh." "Has Nausicles a special complaint against them?" asked Cnemon, and the old man answered. "They have abducted his sweetheart, an Athenian named Thisbe." "Ah," said Cnemon, but immediately fell silent, as if catching himself; and when the old man asked what the matter was, Cnemon diverted the conversation. "I wonder," said he, "how he is so confident and what forces he has for his expedition." "The Great King's viceroy for Egypt, friend," said the old man, "is Oroondates, and under his orders the commandant Mitranes is governor of this village. Him Nausicles has induced, by generous payment, to march with a large force on foot and horse. He is annoyed at the loss of the Athenian girl, not only because he was in love with her and she was an excellent musician, but because he was going to take her to the king

of the Ethiopians, as he himself said, to be a playfellow
and companion to his queen after the Greek fashion. Disappointed of his large expectations of profit by the girl, he
is putting into motion every possible means of recovering
her. I myself encouraged him in this enterprise, thinking
it possible that he might save my children also." "Enough
of herdsmen and satraps and even of kings," interrupted
Cnemon. "You have almost eluded me again by diverting
me to another subject. You have brought on the stage a
tableau which, as the saying is, has naught to do with
Dionysus. Turn your discourse back to what you promised. I find you are like Proteus of Pharos: you not only
transform yourself into deceptive and fleeting appearances
but you try to divert me also." "You shall know my story,"
said the old man. "First I shall set it forth succinctly, not
to trick you of any part, as you imagine, but in orderly
and consistent fashion, and prepare you for the sequel.

"My city is Memphis; my father's name and my own,
Calasiris. My life is now a wanderer's; not long since I was
a prophet. I had a wife, according to the law of my city,
and lost her by the ordinance of nature. When she was
liberated for a different sojourn, I spent some time without
tribulation, finding delight in my two children by her.
Not many years later the circuit of the celestial luminaries
altered our fate: the eye of Saturn smote our house and
brought a change for the worse. This my sagacity foresaw, but could not avail to escape. The immutable decrees
of fate can be foreseen, they cannot be evaded. Foreknowledge in these matters affords the advantage of blunt-
ing the edge of affliction. Unforeseen calamity, my son,
is unbearable; what is foreknown is tolerable. In the former
case the mind is seized by fear and crushed; in the latter
reason renders the evil familiar.

"What happened to me was this. There came to Egypt,
I know not how or whence but to the ill hap of all who

knew her, a Thracian woman named Rhodopis. She was at
the height of her bloom, and second only to Charicleia in
beauty. In her bawdy travels she came to Memphis also,
escorted by a rout of attendants and great luxury. In all
the arts of seduction she was a practiced expert. None that
encountered her could avoid entanglement; fascination irresistible and ineluctable emanated from the courtesan's
eyes. She frequented the temple of Isis, of which I was
the prophet, and regularly worshipped the goddess with
costly sacrifices and offerings. I am ashamed to say it,
but said it shall be: seeing her so frequently, I too suffered
defeat. She vanquished the self-control which had been
my lifelong practice. Long did I resist the eyes of the body
with the eyes of the soul, but I came off the loser and succumbed to the burden of love. I perceived that this woman
was the inception of those evils of which I was divinely
forewarned; I understood that she was a personification
of fate and that the deity who governed my lot had clothed
himself with her as with an actor's mask. I resolved not to
bring shame upon the priesthood to which I had been
brought up from childhood and to refrain from sullying
the shrines and altars of the gods. The appropriate penalty
for my sin—not in act, heaven forbid, but only in desire—
I inflicted upon myself; I appointed reason my judge and
punished my lust with exile. Heavy laden as I was, I departed from my native land, partly yielding to inexorable
fate and suffering it to do with me as it willed, and partly
fleeing the curse of Rhodopis. I was afraid, friend, that
under the baleful influence of the stars that governed me
I might be reduced to some more shameful act. But before
all else the principal consideration that drove me forth
was my children, of whom it was frequently foretold me,
by the arcane wisdom bestowed upon me by the gods, that
they would fall upon one another, sword in hand. Averting
my face, therefore, from a spectacle so abominable that

the sun, I imagine, would veil its rays in a cloud to avoid it, and sparing the father's eyes the repulsive sight of his sons' slaughter, I removed myself from my country and my father's house. My purpose I communicated to no one, but pretended that I was setting out for great Thebes, there to visit my elder son who was sojourning with his maternal grandfather. That son's name, friend, was Thyamis." Again Cnemon was startled, as if the name of Thyamis had boxed his ear; but he governed himself to silence for the sake of the sequel, and the old man continued his discourse as follows: "I will omit my wanderings in the interval, my young friend, for they are not relevant to your inquiry.

"When I learned that there was a city in Greece called Delphi, which was sacred to Apollo and was the seat of other gods also, that it was a laboratory of sages and remote from the tumult of the mob, I took my way thither, judging that a place devoted to sacred mysteries was a suitable lodging for the prophetic kind. I crossed the Crissaean Gulf, landed at Cirrha, and immediately hurried to the city. As soon as I arrived a sound truly divine struck my ears. In all respects the city seemed a fit abode of the gods and not least in the character of its site. Like a citadel or acropolis shaped by nature Parnassus hangs over the city and the spurs at its feet shelter it in the mountain's bosom." "Excellently described," said Cnemon, "as if your perception had been touched by true Pythian inspiration. So my father described the site of Delphi to me when the city of Athens had sent him there on an official mission." "Then you are an Athenian, my boy?" "Yes," said Cnemon. "And your name?" "Cnemon," he replied. "The other details you shall hear presently, but now please go on." "I shall," said the old man. "I went up to the town. I admired the city with its promenades, open places, and fountains, and in particular that of Castalia, where I performed ablutions. Then I hurried to the temple, for the murmur of the crowd, indicating that the hour for the priestess to be inspired was at hand, put wings to my feet. I entered, bowed down, and pronounced a prayer for myself, and the Pythia pronounced the following oracle:

> Tracing your steps from fertile Nile
> You flee the strong spindle of the Fates.
> Endure, for to you dark Egypt's plain
> I shall soon restore. Now be thou my friend.

"When this oracle was delivered I prostrated myself at the altar and besought the deity to be propitious to me in all things. The large crowd which surrounded me rendered praise to the god for having vouchsafed me a response at my first entreaty. Me they felicitated and showed every attention, saying I was most favored by the god next after Lycurgus the Spartan. They permitted me to reside in the precinct of the temple if I wished and voted to supply my sustenance at public charge. In a word, they left nothing to be desired. I attended and studied the rites and sacrifices, of which a great number and variety were performed daily as offerings to the gods by natives and strangers alike, or I conversed with the philosophers, for a great number of them flocked about the Pythian temple. The city is a veritable seat of the Muses, inspired by the god who presides over them. In the beginning they broached various inquiries. One asked how we Egyptians worship our native gods, another why certain animals are deified in one place and others in another and what stories were told of each. One inquired about the construction of the pyramids, another about the cause of the subterranean galleries. In a word, there was nothing Egyptian into which they did not inquire, for anything heard or told of Egypt has a special charm for Greek listeners.

"Finally one of the shrewdest introduced questions about the Nile—what its sources were, how it was particularly distinguished from other rivers, and why it alone of rivers floods in the summer. I told them what I knew and what was written about the river in the sacred books, which only priests may read and understand. I explained that the river took its source in the mountains of Ethiopia and the extremities of Libya, in the region where the East ends and the South begins. It floods in the summer not, as some think, because it is cut off by the Etesian winds blowing in the opposite direction, but because these same winds, at the time of the summer solstice, drive and push the clouds from north to south. Their further movement is arrested by the torrid heat, and they are compacted and condensed into water, which falls in torrential rains. The Nile rages and is no longer restrained in its channel but spreads over its banks like a sea and fertilizes the tilth it floods. That is why its water is sweet to the taste: it is supplied by clouds in the sky. It is bland to the touch, not hot as at its source, but still tepid from the effect of the source. For this reason too it is the only river which does not exude vapors, which it would surely do if, as certain reputable Greeks themselves, I understand, hold, its rise were due to the melting of snow.

"While I was discoursing in this manner a priest of Apollo whom I had come to know best, Charicles by name, remarked, 'Admirably said! I share your view, for it agrees with what I learned from the priests at the cataracts of the Nile.' 'Have you been there, Charicles?' said I to him. 'I have, wise Calasiris,' said he. 'What errand took you there?' I asked. 'It was a family misfortune,' he answered, 'which turned out to be a cause of happiness.' When I expressed surprise at the paradox, he said, 'You would not wonder if you heard how the thing came about, and hear it you may whenever you choose.' 'Then please

tell it, for I choose now,' said I. 'You must know,' said
Charicles when he had dismissed the bystanders, 'that I
have long wished you to hear my story for a reason of my
own. I was married but had no children, until late in life
and after many prayers I became the father of a little
daughter, but received a divine warning that her lot would
not be auspicious. She reached marriageable age and I
betrothed her to the suitor (she had many) whom I judged
worthiest. On the first night that she lay with her husband
the hapless girl died, for her bridal chamber was set afire,
either by lightning stroke or human hands. The unfinished
hymeneal chant was concluded as a dirge; from her bridal
canopy she was escorted to the tomb, and the torches which
were lighted for her marriage kindled her funeral pyre. To
this tragedy fate added another act: it took from me my
child's mother, who succumbed to her grief. My heaven-
sent calamities I could not endure, but I did not take myself out of life, for I believed the theologians who declare
the deed impious. But I did take myself out of my native
land and fled the desolation of my house. The dimness of
recollection, when the actuality is removed, is a great pal-
liative to grief. I roamed over many lands, and eventually
to your Egypt and to Catadupa, to study the cataracts of
the Nile.

" 'That, my friend, is the explanation of my visit to
Egypt. I now insert a digression which, to speak more truly,
is the principal part of my tale. While I was amusing myself by wandering through the city and purchasing objects
which are rare in Greece (for now the intensity of my sorrow was assuaged and I contemplated returning to my own
country) a man of dignified appearance accosted me. His
countenance reflected high intelligence, his age was just
past student years, and his color was a deep black. He
saluted me and in broken Greek said he wished to speak to
me. I agreed readily, and he took me to a nearby temple.

"I saw you bargaining for leaves and roots from India, Ethiopia, and Egypt," said he. "If you wish to make a good purchase, free of all deceit, I am ready to supply you." "I do," said I, "show me your wares." "Do not be too petty a buyer," said he. "And do not be too difficult a seller," said I. He then produced from under his arm a small pouch and showed me a marvelous collection of precious stones. There were pearls as big as nuts, shaped in perfect spheres and of clear white color. There were emeralds and jacinths, the former a delicate green, like a field of corn in spring, shining and smooth like olives; the latter imitating the color of a sea-beach tinged purple by the changing shadows from an overhanging rock. In a word, the scintillating and coruscating mixture was a delight to the eye. When I saw them I said, "You must find another customer, stranger; I and all my fortune could scarcely amount to the value of a single one of those stones." "If you cannot buy them," said he, "you can surely take them as a gift." "I am certainly capable of taking a gift," said I, "but I cannot conceive why it pleases you to make fun of me." "I make no fun," said he, "but am in deep earnest, and I swear by the gods of this temple that I will give all these to you if you are willing to receive in addition another gift far more precious than these." At this I laughed and when he asked me why I said, "Because it is laughable; you engage to give me such valuable gifts and then promise me another still more valuable as a reward for taking them." "Have faith," said he, "swear to me that you will use the gift well, as I myself shall direct you." I was amazed and perplexed, but allured by the hope of such treasures, I gave my oath. When I had so done, in the terms he stipulated, he took me to his house and showed me a girl of indescribable, and indeed heavenly beauty. He said she was seven years old but to me she seemed nearly of marriageable age, so much did her super-

lative beauty enhance even her stature. I stood dumbfounded, ignorant of what was happening and ravished by
what I saw.'

" 'The man then gave me the following account. "The
child you see, stranger, was exposed while yet in her swaddling clothes by her mother, for a reason you shall presently learn, and abandoned to the chances of fortune. I
found her and took her up, because for me it is not per-
missible to disregard an imperiled soul once it has taken
on human form. This is a precept of our gymnosophists, of
whom I have recently been privileged to be a disciple. Moreover, from the child's eyes there shone a sparkling and
supernatural brilliance, so brightly and engagingly did she
look at me when I examined her. Lying with her was a
necklace of gems, which I have just shown you, and a
ribbon woven of silken thread on which was embroidered
in native characters the story of the child. The mother, I
suppose, had solicitously provided these symbols by which
the child might be recognized. When I read this and
learned whence the child came and whose it was I took it
to a farm far from the city and gave it to my shepherds
to bring up, enjoining them to speak of her to no one.
The valuables exposed with her I kept, so that they might
not give rise to some plot against the child. At first everything was kept secret, but as time went on her bloom of
beauty surpassed all expectations. Not even in the bowels
of the earth could her loveliness, I think, be hidden; even
from there it would shine forth. I was afraid her story
might come to light and endanger her safety and involve
me in unpleasantness also, and so I managed to be sent
as ambassador to the satrap of Egypt. I brought the child
here with me with the intention of making some arrangements for her. As for the satrap, I shall shortly dispatch
my business with him, for he has promised me an audience
today. To you and to the gods who dispose events I deliver

this child upon the condition sworn to between us. You will treat as free born and marry to a free-born man this girl whom you receive from me, or rather, from the mother who exposed her. I have faith that you will perform all your engagements; I trust in your pledges and in your character, which, in the many days you have sojourned here, I have carefully observed and found to be truly Greek. These things I say to you in brief, for the business of my embassy summons me. Tomorrow you will receive more explicit and precise information about the girl if you meet me at the temple of Isis." '

" 'I did as he desired: I veiled the girl and brought her to my house that day. I tended her carefully and caressed her tenderly. I gave hearty thanks to the gods and thenceforward called her my daughter and so regarded her. At dawn the next day I went in great haste to the temple of Isis, where I had agreed to meet the stranger. I walked about for a considerable time, but he failed to appear, and so I went to the satrap's residence and inquired whether anyone had seen the Ethiopian ambassador. I was told that he was gone, or rather that he had been driven out, the satrap threatening death if he were not beyond the borders before sunset. When I asked the reason my informant told me that he had interdicted the exploitation by Egypt of the emerald mines on the grounds that they belonged to Ethiopia. I returned in a depressed mood, as if I had suffered some heavy blow, for now I could not know whence the child came and who her parents were.' " "No wonder," said Cnemon, "I too am disappointed at not knowing. But perhaps I shall?" "You will," said Calasiris, "but let me tell you how Charicles continued his account."

" 'When I returned to my room, I was met by the child. She said nothing, for she did not know Greek, but she saluted me with a gesture, and the sight of her shining face was enough to soothe me. Like good and well-bred puppies who fawn upon people whom they have newly come to know, so she, I was pleased to see, quickly perceived my affection for her and treated me like a father. I resolved not to dally in Catadupa lest some malignant deity should again deprive me of a daughter, so I descended the Nile to the sea, where I found a ship and embarked for home. The child is now here with me; she is indeed my child and is called by my name and my whole life is centered upon her. She has surpassed my fondest hopes. She was quick in learning Greek, and quickly did she reach maturity, like the scion of noble stock. In physical beauty she so far transcends all her sex that every eye, Greek or foreign, turns to her. Wherever she appears, in temple, promenade, or public square, she is the cynosure of all eyes and all attention like a model work of art. But though her qualities are such, she is causing me much vexation. She rejects matrimony and insists on a virgin life. She has devoted herself as acolyte of Artemis and spends her time in hunting and practicing archery. To me life is intolerable. I had hoped to marry her to my sister's son, an amiable young man, accomplished in speech and character, but have no success because of her stubborn decision. Neither entreaties nor promises nor reasoning can move her, and what is most annoying, she uses my own shafts against me, as the saying goes. The versatile eloquence which I taught her she uses to argue that she has chosen the best of lives. Virginity she glorifies and represents as an approach to the immortals. She calls it immaculate, untainted, incorruptible. Love, Aphrodite, and the married state she despises and rejects.'

" 'It is here that I request your assistance, and that is why I seized the opportunity which was so aptly offered to trouble you with my long story. Do me this kindness, Calasiris. Bring to bear upon her some Egyptian science or magic. By word or deed bring her to realize her own nature and to understand that she was born a woman. For

you the matter is easy if you are willing. She is not averse
to conversation with men, but despite her association with
them she insists on virginity. She lives here as you do, I
mean within the precincts of the temple. I am your suppliant: do not disregard me, do not suffer me to spend a
grievous old age, childless, comfortless, and without hope
of descendants; do not, by Apollo here and by your native
gods.' I wept when I heard this, Cnemon, for he too shed
many a tear as he pleaded, and I promised that I would do
what I could to help him.

"We were still deliberating about these matters when
word was hurriedly brought that the chief of the sacred
delegation of the Aenians had long been at the door and
was impatiently asking that the priest appear to inaugurate
the ritual. I asked Charicles who the Aenians were, what
their observances were, and what sacrifice they were offering. 'The Aenians,' he said, 'are the noblest part of the
Thessalians. They are thorough Hellenes, being descended
from Helle, son of Deucalion. Their country extends along
the Malian Gulf. Their capital they call by the proud name
of Hypata (or "Eminent") because, as they say, it is most
eminent and bears sway, or, as others think, because it is
situated at Mount Oeta. Their sacred embassy and ritual is
celebrated every fourth year, at the time of the Pythian
games (which, as you know, are now in progress) to Neoptolemus, son of Achilles. It was here, at the very altar of
Apollo, that Neoptolemus was treacherously slain by Ores-
tes, son of Agamemnon. This year's observance is more
ambitious than others, for its chief claims descent from
Achilles. I happened to meet the young man yesterday, and
he seemed to me to be truly worthy of the race of Achilles;
his handsome figure and noble stature confirm his descent
from a goddess.' I expressed surprise that an Aenian should
claim descent from Achilles, for the Egyptian poet Homer
derives Achilles from Phthia. 'The young man,' said Chari-

cles, 'and the Aenians generally, claim Achilles as their
own hero. They insist that Thetis, who married Peleus,
came from the Malian Gulf and that in antiquity the region about the gulf was called Phthia. Others who claim
the distinction do so falsely. By another connection also
the young man claims relationship with the Aeacidae.
Mnestheus, son of Spercheius and of Polydora, daughter of
Peleus, he asserts was his ancestor. This Mnestheus was one
of Achilles' principal companions in the expedition against
Troy and it was because of their relationship that he commanded the first corps of the Myrmidons. The young man
clings fast to this relationship to Achilles and insists that
the Aenians are Achilles' people. To the other arguments
which he cites he adds the fact that in the matter of the
consecration of Neoptolemus all the Thessalians have
yielded to the Aenians, thus testifying that the Aenians
are the closest relations.' 'I begrudge them not at all, Charicles,' said I, 'whether their claim is an agreeable pretense
or whether it is well founded. But please have the chief
brought in, for I am frantic to see him.'

"Charicles gave a nod, and the young man came in. He
did have the true air of an Achilles in his forthright look
and his proud spirit. His neck was erect, his hair flowed
straight back from his forehead, his nose proclaimed his
impetuous spirit and his nostrils snuffed the free air. His
eyes were not blue but a bluish black; his glance was austere but not unamiable, like the sea smoothed to tranquil-
ity after a tempest. When we had exchanged the customary
greetings he said it was time to proceed to the sacrifice to
the god so that the consecration to the hero and the procession which followed it could be carried out in due season.
'So be it,' said Charicles. As he arose he said to me, 'Today
you will see Charicleia if you have not already done so.
Ancient usage requires that the priestess of Artemis be
present at the procession and consecration to Neoptolemus.'

I had several times seen the girl, Cnemon, for we had offered sacrifice together and she had asked me questions on
religious subjects; but I held my peace and waited to see
what would happen. Together we proceeded to the temple,
where the Thessalians had made all preparations for the
sacrifice. We approached the altar and the young man began the ritual. When the priest had offered the preliminary
prayer the Pythia pronounced this oracle:

Her who is first in grace, in fame last,
Celebrate, ye Delphians, and also him sprung from a god-
    dess.
When they have left my temple and cloven the waves
They will arrive at the dark earth of the Sun.
There will they obtain the great prize of noble life,
White garlands on dusky brows.

"When the god pronounced these words all present were
baffled and at a loss to know what the oracle signified.
Everyone interpreted it in a different sense, each giving
the oracle the meaning he desired. But no one caught its
true meaning. Oracles and dreams generally are judged
only by subsequent events. The Delphians, moreover, were
excited by the lavishly mounted procession and hurried to
see it, and they neglected to investigate the exact sense of
the oracle."

3

"WHEN THE PROCESSION and the consecration were
concluded . . ." "But they have not been concluded,
father," interrupted Cnemon, "for your discourse has not
yet made me a spectator, and I am completely overcome by
eagerness to hear and to see the festivity with my own eyes.
But you evade me, like the man in the story who came after
the party was over; you open your theater and shut it in
the same instant." "I have no wish to trouble you, Cnemon," said Calasiris, "with matters extraneous to our subject. I was proceeding to the relevant parts of my story, the
matters about which you inquired in the beginning. But
since you wish to be a ringside spectator (which is proof
enough that you are an Athenian) I will give you a brief
account of the famous celebration, both for its own sake
and for its consequences.

"In the van was a hecatomb conducted by initiates of
rustic appearance and dress. Each wore a white tunic, girt
so that it reached the knee: the right arm, with shoulders
and breast bare, brandished a two-edged ax. The oxen, all
black, tossed their necks and arched them into curves.
Their horns were of moderate size and came to a point

without bending, one gilt and the other twined with garlands of flowers. They were bandy-legged, and their dew-
laps hung down to their knees. Their number was exactly
a hundred, in accordance with the significance of 'hecatomb.' There followed a multitude of other victims; each
species separately was conducted in orderly fashion to the
accompaniment of flute and pipes which played an initiatory melody indicating that a sacrifice was to follow.

"After the animals and their conductors, came Thessalian maidens with beautiful low-girt robes and flowing
hair. They were divided into two choirs; the first group
bore paniers filled with flowers and fruits, and the others
baskets of spices and incense, so that a fragrant aroma filled
the whole place. For carrying their burdens they made no
use of their hands. Their offerings they carried upon their
heads, and held hands to form straight or oblique lines for
marching or dancing. The first choir called out the burden
of the melody, for it was their part to chant the whole
hymn. The hymn was in praise of Thetis and Peleus, and
then of their son, and after that of *his* son. Afterward,
Cnemon . . ." "Why 'afterward Cnemon?' " said Cnemon.
"Again you deprive me of what is most agreeable, father,
by not reciting the hymn itself. Make me not only a spectator of the procession but an auditor too." "If you are set
upon it," said Calasiris, "you shall hear it. It went somewhat as follows:

> Thetis I sing. Thetis the golden-haired,
> Immortal daughter of Nereus of the sea,
> To Peleus wed at the bidding of Zeus.
> Our Lady of Paphos, bright goddess of the sea,
> Whose loins bore the spear-raging war-god,
> Greece's brilliant glory,
> Divine Achilles of heaven-ranging fame.
> To him Pyrrha bore Neoptolemus,

The sacker of Troy, the bulwark of the Danaans.
Be thou to us propitious, Neoptolemus,
Hero blessedly reposing in Pythian land.
Accept this our offering of hymns,
Keep all fear far from our city.
Thetis I sing, Thetis the golden-haired.

"Such was the text of the hymn, Cnemon, as well as I
can recall it. So well did its melody harmonize with the
dance and so well did the rhythm of the steps suit the ca-
dences that sound diverted attention from spectacle and all
present kept time with the maidens in their paces, as if they
were mesmerized by the chant. But then a mounted band
of cadets and their leader burst brilliantly into view and
afforded a spectacle fairer far than any music. The cadets
numbered fifty, divided into two squads of twenty-five
riding on either side of their chief, who occupied the center.
Their boots were laced with a purple thong tied above the
ankle. Their capes were white, fastened with a golden
brooch over the breast and edged with a blue border in a
circular design. Their mounts were all Thessalian and reflected the freedom of their plains in their proud bearing.
They champed their bits as if disdaining control and were
flecked with foam, but they nevertheless heeded the will of
their riders. They were caparisoned with trappings and
frontlets of silver and gilt, as if the cadets vied with each
other in richness. Magnificent as they were, however, Cnemon, all eyes passed over them with little heed and turned
to gaze at their leader, Theagenes, the object of my special
care. You would say that the previous spectacle had been
dimmed by a lightning flash, so brilliant a show did he
make. He too was mounted, but he wore the dress of a
hoplite and brandished an ashen spear with brazen point.
His helmet was unfastened and he marched bareheaded. He
wore a cloak of purple with gold embroidery representing

the battle of the Lapiths and the Centaurs; the brooch was
of electrum and bore the figure of Athena with a Gorgon's
head on her shield. His charm was enhanced by a light fluttering breeze; it played on his hair which fell down his
neck in waves and divided the ringlets on his brow, and
lifted the edges of his cloak from the croup and withers of
his horse. You would say that the horse was conscious of
his master's beauty and that the handsome mount sensed
that he was carrying the handsomest of riders. He arched
his neck, pointed his ears, held his head erect, rolled his
eyes in their sockets, proud of himself and his burden. He
paced along under a loose rein, putting his weight on either
shoulder in turn, lightly tapping the ground with the tips
of his hooves and adjusting his pace to a tranquil motion.
At the sight all were struck with admiration and voted the
leader the prize for manliness and beauty. All the women
of the street, unable to conceal or control the passion that
mastered them, pelted him with fruit and flowers, thinking
to attract his favorable notice. The sole and universal
judgment was that mankind could never produce beauty
surpassing Theagenes'.

"Came then Dawn, the rosy-fingered, as Homer says,
and when Charicleia, beautiful and clever, emerged from
the temple of Artemis we realized that even Theagenes
might be surpassed—but only because the pure loveliness
of womankind is more attractive than the first among men.
She rode in a carriage drawn by a yoke of white oxen and
was dressed in a purple robe picked out with golden rays
which reached to her feet. Under her bosom was fastened
a cincture on which the artist had bestowed all his skill;
never before had he fashioned anything so fine, nor could
he ever again afterward. Two serpents had their tails inter-
laced behind her back, while their necks crossed under her
breasts and formed a winding noose. The heads emerged
from the noose at either side like knobs for the knot. You

would have said not that the serpents seemed to glide but
that they did glide. Nor did they have a rigid and terrifying look, but rather did they float in a languid slumber, as if
they had been lulled to sleep by the loveliness of the maid-
en's bosom. Their material was gold, their color a dark
blue. The gold was artificially darkened so that the alterna-
tion of black and yellow should imitate the rough and
changeable scales. Such was the maiden's girdle. Her hair
was neither all braided nor all loose. The greater part,
gathered behind her neck, floated in waves on her back
and shoulders; that which descended from her crown and
brow was wreathed with soft branches of laurel, which
prevented the breezes from disturbing it more than was
seemly and gave an appearance of roses in bright sunlight.
In her left hand she carried a bow covered with gilt, over
her right shoulder a quiver was slung, in her right hand
was a lighted torch—but the beam from her eyes shone
brighter than any torches."

"Truly Charicleia and Theagenes!" cried Cnemon.
"Where in the world are they? Do, by the gods, show me
where!" begged Calasiris, thinking Cnemon had caught
sight of them. But Cnemon said, "I imagined I saw them,
father, though they were not present, so vivid was your
description and so closely did your account match my
own recollection of them." "I do not know," said Calasiris,
"whether you saw them as all Greece and the sun viewed
them upon that day—so universally admired were they, so
glorified, she the object of all men's prayers, he of all
women's. Marriage with either of them they regarded as tan-
tamount to immortality, except that the natives were more
smitten with the young man and the Thessalians with the
girl, each admiring more what they saw for the first time.
A novel spectacle is more apt to astonish than a familiar
one. But ah, sweet delusion, delightful fancy! What wings
you gave my spirit when I thought you had seen my dar-

lings and would point them out to me, Cnemon! Really, I
think you have cheated me altogether. At the beginning of
our talk you said they would arrive very soon and show
themselves, and on that condition demanded my account
of them as your reward; but now it is evening and night
is falling and you cannot show me them anywhere." "Courage!" said Cnemon, "be of good heart, for they will surely
come. Perhaps they have encountered some obstacle and
will arrive later than they engaged. But I would in any
case not show them to you unless you produced my full
price. If you are in a hurry to see them, therefore, make
good your promise and carry your account to its conclusion." "I myself find it irksome to speak of matters which
recall my sorrows, and I thought my garrulity had satiated
you and was now cloying. But since you are an avid listener
and insatiable in your appetite for good stories, come, let
us resume our discourse where we digressed. But first let
us light a torch and pour bedtime libations to the deities
of the night, so that when we have performed the customary rites we may spend a tranquil night in discourse."

So the old man said, and at his bidding the maid brought
in a lighted lamp. Then he poured a libation, and among
other gods specially invoked Hermes. To him he prayed
that the night would bring agreeable dreams and that those
he most loved might appear to him in his sleep. When these
observances were completed he resumed: "When the procession had encircled the tomb of Neoptolemus, Cnemon,
and the cadets had ridden round it thrice, the women raised
a wail and the men a war cry. Then at a single signal oxen,
lambs, goats were sacrificed, as if the slaughter had been
carried out by a single hand. A huge altar was piled with
an immense amount of kindling, the customary portions
of the victims were placed upon it, and the priest of Apollo
was requested to inaugurate the libation and light the altar.
Charicles said that the libation was his function, but that

traditional usage required that the chief of the sacred embassy should kindle the altar with the torch he received from the priestess. So saying he performed the libation, and Theagenes received the fire.

"We understand, my dear Cnemon, from the effects souls exhibit that they are divine and have primordial affinities. As soon as those two young people looked on one another they fell in love, as if from the first encounter the soul recognized its like and hastened to its proper domicile. At first they stood in sudden amazement, and then, very slowly, she handed him the torch. He received it, and they fixed each other with a rigid gaze, as if they had sometime known one another or had seen each other before and were now calling each other to mind. Then they gave each other a slight, and furtive smile, marked only by the spreading of the eyes. Then, as if ashamed of what they had done, they blushed, and again, when the passion, as I think, suffused their hearts, they turned pale. In a single moment, in short, their countenances betrayed a thousand shades of feeling; their various changes of color and expression revealed the commotion of their souls. These emotions escaped the crowd, as was natural, for each was preoccupied with his own duties; they escaped Charicles also, who was busy reciting the traditional prayer and invocation. But I occupied myself with nothing else than observing these young people from the time that the oracle upon Theagenes was chanted in the temple as he was offering sacrifice. I was moved by their names to form conjectures concerning the future, but I could not conceive precisely what the remainder of the oracle portended.

"Slowly and as if perforce Theagenes tore himself from the girl, applied the torch, and kindled the altar. The procession dispersed; the Thessalians addressed themselves to their feast, and the rest of the people departed each to his own house. Charicleia put on a white mantle, and with a few familiars went to her lodging in the temple precinct; she did not live with her supposititious father but kept apart because of her religious duties. What I had heard and seen made me curious, and so I contrived to encounter Charicles. 'Have you seen Charicleia,' he asked, 'my glory and the Delphians'?' 'This is not the first time,' said I. 'I have frequently encountered her in the temple, and not incidentally, as the saying goes: she has offered sacrifice with me and has questioned me and received my answers whenever she was in doubt on matters human or divine.' 'But what did you think of her today, my friend? Was she not an ornament to the procession?' 'Hush, Charicles,' said I, 'it is as if you asked whether the moon is not brighter than the stars.' 'But some,' said he, 'praise that Thessalian youth also.' 'One may assign him the second or third place,' said I, 'but one must acknowledge that the crown of the procession and indeed its very eye was your daughter.' Charicles was delighted, and speaking the simple truth promoted my own purpose, for I wished to build up his confidence. Smiling, he said, 'I am going to her; if you like come with me and see whether she has been fatigued by the crowd and the tumult.' I was happy to consent, but indicated that I regarded his invitation as more urgent than any business of my own.

"When we arrived at her lodging we found her on her bed, ill at ease and with eyes swimming with love. She saluted her father with her customary embrace and, when he asked what ailed her, said she had a headache and would like to rest if she might. At this Charicles was alarmed and left the chamber with me, enjoining the maids to keep silence. In front of the house he said to me, 'What is this, Calasiris? What is the indisposition that has attacked my little girl?' 'Do not wonder,' said I, 'if, being exhibited to such a multitude, she has attracted some evil eye.' He smiled ironically and said, 'So you, along with the common herd, believe in the evil eye?' 'As I believe in anything which is manifestly true,' I said. 'This is how it works. The air by which we are surrounded and which reaches our inward parts through eyes, nostrils, breath, and other passages, brings with it qualities it has received outside and implants in the person receiving it whatever affections it has acquired. Thus when one looks upon a beautiful object with envy he fills the surrounding air with this malignant quality and transmits his own pernicious breath to whatever is near. Being thin and subtle, this breath penetrates to the bones and marrow, and thus envy under its commonly accepted designation of "evil eye" is a disease which affects many people. Consider also, Charicles, how many people are infected with eye disease or other contagions when they have never touched anyone suffering from the disease or his bed or his table; the air itself is infectious. One proof of this argument is the genesis of love, in which mere sight provides a beginning and a leverage; it is through the eye that the passion penetrates to the soul. It is obvious that it must be so. Sight being the most mobile and the hottest of all our perceptions and accessibilities, it is most receptive to emanations and with fervent spirit attracts passing elements of love. If you wish an example from natural history, here is one taken from our sacred books on animals. The thick-kneed bustard cures persons suffering from jaundice. If anyone so afflicted looks at the bird, it runs away, shuts its eyes, turns its back—not, as some think, begrudging its help, but because when it looks it naturally draws the disease to itself like a flux, and therefore it dodges sight as it would a blow. You have doubtless heard of the serpent called basilisk, whose breath and look alone is enough to parch and corrupt whatever it encounters. We must not be surprised that some people cast an evil eye even upon those they love and wish well; since they are by nature envious they act not as they wish but as their nature compels them.'

"Charicles paused for a moment and then said, 'Your solution of this problem is sagacious and plausible. I only wish that Charicleia did feel love and desire, for then I should consider her not diseased but cured. You know I have solicited your help in this matter. But there is no fear —such is her hatred of love and marriage—that this is her ailment; no, it is really of the evil eye that she is suffering. Surely you will be willing to solve this difficulty, for you are a friend and very competent.' I promised that I would do all I could to help if I perceived that she was in any way diseased.

"While we were yet deliberating a man came up in haste and said, 'Good people, you are dallying as if it were a battle or a war you were invited to and not a feast organized by excellent Theagenes and presided over by Neoptolemus, the greatest of heroes. Come! Do not drag the banquet out till evening; you are the only ones missing.' Charicles bent over to my ear and said, 'The fellow invites me with a cudgel. He is importunate, and drunk too. But let us go; he may end by beating us.' 'You are joking,' said I, 'but in any case, let us go.'

"When we arrived Theagenes placed Charicles next to himself and bestowed an honorable place on me too for Charicles' sake. There is no point in boring you with the details of the feast—the dancing girls, the flautists, the dance of cadets in arms, the pyrrhic dance, the sumptuous viands which Theagenes provided to enhance conviviality and joviality. But here is a thing which is necessary for you to hear and pleasant for me to tell. Theagenes exhibited a cheerful face and forced himself to show the company friendly courtesy, but I could perceive the course of his thoughts. Now his look wandered, now he heaved a deep sigh for no apparent reason; now he was melancholy and thoughtful, and suddenly he put on a brighter look, as if he had become aware of his surroundings and recalled him-

self. He moved from one mood to another easily, for the
mind of a lover, as of a man drunk, is variable and unable
to remain fixed. Each teeters on a slippery emotion; that is
why a lover is inclined to drink and a drinker to love.

"When his boredom and anxiety became increasingly apparent, the others present also noticed that he was not well.
Even Charicles, who had observed nothing else unusual,
whispered to me, 'The evil eye has hit him too; he seems
to have the same ailment as Charicleia.' 'By Isis, the same,'
said I, 'and quite naturally, for he was second to her in
beauty in the procession.' So we remarked. When it was
time for the cups to be carried around, Theagenes, though
not disposed to do so, toasted each guest. When it came my
turn I said I accepted his good wishes but would not take
the cup; he thought I insulted him and gave me a sharp
and burning look. Charicles, who understood the situation,
said, 'He abstains from wine and animal food.' When
Theagenes asked the reason, he said, 'He is an Egyptian
from Memphis, and a prophet of Isis.' When Theagenes
heard the words Egyptian and prophet he was filled with
sudden delight, and as if he had come upon some treasure
he rose upright, called for water, drank the toast, and said,
'Wise sage, accept this loving cup, which I drink to your
health in the beverage most agreeable to you; may this
table consecrate our friendship!' 'May it consecrate, excellent Theagenes,' said I, 'the friendship I have long felt for
you'—and I accepted the cup and drank it off. At this the
banquet ended, and each departed to his own house. At
parting Theagenes embraced me much more warmly than
our acquaintance warranted.

"When I came to my lodging I spent the first part of
the night sleepless on my bed, turning my thoughts on the
young people up and down and seeking to decipher the
last words of the oracle. At midnight I saw Apollo and
Artemis, as I imagined (if imagine I did, and not actually

see) ; the god put Theagenes into my hands and the goddess, Charicleia. They called me by name and said, 'It is time for you to return to your country; such is the decree of the fates. Go yourself and take these along as your companions. Treat them as your children. Escort them out of Egypt in what manner and to what place the gods please.' When they had so said they departed, thus showing that the vision was no dream but actuality. What I had seen I understood, except that I was at a loss to know to what people or what country the gods wished me to escort the young people." Cnemon interposed. "That, father, you will tell me later if you found out; but how did you say the gods revealed to you that they appeared in actuality and not in a dream." "In the same manner, my son," said Calasiris, "as the wise Homer intimates. Many readers are oblivious to his enigmatic lines: 'Easily I knew the tokens of his feet and knees as he turned away; the gods are easy to discern.' " "I seem to be of the many," said Cnemon, "and perhaps that is what you meant to prove by citing his lines. Ever since I learned the words I have taken them in the ordinary sense, and was not aware of any hidden theological meaning."

Calasiris hesitated a moment in order to rouse his mind to the domain of the mysterious, and then said, "When gods and divinities visit us and depart from us, Cnemon, they seldom take the form of other creatures but frequently that of humans; this similitude has greater effect upon our imaginations. Even if they are not noticed by the profane, they cannot be concealed from the sage. They can be recognized by their eyes, for their gaze is fixed and they never shut their lids, and even better by their gait, for they do not move by alternate steps but by an aerial gliding motion, cutting the air rather than walking through it. That is why the Egyptians join the feet of the gods in their statues and unite them into a single whole. Homer, being an Egyptian and instructed in their sacred lore, knew

this and represented it symbolically in his verses, leaving it
to those capable of doing so to understand it. Of Athena
he says 'Fierce glared her eyes,' of Poseidon, 'Gliding in his
gait,' not, as some wrongly hold, 'I easily knew him.' "

"This is for me an initiation, divine Calasiris," said Cnemon. "But you have several times called Homer an Egyptian, a thing unheard of to this day. I cannot disbelieve
you, but I find it strange, and beg you not to pass over the
matter without a plain explanation." "Exposition of this
question is not germane to our present subject," said Calasiris, "but I shall give you a brief account nevertheless. Different authors have ascribed different countries to Homer,
and indeed the sage is at home everywhere; but it is certain that Homer was an Egyptian and that his city was
Thebes of the Hundred Gates, as he himself declares. His
father, men think, was a priest of Hermes, but in fact it
was Hermes himself. When the priest's wife had completed
a certain traditional ceremony and had gone to sleep in the
temple, the god consorted with her and begot Homer. The
mark of his ill-assorted parentage Homer bore from his
birth—a long strip of hair growing on one of his thighs.
That is how he got the name Homer (or 'The Thigh')
when he wandered over Greece and other countries chant-
ing his poems. His true name he never told, nor his city or
family, but those that knew the mark on his body made it
into a name." "But why did he conceal his country,
father?" asked Cnemon. "Possibly because he was ashamed
of being an exile; when he left the cadet stage and was
examined for the priesthood, his 'father' banished him
because the blemish on his body proved him illegitimate.
Or possibly he purposely kept his true origin secret so that
he could claim every country as his fatherland."

"Well and truly said, it seems to me," said Cnemon. "I
find evidence in the man's poetry, its sweetness shows an
Egyptian temperament; nor would it so far surpass all

others in merit if Homer did not derive his genius from
some divinity. But now that you have apprehended the
gods in Homeric fashion, Calasiris, tell me what happened
next." "Much the same as before, Cnemon," said Calasiris,
"sleeplessness, deliberation, and cares which flourish by
night. I was glad to discover expectations but I was sorry
to think that Charicles would be deprived of his daughter.
I was in a quandary as to how the young people could be
carried off together and how we could concert measures for
departure. I was anxious about how we could keep our
escape secret, whither we should turn, whether by land or
sea. In a word, I was overwhelmed by a storm of worries
which harried me the rest of the night and kept me sleepless.

"Day had not fully dawned when there was a noise at
the yard door and I heard a boy calling. When the servant
asked who it was that knocked and what he wanted, the
caller replied, 'Say that it is Theagenes the Thessalian.' I
was happy to hear the young man announced, and ordered
him to be invited in. Here, I thought, was an unplanned
opportunity to get my designs afoot. I supposed that Theagenes, who had heard at the banquet that I was an Egyptian and a priest, had come to find a helper for his love
affair. He labored, I supposed, under the common and ill-
informed error which regards all Egyptian wisdom as the
same. One form of it is vulgar. It creeps, one might say,
on the ground. It involves service of idols and is preoccupied with the bodies of the dead; it pores over herbs and
mumbles incantations. Neither this science nor those who
employ it reach any good end. Generally, it stumbles in its
own endeavors, and when it does produce effects they are
gloomy and lamentable. It represents illusion as reality,
disappoints hopes, invents lawless practices, and ministers
to licentious pleasures.

"But the other, my son, is the true Egyptian wisdom, of

which the vulgar science is a bastard progeny. It is this which our priests and prophets cultivate from their youth. Its look is upward to heaven, it is a companion of the gods and a partner in the nature of the divine, it studies the motion of the stars, and from them gains foreknowledge of the future. It is remote from the earthy matters of our world, and concerns itself with all that is noble and profitable for mankind. Because of it did I depart from my country betimes, as I have already explained, to avoid the evils and the fratricidal war of my children which it enabled me to foresee. But these matters must be entrusted to the gods and in particular to the fates, who have power to accomplish or to hinder. It is they, doubtless, who have ordained my exile from my country, not for the apparent reasons but in order that I might find Charicleia. Now you will hear how I did so.

"After Theagenes had entered and we had exchanged greetings, I made him sit on a couch near me and asked, 'What brings you to me so early?' He stroked his face several times and said, 'I am under great strain but am ashamed to say why,' and then he fell silent. I saw that it was time for me to play the wonder worker and to 'divine' what I already knew perfectly well. I gave him an arch look and said, 'You may be timid about speaking but nothing is concealed from my science and the gods.' I paused impressively and then arranged counting pebbles in my fingers (though I had nothing to calculate) and shook my hair and pretended to be possessed and then said, 'My son, you are in love!' At this divination he started up, and when I added 'with Charicleia' he thought my knowledge was inspired. He all but prostrated himself at my feet, and when I prevented him he leaned over and kissed my head repeatedly and thanked the gods that, as he said, he had not been disappointed in his expectations. He asked me to be his savior; if he did not obtain assistance, and that quickly, he could not survive, so great a malady had attacked him, so ardently did his desires burn. This was his first experience of love. He insisted, with many oaths, that he had never associated with women and had always rejected marriage and love when anyone suggested it. Charicleia's beauty had now convinced him that he was not by nature abstemious but that until the present he had never seen a woman worthy of his love. With these words he wept, as if he had succumbed to a girl perforce. I encouraged him and said, 'Take heart, now that you have had recourse to me. The girl cannot be stronger than my science. She is austere and difficult to subdue to love. She disdains Aphrodite and marriage, and will hear nothing of it. But for you every shift must be made: art can constrain even nature. Only be confident and follow the instructions I find necessary.' He promised to do whatever I should order, even if I should bid him walk on swords.

"While he was thus beseeching me and promising me all his fortune as a fee, a messenger from Charicles came in and said, 'Charicles requests you to come to him. He is in the shrine of Apollo nearby, where he is offering a hymn to the god because of certain disturbing dreams.' I arose at once, and when I had dismissed Theagenes, went to the temple. I found Charicles in a chair, very sorrowful and sighing continually. I advanced and asked, 'Why so sad and melancholy?' 'How should I not be?' said he. 'I am terrified by dreams and I hear that my daughter is worse and has spent a sleepless night. I am anyhow distressed about her ill health but particularly because tomorrow is the day fixed for the contest in which it is a tradition for the priestess to present the torch to the armed runners and award the prizes. Either, then, she must stay away and thus desecrate the ancestral law, or, if she attends against her will, her disease will be aggravated. If you have yet done nothing, do help now and apply some remedy: so you will duly discharge the obligations of friendship, of piety to me and of piety to the divine. I know that if you will it is no great task for you to cure what you say is the evil eye; for prophets no remedies are impossible.' I confessed that I had been negligent, the better to carry on the deception, and asked for a day to make necessary preparations for the cure. 'For the present,' said I, 'let us go to the girl and diagnose her state more accurately and do what we can to comfort her. Please say a few words about me to the child, Charicles. Let her see your confidence in me so that she may accept me on familiar terms and have greater confidence in my treatment.' 'So be it,' said he, 'let us go.'

"What need to elaborate on the state in which we found Charicleia? She had succumbed completely to her malady. The bloom had flown from her cheeks, and tears flowing like water had extinguished the luster of her eyes. When she saw us she tried to compose herself and force herself to resume her normal expression and voice. Charicles embraced her and showered a thousand kisses and every tenderness upon her, and said, 'Child, little daughter mine, why do you hide your suffering from your father? You have been attacked by an evil eye, and yet you keep silent as if you had done some wrong, when it was you that was wronged by the evil looks of others. But take heart. Wise Calasiris here has promised to provide a remedy for you. He can do so if anyone can, for he is expert in the divine art. He is a prophet by profession and has been devoted to sacred matters from childhood, and most of all, he is a true friend. It is best for you to be co-operative and allow him to pronounce incantations over you or employ any other remedies he chooses; I know that you welcome association with scholars.' Charicleia remained speechless but nodded to indicate that she would welcome my advice. We then took our leave. Charicles reminded me to take thought of his earlier request and consider methods which might produce in Charicleia an inclination to love and marriage. I sent him away in good spirits, assuring him that I would shortly accomplish all his desire."

4

"THE FOLLOWING DAY was the last of the Pythian competition, but on it the contest of our young pair reached its height. The master of the games, I would say, and their arbiter was Eros, who, by pairing two such champions, strove emulously to demonstrate that the contest of love is the major event. The proceedings took the following course. All of Hellas were spectators, and the Amphictyons presided over the games. Contests in running, in wrestling, and in boxing were run off magnificently, and then the herald cried out, 'Those in heavy armor forward!' Suddenly, at the head of the lists, Charicleia, Artemis' acolyte, appeared in all her splendor. She had come in obedience to ancestral usage, or perhaps, as I rather think, in the hope of glimpsing Theagenes. In her left hand she carried a lighted torch, and in the other waved a palm branch. Upon her appearance, the whole assembly turned their attention toward her, but no eye was quicker than Theagenes', for keen is a lover's lookout for his beloved. He had heard that she might come, and his whole mind was preoccupied with that expectation; and so he could not govern himself to silence, but murmured softly to me (his seat was conveniently close to mine), ' 'Tis herself, 'tis Charicleia.' I bade him keep the silence.

"At the summons of the herald there appeared a warrior splendidly accoutered, proud, and, as it seemed, famous; he had won crowns in many previous contests, but on this occasion had no opponent because, I suppose, none was so bold as to compete with him. The Amphictyons bade him retire, for according to the law only a man who actually competed could obtain a crown. He then suggested that volunteers for the contest be invited by herald's proclamation; the presidents so ordered, and the herald announced that any who would should come forward.

" 'The man is calling me' Theagenes said to me, and when I said, 'What makes you say so?' he answered: 'This is how it is, father. As long as I am here and can see, no other man is going to receive the prize from the hand of Charicleia.' 'But what if you fail,' said I, 'have you given no thought to the disgrace involved in defeat?' Said he: 'Who can be so madly eager to see and be near Charicleia as to outrun me? Whom can the sight of her give such wings to swoop through the air? You know that artists furnish Eros with wings: that is to show how volatile are those he governs. Besides, if I may reinforce these arguments with a personal boast, no one heretofore has been able to brag that he has outrun me.'

"So he said, and sprang forward, entered the lists, gave his name, declared his origin, and was allotted his position in the course. Attired then in full panoply he took his stand at the barrier, panting, scarcely able to await the signal blast of the trumpet. A noble and engrossing spectacle it was, like Homer's representation of Achilles contending in battle at the Scamander. All Hellas was stirred by the unexpected turn, and each man strained for Theagenes to win as if he were himself in the struggle—such power has beauty to win the favor of those who first behold it. But most of all was Charicleia stirred; I had long been watching her, and I observed the changes in her countenance. The herald announced the runners so that all could hear, crying out, 'Ormenos the Arcadian and Theagenes the Thessalian!' The barrier was down and the race was on, so swift that it almost defeated the power of vision. Then could the girl neither keep still nor contain herself; her limbs trembled and her feet quivered as if, I should say, her very soul shared Theagenes' exultation and the eager intensity of his effort. Every one of the spectators was in suspense for the outcome and consumed with anxiety, but I more than all, for I was now resolved to regard him as my son for the future." "No wonder," said Cnemon, "that the spectators there present were in such agony when even I, here and now, am trembling for Theagenes. Tell me quickly, I beg you, whether he was proclaimed victor."

"When Theagenes reached the halfway mark, Cnemon, he turned a little, glowered at Ormenos, raised his shield aloft, craned his neck to gaze full upon Charicleia, and then sprinted to the goal like a bolt, leaving the Arcadian behind by more than a furlong, as was subsequently determined by exact measurement. He dashed full up to Charicleia and fell into her bosom—purposely, but as if, forsooth, the exertion of running had exhausted him, and I noticed that when he received the palm from the girl he kissed her hand."

"You have restored me to life," said Cnemon. "So he won the race and kissed the girl. What comes next?" "You are not only a glutton for listening, Cnemon, but impregnable to sleep. No small part of the night is spent, yet you persist in keeping awake and do not grow restive at my tedious tale." "For my part I find fault with Homer, father, for saying that love, like everything else, cloys with satiety. In my judgment no one can ever get his fill of it, either in experiencing its pleasures or in hearing tales

of love. Can there be a heart of such unfeeling stone or
steel as not to be entranced with the story of the love of
Theagenes and Charicleia, even if he listened all year? So
do go on with what followed."

"Well then, Cnemon, Theagenes was crowned and proclaimed victor, and escorted by a cheering crowd; but
Charicleia suffered a resounding defeat. When she saw
Theagenes for the second time her yearning made her a
more abject slave than before. The sight of lovers recalls
passion, and seeing makes the imagination flare as fuel does
fire. Charicleia went home and passed a night like the
others, or even thornier. I too was again sleepless, pondering how we might manage a clandestine escape, and to
what country heaven purposed to dispatch the young folk.
I only knew that our flight must be effected by sea, basing
my conjecture on the language of the oracle: 'Cloven the
waves, they will arrive at the dark earth of the Sun.' But
to discover whither they were to go I could find but one
solution, and that was to obtain, if possible, that ribbon
which had been exposed with Charicleia, upon which, as I
had heard Charicles say, her story was embroidered. It was
likely that from it I might learn her country and her
parents (whose identity I had already surmised), and perhaps it was thither that fate directed their course.

"Early in the morning, then, I went to Charicles, where
I found the whole household in tears, and Charicles more
so than the rest. I approached him and asked, 'Why this
uproar?' 'My daughter's disease is growing upon her,' he
said. 'Last night she was more wretched than before.' 'Up,'
said I, 'and all the rest too leave the room. Someone bring
me a tripod, laurel, fire, and frankincense, and let no one
disturb me until I call.' Charicles issued the orders, and it
was done. When I had obtained quiet I began enacting a
role as on the stage. I burned the incense and mumbled
some prayers in a whisper and stroked Charicleia from head

to foot with the laurel branch several times, and at long
last when I had drenched myself and the girl with a plethora of such foolishness I stopped and yawned like a man,
or rather like an old hag, falling asleep. The girl kept shak-
ing her head and smiled detachedly, to signify that I was
far from the mark and did not understand her malady.
But I took a seat by her and said, 'Courage, my child. The
disease is simple and easy to cure. You have been bewitched,
possibly when you attended the procession, probably when
you presented the prize. I even suspect the culprit: it was
Theagenes, the man who ran in armor. I noticed him staring at you especially and casting an undeviating eye upon
you.' 'Whether he looked at me or no,' said she, 'farewell
to him!—But who are his family, where is he from? I noticed he was surrounded by a crowd of enthusiasts.' 'That
he is a Thessalian you have already learned from the an-
nouncement of the herald. He claims descent from Achilles,
and I think truthfully, if one may conjecture from the
young man's stature and bearing; these do vouch for nobility like Achilles! Yet he is not as proud and arrogant as
Achilles; the intensity of his character is tempered by
sweetness. And although he has a baneful eye and has bewitched you with his glance, his own sufferings are sharper
than those he has inflicted.' 'Father,' said she, 'thank you
for sympathizing with my suffering, but why do you speak
ill of a man who has probably done no wrong? It is not of
witchery that I am ill but some other malady, I think.'
'Why do you conceal it then, my child, why do you not
take courage to speak out so that we may provide some
remedy? Am I not a father to you in age, and more so in
affection for you? Am I not well known to your own
father and a kindred spirit? Tell me what is troubling you.
I will keep your confidence and, if you like, even swear
to it. Speak freely, and do not nurture and augment your
sorrow by keeping it silent. Any disease quickly diagnosed

is easily cured; one neglected becomes in time incurable. Silence is the nourishment of disease; a malady spoken of is easily relieved.'

"These remarks checked her for a while, and her expression betrayed a thousand directions and impulses in her mind. 'Bear with me this day,' she said, 'and you shall hear my story another time—if you have not already conceived it in your mind, for you claim mantic powers.' I rose and departed, to give the girl an interval in which to overcome her sense of shame. Charicles met me and asked, 'What do you have to tell?' 'Everything is going well,' I said. 'Tomorrow she will be relieved of her troublesome complaint, and another thing agreeable to you will take place. In the meanwhile nothing prevents you from calling in a physician.' I hurried away upon saying this, to forestall Charicles' further questions.

"I had gone but a little way when I saw Theagenes strolling about the temple and its precincts and talking to himself, as if it gave him satisfaction merely to look at Charicleia's house. I turned aside and passed as if I had not noticed him, but he spoke: 'Hello, Calasiris, listen, I've been waiting for you.' I turned quickly and said, 'Handsome Theagenes, and I did not see him!' 'How handsome,' said he, 'when he does not please Charicleia?' I assumed an angry pose and said, 'Will you not stop insulting me and my art? By my art she has been captivated and constrained to love you, and she prays to see you as if you were a heavenly being.' 'What!' said he, 'you say that Charicleia loves me? Why don't you take me to her?' And he started to run. I grabbed his cloak and said, 'Halt, you, even if you are a fast runner. This is not merchandise to be snatched, to be bought cheap, available to all comers; it requires much planning to ensure success and much preparation to ensure safety. Do you not know that the girl's father is an important figure in Delphi—do you not realize that the laws

provide capital punishment for such offenses?' 'I am indifferent to death,' said he, 'if I can get Charicleia. However,
if you think it best, let us go and ask her father for her.
I am after all not unworthy of marriage into Charicleia's
family.' 'We would never succeed,' said I, 'not because any
fault can be found with you, but Charicles has long ago
betrothed the girl to his sister's son.' 'He will rue it,' said
Theagenes, 'whoever he is. No man shall make Charicleia
his bride while I am alive. My hand and sword have not
grown so sluggish.' 'Stop,' said I, 'there will be no need of
that. Just be guided by me and follow my directions. Go
away now, and take care not to be seen too often in my
company. Make your visits to me quietly and alone.' He
went off downcast.

"On the next day, when Charicles met me he ran up as
soon as he saw me and kissed my head again and again, and
cried out repeatedly, 'This is wisdom! This is friendship!
The great fact is achieved, the impregnable is captured,
the invincible is vanquished. Charicleia is in love!' At this
I preened myself and arched my brows and paced delicately
about. 'Obviously,' said I, 'she was not able to resist my
first essay, and the means I employed were far from my
most potent. But Charicles, how did you discover that she
is in love?' 'By your advice,' said he, 'I called in the most
highly reputed physicians, as you suggested, to examine her,
and promised them all my fortune as a fee if they could
help her. As soon as they came in they asked what her pain
was. She turned away and made them no answer at all,
but kept repeating a verse from Homer, "O Achilles, son
of Peleus, most excellent of the Achians." The learned
Acesinus, (you probably know the man) laid his hand on
her wrist, though she was unwilling, and appeared to be
diagnosing her condition from her pulse, which, I imagine,
indicates the movement of the heart. He continued his
examination for a long while, observed her narrowly up

and down, and then said, "Charicles, your calling us here
is futile. Medical skill cannot help in this case." I cried out,
"Ye Gods, what are you saying? Is my darling daughter
gone? Is she beyond hope?" "There is no occasion for excitement," said he, "just listen." He drew me aside from
the girl and the others and said: "Our art professes to
minister to afflictions of the body, and not of the soul, except only when the soul shares the suffering of the afflicted
body, and is therefore relieved when the body is cured.
Your daughter is suffering from a malady, indeed, but it
is not of the body, for there is no plethora of humors, no
heavy pains of the head, no burning fever. Nor is there
any other infection either of a member or of the whole
body. This is so beyond doubt." When I insisted and begged
him to tell me if he had discovered anything further he
said: "Could not even a child know that her suffering is
of the soul and that she has a plain case of love? Do you
not observe how her eyes are swollen, her look unsteady,
her face pale? She does not complain of internal discom-
fort, but her wits wander and her speech is incoherent. She
is sleepless for no apparent reason, and is rapidly losing
weight. You must find the man who will cure her,
Charicles, and he can be none other than the man she
yearns for." So saying he departed, and I have come to
you on the run, my savior and my god, who are the only
one able to do us this kindness. This Chariclea too knows,
for when I begged and implored her to tell me what ailed
her, she answered only that she did not know what her
malady was and that only Calasiris could cure her, and
she besought me to call you to her. To me this is clear proof
that she is profoundly impressed with your wisdom.'

" 'You tell me she is in love,' said I to him. 'Can you tell
me with whom?' 'By Apollo, I can't,' said he. 'How or
whence could I know that? Above all the money in the
world I would pray that she be in love with Alcamenes,

my sister's son. I have long pledged him as her bridegroom, as far as my wishes can be realized.' I said that it was easy to make the experiment of introducing the young man to her inspection, and he thanked me and went away. At the hour of the full market he met me again. 'I have foul news,' he said, 'the child must be possessed, for her conduct is very strange. I brought Alcamenes in, as you bade me do, all elegantly groomed, but as if she had seen the Gorgon's head or something more awful still she uttered a piercing shriek and turned to the opposite side of the room, and put her hands around her neck like a noose, and threatened upon oath to do away with herself if he did not immediately leave the room. Quicker than you could say the word, we departed, for what could we do in the face of such extraordinary behavior? Again we are your suppliants: do not look on while she perishes and I fail of my prayers.' 'Charicles,' said I, 'you were not mistaken when you said the girl was possessed. She is troubled by the powers which I myself employed against her, and as they were no slight powers, she is forced to do things contrary to her nature and her wishes. But it seems to me that some counterdeity is blocking my measures and combating my agents. It is therefore time that you showed me the ribbon which you told me was exposed with the child and which you received with the other tokens. I fear it may be filled with some sorceries and be inscribed with maleficent imprecations which make her spirit savage; it may be the work of some enemy who has plotted to have her live her life out without love and without posterity.'

"Charicles agreed with what I said, and soon brought me the ribbon. I asked him to give me a little time, and when he agreed I hurried to my lodgings and without waiting an instant read the letters embroidered on the ribbon. The characters were Ethiopic, not, however, of the demotic variety but the royal script, which is like the Egyptian writing called hieratic. When I had deciphered it I found it to say: 'Persinna, Queen of the Ethiopians, inscribes this lament as a last gift to her daughter who has no name and is known to me only by travail pangs.' When I came upon the name of Persinna, Cnemon, I shuddered; nevertheless I read on, as follows: 'I call to witness the Sun, the first begetter of our race, that it was not because of any crime of mine that I exposed you at your birth and kept the sight of you from your father Hydaspes. Yet do I make my defense to you, my daughter, if you survive, and to him who shall take you up, if heaven provide any such, and to all the human race, by revealing the cause of my exposing you. Our ancestors are of the gods Sun and Dionysos, and of heroes Perseus and Andromeda, and in addition Memnon. Those who, at various times, have builded our royal courts have adorned them with pictures of these personages. Portraits of the others and representations of their exploits they painted in the men's apartments and the colonnades; the women's apartments they decorated with colorful representations of the love of Perseus and Andromeda. Once in the tenth year after Hydaspes knew me as his wife, when we were still childless, it happened that when I retired to the women's apartment one summer noon for a siesta, your father consorted with me, bidden to do so, he swore, by a dream; and I perceived straightway that I was pregnant.'

" 'The whole period of my pregnancy was kept as a public festival, and sacrifices of thanksgiving were offered to the gods in the hope of an heir of the blood royal. When I brought you to birth I found you white, a complexion alien to the native Ethiopian tint. I knew the reason for this: when I consorted with my husband I was looking at the picture which represented Andromeda just as Perseus had brought her down from the rock, and my offspring unhappily took on the complexion of that body. I re-

solved to deliver myself from a shameful death, persuaded
that your complexion would entail a charge of adultery
and that no one would credit my story of the transformation. You I preferred to deliver to the hazards of chance
rather than to certain death or, at any rate, the infamy of
bastardy. To my husband I pretended that you had died
at birth, and I surreptitiously exposed you, depositing with
you the greatest amount of treasure I could as a reward
for him who should save you and decking you with other
adornments and wrapping about you this ribbon. It has
your pitful story and mine, which I have broidered in
blood and tears, when I newly became a mother and a thing
full of grief. But ah, my sweet, my daughter only for an
hour, if you survive do be mindful of your good birth
and honor chastity, which is the sole virtue that distinguishes womenkind, and cultivate the queenly temper appropriate to your high descent. Among the jewels exposed
with you remember above all to seek out and claim for
yourself a particular ring. That ring your father gave me
when he asked for my hand; its circlet is inscribed with
the royal symbol and its setting is hallowed by the stone
Pantarbe, which possesses secret power. I speak to you
now through the medium of writing because some divinity
has deprived me of living conversation with you, face to
face; perhaps my words will be mute and futile, perhaps
they will some day come of use. Fortune is uncertain and
man cannot know it. If you survive—O beautiful in vain,
beauty which imputes guilt to your mother!—this writing
will serve as a token of recognition; if you fare as I hope
I may never hear, it will serve as your shroud, and your
mother's tears as your mourning.'

"When I read this, Cnemon, I acknowledged the miraculous dispensations of the gods. I was filled at once with
pleasure and pain, and I partook of a strange combination
of grief and happiness. My spirit exulted at the discovery

of what had been dark and at the solution of the oracles; but it was apprehensive of the outcome and filled with pity for the life of man, whose instability and uncertainty and violent vicissitudes were now so singularly illustrated by the fortunes of Charicleia. My mind was occupied by many reflections: who her true parents were and who the reputed; how far she was banished from her native country; how she had acquired a false title of daughter and had lost her true family of Ethiopian royalty. For a long while I wavered between pity for the past and timorous joy for the future, until reason recalled sobriety and I determined to dally no longer but set to work. I went to Charicleia and found her alone. Her condition was desperate; though her mind struggled to bear up, her body was exhausted and too weak for further resistance, it yielded to disease.

"I sent away everyone present and gave orders that I was not to be disturbed for I was going to perform certain rites and incantations on the girl. Then I said: 'Charicleia, it is time for you to tell me your trouble, as you promised to do yesterday, and not mystify a man who wishes you well—and has the capacity of discovering all even if you remain silent.' She took my hand and kissed it and wept over it and said, 'Wise Calasiris, do me this kindness, let me suffer in silence; you yourself may identify the disease as you will, but suffer my modesty to keep secret a thing that is shameful to feel but more shameful to reveal. I suffer indeed from a malady which is now at its height, but I suffer more from not having overcome the disease at its beginning, and at being worsted by an affliction which has always been abhorrent to me and of which even the sound contaminates the pure title of virginity.' I comforted her and said, 'My daughter, you have two good reasons for keeping your affairs to yourself; I have no need to learn what my art has long ago taught me, and your modesty naturally forbids you to speak of matters seemly

for women to hide. But since you have once felt love, and
are manifestly smitten with Theagenes (as I am apprised
by divine intimation) you must realize that you are neither
the only nor the first woman to succumb to this passion;
it has been the lot of numberless women, many celebrated
maidens in other respects irreproachable. For Eros is the
greatest of the deities and is reputed to hold dominion
even over the gods. Consider then how you may best confront your present situation. To be unaffected by love in
the first place is a blessing; but once being smitten, it is
wisest to direct your desires with prudence. If you are
willing to trust me, you can repel the shameful imputation
of sensuality and substitute union in lawful wedlock—you
can transform your malady to marriage.'

"At my remarks, Cnemon, she fell into a copious sweat.
Her gamut of emotions was obvious: she was rejoiced by
my suggestions, in agony for the realization of her hopes,
and embarrassed by the discovery of her weakness. After
a long silence she said: 'Father, you speak of marriage and
recommend it as if it were certain either that my father
would consent to it or that my adversary would recipro-
cate my feelings.' 'As for the young man,' said I, 'we are
on certain ground; he is moved by the same impulses as
you, and even more deeply smitten. It seems that from
your first encounter your souls somehow recognized their
suitability for one another and were inflamed with equal
desire. The young man's desire I myself augmented by my
art, out of affection for you. But your reputed father is
preparing a different bridegroom for you, Alcamenes,
whom you know.' 'He shall prepare Alcamenes a grave,'
said she, 'sooner than marriage with me. Either Theagenes
shall wed me, or fate shall inherit me. But you spoke of
Charicles as my *reputed* father; tell me, I beg of you, how
you discovered it.' 'From this,' said I, displaying the ribbon. 'Where did you get it, and how?' she cried. 'From the

moment Charicles received me from him that nurtured me and somehow brought me here, he has kept it in a box, most carefully, to prevent the injuries of time.' 'How I got it,' said I, 'you shall hear another time. For the present, tell me whether you know what is written on it.' She confessed that she did not: how should she? 'It declares your race and fortune,' said I. She begged me to reveal all that I knew, and I told her all that was written, reading it clause by clause and interpreting it word for word.

"When she knew who she was her mood expanded and she rose to the dignity of her blood. 'What must I do?' she asked, and I began a more explicit explanation of my design and revealed the actual state of affairs to her. 'Daughter,' said I, 'I have been in Ethiopia to study their wisdom. I became acquainted with your mother Persinna, for the royal court is hospitable to scholars, and I acquired some reputation by enriching my Egyptian attainments with an increment of Ethiopian wisdom. When the queen perceived that I was on the point of returning to my home, she told me her whole story, first exacting a pledge of silence upon oath. She said she dared not confide in the native sages and besought me to inquire of the gods whether, in the first place, you survived your exposure, and then in what part of the world you were; she had made diligent inquiry among her own people, but could learn nothing of such a girl as you. The gods did reveal the facts to me and I told her that you were alive and your whereabouts. She then implored me to seek you out and prevail upon you to return to your native land. After her travail with you, she had lived without chick or child, and was now resolved, if you should come to light, to confess the whole transaction to your father. She knew that he would now believe her, for their long life together had supplied proof of her fidelity, and that he would seize upon the unexpected realization of his hope for a successor of his own blood.'

" 'Thus she said and thus she implored me to do, frequently conjuring the Sun—an oath which it is unlawful for any sage to transgress. Her petition confirmed by oath I come to fulfil. It was not just for that purpose, to be sure, that I journeyed hither; but by divine providence I have this much greater profit of my wandering. For a long time, as you know, I have lain in wait for you. I have omitted no jot of the tendance which has always been your due, but I have concealed the facts and have awaited an opportunity to procure the ribbon by some expedient and so to bring you confirmation of what I say. If you heed my advice, it is now possible for you to escape hence with us, before you are forced to submit, against your will, to the marriage with Alcamenes which Charicles is eagerly promoting; possible, too, for you to recover your family, your country, your parents, and to be united to Theagenes as a husband, who is ready to follow wherever we choose to go. In exchange for this alien and orphan life you will obtain nobility and sovereignty, and you will bear rule with your dearly beloved, if any trust is to be placed in the gods and in the Pythian oracle.' I reminded her of the oracle and explained its meaning; it was not unknown to her, for it had been much cited and its meaning inquired into. At my words Charicleia grew tense and said: 'Since you assert that such is the will of the gods, and I trust you, what must I do, father?' 'Pretend,' said I, 'that you consent to marriage with Alcamenes.' 'It is a difficult,' she said, 'and an odious thing to prefer anyone to Theagenes, even in appearance; but since, father, I have entrusted myself to the gods and to you, what is the object of this pretense, and how can its veritable realization be avoided?' 'The event will show you,' said I. 'Advance knowledge conduces to hesitation in women, whereas sudden action frequently produces boldness and success. Only follow my instructions, both in other matters and in respect to the present marriage. Then yield to Charicles, for he will do nothing without my direction.' To this she agreed, and I left her in tears.

"Soon after I left her room I saw Charicles, very downcast and covered with gloom. 'You are a strange man,' I said to him. 'When you ought to be wreathed with happiness and offering thanksgiving sacrifices for the realization of your prayers, now that Charicleia has at last, by my wisdom and skill, been brought to the point of desiring marriage, you go about gloomy-faced and distracted and all but lamenting. What can have happened to you?' And he: 'Why should I not grieve? My darling is more likely to pass from life than, as you say, contract a marriage, if any heed is to be paid to my dreams. Last night, in particular, I was terrified by a dream in which I thought I saw an eagle swoop down from the hand of Apollo, snatch my daughter who was clinging to my bosom, and carry her off to a remote region of the earth filled with dark and shadowy forms. In the end I could not know what happened to her, for the vast intervening space blocked my vision from following further.'

"When he told me this I conjectured what the dream portended, but I wished to rouse his spirits and distract him from any suspicion for the future. 'As a priest,' said I, 'and of the most prophetic god at that, you seem to me ill-founded in the interpretation of dreams. The dream signifies the impending marriage of your child, and the eagle prefigures the groom who will take her; and when Apollo nods his approval and leads forth her husband—as it were, out of his own hand—you are annoyed at the vision and find the dream disturbing. Let us keep our utterances good-omened, Charicles, and let us gladly accommodate our-

selves to the will of the gods and turn our efforts towards
obtaining the girl's full consent.' He asked me what he
might do to make her more compliant, and I said, 'If you
have some valuable heirloom, a gilded robe or a jeweled
necklace, take them to her as a present from her bridegroom
and break Charicleia's resistance down by gifts. Gold and
precious stones work irresistible magic on a woman. In
other things too you must be deft in preparing for the
festivity; it will be necessary to press the marriage forward while the cohesive elements of my art still hold the
girl's will under constraint.' 'Be sure that I shall not be
found wanting,' said Charicles, and hurried off, spurred
on by his joy, to put my words into effect. And, as I subsequently discovered, he did precisely as I had suggested,
omitting no jot. The precious robe and, in particular, the
Ethiopian jewels which had been exposed by Persinna as
tokens he brought to Charicleia as if they were presents
from Alcamenes.

"I encountered Theagenes and asked him what had become of his countrymen who had formed his company in
the procession. He told me that the girls were gone, having
taken a head start for the sake of easier travel: the young
men were becoming impatient of delay and eager to start
on the road home. When I had this information I instructed him what to say to them and what to do himself
and bade him observe the signal I would give at the opportune moment. Then I turned my steps to the temple of
Apollo to petition the god to guide my flight with my
young friends by some oracle. But the god was quicker
than my thought; he is a present help to those who act in
accordance with his will, and with benevolence unsolicited
often anticipates their desire. So on this occasion, before
my inquiry was formed, Apollo's answer forestalled it and
by his action demonstrated his guidance. For as I was preoccupied with my calculations and turning my steps, as I

have said, towards the oracle, I was arrested by a voice saying: 'Join in our libations, good sir.' The invitation came from some visitors who were feasting, with flute accompaniments, in honor of Heracles. When I became aware of this I checked my steps, for it is not lawful to pass by a sacred summons. I took frankincense and offered it and poured a libation of water; they were surprised at my paltry offerings, but nevertheless asked me to share their feast. This invitation too I heeded and took my place on the couch strewn by the visitors with myrtle and laurel, and tasted such food as is my wont to take. Then I said to them: 'Sirs, of good cheer I have no lack, but concerning yourselves I am uninformed. It is now time for you to say who you are and whence, for I think it vulgar and rude for people who have shared grace and meat to separate with no further knowledge of one another after having initiated the bond of friendship with sacred salt.' They said then that they were Phoenicians from Tyre, merchants by profession, sailing to Libyan Carthage in a large trading ship carrying wares of India, Ethiopia, and Phoenicia. At the moment they were celebrating a feast of victory to the Tyrian Heracles because a young man of theirs (and they pointed to him sitting at the head of the table) had won the crown in a wrestling contest and so had given Tyre the honor of a victory in Greece itself. 'When we had passed Malea and were driven to Kephallene by contrary winds,' they said, 'this young man swore to us by this our ancestral god that a Pythian victory had been prophesied to him in a dream, and persuaded us to turn out of our intended course and touch here. Events have confirmed the prophecy: our erstwhile merchant is now proven an athletic champion. This is his thanksgiving celebration to the god who revealed his victory, and at the same time a celebration for propitious embarkation. For, good sir, we purpose to sail at dawn if the breezes favor our design.'

" 'Is that truly your purpose?' I asked, and they answered, 'It is indeed.' 'You shall have me as a fellow voy-
ager then, if you wish,' said I, 'for a certain errand takes
me to Sicily, and that island, as you know, lies on the way
of your voyage to Libya.' 'If only you *would* be willing
to sail with us!' said they. 'We anticipate nothing but good
from having as our fellow traveler a man who is a sage, a
Hellene, and, as our experience suggests, is favored by the
gods.' 'I *shall* wish to join you,' said I, 'if you would give
me one day to make ready.' 'You shall have tomorrow,' said
they, 'but you must be at the shore in the evening; the
nights are favorable for sailing, for land breezes then drive
our boat without ruffling the sea.' I promised to be there,
and pledged them upon oath not to sail before the time
appointed.

"I left them busy with their fluting and dancing. It
was a round dance to a rapid Assyrian strain; now they
leapt high in the air, now crouched down to the ground,
and now whirled their whole bodies about like men possessed. I then went to Charicleia, who held in her lap and
was admiring the jewels Charicles had given her, and on
next to Theagenes. I told each of them what they must do
and when, and then went home, intent on our plans,
which proceeded as follows. At midnight, when the city
was plunged in sleep, an armed band attacked the residence
of Charicleia. Of this amatory expedition Theagenes was
the general, and his henchmen were the young men of
the processional troop. They created a tumult with shouts
and crashing shields to frighten off any observers. With
lighted torches they dashed into the house, easily wrenching
open the door, the bars of which had been purposely arranged for easy ingress. Charicleia was privy to their design and ready, and she only pretended to resist their violence when they seized her; with her they carried off a
quantity of stuff which the girl pointed out to them. Out-

side the house again, they uttered a war whoop and made a terrible din with their clashing shields, and as they marched through the city threw all the inhabitants into indescribable panic. They had chosen this eerie hour in order to be more terrifying, and Parnassus re-echoed their brazen clangor. And so they made their way out to Delphi, constantly calling out to each other the name of Charicleia.

"As soon as they were outside the city they galloped to the mountainous region of Locris and Oeta. Here Theagenes and Charicleia left the Thessalians, by preconcerted arrangement, and secretly fled to me. They fell at my knees, which they long clung to, and repeatedly cried, 'Father, save us!' This was all Charicleia could say, for she hung her head in embarrassment at the bold venture she had made; but Theagenes enlarged his petition, saying: 'Calasiris, protect strangers, fugitives, and suppliants, who have given everything up in order to possess one another. Save these playthings of fortune, prisoners enslaved by a chaste love, voluntary exiles, yet uncondemned, who give all their expectation of safety to your care.' I was deeply affected by these words, and in my mind, but not with my eyes, I wept in sympathy for the young pair; but I recovered myself without their notice, and raised them up and comforted them. I bade them have high hopes for the outcome of an undertaking whose inception had received divine approval, and then said: 'I go to attend to what must next be done; you wait here and take the greatest care not to be seen by anybody.' So saying, I made to hurry off, but Charicleia seized my cloak to keep me back and said: 'Father, the inception will be unjust, nay, treacherous, if you go off and leave me and entrust me to Theagenes. You do not realize how untrustworthy a guardian is a lover if he has his beloved in his power, and especially if he is left alone with no one to shame him into propriety.

His passion will flare the brighter, I think, when he sees
its coveted object without a defender. I will not let you
go, therefore, until I have exacted an oath from Theagenes,
in view of our present situation and still more of the future, that he will not consort with me in the uses of Aphrodite before I have recovered my own family and house, or,
if some deity prevent such recovery, not before I myself
consent to be his wife.' I marveled at what she said, and
pronounced my judgment that her request must be carried
out. I lighted the hearth to serve as an altar and burned
frankincense upon it, and Theagenes took the oath, pro-
testing that it impugned the loyalty of his character and,
by invoking fear of divine compulsion, prevented him from
demonstrating his voluntary restraint. Nevertheless, he
swore by Pythian Apollo and Artemis and Aphrodite herself and the Loves, that he would in every respect conform
to the desires and mandates of Charicleia.

"These and other vows they solemnly exchanged under
divine auspices, and then I hurried off to Charicles' house,
which I found in a tumult of shrieks and lamentations.
His servants had already come and reported that the girl
had been kidnaped, and a crowd of sympathetic citizens
surrounded Charicles, who was lamenting, ignorant of
what had happened and at a loss to know what to do next.
'You miserable creatures,' I called out, 'you behave like
simpletons. How long will you sit there dumb and helpless? Has misfortune bereft you of your wits? Why aren't
you under arms pursuing the enemy? Why don't you catch
and punish those ravishers?' Charicles replied: 'It is probably useless to fight against our plight. I am paying this
penalty, I see, by the wrath of heaven. Once I entered
the shrine at a forbidden hour and my eyes saw what was
unlawful; because I saw what I should not have seen the
god foretold that I should be deprived of seeing what I
most delight to see. Nevertheless, there is nothing to pre-

vent struggling against a deity, as the saying goes, if we
knew whom we must pursue and who it was that brought
this heavy calamity upon us.' 'It is that Thessalian whom
you admired and introduced to me,' I said. 'It is Theagenes
and the boys with him. You will find that not one of
them has lingered in the city until evening. Rise, then, and
summon the people to council.'

"So it was done. The magistrates proclaimed a special
meeting of the assembly and published their proclamation
to the city by trumpet blasts. The populace assembled at
once and the theater was transformed into a night council.
Charicles stepped forward, and the mere sight of him
moved the multitude to sighs and groans. Swathed in a
black robe and with his face and head covered with dust,
he spoke as follows: 'When you see the extent of my
calamity, men of Delphi, you may think that I have con-
voked this assembly and come forward here to plead for
myself, but that is not the case. I do, indeed, suffer a hundred deaths, deserted and smitten by god, my house robbed
of its most precious solace; nevertheless, hope, the common and empty lure of all mankind, persuades me to persevere by suggesting that I may yet find and recover my
daughter. Even more am I persuaded to persevere by the
hope of seeing my city exact vengeance from those who
have outraged it—unless the Thessalian striplings have
robbed you too of your free spirit and your indignation
on behalf of your native land and its ancestral gods. What
is most grievous of all is that dancers, children, a mere
handful, spectators of a rite, should with impunity have
trampled upon the first city of the Hellenes, should have
robbed the temple of Apollo of its most precious possession
—of Charicleia, alas, my very eyes. Ah, how inexorably
has divine jealousy visited me. The life of my first daughter,
born of my body, was, as you know, extinguished along
with her marriage torches; and the fresh grief ravished

away her mother, and drove me from my country. But those things I could endure after I found Charicleia. Charicleia was my life, my hope, and the successor of my family; Charicleia was my only comfort, and, so to speak, my sheet anchor. And that has now been cut off and carried away by tempestuous seas called down upon me by some fate, not at random on an indifferent occasion, but precisely at the least opportune moment, as if to make a cruel plaything of me. So near was her bridal bed; you had all been informed of her impending marriage.'

"While he was still speaking and wholly dissolved in lamentation, the magistrate Hegesias interrupted and stopped him short and addressed the assembly: 'Charicles may lament now and later, but we must not be submerged in his grief and disappear from view in the torrent of his tears. We must not lose the opportune moment, which is of great weight in all matters and particularly so in war. If we march directly from this meeting there is some hope that we can overtake the enemy, for their progress will be leisurely in the expectation that our preparation will take time. But if we sit here expressing pity, or rather, being women, our delay will give them an even longer head start and we shall do no more than give the boys a good laugh—boys who, in my judgment, should be caught at once and impaled and their descendants disenfranchised and their whole race punished. This can be easily effected if we stir up the indignation of the Thessalians themselves against any that escape us, and by official decree prohibit them from performing the procession and sacrifices appropriate to their hero at Delphi and decide to carry out the ritual at our own expense.'

"These proposals were approved, and the people ratified the decree. Then the magistrate continued: 'I should like a further vote on the proposition that in the future the priestess must not appear to the runners in the armor race.

In my opinion that was the inception of Theagenes' impiety; he conceived his mad passion to ravish the girl, I believe, on his first sight of her. It is therefore desirable to forestall any such attempt for the future.' This proposition too was carried by a single unanimous vote. Then Hegesias gave the signal for marching and the trumpet was sounded. The theater broke up to form an army and there was an uninterrupted rush from the meeting to the battle. Not only robust men capable of bearing arms, but adolescents and mere boys, substituting zeal for maturity, boldly joined the expedition. Even women showed a spirit superior to their nature and, snatching up whatever implement came to hand, joined in the chase—in vain, for being outdistanced they were forced to acknowledge the natural feebleness of their sex. You might have seen even old men struggling with their age, their minds dragging their bodies along, as it were, and their zeal reproaching their weakness. Anguish for the loss of Charicleia gripped the entire city, and without waiting for daylight the whole populace, as if moved by a single impulse, poured forth in pursuit."

5

"SUCH WAS THE TEMPER of the people of Delphi and such their behavior, but how they succeeded I could not know, for their pursuit provided opportunity for my flight. In the dark of night I collected the young pair and took them, just as they were, down to the sea and embarked them on the Phoenician ship, which was ready to loose its moorings; though day was just beginning to dawn the Phoenicians thought they would not be transgressing their engagement to me, for they had agreed to wait a day and a night. They were very glad to see us come and welcomed us on board. At once they rowed out of the harbor, and then a gentle land breeze raised ripples which smilingly, as it were, followed our stern; the sailors then hoisted their canvas and let the vessel run. We all but flew past the Gulf of Cirrha, the foothills of Parnassus, the Aetolian and Caledonian cliffs; the rocks which are called and are Sharp and the sea of Zacynthus hove into sight as the sun was going down in the west.

"But why am I so unseasonably tedious? Why can't I remember that it *is* upon a veritable sea that I am launching my narrative, which has only left its base? Let us stop our tale for a while, and both snatch a little sleep. You have shown yourself an extremely patient listener and are manfully struggling against slumber, Cnemon, but now that I have spun my adventures out to so late an hour I think that even you are beginning to flag. As for me, son, old age weighs me down and the recollection of my afflictions deadens my intellect and conduces to sleep." "Hold then, father," said Cnemon, "but not because I am weary of your narrative; for my part I could go on listening to it for many nights and more days, so insatiable am I and so enchanted with its Siren's charms. But for some time I have been hearing confused voices in the house and the humming of a crowd. I was really disturbed by it, but forced myself to silence because I was drawn on by eagerness to hear what you were going to say." "I had not noticed it," said Calasiris, "doubtless because age has made my hearing dull—old age is a disease of the ears as of other organs—and perhaps because I was absorbed in my narrative. It must have been Nausicles, the master here, coming home. Heavens! I wonder what success he has had." "All the success I could wish," said Nausicles, making a sudden appearance. "I have been aware, my good Calasiris, how solicitous you have been for my affairs and how you have accompanied me in mind. I have had other evidence of your good will besides that last remark of yours which I overheard as I came in. But who is this stranger?" "A Greek," said Calasiris, "the particulars you will hear later. But if you have had good success tell me quickly, so that I may share your satisfaction." "You too shall learn the details in the morning," said Nausicles. "For the present, suffice it to say that I have obtained a better Thisbe. But I must take a little sleep to recover from the fatigue of my journey and my other cares."

Having said this he hurried off to do as he said, but Cnemon was petrified at hearing Thisbe's name. He was

perplexed and wracked his brain with a thousand vain
thoughts; the rest of the night he was miserable and
fetched such heavy and frequent sighs that even Calasiris,
though he was sunk in profound sleep, finally took notice.
The old man raised himself, leaned on his elbow, and asked
Cnemon what the trouble was and what agitation was
driving him frantic. "Should I not be frantic," said
Cnemon, "when I hear that Thisbe is alive?" "And who
is Thisbe?" said Calasiris. "How do you know her? Why
does a report of her being alive disturb you?" Said Cnemon:
"The rest you shall hear later, when I come to tell you my
own story. But I tell you now that I recognized her dead
body with these my eyes, and buried her with these my
hands among the buccaneers." "Go to sleep," said Calasiris;
"we shall soon know the facts of the case." "I could not
sleep," said Cnemon. "Do you take some rest. I could not
live another minute unless I somehow manage to find out
what delusion has affected Nausicles—or whether among
the Egyptians the dead really come to life." At this
Calasiris smiled a little and went back to sleep again.
Cnemon left the room and stumbled about, as was natural
for a man wandering around a strange house in the dark
of night, but he minded nothing in his eagerness to be
rid of his terror of Thisbe and his apprehensions. After
he had many times unwittingly traversed the same parts
of the house he became aware of a woman quietly lamenting in the night, like a nightingale giving voice to its dirge
in the springtime. Guided by the lament he made his
way towards the room, put his ear to the crack between
the doors, and listened. The woman was still lamenting,
and this is what he heard:

"Altogether hapless am I. I had escaped the robber band,
I thought I had avoided the cruel death I always expected.
I thought I should spend the rest of my life with my be-
loved, the life of an alien and vagabond, but with him it

would have been sweet. For me nothing can be so difficult that I would not, with him, find it tolerable. But now that deity who has governed my lot from the beginning and is never at all satiated has given me a brief glimpse of pleasure and then again disappointed me. Slavery I thought I had escaped, again I am a slave; prison, and again I am under guard. An island constrained me, and darkness; I suffer the like now, and truth to tell, more bitterly, for he that was willing and able to be my solace is now separated from me. Yesterday a robbers' cave was my shelter, a pit of hell: how was my dwelling place other than a grave? But all this the presence of my dearly beloved made light; there he sorrowed for me when I was alive, and when I was, as he thought, dead, he wept for me and grieved at his loss of me. Now I am deprived even of that; the partner of my misfortunes, who took the burden of my troubles upon himself, is departed. I am solitary and deserted, a wretched captive exposed to the assaults of a bitter fortune; yet do I endure to live because I hope my sweetest may be alive. But oh, my darling, wherever are you? What fortune is yours? Are you too, alas, a slave, you whose spirit is so free and unfettered except by love? But I pray only that you survive, and once again see your Thisbe—so must my name be called, though you like it not."

Cnemon could contain himself no longer when he heard these words. He did not wait to listen to the rest, but supposed it would be like the first, and believed from the last expression that the woman was really Thisbe. He all but collapsed at the very doors. Holding himself up with difficulty and apprehensive of detection (for by now the cocks had crowed for the second time), he ran stumbling away, now bruising his feet and now falling full against the walls, once banging his head against a door lintel, and again against utensils hanging from the ceiling. After much

straying he reached the room where they lodged and fell
in a heap on his bed. His body was palsied with quivering,
and his teeth chattered violently; he would have been in
peril of breathing his last if Calasiris had not quickly noticed his state and warmed him and comforted him. When
he had got his breath a little Calasiris asked what had so
affected him. "I am lost," he said, "that vile Thisbe is
really alive." So saying he fainted away again. Calasiris
again had much ado in his efforts to restore him. Some
demonic power was making sport of Cnemon, a power
which produces wild mockeries in many human affairs
and in particular suffers man to reap no pleasure without
accompanying pain. A thing which will presently afford
the greatest happiness it first endows with the aspect of
calamity, either because the nature of that power is such
as was now manifested, or because the nature of man
cannot admit joy pure and unalloyed. So on that occasion
Cnemon fled what he most of all desired and supposed the
most agreeable thing was the most repulsive: for the grieving woman was not Thisbe but Charicleia. This is what had
befallen her.

When Thyamis had been taken alive and made prisoner,
and the island set afire and emptied of the buccaneers who
had made it their home, Cnemon and Thermouthis,
Thyamis' squire, crossed over the lake in the morning to
discover how the enemy had disposed of the robber chief.
Their adventures on this occasion have already been told.
Theagenes and Charicleia had been left alone in the cave,
but reckoned their perilous situation a great windfall. Finding themselves for the first time alone and free of any
disturber, they took their fill of uninhibited and whole-
hearted embraces and kisses. Plunged into oblivion of all
else, they clung to one another as if they grew from a
single root, satiating themselves with a chaste and virginal
love, mingling their hot, wet tears, and cleaving to one

another with pure caresses. When Charicleia felt that Theagenes' virility was stirring, she restrained him by admon-
ishing him of his oath, and he, for his part, was easily
checked and without difficulty recalled to temperance, for
though he submitted to pure love he could vanquish sen-
sual pleasure. When they finally came to the realization
that there were things to be done, they forced themselves
to be content with the dalliance they had had, and Theagenes spoke as follows: "To be together, dear Charicleia,
to possess what we have cherished as most precious and for
which we have endured all afflictions, is our dearest prayer:
may the gods of Greece fulfil it. But human affairs are un-
stable and fluctuating; we have suffered much and must
yet expect more. Our present task is to keep our appoint-
ment with Cnemon at the village of Chemmis, but we
cannot know what fortune awaits us there, for an enormous distance still separates us from the land which is our
goal. Let us therefore devise some token of recognition by
which we may secretly communicate in one another's presence and by which each may trace the other if it is our
lot to be separated. It is a good precaution in wandering
about to keep a shared token for finding one's friend."

Charicleia approved the scheme, and they agreed, if
they should become separated, to write on temple walls
or notable monuments, herms, or crossroad pillars, Theagenes the name "Pythios," and Charicleia, "Pythias," with
the notation "Pythias has gone to the right or the left,
towards this or that city, village, or people," specifying the
day and hour. If they should find themselves in the same
place it would be sufficient merely for one to see the other,
for no lapse of time could efface the recognition of love
from their souls. Nevertheless Charicleia showed Theagenes
the ancestral ring which had been exposed with her, and
Theagenes showed Charicleia a scar on his knee made by
a wild boar. For words to be used as tokens, she chose

"lamp," and he "palm." Upon concluding this agreement
they again embraced one another and again wept, making
their tears serve as sacred libations, as it were, and their
kisses as oaths. After these pledges they withdrew from
the cave, but touched none of the treasures laid up there,
for they thought wealth gotten by plunder an abomina-
tion; but they did take what they had brought from
Delphi and the robbers had taken from them. Charicleia
changed her dress. Her jewels, fillets, and sacred robe she
put into a wallet, and to conceal them, placed cheaper
articles on top. Her bow and quiver she gave to Theagenes
to carry; these were the arms of the deity whose sway he
acknowledged, and to him a sweet burden. They had just
approached the lake and were about to embark in a boat
when they saw a troop of armed men moving towards
the island.

The sight made them dizzy, and for a long while they
stood gaping, as if the repeated assaults of fortune had
deprived them of sensation. At long last, when the newcomers had all but landed, Charicleia proposed that they
run back to the cave, if they could elude the men, and
hide themselves there. But Theagenes held her back and
said: "How long shall we keep fleeing from a fate which
is everywhere pursuing us? Let us yield to fortune and
meet it with fortitude. Flight would only gain us futile
wandering, a vagabond life, and the incessant assaults of
our hostile deity. Do you not see how his savage zeal has
heaped piratical attacks upon the misfortunes of exile,
cruelties by land upon those by sea, and pitched battles
upon brigand raids? A little while ago he made us captives,
but then he left us deserted; he held out the prospect of
deliverance and flight to freedom, and now sends ruffians
to destroy us. It is a game of war he is playing against
his victims; he has staged our drama like a play in the
theater. Why should we not cut his tragic composition off

here, why not deliver ourselves to those who wish to
kill us? Perhaps he may yet be ambitious to give the denouement of his play a stunning curtain and force us to
take our own lives."

With these sentiments Charicleia did not wholly agree.
His expostulations with fortune she declared were just, but
she did not approve of voluntarily surrendering themselves
to the enemy. It was not certain, in the first place, that
if caught they would be killed: the deity against whose
power they wrestled was not so benevolent as to give them
so speedy a release. Probably he preferred to preserve them
for slavery, and it might be a fate more bitter than death
to be delivered to cruel barbarians and be exposed to their
unspeakable and nameless outrages. "These let us avoid in
every possible way," said Charicleia, "and let us take hope
for the future from our experiences of the past, for many
times now have we survived situations more desperate."
"Let us do as you will," said Theagenes, and followed her
lead as if he were being dragged. But they were not quick
enough to pass the whole distance to the cave, for while
intent on the men advancing in front they had failed to
notice that they had been cut off by another party of the
enemy which had landed to their rear. They were terrified
into immobility, and Charicleia cringed close to Theagenes,
so that if die they must she might die in his embrace. Some
of the advancing party tensed themselves to strike, but
when the young pair looked up they were dazzled by their
beauty, their hearts failed, and their right hands fell slack;
for beauty, it appears, awes even barbarian violence, and
fierce eyes grow gentle at the sight of loveliness.

They arrested them, then, instead, and took them to
their commander, very eager to be the first and to bring
the fairest spoil. No other spoil at all could they bring, for
nothing else did anyone encounter, though they ransacked
the island from one end to the other and covered it all

with their weapons as with nets. All the rest had been consumed with fire in the previous fighting; only the cave
remained undiscovered. The commander to whom our captives were taken was Mitranes, lieutenant of Oroondates,
viceroy of Egypt for the Great King. Him Nausicles had
induced for a large fee to make a descent upon the island
in search of Thisbe. Theagenes and Charicleia were brought
up, loudly invoking the savior gods, and Nausicles, seizing
his cue with a merchant's shrewdness, sprang forward, and
as he ran shouted, "This is Thisbe, whom those blackguard pirates ravished from me; thanks to you and the
gods I have her back." He laid hold of Charicleia with
great demonstrations of joy; but speaking softly and in
Greek to elude those present he advised Charicleia to pretend that her name was Thisbe if she valued her life. His
ruse succeeded. When Charicleia heard Greek spoken she
assumed that the man who spoke it would aid and assist
her, and entered into the plot; and when Mitranes asked
her name she answered that she was Thisbe. Then Nausicles
ran up and showered kisses on Mitranes' head and extolled
his fortune, and inflated the barbarian's conceit by admiring his other military successes and in particular the happy
conclusion of the present expedition. Mitranes was flat-
tered by this praise and was deceived by the pretended name
into accepting Nausicles' claim. He was smitten by
Charicleia's beauty, which, though she was dressed in tat-
ters, shone forth like the moon's beams from under a
cloud; but his feather brain was overwhelmed by the
sharpness of the deceit, which afforded no opportunity for
reconsideration. "She is yours, then," he said, "take her,"
and with that he handed her over. But he looked back at
her constantly, and made it plain that he was unwilling
to surrender the girl and did so only because he had been
paid in advance. "But this man, whoever he is," he said,
meaning Theagenes, "shall be my booty; let him follow

under guard. He shall be sent to Babylon, for he is hand-some enough to serve at the King's table."

After these exchanges they crossed the lake and went their several ways. Nausicles proceeded to Chemmis with Charicleia; Mitranes turned to other villages under his administration, and with no delay sent Theagenes to Oroondates, who was in Memphis, accompanied by a letter as follows: "To Oroondates, Viceroy, from Mitranes, Com-mandant: A Greek youth too fine for my service, worthy to appear before and serve our divine Greatest King alone, I have taken captive and send to you, enjoining you to conduct to our common master this inestimable present, such an ornament as the royal court has never before seen and will never hereafter see." Such was that message.

Before the day was fully light Calasiris along with Cnemon hastened to Nausicles to hear his news. Upon being asked what he had accomplished, Nausicles re-counted the whole story: he had gone to the island, found it desolate and at first encountered no one; another girl had appeared and he had circumvented Mitranes and ob-tained the girl by pretending she was Thisbe; he had man-aged better by coming upon this girl than he would have by finding the other. The difference between the two was no less than between god and mortal. So superlative was the girl's beauty that he could find no words to express it; in any case she was here, and they could see for themselves.

From what Nausicles said they scented a suspicion of the truth, and besought him to send for the girl at once; indescribable beauty, they knew, could only apply to Charicleia. She was brought in, her head downcast and her face veiled. When Nausicles bade her take heart, she saw and was seen—beyond the hopes of all. All were moved to cry out, and as by a single signal or the same downbeat they all wailed. What one could hear was "Oh, father!"

"Oh, daughter!" "Really Charicleia, and not Thisbe!"
Nausicles was dumbfounded when he saw Calasiris embracing Charicleia as hard as he could and weeping, and
could make nothing of the recognition scene, so like a
stage play, until Calasiris, warmly embracing and kissing
him, said, "Ah, best of men! For your good deeds may
the gods requite you with your heart's desire, full and
overflowing. You have proved to be the savior of the
daughter I had never hoped to find; you have brought
to my eyes the sweetest of all sights. But dear daughter
Charicleia, where did you leave Theagenes?" At this query
she raised a wail, and after a speechless moment said, "He
was taken captive by the man, whoever he may be, who
gave me to this gentleman." Calasiris then besought Nausicles to tell him what he knew about Theagenes: who
had got possession of him, and whither was he carrying
him. Nausicles told him all. He sensed that these were the
pair about whom the old man had so often spoken to him,
and in sorrowful search of whom he knew the old man
had gone on his wanderings. He added that his information would be of little advantage to people in humble circumstances, for it would be strange indeed if Mitranes
would release his young captive for any sum of money.
"I have money," said Charicleia softly to Calasiris. "Promise as much as you like. I have kept safe and carry with me
the jewels you know of."

What Charicleia said raised Calasiris' spirits, but for
fear that Nausicles might suspect the facts and covet the
wealth that Charicleia was carrying, he said, "My good
Nausicles, the sage cannot be in want. He limits his desires
by the measure of his resources, and from the gods receives so much as he knows it is proper to ask of them.
Only tell me, then, where that person is who has Theagenes
in his power; providence will not be indifferent to our
need but will supply whatever we may wish to overcome

the avarice of the Persian." At this Nausicles smiled and
said, "You will be able to persuade me that you can suddenly grow rich, as by magic, if you first pay me the ransom for this girl; surely you know that merchants love
money no less than Persians." "I do know it," said Calasiris,
"and you shall have the money. But why are you slow in
anticipating my request and why do you not, in keeping
with your wonted courtesy and without waiting for my
solicitation, yourself offer to return my daughter? Must
I entreat you?" "No ill will," said Nausicles. "If you like,
attend the thanksgiving sacrifice which I am about to offer
to the gods and pray they make me rich; for yourself you
need only reach out for riches." "Do not mock me, and
do not be incredulous," Calasiris said to him, "but go and
make your preparations for the sacrifice; we will join you
when everything is ready."

So they did, and presently a message from Nausicles invited them to hasten to the sacrifice. They had concerted
what they were to do, and came cheerfully. Nausicles and
his party and a crowd of other guests—the sacrifice was
to be a public celebration—attended, and Charicleia came
with Nausicles' daughter and other women of his household. These had urged and entreated Charicleia to come,
but would never have persuaded her if she did not think
the sacrifice would afford her a pretext for offering prayers
for Theagenes. The god to whom Nausicles paid special
reverence as the patron of merchants and traders was
Hermes, and it was to Hermes that the sacrifice was offered.
When they reached the temple of Hermes and the victims
had been slaughtered, Calasiris inspected the entrails and
by the alterations of his expression indicated the variations
of fortune, good or bad, that were to come. Then he placed
his hands on the altar, pronouncing certain words the while,
and pretended to take from the fire a thing he had brought

with him. "This the gods bring you through me, as a ransom for Charicleia," he said, and at the same time handed Nausicles a royal ring, an object extraordinary and even divine. The circlet was of amber, and the gem in its setting was a brilliant Ethiopian amethyst of the size of a maiden's eye, finer far than those of Spain or Britain. These latter have a dullish tinge, like a rose first bursting from its bud and forming petals and just becoming a deeper red under the rays of the sun. But the Ethiopian amethyst is clear and deep in color, and flames out with a fresh beauty like the spring's. If you turn it in your hand it sends forth a golden ray, not dulling the sight by its rough strength but illuminating it with a gentle glow. Furthermore it possesses much more genuine power than Western stones; the Ethiopian amethyst does not belie its name but is truly *amethyst* ("uninebriate") for him who wears it, and in drinking parties keeps him sober.

All Indian and Ethiopian amethysts have this character, but the one which Calasiris now gave to Nausicles was even finer. An animated design was engraved upon it in intaglio. A young shepherd was represented as pasturing his sheep. He was standing on a slightly raised rock to survey his flock and was directing them to their pasturages by the notes of his transverse flute. The sheep seemed to hearken and to regulate their pace by the pasturing signals of the pipes. One would imagine that their heavy fleeces were of gold; this effect was not produced artificially, but the native ruddiness of the amethyst tinted the backs of the sheep. The light frolicking of lambs was also represented. Some scampered up the rock in a troop, others gamboling friskily about the shepherd in a ring gave the rock the appearance of a rustic theater. Some wantoning in the flame of the amethyst as in the sun bounded over the rocks on the tips of their hooves. The rock was not counterfeit but real; at the edges of the stone the artist had marked off the space he desired, thinking it otiose to feign stone in stone. Such was that ring.

Nausicles' admiration of the marvel was surpassed by his pleasure at its value, for he judged the stone was worth his whole fortune. "I was only joking, my good Calasiris," said he. "My request for ransom was nothing more than talk; it was my intention to release your daughter to you without price. But since the worthy gifts of the gods are, as you sages say, not to be rejected, I receive this heaven-sent stone, persuaded that it has come from Hermes, always to me the fairest and most generous of gods. Truly it was through the fire that he sent this stone, through your ministry, as may be seen from the blaze shining in it. Besides, I think the fairest gain is that which makes the receiver rich without impoverishing the giver." Thus he spoke and did, and then he and the others addressed themselves to the feast. For the women he assigned a separate place in the interior of the temple; the men he made recline in the outer precinct. And when their good cheer had satisfied their appetites, and tables had made way for mixing bowls, the men sang marching songs to Dionysos and poured libations, and the women danced a thanksgiving hymn to Demeter. Charicleia drew apart and attended to her private business: she prayed that Theagenes keep safe and be preserved for her.

Now, when the drinking had produced a luminous warmth and the guests turned to merriment, Nausicles held up a cup of pure water and said: "My good Calasiris, to you I drink the pure water Nymphs, as you would have me to do, virginal Nymphs that have no share in Dionysos. If you return our pledge with the tale we desire to hear, you will provide us with better entertainment than the most generous wine bowls. The ladies, as you hear, are following their drinking with the dance for their pastime.

But the story of your wanderings, if you would kindly tell it, would be a far more agreeable conclusion to our banquet than any dance or music. You have often put off my request that you tell the tale on the grounds that you were still steeped in your miseries; but you can never expect an occasion better than the present, when one of your children is here safe and before your eyes, and your son, with the gods' help, you will soon see—especially if you do not affront me by again deferring your narrative." "All blessings upon you, Nausicles," put in Cnemon. "Though you have provided every kind of music for our entertainment you are willing to forgo ordinary kinds of amusement and are eager to listen to arcane matters tempered with a pleasure truly divine. In my opinion you show admirable judgment in coupling Hermes with Dionysos, thus mingling the pleasures of discourse with those of wine. I am filled with admiration for the sumptuousness of your sacrifice, and I cannot think how anyone could render Hermes more propitious than by making a contribution to the feast of the thing which is appropriate to Hermes—discourse." Calasiris yielded, to please Cnemon and to oblige Nausicles, whose assistance he might yet require. He told his whole story, abridging and, as it were, summarizing the first portion which he had already recounted to Cnemon. Some parts which he did not regard it convenient for Nausicles to know he passed over. He began where the fresh matter followed upon what had already been told, and continued as follows.

"So, to escape the Delphians we embarked upon the Phoenician ship. The beginning of the voyage was altogether satisfactory, for a moderate wind from the stern drove the ship forward; but when we reached the Caledonian strait the sea was agitated by a strong wind, which disturbed us greatly." Here Cnemon begged him to include any explanation he might have heard for the constant agitation of the sea in that locality. "At that place," Calasiris complied, "the Ionian Sea contracts from a great width and pours into the gulf as through a funnel. As it rushes to mingle with the Aegean its advance is cut off by the Peloponnesian isthmus, which, seemingly by divine providence, has interposed the neck as a wall to prevent inundation of the mainland opposite. Thus a countercurrent naturally arises, with greater force in the strait than in the rest of the gulf; the inrushing waves strike those flowing in the opposite direction, produce a swirl of water, and build up boiling waves which break tumultuously over one another." This explanation was received with applause and approval, all present testifying that it was true. Then Calasiris continued as follows: "When we passed the strait and lost sight of the Sharp Islands, we thought we sighted the Zacynthian promontory, for a misty cloud obscured our vision, and the pilot gave orders to reef sail. When we asked why he slackened speed when we had a tail wind, he replied: 'Because if we used the full wind we would arrive at the island about the first watch, and in the dark there is danger of foundering on the inshore reefs which abound there. It is therefore better to spend the night at sea, carrying only so much sail as will suffice to bring us to land in the morning.'

"So the pilot said, but it did not turn out so, Nausicles, for the sun was already risen when we dropped anchor. The islanders who lived near the harbor, which was not far distant from the city, flocked to see us as to some strange spectacle. They appeared to admire the maneuverability of the ship, its size, and its excellent construction, and they spoke of its fine Phoenician craftsmanship. Still more did they wonder at our uncommon good fortune in having enjoyed so fair and painless a passage in the winter season, when the Pleiades were already setting. Almost all

the company left the ship while the hawsers were still being made fast and hurried to Zacynthus to make purchases.
I happened to have overheard the captain say we would
winter in the island, and began to look about for lodgings
near the shore. The ship I thought an unsuitable residence
because of the boisterous crew, and the city I rejected as
an unsafe asylum for the young people.

"I had gone but a little distance when I spied an old
fisherman sitting before his door and mending broken nets.
I approached him and said, 'Good morning, friend; tell
me where a man might find lodgings.' 'At the nearest
promontory,' said he, 'on a hidden rock; it was broken and
torn yesterday.' 'That is not what I wanted to know,' said
I. 'You would do me a great kindness if you would receive
me into your house or direct me to another.' 'I didn't do it,'
said he, 'I was not in the boat. Tyrrhenus is not so awkward
nor so heavy with age. It was the fault of those green
hands who spread the nets in the reefs where they shouldn't
have.' I finally realized that he was hard of hearing and so
I shouted: 'Good morning; tell me a lodging for strangers.'
'The same to you,' he answered, 'you can stay with me if
you like, unless you are one to demand many beds and
bring a crowd of servants.' When I said that I had two
children besides myself, he said, 'A proper number. You
will find that we are one more. I have two sons that live
with me—the older ones are married and run their own
houses—and the fourth in the house is the boys' nurse;
their mother died not long ago. So, good sir, do not hesitate
or doubt that we shall be glad to receive a man who shows
good breeding at the first encounter.' I accepted his offer,
and in a little while, when I returned with Theagenes and
Charicleia, the old man received me cordially and assigned
us the warmest part of the house. The first part of the
winter season we passed agreeably enough. We spent our
days together, but when it came time to sleep we separated.

Charicleia slept with the nurse, I and Theagenes in one room, and Tyrrhenus and his boys in another. Our table was in common. We provided other victuals, and Tyrrhenus feasted the young people with an abundance of fish. Most he caught himself; but sometimes, to amuse our leisure, we joined his fishing trips. He used various techniques, appropriate for every season. He was extremely skillful, and the fish were plentiful, so that many people attributed to luck what was due to his skill.

"But the unlucky, as the saying goes, must everywhere be unlucky. Even in that desert Charicleia's beauty brought trouble. That Tyrian merchant, the Pythian victor with whom we sailed, kept bothering me with frequent private visits and tedious requests that I, as her father, give him Charicleia in marriage. He put on great airs, gave a catalogue of his noble family and an inventory of his present wealth. He said that the ship was his own property and that he owned most of its cargo, which consisted of gold, precious stones, and silk. He cited his victory at Delphi as no small increment to his reputation, and made many other claims besides. I objected that we were poor, and that I would never think of marrying my daughter to a foreigner whose country was so remote from Egypt. 'Say no more of that, father,' said he. 'As for the absence of dowry, I value the girl beyond all wealth in money. As for race and country, I shall accept yours. I will give up my voyage to Carthage and sail with you wherever you please.'

"I saw that the Phoenician, so far from relaxing his ardor, grew even warmer and let no day pass without his tedious importunities, and so I resolved to put him off for the present with fine promises, for I feared we should be liable to violence in the island. And so I promised that I would give him satisfaction when we reached Egypt. But I had scarcely got rid of this embarrassment when, as the saying goes, fate rolled wave upon wave. Only a few days later Tyrrhenus accosted me in a remote bend of the shore and said: 'Calasiris, I swear to you by Poseidon and the other deities of the sea that I regard you as my brother and your children as my own. I come to inform you of a gathering danger of which you must by all means be told, and concerning which it would be impious of me, who have shared a hearth with you, to keep silent. A pirate band concealed in a fold of yonder promontory is lying in wait for that Phoenician vessel and has posted relays of sentinels to watch for its sailing. Take care, then, be vigilant, and calculate what you must do, for it is because of you, or rather of your daughter, that they have conceived this bold but to them commonplace design.' 'May the gods give you due requital for your kindness,' said I to him, 'but how did you discover this plot?' 'My trade makes me acquainted with these men. I supply them fish, and receive a higher price than others pay. Yesterday as I was taking up my weirs among the rocks the robber chief encountered me and asked, "When are the Phoenicians going to sail, if you know?" I understood the purport of the question and said, "I cannot say exactly, Trachinus, but I suppose they will sail in the early spring." "Will that girl lodging with you sail with them?" he asked. "I do not know," I said, "but why are you so curious?" "Because I fell madly in love with her as soon as I saw her," he said. "I have never come upon such beauty, though I have taken many captives and very handsome ones too." I wished to draw him on to reveal his whole plan, and said, "Why must you come to blows with the Phoenicians? Why not, without shedding blood and before they put to sea, kidnap her out of my house?" "Even among thieves," he said, "there is conscience and feelings of humanity towards acquaintances. I wish to spare you the troubles you would experience if the strangers were to be sought at your hands. Furthermore, the single stroke would get me two great advantages, the

wealth of the ship and marriage with the girl; if I made
my attempt by land I would certainly lose one of these.
Moreover, an attempt so near the city is not safe; news of it
would spread at once, and there would be pursuit." I
praised his prudence and departed, and come to inform you
of the dastardly plot prepared against you. I implore you
to take thought for saving yourself and yours.'

"When I heard all this I went off in sorrow and turned
various plans over in my mind. By pure chance the merchant met me, and by talking on the old subject gave me
a handle for a new scheme. Concealing those parts of Tyrrhenus' information I thought advisable, I revealed only
that a local personage whose power was irresistible was
planning to abduct the girl. 'I would much prefer,' said I,
'to marry her to you, because of your previous acquaintance
and your wealth, and above all because you have voluntarily promised to settle in our country if you marry her.
If you have the matter at heart we must hasten our departure to prevent irresistible violence.' He was overjoyed
and said, 'Bravo, father!' and ran up to kiss my head and
asked when I would have him weigh anchor; if the weather
was too bad for sailing, it was possible to remove to another anchorage where we would be beyond reach of the
plot and could await full spring. 'If my suggestion has
weight,' said I, 'I advise sailing this very night.' 'So be it,'
said he, and departed. I went home. To Tyrrhenus I said
nothing, but I told the children that at dark of night we
should again have to take ship. They were surprised at the
suddenness and asked its reason; I said I would tell them
another time, and added, 'Now we must act.'

"After a light repast we retired to sleep. In a dream there
appeared to me an old man. Though shrunken, his girt
robe revealed thighs that had been powerful in youth; on
his head was a dogskin cap; his look was intelligent and
cunning; and he dragged one leg that limped because of

some wound. He approached me and with an ironic smile said, 'My fine friend, you are the only one who has no regard for me. Everyone that sails by Kephallene visits my house and eagerly contemplates my glory; but you have been so indifferent as not even to give me a perfunctory greeting, though I am your near neighbor. For this neglect you shall pay, and quite soon. You will experience afflictions like mine, and encounter enemies both by sea and land. But the girl you carry with you salute in the name of my wife Penelope, who says she is pleased with her because she values chastity above all else; Penelope promises a happy issue to her fortunes.' From this vision I sprang up trembling, and when Theagenes asked what the matter was, I said, 'We may be late for the sailing, and the thought of it troubled my sleep and awakened me. Get up and pack our things. I will go for Charicleia.' The child came at my first summons, and Tyrrhenus, who overheard, arose and asked what was happening. 'What is happening,' I said, 'is by your advice. We are trying to escape those plotting against us. Heaven preserve you for proving so excellent a friend to us; but do us this final kindness. Sail over to Ithaca and offer sacrifice to Odysseus on our behalf. Beg him to mitigate his resentment; this night he appeared to me in a dream and signified his anger.' Tyrrhenus promised to do so and escorted us to the ship, shedding many tears and wishing us as prosperous a voyage as we would ourselves desire.

"But why weary you with details? When the morning star shone forth, we put to sea. At first the sailors objected, but they were finally persuaded by the Tyrian merchant, who told them they were escaping a pirate attack of which he had been warned. He did not realize that his fiction was literal truth. We ran into gales, and in the irresistible storm and monstrous waves we almost foundered; but after losing one of our rudders and having most of our yard-arms broken we finally reached shelter at a promontory of Crete. On that island we decided to stay for some days, to repair our ship and refresh ourselves. We did so, and the resumption of the voyage was announced for the first day of the new moon, after its conjunction with the sun. We set sail and spring zephyrs carried us forward night and day. The pilot steered for Libya, for he said that the wind favored a direct and uninterrupted crossing of the sea and that he was eager to reach the mainland and make harbor because he suspected that the brigantine which could be seen at our stern was a pirate boat. 'She has followed our track,' said he, 'from the moment we left the Cretan headland, and she has maintained the same distance from our course as if she were impelled by the same motion. Whenever I have purposely deviated from the straight course I have observed her do the same.'

"At this intelligence some of the crew were stung into action and urged preparation for defense; others dismissed it and said it was usual for a small vessel to follow a larger at sea, to have the advantage of a more expert pilot. While these views were being disputed, the time of day came on when the farmer looses his ox from the plow; the wind slackened and gradually fell, striking the sails softly and ineffectively, fluttering rather than swelling them. Finally, it subsided into a dead calm, as if it were setting with the sun, or to speak more truly, as if it were co-operating with our pursuers. For as long as the wind blew, the brigantine was left far behind the merchant ship, whose larger sails received more wind. But when the dead calm flattened the sea and called for the use of oars, they were upon us quicker than the words could be pronounced. All the brigantine's crew, I suppose, were rowers, and their light craft was amenable to the oar.

"When they had come alongside, a man who had embarked at Zacynthus cried out, 'This is it, men, we are done

for. That is a pirate craft. I know Trachinus' brigantine.'
At this news the ship shook. Though the sea was calm it
was overwhelmed by a wave. The ship was battered by
shouts, wails, running to and fro. Some ducked down into
the hold of the ship, others stood on the bridge and encouraged one another to fight, others advised leaping into
the skiff and attempting escape. In this confusion instant
war overtook them, unwilling though they were, and each
man armed himself with whatever came to hand to defend himself. I and Charicleia clung to Theagenes, who
was boiling with eagerness to join the fight, and with difficulty restrained him. She declared that not even death
would separate them and that one sword and a single stroke
would inflict the same destruction upon them both. For my
part, as soon as I recognized that the aggressor was Trachinus, I resolved to contrive some plan for our future safety.
And so it came about. The pirates crossed our bow in an
endeavor to get possession of our ship without striking a
blow. They hurled no weapons, but by rowing round us
they prevented us from moving. Like besiegers, they were
anxious to take our ship by capitulation. 'Unhappy men,'
said they, 'why are you so mad as to lift your hands against
so superior and irresistible a force? Why do you throw
yourself to certain death? We are charitable, and advise
you to embark in your skiff and save yourselves wherever
you will.' Such was the pirates' offer, but those on the
merchantman were bold as long as the battle was without
peril and the war without blood, and declared that they
would not abandon ship.

"But when the boldest of the pirates leapt onto the ship
and by striking right and left with his sword demonstrated
that war is decided by slaughter and death, and when the
other corsairs leaped after him, then the Phoenicians repented and fell at their feet and begged for quarter, agree-
ing to do whatever they were commanded. Although the

corsairs were already deep in slaughter and the sight of blood whets the passions, at the command of Trachinus they spared the suppliants, beyond all hope. There ensued a truce—or rather, the most horrible aspects of war were terminated by the false title of peace, for the terms imposed were more grievous than the fighting. They ordered that each man leave the ship with one shirt, and threatened death for any that violated these terms. But life, it seems, is more precious to man than anything: so then the Phoenicians, robbed of their ship and hope of wealth, behaved as if they had profited rather than lost, and each hurried to be ahead of his fellows in getting into the boat, each competing to be the first to be saved.

"In obedience to the order we too stepped forward; but Trachinus laid hold of Charicleia and said, 'This war is not against you, my darling, but rather for you. For a long while I have been following you, ever since you left Zacynthus; for your sake I have encountered so much sea and so much danger. Take heart, then, and know that with me you will be mistress of all this treasure.' So Trachinus said, and Charicleia, like the clever creature she was, was quick to use the opportunity. Putting into practice some of my instruction, she smoothed her brow which the sudden storm had ruffled, and put on a winning look. 'Heaven be thanked,' she said, 'for disposing your mind kindly towards us. But if you really wish me to be and remain cheerful, give me first this mark of your good will. Save my brother here and my father, and do not force them to quit the ship; I cannot live apart from them.' So saying, she fell at his knees and clung to them in supplication. Trachinus was thrilled by this embrace, and purposely delayed promising. But when he was moved to pity by her tears and subdued to obedience by her looks, he raised the girl up and said, 'Your brother I grant you, and very cheerfully, for I see that he is a manly fellow and a proper comrade for our

way of life. This old man is only useless baggage; but to
please you, let him stay.'

"While these things were being done and said, the sun
reached its setting and produced the twilight dusk which
separates day and night. Suddenly, the sea grew rough,
perhaps because of the change of seasons, perhaps by the
changed will of some fate. The whistle of a rushing wind was
heard; in a moment it swept down upon the sea in stormy
gusts and filled the pirates with sudden consternation. They
had left their own brigantine to plunder the cargo of the
merchantman, and they were caught on a big ship whose
management they had no experience of. The various tasks
of navigation they undertook at hazard, each man boldly
improvising procedures he knew nothing of. Some reefed
the sails lubber-like, others clumsily pulled at ropes. One
bungler inherited the prow, another attempted to manage
the tiller at the stern. It was not so much the violence of
waves that threw us into the extreme of danger—the storm
had not reached its height—as the awkwardness of the
pilot. He persisted in steering as long as the afterglow of
the sun provided light, but when darkness prevailed he re-
signed. When we were already washed by the sea and
wanted but little of drowning, some of the corsairs at first
attempted to transfer to their own brigantine, but they
were prevented by the beating of the sea and by Trachinus,
who urged that if they saved the merchant ship and its
wealth they could buy a thousand such brigantines. Finally he cut the cable by which the brigantine was kept in
tow, maintaining that it might bring on a new storm, and
explaining also that he was providing for future safety, for
to arrive anywhere with two vessels would create suspicion,
and the crew of at least one would be narrowly examined.
This seemed reasonable, and of the two reasons preferred,
the one relating to the present proved valid immediately,
for from the moment the brigantine was set adrift a brief

respite from the storm was perceptible. But we were by no means out of our peril; we had to struggle against enormous waves; parts of the ship and its freight were jettisoned, and we were subjected to a thousand dangers. That night and the day following we weathered with difficulty, and towards evening made land at the Heracleot mouth of the Nile, where, with no desire to do so, our wretched company landed on Egyptian soil.

"The pirates were happy, but we were full of sorrow and reproached the sea for preserving us: it had begrudged us a death free of outrage and had now delivered us to a more dreadful expectation by land, where we would be exposed to the lawless whims of the pirates. Those villains had hardly set foot on land when they showed their nature. Declaring that they wished to offer thanksgiving sacrifices to Poseidon, forsooth, they fetched Tyrian wine and other such luxuries from the ship and sent men to buy cattle in the surrounding district; these they provided with large sums and bade them pay the first price asked. These men soon returned, driving a whole herd of sheep and pigs, and those who had stayed behind welcomed them, lighted a fire, flayed the victims, and prepared the feast. Trachinus took me aside so that the others might not hear, and said: 'Father, I have betrothed your daughter to be my wife and intend to celebrate the marriage today, as you see, combining the most delightful of festivals with a sacrifice to the gods. So that you will not (as you otherwise might) be a gloomy guest, and so that your daughter, learning of my intention from you, might rejoice at her lot, I have thought it right to inform you of my purpose in advance—not that I desire you to confirm it, for my power is sufficient to enforce my will, but because I regard it more proper and propitious for the bride to be prepared in advance by learning of her marriage from her parents.' I approved of his sentiments and put on a happy expression, and said I gave great thanks to the gods for making my daughter's master her husband.

"I retired for a moment to reflect on what could be done at this conjuncture. Then I returned and petitioned that the affair be carried out more ceremoniously and that the ship be assigned to the girl as a bridal chamber. No one must enter it or disturb her, so that she might have time to arrange her wedding costume and make other proper preparations, 'for,' I added, 'it would be most unseemly if a young lady of her birth and wealth and in particular when she is to be the bride of a Trachinus, should not make herself as fine as possible even though the circumstances and the place might diminish the splendor appropriate to such a marriage.' Trachinus was overjoyed and issued the necessary orders. He directed that the men should carry whatever was needed out of the ship and then not go near it. They did as they were bidden and brought out tables, mixing bowls, carpets, hangings—of Sidonian and Tyrian workmanship—and all other appliances for a rich feast. Upon their shoulders they carried in disorderly piles wealth which toil and frugality had accumulated, and which fate now bestowed upon a riotous and gluttonous revelry.

"I took Theagenes aside and went to Charicleia, whom I found in tears. 'Daughter,' said I, 'this is all familiar to you, there is nothing new. Is it for the past you are weeping, or is there something else?' 'Everything,' said she, 'but above all, the prospects held out by Trachinus' hateful good will, which he is likely to insist upon at this time, for unexpected success naturally provokes outrageous conduct. But Trachinus and Trachinus' abhorred love will rue it, for he will be balked by my death. It is the thought of you and of Theagenes, if I must be separated from you before my end, that drives me to tears.' 'Your conjectures,' I said, 'are correct. Trachinus will turn the banquet which follows the sacrifice into a marriage celebration for him-

self and you. He confided his design to me, as being your
father, but I knew of his violent passion long ago, when
Tyrrhenus told me of it in Zacynthus. I said nothing to
you at the time, not to prematurely afflict your minds with
impending misfortune when it was still possible to escape
his designs. But since, my children, fate has opposed this
hope and we are still in the same peril, let us dare some
noble and decisive deed to meet this critical danger, and
either succeed as becomes noble men and free, or gain a
glorious death, as becomes chaste men and brave.'

"They promised to do whatever I ordered. I gave them
instructions, left them to carry them out, and sought out
Trachinus' second in command, Pelorus I think he was
called, saying I had something of the highest importance
to tell him. He was very ready to listen, and took me aside
where no one could overhear. 'I shall be very concise,' said
I, 'for time does not admit of long speeches. My daughter
is in love with you, and no wonder. Your high merit has
captivated her. She suspects that your commander is preparing to make the festival a marriage, and he has in fact
shown some such intention by ordering her to deck herself
out elegantly. Consider how you may combat this plan and
get the girl for yourself. She declares she would sooner die
than be married to Trachinus.' 'Courage,' said he, 'I myself
have long been in love with the girl and only prayed for
some favorable opportunity. Now Trachinus shall either
yield her to me voluntarily on my just claim as having
been the first to board your ship, or else his will be a bitter
marriage when he gets his deserts from this right hand of
mine.' When I heard this I hurried away, so that no suspicion might arise. I then went to the children and comforted them with the good tidings that our plan was off to
a good start.

"A little later we partook of the feast, and when I observed that the men were well soaked and ready for any

violence, I said softly to Pelorus (I had purposely taken a place near him), 'Have you seen how beautifully dressed the girl is?' And when he said 'No,' I said, 'You could, if you went aboard the ship, but secretly, for you know that Trachinus has forbidden anyone to go near it. You will see Artemis herself sitting there. But for the moment you must control yourself when you see her, otherwise you will invite death for yourself and for her.' Without delay, then, he arose, as if to answer a call of nature, and surreptitiously hurried to the ship, where he saw Charicleia. She wore a crown of laurel upon her head and was resplendent in a gold-embroidered robe; she had dressed herself in the priestly vestments of Delphi, to serve as the habiliments of triumph or of death. Everything about her was splendid and bespoke the array of a bridal canopy. The spectacle set Pelorus afire, as it naturally would, with desire and jealousy, and when he returned his looks plainly showed his furious temper.

"He had scarcely resumed his place when he broke out, 'Why have I not received my prize for being the first to board the ship?' 'Because you haven't asked for it,' said Trachinus, 'and besides our booty has not yet been distributed.' Said Pelorus, 'Then I ask for the captive girl.' Said Trachinus, 'Take anything you like except her.' Pelorus interjected, 'You break the pirate law which gives first and unrestricted choice to the man who is first to board an enemy vessel and first to encounter danger.' 'I do not break that law, my fine fellow,' said Trachinus, 'but I do insist upon another law which requires subordinates to yield to their commanders. I have a violent passion for that girl and propose to marry her. I think it right that my preference be respected in this matter, and if you do not obey orders you will soon rue it, when I smash you with this cup I hold.' Pelorus looked at the rest of the company and said, 'You see how our toils are requited? Just so will each of you at one time be deprived of his prize and be made to feel the tyranny of this law.'

"What a spectacle ensued, Nausicles! You might liken the company to a sea churned up by a cyclone. Blind impulse drove them to indescribable tumult, ruled, as they were, by wine and passion. Some inclined to Trachinus, some to Pelorus, these shouting that the commander must be respected, those that the law must not be violated. At length Trachinus brandished his cup to strike Pelorus, and Pelorus, who was ready on his guard, was beforehand in plunging a dagger into the breast of Trachinus, who fell mortally wounded. Among the others war without quarter became general. They fell upon and struck one another mercilessly, some in revenge for their commander, others defending Pelorus' right. There was a continuous din as clubs, stones, cups, torches, tables, were hurled and found their marks. I withdrew as far as I could and got a safe view of the spectacle from a hilltop. But Theagenes did not stand outside the fight, nor, indeed, did Charicleia, but they acted according to our previous arrangement. Sword in hand, Theagenes at first fought on one side, laying about him in a seeming fury. And Charicleia, as soon as she saw that war had broken out, shot her unerring arrows from the ship, sparing none but Theagenes. She aimed without distinction of party, and carried off any fair mark she saw, herself being invisible but able to see her opponents very well by the light of the torches. These were ignorant of the source of their distress and some thought the blows were heaven-sent. At length all had fallen except Theagenes, who was left in single combat with Pelorus, a brave man and well schooled by many bloody actions. Nor could Charicleia's archery now support him; though she was in an agony of anxiety to help him, she was afraid, since the combat was hand to hand, that her arrows might miscarry. But in the end Pelorus' resistance failed. When Charicleia's active support was thwarted, she used words instead of arrows to reinforce Theagenes. 'Play the man, my darling!' she cried. These words supplied strength and courage to Theagenes, and reminded him that the prize of the fighting was still alive, and now Theagenes easily gained the upper hand. Though he was oppressed by numerous wounds he roused his spirit and leapt upon Pelorus and struck at his head. The head he missed, because Pelorus dodged, but the sword slipped down Pelorus' shoulder and lopped off his arm above the elbow. Pelorus turned to flight with Theagenes after him in pursuit.

"What followed I am not able to say, except that Theagenes came back without my noticing it. Myself I remained on my hill, because I would not venture to be involved in an embattled area at night. Not so Charicleia. When day broke I saw Theagenes lying stark on the field, and Charieleia sitting by and lamenting and patently wishing to slaughter herself, but restrained by a glimmer of hope that the young man might yet survive. I had not presence of mind, ill-starred as I was, to speak or make inquiry or lighten her woe with words of comfort, nor to minister to their needs—so close did afflictions by land follow those by sea. In daylight, as I was descending from my hill I saw a crowd of Egyptian brigands who had apparently run down the side of the mountain which stretched down to the sea; these brigands already had the young people in their power, and a little later, when they had brought as much plunder as they could out of the ship, they went off. I helplessly followed at a distance, bewailing my own lot and theirs. I could do nothing to assist, so thought it best not to join them, but to hoard my efforts against some future hope of aiding them. But my strength was inadequate. Old age hampered my efforts to keep up with the Egyptians in the mountainous roads, and I was left behind. Until the present moment, when I have recovered my daughter by the benevolence of the gods and your kindness, Nausicles, I have contributed nothing to her welfare except tears and lamentations without end."

Thereupon he fell to weeping, and all present wept with him, and the banquet was transformed to a scene of mourning mingled with pleasure, for wine is somehow conducive to tears. At length Nausicles said, to encourage Calasiris, "Father, from now on you can be cheerful. Your daughter you already have, and only the night prevents you from seeing your son. In the morning we shall visit Mitranes and put forth every effort to procure the release of your excellent Theagenes." "My fondest wish!" said Calasiris. "But now it is time to break up our feast. Let the divine be held in mind, and let someone pour the libations of consummation."

Thereupon the libations were passed around and the banquet dissolved. Calasiris looked for Charicleia, but though he scrutinized the crowd as they filed out, he could not find her. Then at the suggestion of one of the women he went to the temple and came upon her clinging to the feet of the statue. The long-drawn prayers and excess of sorrow had plunged her into a deep sleep. He wept a little and prayed heaven to change her fortune for the better, and then he gently woke her and escorted her, blushing at having unwittingly succumbed to sleep, to their lodging. There she retired to the women's apartment and went to rest with the daughter of Nausicles. But her cares kept her wakeful.

6

CALASIRIS AND CNEMON went to rest in their room in the men's wing. The remainder of the night passed more slowly than they wished but more quickly than they thought, for the greater part of it had been consumed by the feast and by the charming but lengthy narrative. Without waiting for full daylight they approached Nausicles and requested him to say where he thought Theagenes might be and to take them there as promptly as possible. Charicleia begged to go along, but was obliged to remain where she was, Nausicles assuring her that they were not going far and would soon come back with Theagenes. And so they left her behind, oscillating between chagrin at the separation and exultation at her expectations.

They had barely left the village and were passing along the banks of the Nile when they saw a crocodile making its way from the right bank towards the left and plunging into the channel of the river with rapid thrusts. The others were undisturbed at the familiar sight, except that Calasiris thought it portended some hindrance on the road; but Cnemon, though he had not clearly seen the creature itself, but rather a depressed and fugitive shadow, fell into a transport of alarm and could barely keep from running away. Nausicles burst into laughter and Calasiris said, "Cnemon, I thought it was only by night that you were subject to panic and trembled at rustling darkness; but now, it seems, you are singularly courageous by day also. It is not only *names* you hear that put you in a fright, but even the most ordinary and harmless sights." "What god is it," asked Nausicles, "or what demon, whose name our hero cannot endure to hear?" "Whether gods and demons so frighten him I cannot say," answered Calasiris. "It is a mortal, and not one renowned for prowess—not even a man, but a mere woman, and at that a dead one, as he himself says, at the mention of whose name he shivers. The night when you returned from the buccaneers and brought Charicleia back to us safe, dear friend, the name of the person I speak of was mentioned—I do not know how or whence—and he did not let me get even a wink of sleep; all night he kept dying of terror and I had much ado to restore him. If I were not going to set him off in another transport of terror I would repeat the name now, Nausicles, to give you a good laugh." Then he uttered "Thisbe."

But Nausicles laughed not at all. Rather was he sobered by what he heard and stood pondering, at a loss to know how Cnemon came acquainted with Thisbe, what their relations had been, and why he was so affected by her name. But now Cnemon burst into a laugh and said, "You see, good Calasiris, what a power the name possesses. It is a bugbear, as you say, not for me alone but for Nausicles too. But the effects are completely reversed. Now I laugh, because I know she is dead, but our brave Nausicles, who laughs and mocks at others, is now somber." "Stop," said Nausicles, "you have full revenge, Cnemon. But in the name of the gods of hospitality and friendship, in the name of the salt and the table which you have shared, I think generously, in my house, tell me whether you know the name of Thisbe and actually feared it or whether you are making sport of me." "It is your turn, Cnemon," interposed Calasiris, "to deliver the account of your adventures which you have frequently promised to relate but have always put off with various dodges. This is the proper occasion, for your story will gratify Nausicles as well as me and will lighten and speed our journey."

Cnemon consented and recounted his whole story, abridging what he had already told Theagenes and Charicleia—that he was Athenian by country, that his father was Aristippus, and that Demainete had become his stepmother. He spoke of Demainete's lawless love for him and how, when it was thwarted, she laid a plot against him, employing Thisbe as her agent. He explained how he was banished from his country, condemned as a parricide by vote of the people, and how, when he was living in exile in Aegina, a classmate named Charias told him that Demainete was dead, that she had been betrayed by her accomplice Thisbe. He told how he had then heard from Anticles that his father's property had been confiscated on a charge concerted against him by her family—which persuaded the people of its truth—that he had murdered Demainete. He spoke of Thisbe's eloping from Athens with a merchant of Naucratis who was her lover. Finally, Cnemon told how he sailed for Egypt with Anticles in search of Thisbe, to bring her to Athens, if he could find her, in order to absolve his father of the false charge and to punish her; and how, after encountering many changes and vicissitudes of fortune he had been taken captive first by pirates, and then, after he escaped them and arrived in Egypt, again by the buccaneers. Speaking of these he told of his encounter with Theagenes and Charicleia and of the death of Thisbe. So he continued his tale until he came to the events known to Calasiris and Nausicles.

When Cnemon finished Nausicles turned many thoughts

over in his mind. Now he was minded to tell the story of himself and Thisbe, and now he judged it better to postpone it to another time. Finally, though he wished to speak, he held back, partly because he thought it better to say nothing, and partly because he was prevented by an accident. They had gone about sixty furlongs and were near the village where Mitranes resided when they met an acquaintance of Nausicles and asked him where he was going in such haste. "Nausicles," said he, "you inquire about my exertions as if you did not know that just now all my efforts are concentrated upon a single object, which is how I may serve and execute the behests of Isias of Chemmis. It is for her I work the land, for her needs that I toil, for her sake that I take no rest night or day. I refuse no task, great or small, that Isias imposes upon me—and all I get is toil and pain. Now, as you see, in obedience to her command, I am running to bring my darling this Nile phoenicopter bird." "It is a most amiable sweetheart you have got," said Nausicles, "and her commands are trifling. Instead of a phoenicopter she might have ordered you to bring the phoenix itself, which comes from Ethiopia or India." "That is her regular way," said he, "she mocks at me and my efforts. But where are you going, and what is your business?" When they said that they were bent on seeing Mitranes, he answered, "No use, your hurry is wasted, for Mitranes is not at home. Last night he went on an expedition against the buccaneers of Bessa. He had sent to Oroondates at Memphis a young Greek captive who, I imagine, was to be sent to the Great King as a present, and the Bessaeans under their newly elected leader Thyamis seized the young man in a raid and hold him prisoner." Even as he was speaking he began to run. "I must hurry to Isias," said he, "she is looking for me now with many eyes, and if I linger there will be a jealous scene. She is a terrible woman and for most unaccountable reasons frames reproaches and bickerings against me."

His intelligence left the others long dumbfounded by the unexpected disappointment of their hopes. At length Nausicles tried to encourage them, urging that there was no occasion to despair of their undertaking because of a slight and momentary setback. For the present they must return to Chemmis to consider what must next be done and to prepare for a longer journey in search of Theagenes, whether he was still with the buccaneers or whether they should learn that he had gone elsewhere. In any case they must always keep up their hopes of finding him, for it was by the interposition of providence that they had encountered the acquaintance whose information directed them to Theagenes' whereabouts and guided them in a straight line to the buccaneers' village.

Nausicles' suggestions were accepted without demur; for one thing, the news admitted a glimmer of hope, and for another, Cnemon privately gave Calasiris strong assurances that Thyamis would certainly keep Theagenes safe. They decided then to return, and found Charicleia at the house door, peering in all directions for their appearance. When she saw that Theagenes was not with them she uttered a sorrowful wail: "Are you returning alone, father, just as you left? Theagenes must be dead. If you have anything to tell, tell it quickly, in heaven's name, and do not prolong my agony by dragging out your tidings. Quick revelation of calamity is charity; the soul collects its powers to meet the evil, and the shock is soon relieved." Cnemon cut her excessive distress short, saying, "How troublesome you are, Charicleia! You are always ready to divine the worst, and are wrong, for you are in no trouble. Theagenes is alive and safe, thank heaven." He told her briefly how and where he was. "Your words clearly show, Cnemon," remarked Calasiris, "that you have never been in love. Otherwise you would surely know that lovers are apprehensive of the most harmless trifles, and where the beloved is concerned, trust only their eyes. Absence always fills their languishing souls with torment, for they are convinced that only the direst obstacles could ever keep their darlings away. So, friend, let us forgive Charicleia, who shows all the symptoms of a serious case of love, and let us get indoors and consider what we have to do."

At this Calasiris took Charicleia by the hand and with paternal tenderness brought her into the house. Nausicles, who wished to cheer their spirits—and had another project of his own also—prepared a more elegant dinner than was his habit, and invited only them and his daughter, whom he titivated and adorned to make a finer show than usual. When the company seemed satisfied with their cheer, he began to speak to them as follows: "The gods be my witness, friends, that I should be happy if you would wish to stay here with me for all time and share my treasures and my pleasures. I do not regard you as sojourning visitors but as friends true and tried, and I should consider nothing that conduces to your welfare as onerous. In your desire to recover your kindred I am ready to co-operate so far as in me lies. But you know very well that mine is a merchant's career: that is how I plant and reap. Now the bright zephyrs have begun to breathe again and have smoothed the sea for navigation and bring promise of fair voyages to merchants. Like a clarion call my affairs summon me to a sojourn in Greece. You would be doing me a fair grace if you could communicate your own desires to me, so that I may make my dispositions in accordance with yours."

After this speech Calasiris paused a moment and then said: "Nausicles, may your sailing be auspicious. May Hermes of Gain and Poseidon of Safety join in your voyaging and foster it. May they make every sea smooth and every

wind fair; may they render every harbor a haven, every
city accessible and hospitable to the merchant. Us have you
courteously treated while here and graciously dismissed
when we wished to depart; the laws of hospitality and
friendship have you scrupulously observed. Though it is
painful for us to be separated from you and from your
house, which you have generously taught us to consider
our own, nevertheless ineluctable necessity imposes upon us
the search for what is dearest to us. Such is my own and
Charicleia's resolve; what Cnemon's purpose is, whether
he is ready to do us the grace of sharing in our wanderings
or whether he is otherwise minded, he himself is here to
say."

Cnemon indicated his desire to respond and was on the
point of utterance when sudden sighs and a hot spate of
tears stopped his tongue. At long length he collected his
breath and with a deep sigh said: "Ah, the vicissitudes
which fickle and incalculable fortune sends upon men!
What a flood tide of afflictions have you been pleased to
sweep over others, over me! Of my family and father's
house you have deprived me; from my country and dearest
city you have alienated me; upon Egyptian soil, after intervening trials, you have cast me up in a shipwreck; to piratical buccaneers you have delivered me. A brief ray of
hope you showed by giving me companions, as unfortunate
as myself indeed, but Greeks, and with them I hoped to
pass my remaining days; but now this solace, too, you
cut off. Whither should I turn? What must I do? Should I
desert Charicleia before she has found Theagenes? That
would be infamous—Holy Earth!—and impious. But must
I follow her and join in the search? If there were good
prospect of finding him, the labor would be well ventured; but the future is uncertain and difficult and there
is no telling where and when my wandering may end. Why
should I not ask pardon of you and the gods of friendship

and venture to speak now of returning to my country and family? If Nausicles is sailing, as he says, to Greece, the opportunity comes heaven sent. If anything has happened to my father, our house would be altogether desolated, with no successor and no heir. Even without the property, it would be a good and sufficient thing for a shoot of his line to survive in my person. But, dear Charicleia, it is to you that I am most anxious to excuse myself. I ask your pardon; please grant it. I will follow you to the country of the buccaneers and ask Nausicles, however urgent his haste, to wait a little. If I can actually put you into Theagenes' hands I shall have proved to be an honorable guardian of the deposit in my care and shall myself start out with high hopes and a serene conscience. But if I should, heaven forbid, fail, I might still be pardoned, for I am not leaving you solitary but putting you into the hands of an excellent guardian, your father Calasiris."

Many signs had led Charicleia to conjecture that Cnemon was in love with Nausicles' daughter, for a lover is quick to perceive another governed by the same passion. From what Nausicles had said she understood too that he would be very pleased with the alliance and that he had long been endeavoring to bring it about and to induce Cnemon's interest in various ways. Furthermore she thought it was neither proper nor above suspicion to have Cnemon as a companion on her travels. "Do what is agreeable to you," she said. "The good offices you have shown us we acknowledge, and we express our gratitude; but for the future there is no need for you to occupy yourself with our cares or, contrary to your own desires, to incur the dangers of fortunes that do not concern you. Go to Athens and recover your house and home. Nausicles, as you say, luckily offers the opportunity; do not neglect it. Calasiris and I will struggle with whatever befalls until we find the end of our wanderings, and if there are no humans to take our part we shall trust the gods to be our companions."

Nausicles now interposed, saying, "May Charicleia's wishes come true; may the gods accompany her on her quest and may she recover her own, so noble is her character, so intelligent her understanding. And do you, Cnemon, no longer distress yourself at not bringing Thisbe back to Athens. I am the culprit who abducted her from Athens, for I am the merchant of Naucratis who was Thisbe's lover. Nor grieve that you will be reduced to beggary. If your desires coincide with mine you will have ample wealth and, under my guidance, recover your house and your country. If you are willing to marry I offer you my daughter Nausicleia, with the largest possible dowry, and will consider, knowing your family, house, and race, that I have received no less from you." Not a moment did Cnemon hesitate. The thing he had long desired and prayed for without hope of obtaining he now received unexpectedly and more generously than he had dared pray. "All your offer I accept very gladly," said he, and stretched out his hand. Into his hand Nausicles placed his daughter's in token of betrothal and bade his household raise the hymeneal chant. He himself opened the dance, transforming the banquet into an improvised marriage.

The company were happily dancing and celebrating the impromptu marriage, and through the night the house was bright with nuptial torches. But Charicleia went apart from the rest, retired to her own room, locked the door securely, and believing that no one would disturb her, she surrendered herself to a bacchant frenzy. She pulled her hair loose and ripped her garments and said: "On! I too will dance, after the fashion appropriate to him, to the demon who holds me in sway. To him will I chant dirges and writhe in a dance of lamentation. Let murky gloom pour over and let unillumined night preside over my ritual; this lamp I dash to the ground. Such is the dainty marriage canopy he has rigged for me, such the bridal bed to which he leaves me. Solitary he keeps me, and unwed—in name Theagenes'

bride, but, alas, a widow. Cnemon marries, but Theagenes
wanders, and at that a captive, perhaps in chains. But even
that would be happiness if he is only safe. Nausicleia is a
bride, and my bedfellow until tonight is unyoked from
me; Charicleia is desolate and deserted. But not for them
is my reproach, fortune and ye other powers; let them be
happy to their heart's content. But why have you not used
me as you used them? My tragedy you have prolonged end-
lessly; its horror transcends any stage. But why do I reproach the powers divine? Let the rest be accomplished as
the gods will. But oh, Theagenes, my sole and sweetest care,
if you are dead, if I hear what I hope I may never know,
I will never put off joining you. For the present let me bestow upon you these funerary offerings"—plucking out
hair and throwing it upon the couch—"and let me pour
libations from these eyes which you held dear"—and a del-
uge of tears moistened her bed. "But if you are alive and
safe, come to me now, dear friend, and lie by my side, in
a dream. But even then, my dear, preserve my maidenhood
for legitimate marriage. Look, see how I embrace you, how
I imagine I hold you and see you."

So saying she flung herself upon the bed, face down,
and embraced it close with moans and broken sobs. Her
excess of agitation induced torpor and dizziness and
clouded her reasoning faculties. Insensibly, she fell into a
sleep, which held her fast until broad daylight. When he
did not see her at the customary hour Calasiris was disturbed and went to seek her. He went to her room, knocked
sharply at her doors, and called her repeatedly by name,
and she awoke. Charicleia was confused by this sudden
awakening; she hurried to the doors, dressed as she was,
unbarred them, and let the old man in. When he saw
her disheveled hair, her dress torn over her bosom, her eyes
inflamed and showing signs of the frenzy she was in before
she fell asleep, he surmised the cause. He led her to her bed,

sat her down upon it, covered her with a robe which he
pulled decently about her, and said, "What is this, Charicleia? Why this excessive and immoderate agony? Why are
you so abjectly defeated by events? I have always known
you to bear your lot nobly and sensibly; now I cannot
recognize you. Will you not give over this folly? Will you
not remember that the human lot is unpredictable and
subject to extreme turns of fortune? Why do you destroy
yourself on what may be the eve of better hopes? Spare
me too, my child, spare me if not yourself, and spare Theagenes, for whom life has meaning only with you and is a
boon only if you are safe."

Charicleia blushed at his chiding and even more when
she thought of the condition in which he found her. For
a long while she remained silent, and when Calasiris pressed
her for an answer she said: "You are right to blame me, but
perhaps I should be pardoned, father. It is no vulgar or
capricious passion that drives me to wretchedness; it is a
pure and chaste longing for a man whom I regard, though
he has never known me carnally, as my husband, and that
man is Theagenes. I grieve at his not being here, but even
more I am afraid of his not being at all." "As for that,"
said Calasiris, "take heart. That he is alive and will soon
be with you is confirmed by the oracles concerning you
two, if we may trust the gods and yesterday's news that
he was captured by Thyamis and sent to Memphis. If he
is a captive it is certain that he is safe, for there is an old
familiarity and friendship between him and Thyamis. Now
we must delay no longer but hasten as quickly as we may
to the village of Bessa, and we must seek your Theagenes,
and also my son; you must surely have heard that Thyamis
is my own son." Charicleia became pensive. "If Thyamis
is your son," said she, "and this is your Thyamis and not
another, our affairs are in great jeopardy." Calasiris wondered why, and asked. "You know," she answered, "that

I was a captive among the buccaneers. There Thyamis, attracted by that appearance of beauty which has been my affliction, fell in love with me. There is a danger, if we encounter him in our search, that he will recognize me as the girl he saw and force the consummation of the marriage which he proposed before and which I put off by trickery." Said Calasiris: "Never would his passion be so ungovernable as to disregard the sight of his father. His begetter's eye will evoke the son's reverence and restrain his lawless passion, if such he has. Still, nothing prevents you from contriving some expedient for circumventing what you fear; you seem very clever at inventing dodges and subterfuges to put off importunate suitors."

At this pleasantry Charicleia recovered her spirits a little and said: "Whether you are in earnest or are making sport of me, enough of that for the present. I shall explain to you the ruse which Theagenes and I concerted before but which events forestalled; now we may use it with better luck. When we were contemplating escape from the buccaneers' island we decided to change to tattered garments and to pass through towns and villages disguised as beggars. If you agree, let us disguise our appearance and act the beggar so we will be less liable to embarrassing encounters. For such people lowliness insures safety; poverty arouses pity, not envy. Our daily needs we shall procure easily, for in a foreign land purchases are difficult for strangers but requests are readily granted to the pitiful."

Calasiris approved the project and was impatient to start. They announced their departure to Nausicles and Cnemon and their party, and on the third day they set out, taking no pack animal, though one was offered, and no human attendant. Nausicles, Cnemon, and their household escorted them. Nausicleia, too, begged her father to allow her to join the escort, her bride's shyness overcome by her love for Charicleia. When they had gone about five fur-

longs there was general leave-taking, and they shook hands
and wept copiously and exchanged wishes for prosperity.
Cnemon asked pardon for not accompanying them on the
grounds of his new marital tie, and implied that he would
overtake them if opportunity offered. And so they parted,
and Nausicles' party went back to Chemmis.

As for Charicleia and Calasiris, their first care was to
transform themselves into beggar's guise. They demeaned
themselves with rags which they had got ready, and then
Charicleia defiled her face by rubbing soot on it and smear-
ing mud over it. On her head she stuck a tattered veil whose
hem hung crooked from her brow over one eye. Under her
arm hung a wallet which appeared to contain broken
victuals and crusts but actually held the Delphian priestess'
robe, the fillets, and the jewels and tokens her mother had
exposed with her. Charicleia's quiver Calasiris wrapped in
a worn-out sheepskin and carried across his shoulders like
a piece of baggage. He loosened the strings of the bow,
and when it lost its curve he used it as a stick. He leaned
heavily upon it, and if he saw anyone coming along he
stooped his back more than his age constrained him to
do and dragged one leg. Sometimes Charicleia led him by
the hand.

When their costumes accurately represented their im-
posture, they joked a little, and bestowed mocking compli-
ments on the suitability of their attire, but they prayed
that fate would carry their wretchedness no further than
their appearances and would put a stop to their afflictions.
Then they hurried towards the village of Bessa where they
hoped to find Theagenes. But they were disappointed.
When they approached Bessa about sunset they saw the
ground strewn with a mass of bodies newly slain. Most,
their dress and weapons showed to be Persians, but some
were natives. They supposed it was the tragedy of war
they saw, but who the actors were they could not tell.

Passing through the carnage and looking to see if there were any they knew—our faint hearts fear the worst where loved ones are concerned—they came upon an old woman clinging to the body of a native and uttering a gamut of laments. They resolved to make inquiries of the old woman if they could. First they sat by her and tried to comfort her and to quiet the vehemence of her lamentation. When she relaxed a little they asked, Calasiris speaking to her in Egyptian, whom she mourned and what the war was. She replied succinctly: her grief was for her son, who lay dead before her; she had purposely come to the scene of the carnage in the hope that some one might attack her and release her from life; in the meanwhile she was offering her son what funeral rites she could—tears and lamentations.

Of the war she gave the following account: "A foreign young man of singular beauty and stature was being taken to Oroondates, viceroy of the Great King, to Memphis. He was sent, I believe, by the commandant Mitranes, who had taken him captive and was offering him, they say, as a very valuable gift. The people of the village here"—and she pointed to a nearby village—"claimed they knew the young man, whether truly or for a pretense, attacked the convoy, and abducted the young man. When Mitranes heard of this he was naturally angry and the day before yesterday marched against our village. (Our village is a very warlike breed; they live by brigandage and despise death, and they have widowed and orphaned many women, as now me.) When our people received intelligence of the expedition they laid several ambushes where they received the enemy and defeated him. Part fought them directly in the van, others with a shout sprang upon the unsuspecting Persians from the ambushes at their rear. Mitranes fell fighting among the foremost and with him almost all his men, for they were surrounded and could not escape. A few of ours fell, too, and among those few, by the heavy hand of fate, my son, his chest pierced, as you see, by a Persian dart. And now, a wretched woman, I grieve for him that is lying here and am likely to grieve for my one remaining son, for yesterday he marched against Memphis with the others."

Calasiris inquired the cause of their expedition, and the old woman told what she had heard from her surviving son. Having killed the King's soldiers and a commandant of the Great King, they saw well enough that their ill deeds would bring them no small jeopardy but utter destruction. Oroondates, the viceroy at Memphis, had very strong forces at his disposal and as soon as intelligence reached him he would immediately seal the village off on all sides and exact vengeance by a general massacre of its inhabitants. "Since the risk they ran was total, they determined to remedy their great daring with even greater, to anticipate Oroondates' expedition and to attack him unexpectedly. Either they would kill him, if they caught him in Memphis, or if he were absent, as some reported, on a campaign in Ethiopia, they would the more easily occupy a city bare of defenders. For the time they would be free of danger and could render a service to their chief Thyamis by restoring him to the dignity of the priesthood of which he had been unlawfully deprived by his younger brother. Even if they should fail, they would die fighting, and not merely be corralled and exposed to Persian insult and abuse. But you, strangers, where are you bound for?" "To the village," said Calasiris. "It is not safe for people they do not know to mingle with the few remaining villagers at this hour," said she. "But if you would conduct us," said Calasiris, "we should doubtless be safe." "I haven't time," answered the old woman, "there are certain nocturnal rites I must perform. But if you can tolerate it (and indeed you have no choice) move apart from these bodies to a clear space and make the best of it through the night. In the morning I will be your guide and sponsor for your safety."

Calasiris translated all she had said to Charicleia. Together they passed beyond the prone bodies and came upon a low hill. There Calasiris lay down, with his head on the quiver, and Charicleia made a seat of her wallet and reposed on it. The moon was just rising and, it being the third day from the full, illuminated the scene with bright rays. Old as he was, and fatigued by his journey, Calasiris fell asleep, but Charicleia's flood of thoughts kept her awake, and so she witnessed a scene that was diabolical but commonplace among Egyptian women. The old woman, supposing she would be undisturbed and unseen, began by digging a trench, and then on each side of it lighted a fire. Between the fires she placed the dead body of her son. Then from a tripod nearby she took an earthenware cup from which she poured honey into the trench, from another milk, and from a third she poured wine. Then she molded a lump of dough into the likeness of a man, crowned it with laurel and fennel, and threw it into the trench. After all this she snatched up a sword, gesticulated with it frantically, invoked the moon in a barbarous jargon strange to the ear, made an incision in her arm, caught the blood with a branch of laurel, and sprinkled it on the fires. After other eerie motions she stooped over the body of her son and murmured incantations in its ear. By her sorcery she roused the body and forced it to stand upright.

Charicleia had been frightened enough by the preliminaries, but now she shuddered in terror of the unearthly proceedings and awakened Calasiris so that he too might witness the scene. The two were in darkness and could not be seen, but the light and the fire made it easy for them to see, and they were near enough to overhear the old woman's loud voice when she questioned the corpse. She inquired whether its brother, her surviving son, would return safe. The corpse did not reply but only nodded, which the mother could interpret as a hopeful sign. Then it collapsed and fell on its face. She turned the body over on its back and questioned it more vehemently, repeating apparently more compelling incantations in its ears. She bounded about, sword in hand, brandishing it now towards the fire and now towards the trench, and again aroused the corpse upright and put the same question, compelling it to answer now not merely with a nod but in distinct words. While the old woman was thus occupied Charicleia begged Calasiris to approach her and make inquiries concerning Theagenes, but he refused. It was only by constraint, he said, and by accident that he witnessed so diabolic a scene. It was not the business of a prophet to engage in, or even be present at, such practices. Only through lawful offerings and pure prayers did prophets exercise their mantic art, not by literally groveling over the earth and over cadavers, not by such wickedness as the Egyptian woman had perpetrated and a chance circumstance had made them witness.

While Calasiris was still speaking there resounded from the corpse a deep and raucous voice as from a cleft of the earth or the windings of a cavern. "I spared you at first, mother," it said, "though you violated human nature and the decrees of the fates; I restrained myself when by your sorceries you moved what is immovable, for even the departed preserve reverence for parents so far as they may. But you yourself have abolished that reverence. Not content with the first stages of your execrable undertaking you pursue it to the very limits of the diabolic. You compel a dead body not only to rise and nod, but to speak. The rites due me you neglect; concerned only for your selfish desires you prevent me from mingling with the other souls. Hear then what I have been careful to keep from you. Your son will not return to you safe, nor will you escape death by the sword. Your life you have spent in these unholy practices; the violent death which is the legacy of such practices will not be long deferred. These unspeakable mysteries which should be covered by silence and darkness, furthermore, you boldly perpetrate in the presence of others; it is before witnesses that you betray the secrets of the dead. One of them is a priest, and this is the less serious, for he is wise enough to seal the ineffable with silence. Furthermore, he is dear to the gods; his sons, who have engaged to settle their conflict with the sword, his very appearance will stop from bloody combat hand to hand, if he hastens his journey. But more serious: a girl has witnessed all that was done to me and has overheard everything. She is deeply in love and has roamed the world over for her beloved's sake. After myriad labors and myriad dangers she will find him in a remote country and with him spend a brilliant and royal life."

After this utterance the corpse collapsed and lay still. The old woman understood that it was the strangers who were the witnesses, and so just as she was, sword in hand and in a frenzied mood, she rushed about among the dead bodies, where she suspected they had hid themselves. When she found them it was her purpose to destroy them, because their presence had militated against the success of her witchcraft. But her fury blinded her caution, and so in her search she failed to notice a fragment of spear sticking upright. Upon this spear she fell and was transfixed, and thus promptly fulfilled the prophecy of her son.

Calasiris and Chariclea had been exposed to a grave danger. To shake off the scene of horror, and spurred on by the prophecies they had heard, they hastily resumed their way to Memphis. Even as they approached the city the events foretold in the incantation scene were transpiring in it.

7

WHEN THYAMIS ARRIVED with his brigand band
from Bessa the inhabitants of Memphis barely had time to
bar their gates. One of Mitranes' soldiers who had escaped
from the battle at Bessa had foreseen the foray and had
warned the townspeople. Thyamis ordered his men to
ground arms before a portion of the wall. His purpose was
to refresh his men from the fatigue of the march and apparently to lay siege. At first the people in the city feared
the onset of a host, but when they saw from the walls that
the brigands were few, they forthwith collected the few
archers and cavalrymen that had been left behind to garrison the city, armed the citizens with whatever weapons
came to hand, and were eager to sally forth and fall upon
the enemy. But an elderly gentleman of high repute prevented them and explained that even if, as was the case,
the satrap Oroondates was absent on an expedition against
Ethiopia, still it was proper to communicate their design
to his wife Arsace. With her approval the soldiery to be
found in the city would more readily be mustered and
would fight with greater zeal. This advice met with ap-

proval, and all proceeded to the palace which served as the satrap's residence in the king's absence.

Arsace was a tall and handsome woman and a shrewd one. She was sister to the Great King, and her noble birth made her proud. But her life was not beyond reproach, for she indulged in lawless and dissolute pleasures. Among other offenses she shared the responsibility for Thyamis' exile from Memphis. When Calasiris had been divinely fore-warned of the coming rivalry between his sons, he had secretly withdrawn from Memphis. When he was nowhere to be found and was thought to have perished, Thyamis, as elder son, was called to the priesthood. While he was performing the public initiatory sacrifices, Arsace visited the temple of Isis and noticed the charming and blooming priest, who was beautifully vested for the ceremony. She turned unchaste eyes upon him and intimated her wanton desires by her nods. Thyamis took no notice whatever. He was naturally modest and had been educated to self-control. He had no suspicion of what her conduct meant and, being wholly intent on his sacred duties, thought it might have some different significance. But his brother Petosiris, who had long envied Thyamis' elevation to the priesthood, ob-served Arsace's behavior and made her lawless attempt the basis of an intrigue against his brother. He went to Oroon-dates secretly and not only informed him of Arsace's con-cupiscence but falsely added that Thyamis had complied. Oroondates was easily persuaded, for he had had suspicions of Arsace. He left her in peace, for he had no clear proof and was constrained to control his suspicions by fear and respect for the blood royal, but he openly and incessantly threatened Thyamis with death, until he forced him into exile and elevated Petosiris to the priesthood.

These events had transpired long before. At the time we speak of the crowd surged about Arsace's house and informed her of the incursion of the enemy (which she al-ready knew) and petitioned her to order the soldiery present to march out with them. She declared that she was not ready to issue such an order for she did not know the number of the enemy, nor their identity, nor their origin, nor was she aware of the nature of their aggression. It was necessary, she said, first to proceed to the walls, from there to survey the entire situation, and then with additional forces to undertake whatever measures were possible and profitable. The people approved of her remarks and at once proceeded to the wall. There, by the orders of Arsace, a pavilion with curtains woven of purple and gold had been erected. She herself, royally attired, took her place upon a lofty throne, surrounded by bodyguards in gilt armor. She displayed the herald's wand as symbol of peaceful parley and invited the chiefs and notables of the enemy to approach the wall. Thyamis and Theagenes came forward as deputies and took their stand under the wall; they were fully armed except that their heads were bare. The herald then spoke as follows: "In the name of Arsace, wife of the Prime Satrap and sister of the Great King: What do you wish? Who are you? Upon what claim do you venture on this incursion?" They answered that they were of Bessa. Thyamis declared who he was and explained that he had been unlawfully deprived of his priesthood by the intrigue of his brother Petosiris and Oroondates and that the Bessaeans had come to restore him. If he should recover the priesthood there would be peace and the Bessaeans would return home without working injury to anyone. But if not, the issue must be committed to the arbitrament of war and arms. If Arsace took any thought for the proprieties she would use this opportunity to avenge herself on Petosiris for his plot against her and for the wicked calumnies which he had falsely reported to Oroondates—calumnies which had implanted in her husband suspicion of a shameful and adulterous passion and which had imposed upon himself exile from his country.

At these words the populace of Memphis was troubled.

They recognized Thyamis, the cause of whose flight had
been inexplicable. His revelations now awoke suspicion
and they were disposed to believe that he spoke the truth.
But more disturbed than the rest was Arsace, whose mind
was distracted by a tempest of anxieties. She was furious
with Petosiris; she called what he had done to mind and
meditated vengeance upon him. She looked at Thyamis
and again at Theagenes, and was alternately attracted by
each and had a passion for both; the old flame was re-
newed, but the new was more intense. Even the bystanders
could perceive her perplexity. But after a little she recovered, as from an attack of epilepsy, and said: "This is
madness for all the Bessaeans, but most of all for you
graceful young men in your prime, and surely of good
family, as is plain to see. You expose yourselves to imminent peril on behalf of brigands, who are incapable of
withstanding the first shock of battle if it should come to
fighting. Do not imagine that the forces of the Great King
are so feeble that, though the satrap happens to be abroad,
the remnant left behind here could not take all of you
with a net. But since the pretext for your incursion is of
a private and not of an official or public nature, there is
no occasion, I think, for the people at large to suffer. Your
quarrel should be adjudicated privately, and you should
accept the decision of the gods and of justice itself. This
is my opinion, and I ordain that the people of Memphis
and Bessa keep the peace and refrain from unprovoked war
against one another, and that the contestants for the priesthood engage in a single combat, with the sacred office the
prize of victory."

At Arsace's words all the townfolk shouted approval.
They had been moved to suspect Petosiris' wicked treachery—and everyone was very willing to transfer his own
immediate perils into a struggle to be waged by others. But
the Bessaean rank and file seemed dissatisfied and were

averse to allowing their chief to undertake the danger on their behalf. Thyamis obtained their consent, however, by reminding them that Petosiris was weak and without military experience, and he assured them that all the advantages of combat would be on his side. It was doubtless this consideration that had caused Arsace to propose the duel. In it she saw a means of achieving her goal without involving herself: his far superior adversary would inflict upon Petosiris the punishment she desired. Orders appeared to be executed more quickly than they could be uttered. In high spirit Thyamis immediately sent his challenge and eagerly put on the remainder of his handsome armor. Theagenes gave him much encouragement and fitted upon his head his helmet of flashing gold surmounted by a fine plume, and fastened the rest of his armor to make it secure. Petosiris, on the other hand, had to be pushed out of the gates, at Arsace's order, despite his cries and excuses, and was armed perforce. When Thyamis saw him he said, "Good Theagenes, do you see how Petosiris is quaking with fear?" "I do," said Theagenes, "but how will you use your advantage? Your adversary is no ordinary enemy but your brother." "You are right," said Thyamis, "and have correctly divined my own thoughts. My intention is to conquer him, god willing, but not to kill him. Anger and resentment of past injuries must not so far govern me as to purchase revenge for bygones and honor for the future at the price of a brother's blood and the pollution of fratricide." "Nobly spoken," said Theagenes, "and with full understanding of the ties of nature. But have you any instructions to give me?" "The contest before me is mere child's play," said Thyamis, "but fortune frequently surprises mankind with paradoxes. If I prevail, you will enter the city with me and share my life on terms of equality. But if my expectations are disappointed you shall take command of the Bessaeans, who are very favorably dis-

posed to you, and lead a brigand existence until heaven
reveals a more suitable end." With these words they bade
each other farewell, amid tears and kisses. Theagenes sat
down where he was to observe the outcome and thus unwittingly afforded a delicious repast for the eyes of Arsace,
who could satisfy her desires as far as seeing goes.

Thyamis advanced upon Petosiris, who was unable to
face the charge but turned in flight at the first move and
made for the gates in order to dash back into the city. But
his hope was in vain; those in charge of the gates thrust
him back, as did those on the walls, in whatever sector he
sought entry. Petosiris then threw away his weapons and
ran around the city in a circle as fast as he could. Theagenes followed Thyamis as he pursued, being solicitous
for him and unwilling to miss anything that might happen. But Theagenes went unarmed, so that no one should
suspect that he would actually assist Thyamis. He put
down his shield and spear where he was sitting in the
sight of Arsace, and left these for her to look at instead
of himself when he followed the runners. Thyamis could
not overtake Petosiris, nor could Petosiris increase his
distance from Thyamis. Always he seemed on the point of
being overtaken, but he got away, for it was natural that,
being unarmed, he should have an advantage over Thyamis,
who was in armor. Once and a second time they circled
the wall, but before the third circle was completed,
Thyamis was brandishing his spear against his brother's
back and threatening to hurl it if Petosiris did not halt.
The populace, ranged upon the walls as in the seats of a
theater, followed the spectacle attentively.

It was then that some divinity or fortune which is the
arbiter of human destiny introduced a novel episode into
the tragedy being enacted, as if to prevent the opening of
a new drama to compete with the old. At that very day
and hour it prepared an entry for Calasiris, like a *deus ex*

machina, and made him an unhappy witness of the mortal
struggle of his sons. To avoid that odious spectacle he had
endured many tribulations, had employed every expedient,
had inflicted exile upon himself, and had roamed strange
lands, but now an implacable destiny compelled him to
witness the encounter of which the gods had long before
warned him. He saw the pursuit from a distance, and from
the repeated prophecies he had had he knew that his own
sons were involved. Doing violence to his age, he ran
faster than his years would admit in order to prevent the
final clash.

When he had drawn near and was running at their
side he shouted repeatedly, "What is this, Thyamis and
Petosiris?" Again and again he called to them, "What is
this, my sons?" But they did not recognize their father,
for he was swathed in beggar's rags and they were preoccupied with their fight, and so they ignored him as a
vagrant or madman. On the walls some were astonished at
his unflinchingly exposing himself to the combatants and
others laughed at his mad and fruitless efforts. But when
the old man realized that it was his ragged clothes which
prevented recognition he stripped them off, unbound his
hair and let it flow in priestly manner, and flung away
the bundle on his shoulder and the staff in his hands. He
stood facing them, and his venerable and priestly presence
was impressive. He bowed slightly and extended his hands
in a suppliant gesture. "My children," he said, in a sad and
tearful voice, "I am Calasiris, I am your father. Stay your
hands; stay this frightful madness. Do so out of regard
and reverence for him that begot you." Then did the
young men soften and all but swoon. Both fell at their
father's feet and embraced his knees. They gazed upon
him fixedly to make sure of his identity and were satisfied
that it was no phantom they saw but truly their father.
Many and conflicting feelings agitated them. They were

delighted to find their father unexpectedly safe; they were distressed and ashamed of the situation in which he found them; they were anxious about the uncertain future. The townfolk were astonished. They said nothing and did nothing but stood like statues, mute and unknowing, enthralled by the spectacle, when the inner curtain opened on a new character—Charicleia.

Charicleia had followed on the heels of Calasiris and had recognized Theagenes at a distance, for the lover's eye is quick to recognize the beloved; often a gesture or a posture, seen even from a distance or from the back, confirms a fancied resemblance. Frantically, as if sight of him had stung her, she ran to him, clasped him close, hung upon his neck, and caressed him with inarticulate sighs and tears. When he saw her face, begrimed and purposely discolored, and her torn and tattered garments, he took her for a shameless beggar. He pulled her off and thrust her away, and when she would not let go he struck her for troubling him and blocking his view of Calasiris and his sons. She said to him softly, "Pythias, have you forgotten the lamp?" The words struck Theagenes like a bolt. He remembered that the lamp was a token they had agreed upon and gazed into Charicleia's eyes, whose brilliance broke upon him like the sun's rays through a cloud. He threw his arms about her and embraced her. Upon the wall the audience was filled with wonder at the marvelous scene which was being enacted before them; among them sat Arsace, swollen with passion and already viewing Charicleia with no little jealousy.

The impious war of brothers was now ended. The contest, whose issue had been expected to be adjudged in blood, was transformed in its denouement from tragedy to comedy. A father had looked upon his armed sons in single combat with one another; the unhappy eyes of their begetter had all but witnessed his children's death. But the father himself had become the agent of peace. He had not been able to evade the irrevocable decree of fate, but happily had arrived to preside over destiny's issue. The sons recovered their father after ten years of wandering. Shortly after, they themselves crowned him with the priesthood which had nearly been the cause of bloody strife between them, and they adorned him with the symbols of his office and waited upon him.

But in the eyes of all, the flower of the drama was the love scene played by Theagenes and Charicleia. The beautiful and amiable pair who had recovered one another beyond all hope were the greatest attraction of all and pre-empted the attention of the whole city. The crowd poured out of the gates and filled the plain. All ages were represented. The cadets and those newly graduated to manhood ran up to Theagenes. About Thyamis were grouped men in their prime and men of mature years who had known him before. The maidens of the city who were old enough to think of marriage followed after Charicleia. The old men and all the priestly class attended upon Calasiris. A sort of religious procession was formed spontaneously.

Thyamis dismissed the men of Bessa. He thanked them for their loyalty and promised to send them a hundred oxen, a thousand sheep, and ten drachmas for each man at the next full moon. He put his neck under his father's arm to ease the weight and support the steps of the old man, whom unexpected joy had almost paralyzed. On the other side Petosiris did the same. So escorted and with torches lighting the way the old man went to the temple of Isis. He was attended by applause and acclamations and the music of pipes and sacred flutes, which stimulated the lively youth to bacchic dance steps. Arsace too participated in the proceedings. With her own guards and entourage she formed her own procession. Covered with jewels and gold she went inside the temple of Isis, apparently from the same motives which actuated the rest of the city but actually only to see Theagenes. The sight of him she enjoyed more than the rest, but her pleasure was not unmixed. Theagenes was leading Charicleia by the hand and made a way for her through the crowd, and the sight stung Arsace's jealousy to the quick.

When Calasiris reached the sanctuary he prostrated himself to the ground, embraced the feet of the statue, and for a long while remained in this posture, very near to death. Those present raised him up, and with great effort he stood, poured a libation to the goddess and offered a prayer. Then he removed the priestly crown from his own head and placed it upon the head of his son Thyamis. To the assemblage he said that he himself was now grown old and foresaw his end approaching; his elder son was the lawful successor to the symbols of priesthood and moreover possessed the requisite moral qualities and physical vigor for the discharge of the sacred office. By their acclamations the people demonstrated their approval of his conduct. He himself, with his sons and Theagenes, retired to the part of the temple reserved for the priests and remained there. The others dispersed to their own homes.

Arsace found it difficult to go. She turned back repeatedly, as if to pay fuller devotion to the goddess. But finally go she did, turning back to look at Theagenes as long as she could. When she arrived at the royal palace she went directly to her chamber, threw herself upon her bed dressed as she was, and lay there speechless. She had always been inclined to brazen voluptuousness, but now she was inflamed beyond any previous experience by the sight of the irresistible Theagenes. All night she lay there, incessantly twisting from one side to the other, incessantly heaving deep sighs. Now she would rise upright and now fall back on her bedding; now she would tear off part of her clothing and again suddenly fling herself upon the bed. She would summon her maid without cause, and then dismiss her without orders. In a word, her passion would have insensibly proceeded to madness but for the intervention of an old crone named Cybele, who was her chamberwoman and used to serving her amours. Cybele hurried into Arsace's room, for nothing escaped her notice: she was like a lighted lamp and like a lighted lamp she kindled Arsace's passion. "What is this, mistress?" she said. "Is some new or strange pain hurting you? Whose looks have disturbed my pet? Who is so presumptuous and insensible as not to succumb to beauty like yours, as not to account the love you offer as bliss, as to disdain your complaisant nod? Just tell me, my sweetest baby. No one is so adamant as not to be susceptible to my philters. Just tell me, and your desires will be fulfilled at once. You have had enough experience of my talents, I think." Such beguiling words and many others of the same tune Cybele kept murmuring at Arsace's feet, and with all manner of flattery she induced her to avow her passion.

After some moments of silence Arsace said, "Mother, I am smitten as never before. In previous cases of this kind you have time and again rendered me good service, but this time I do not know whether you can mend the situation. The battle before the walls did not reach the point of bloodshed; a sudden peace reconciled the adversaries. But for me it was the inception of a more serious war; I am wounded not in any organ or member but in my very soul. What inflicted the wound was the sight of that young foreigner who ran beside Thyamis in the single combat. You must know, little mother, whom I mean. His transcendent beauty so far outshone all others that it must have been apparent to any rustic with no appreciation of love and beauty, and surely to such a specialist as you. So then, my darling, you know my malady. If you want your baby to get well now is the time for you to bring to bear all your old crone's craft, all your charms and philters. I cannot live if I do not succeed with that man."

"I know the young fellow," said the hag. "He is broad in chest and shoulders, his head is high and forthright, his outstanding stature dwarfs all others, his eyes are blue and at once tender and fierce, his hair falls in long ringlets and his cheeks are wreathed with a fresh yellow down. Some foreign wench who seemed pretty enough but uncommonly impudent dashed up to him and embraced him and hung on his neck. Isn't he the man you mean, mistress?" "The very man, nanna mine," said she. "You do well to remind me of the scandalous behavior of that beggar hussy. She is very proud of that homespun beauty of hers; little enough it is, and common, and made up, but she is luckier than I, for it has gotten her so fine a lover." At this the old woman's lips cracked into a kind of smile, and she said, "Take heart, mistress. Until today the foreigner has thought her handsome, but when I introduce him to you and your beauty he will, as the saying goes, exchange bronze for gold. He will thrust away that bold and conceited little strumpet, whose pretensions will not help her." "If only you would do this, darling little Cybele, you would cure me at once of two distempers, love and jealousy. You would satisfy me with the one, and free me of the other." "So shall it be," said Cybele, "so far as in me lies. But please get some rest and for the present keep calm; do not be disheartened or anticipate trouble. Keep up your hopes."

When she said this she took up her lamp, barred the chamber door, and departed. At dawn she took one of the royal eunuchs, ordered a maid to follow with cakes and other offerings, and hurried to the temple of Isis. Arrived at the vestibule, she said she was bringing an offering on behalf of her mistress Arsace who had been disturbed by bad dreams and wished to propitiate the goddess. One

of the vergers prevented her and sent her away, saying
that all the temple was plunged in sorrow. When the
prophet Calasiris returned home after his long absence, the
verger said, he spent the evening feasting with his friends,
exhibiting a relaxed and cheerful temper. After the repast
he offered libations and addressed a long prayer to the
goddess. He told his sons that they would not see their
father much longer, and enjoined them to take the best
possible care of the young Greeks who had come with him
and to help them realize their desires by every means possible. Then he went to bed. Whether excess of joy had
relaxed and dilated his respiratory passages beyond the
capacities of his aged body, or whether the gods had
granted him his request, at the cock-crow he was found
dead. "And now," the verger continued, "we have sent to
the city to summon all the prophetic and priestly caste so
that we may perform appropriate funeral rites for him
according to our traditional usage. You must go away,
for during all the next seven days it is unlawful for any
but priests even to enter the temple, much less offer sacrifice
in it." "Where will the foreigners you speak of lodge?"
asked Cybele. "Our new prophet Thyamis," said the verger, "has ordered a lodging prepared for them just outside
the temple precinct. There they come now; in obedience
to the law they are removing from sacred ground."

Cybele used this chance as a trap and made ready for
the catch. "God-favored verger," said she, "here is an opportunity to benefit the strangers and to oblige us, especially Arsace, sister of the Great King. You know how
fond she is of Greeks and how hospitable in receiving
foreigners. Tell the young people that by Thyamis' orders
a lodging has been prepared for them in our house." The
verger had no suspicion of Cybele's secret designs and consented. He thought he would be benefiting the strangers
by introducing them into the vice-regal palace and at the

same time, without danger or injury, would be obliging
those who made the request. When he saw Theagenes and
Charicleia approach, mournful and weeping, he said, "Your
conduct in bewailing and grieving for a prophet is forbidden by law and not in keeping with our ancestral tra-
ditions, especially when his departure was foretold. Our
divine and sacred doctrine prescribes that we escort him
with joy and felicitations for having been vouchsafed a
better existence and a seat with the gods. But you must
be forgiven, for it is your father, as you say, your protector, and your sole hope that you have lost. But you
must not wholly despair. Thyamis, it appears, has succeeded not only to his father's priesthood but also to his
affection for you. His first care was to give orders to provide for you. He has prepared a splendid lodging for you,
one that the wealthiest of our own people would envy,
let alone foreigners whose fortune seems humble. Follow
this woman (and he pointed to Cybele), consider her as
your mother, and obey her directions."

Theagenes and Charicleia did as the verger said. Unexpected grief had dulled their faculties, and they were
ready to accept any shelter and refuge. They would surely
have shrunk back if they had foreseen the tragedy that
would be enacted in that proud house and the evils which
awaited them there. Fortune, whose sport they were, had
given them respite for a few hours and allowed them an
ephemeral happiness; but promptly it inflicted new distress
upon them and delivered them, voluntary captives as it
were, into the hands of their enemy. Under the name of
charity and hospitality, she made prisoners of the young
strangers who had no premonition of what awaited them.
Ignorance makes the traveler in a foreign country blind.

As soon as they arrived at the satrap's residence and entered its imposing vestibule, taller and more spacious than

any private house and filled with ostentatious guards and
an array of other attendants, they were surprised and
troubled, seeing that their abode was so far beyond their
present fortune. Nevertheless they followed Cybele, who
exhorted and encouraged them and continually called
them her children and her darlings and assured them that
they would be delighted at the reception which awaited
them. Finally, when Cybele had brought them to her own
private and remote room, she asked everyone present to
leave, and when she was alone she sat down and said to
her charges: "My children, I know the cause of your
present grief. The death of the prophet Calasiris, who took
the place of father to you, has naturally distressed you. But
please tell me who you are and whence you come. That
you are Greeks I am aware, and it is obvious that you are
of good family. Your noble expression and your graceful
and engaging air bespeak high birth. But I should like to
know to what part of Greece and what city you belong.
Who are you and how did your travels bring you here?
It is for your own interest to tell me, so that I can inform
my mistress Arsace, sister of the Great King and wife of
Oroondates, his principal satrap. She is a philhellene, a lady
of delicate sensibilities, and hospitable to foreigners. If she
knows who you are she will treat you with higher regard,
in keeping with your merits. You are speaking to a woman
who is not altogether alien to you. I myself am Greek by
race. My city was Sestos. I was brought here as a captive
and am doing better than I did at home. I am all in all to
my mistress. She all but breathes through me; she sees
through me, I am her mind, her ears, her all. I introduce
fine gentlemen to her and am a faithful keeper of all her
secrets." Theagenes privately compared Cybele's words with
Arsace's conduct the day before. When he remembered her
fixed and immodest stare and her wanton signs and gestures

he boded no good of the future. As he was about to speak to the old woman, Charicleia bent over and whispered in his ear, "Remember your sister in what you say."

Catching the hint Theagenes said, "Mother, we are Greeks, as you are aware. We are brother and sister. Our parents were captured by brigands. We went in search of them but ourselves encountered worse misfortune than theirs. We fell into the hands of savage men who robbed us of our considerable wealth and barely left us alive. By the kind intervention of heaven we chanced upon Calasiris and with him came to this place, hoping to spend the rest of our lives with him. Now, as you see, we are left solitary and abandoned, having lost, besides all else, the man we regarded as our father and who behaved as such. That is our story. To you we are very grateful for your reception and your hospitality, but we should be even more grateful if you enable us to live quietly by ourselves. Forbear the kindness of making us acquainted with Arsace, which you spoke of. Do not introduce to her brilliant and happy fortune lowly alien vagabonds. Acquaintance and sociable relationships should be formed, as you know, among people of like circumstances."

At this speech Cybele could not contain herself. Her beaming face showed how delighted she was at hearing that they were brother and sister; now she was confident that Charicleia would be no obstacle to Arsace's amour. "Handsome youth," said she, "you will not speak so of Arsace when you come to know the lady. She accommodates herself to every fortune, and is the more helpful to those who fare less well than they deserve. Though she is Persian by race, she is a Hellenist by conviction and takes eager pleasure in people from Greece. She is exceedingly fond of Greek ways and Greek society. Do not be uneasy. You will receive all the attention and consideration appropriate for a man, and your sister will be Arsace's play-

fellow and companion. But what names should I an-
nounce?" When she was informed that they were Theagenes and Charicleia she said, "Wait for me here," and
hurried off to Arsace. She instructed her portress, who was
a beldam like herself, to admit no one into the room and
not to let the young people leave it. "Not even if your
son Achaemenes returns?" asked the portress "After you
went to the temple he stepped out to have his eyes swabbed;
you know they still pain him a little." "Not even my son,"
answered Cybele, "lock the door, keep the key, and say
that I have taken it." So the portress did.

No sooner was Cybele gone than Theagenes and Charicleia took advantage of their solitude to lament. Realization of their misery suggested almost identical thoughts
and exclamations to both. "Oh, Theagenes!" and "Oh,
Charicleia!" they repeated, sighing. "What new fortune
has overtaken us?" cried she. And at each cry they embraced each other and wept and kissed. Finally the thought
of Calasiris deflected their grief into mourning for him.
Charicleia, who had known him longer and had more fully
experienced his care and affection, was especially moved.
"Ah, Calasiris," she sobbed, "I may no longer call you by
the sweet name of father, for an envious fate has always
thwarted my use of that title. The father who begat me
I have never known. Charicles who adopted me I have
betrayed. The one that received and educated and preserved me I have lost, and the tenets of the prophets prevent me from paying the customary rites of mourning to
his dead body. But see, my protector and savior, and, yes,
my father, despite envious fate, I pour to you my libation
of tears as well as I can and in the place I can, and I make
you an offering of my own hair." With that she tried to
pluck handfuls of her tresses. Theagenes restrained her,
holding her hands and begging her to forbear. She continued her tragic strain and said, "Why should I go on

living? What hope can I look to? The protector of the
stranger, the staff of the wanderer, the guide to my native
land, the discoverer of my parentage, the solace of my
misfortunes, the support of my helplessness, the solution
of my problems—Calasiris, my stay and anchor in all
things, has perished and left us a wretched pair, helpless
and feckless in an alien land. Ignorance cuts us off from
every road by land or sea. Gone is that reverence and charity, that sagacious and venerable heart, nor will it discover
the final consummation of its beneficence on our behalf."
In such and similar piteous terms Charicleia expressed her
grief. Theagenes was equally sorrowful but repressed his
lamentations out of consideration for Charicleia.

Achaemenes had arrived in the meanwhile. When he
found the doors locked he asked the portress what this
meant, and was told it was his mother's doing. As he stood
at the door wondering at the cause he heard Charicleia
lamenting. He stooped over and through the crack where
the catch of the lock was fastened he saw what was going
on and again asked the portress who the people inside were.
She said that she knew no details but that they were a
foreign girl and boy who, as she conjectured, had just been
brought into the house by his own mother. Again he
stooped over and tried to distinguish the persons he saw.
Charicleia he did not know at all, but he was nevertheless
struck with admiration of her beauty and imagined how
lovely she must be if she were not crying, and his admiration gradually led him to love. Of Theagenes he
thought he had a faint and confused recollection. While
Achaemenes was preoccupied with his peeping, Cybele returned. She had reported to Arsace what she had done
about the young people and felicitated her on her good
luck. Of itself luck had effected more than anyone could
have hoped to procure with a thousand schemes and de-
vices: her beloved was in her own house where she could

see him and be seen by him with perfect security. With much else of this sort Cybele fanned Arsace's eagerness to see Theagenes at once and had much ado to hold her back. She did not wish the young man to see her, Cybele said, with her face pale and eyes swollen from sleeplessness; one day's rest would restore her habitual beauty. With these words she cheered Arsace and put her in a hopeful mood; then she instructed her on how to comport herself in her dealings with her guests.

Finding Achaemenes she said, "What are you so curious about, my boy?" "About the people inside," said he; "who are they and where do they come from?" "You must, my son," said Cybele to him, "hold your peace; keep what you know to yourself and tell nobody, and do not associate with the strangers. These are mistress' orders." He obeyed his mother readily and went off, suspecting that Theagenes was there to supply the customary amatory requirements of Arsace. But as he withdrew he said to himself, "Isn't that the man I lately received from the commandant Mitranes to take to Oroondates, who was going to send him to the Great King, the man who was seized by the Bessaeans and Thyamis at great danger to myself, when I was the only one of his guards who was able to escape? Can my eyes be deceiving me? But they are better and my vision is practically normal. Besides, I heard that Thyamis was here yesterday and recovered the priesthood after single combat with his brother. That is the very man. But for the present I must say nothing of my discovery and wait to find out my mistress' intentions with regard to the strangers." So he soliloquized.

When Cybele bustled in to the young people she detected traces of their lamentations. At the sound of the doors opening they had checked themselves and had hurriedly endeavored to assume their customary posture and expression, but they could not deceive the old woman, for their eyes were still suffused with tears. "My sweets," she cried out to them, "why this till-timed grief when you might be happy and congratulate yourselves on your good fortune? Arsace's feelings towards you are as generous as you could wish. She has consented to see you tomorrow and in the meanwhile has ordered that every kindness and attention be shown you. Away with this silly and really childish grief. Now is the time for you to make yourselves agreeable, to conform yourselves to the wishes of Arsace and hearken to her." "It was the memory of Calasiris' death, mother," said Theagenes, "that moved us to grief; the thought that we had been deprived of his fatherly benevolence made us weep." "All foolishness," said she. "Calasiris was only your pretended father, and was an old man. He succumbed to our common nature and his length of years. But now a single person provides everything—rank, wealth, luxury, and the enjoyment of the flower of your youth; in a word, look upon Arsace as your fortune and do obeisance to her. Only be ruled by me as to how you must approach her and look upon her when she permits you to do so, on how you must conduct yourself and serve her when she is giving you any orders. She has, as you know, a lofty temper, haughty and regal, and her youth and beauty exalt her pride; she will not tolerate disregard of her commands."

Theagenes made no reply and thought to himself that Cybele's remarks hinted at things odious and threatening. Somewhat later eunuchs came in bringing upon golden trays what purported to be leavings from the satrap's table, but were in actuality the most sumptuous delicacies. The eunuchs said, "With these our mistress receives her guests and sends them her first marks of esteem," and then placed the trays before the young pair and withdrew immediately. Because Cybele urged them on and because they did not wish to reject their welcome with insult they tasted

a little of what was placed before them. The same procedure was repeated in the evening and during the days
following. On the morrow, at the first hour of the day,
the same eunuchs presented themselves to Theagenes and
said, "Happy man, you are summoned to our mistress; we
are ordered to bring you into her presence. Come and enjoy a bliss she grants to few persons and on rare occasions."
Theagenes remained motionless for a little and then rose
as if dragged against his will and said to them, "Is the
order to come for me alone or for my sister here also?"
They answered that he was to come alone; his sister would
have an audience by herself. At the moment certain Persian
dignitaries were in attendance upon Arsace, and besides it
was customary for men to be received on one occasion and
women by themselves on another. Theagenes stooped over
to Charicleia and whispered, "There is something queer
and suspicious here." Charicleia whispered back that he
ought not to cross Arsace but at first ought to pretend
to accede to her and indicate willingness to do her will.

Theagenes followed his guides, who instructed him in
the etiquette of addressing the lady, advising him that it
was customary for visitors to prostrate themselves. Theagenes made no reply. Upon entering he found Arsace
seated upon a lofty throne, glittering in a robe of purple
embroidered with gold, proudly displaying precious jewels
and a tiara which symbolized her rank, voluptuously
groomed and rouged, surrounded by armed guards, with
Persian grandees seated on either side of her. Theagenes was
not greatly impressed. As if he had forgotten his agreement with Charicleia to feign a respectful docility, his
pride reasserted itself at the sight of the Persian pomp and
without bending the knee or bowing down, but with head
erect he said, "Hail, princess Arsace." Those present angrily
murmured that Theagenes' refusal to prostrate himself was
a bold and insolent act of sedition. But Arsace smiled and

said, "Forgive an inexperienced foreigner, and particularly
a Greek who is infected with contempt for us Persians." At
the same time she removed the tiara from her head, the
Persian symbol for returning a salutation, though many of
those present tried to prevent her, and then she addressed
him, using an interpreter, for though she understood Greek
she could not speak it. "Take heart, stranger," said she,
"say what you desire; you shall surely have it." Then she
dismissed him, nodding to the eunuchs to accompany him,
and he withdrew with an escort of guards. When Achaemenes saw him again he recognized him more surely. He
wondered why Theagenes was shown such excessive honor,
and though he suspected the reason he held his peace, in
keeping with his orders.

Arsace now feasted the Persian grandees, ostensibly to
pay them the customary respect, but really to celebrate her
meeting with Theagenes. This time she sent the young people not only the customary viands but also tapestries and
embroidered coverlets of fine Sidonian and Lydian workmanship. She also sent them slaves for their personal service, a maid for Charicleia and a valet for Theagenes. They
were of Ionian stock and both adolescents. Being utterly
unable to control her passion she was very urgent with
Cybele to hasten the accomplishment of her desire: there
must be no relaxation of effort and every pressure was to
be applied. Cybele did not, to be sure, openly reveal Arsace's desires, but she made Theagenes understand their purport by circumlocutions and hints. She spoke in glowing
terms of her mistress' warm feelings for him, and under
color of eulogizing her gave him vivid descriptions of her
beauties, not only those that met the eye but also those
her garments concealed. She spoke of Arsace's lovable character, her affability, her complaisance to tender and vigorous young men. In a word she tried every means to discover
erotic inclinations in Theagenes. Theagenes subscribed to

her praise of Arsace's kindness, her affection for Greeks, and such matters, and expressed his gratitude: but her improper suggestions he willfully misunderstood and ignored. The crone fair choked with the vexation that rankled at her heart; she surmised that Theagenes understood her enticements well enough, but was stubbornly repulsing her solicitation. Arsace's pestering was growing unbearable; she declared she could no longer hold out and demanded the fulfilment of her promise, and Cybele put her off with one excuse after another. Now she said the young man was willing but paralyzed by fear; again she pretended that he had fallen ill with a sudden indisposition.

Five and then six days passed. Arsace had twice invited Charicleia to an audience and, to ingratiate herself with Theagenes, had shown her friendly consideration. But now Cybele was compelled to speak to Theagenes in unvarnished terms and to declare her mistress' love without subterfuge. She promised him untold benefits if he would comply and added, "Why this timidity? Why this rejection of Aphrodite? A young man so handsome and vigorous to thrust away a suitable lady who is languishing for him! This thing is an easy windfall and involves no risk. Her husband is away and I, her nurse and the confidante of all her secrets, shall make all arrangements for the meeting. And there is nothing at all to burden you—no wife, no fiancée. Indeed, sensible people make no obstacle of such considerations, for they know that they do no injury to their family and at the same time they themselves are benefited by additions to their fortunes and the enjoyment of pleasure." She ended by subjoining threats to her pleas. "Great ladies who love young men," said she, "are vindictive and inexorable when they are rebuffed and quite rightly avenge the insult of repulse. Remember that the lady in question is a Persian and of the blood royal—those are the terms of your own salutation to her. Her great wealth and power enable her to recompense good will and chastise opposition with impunity. You are an alien, alone and without protection. Spare yourself and spare her too; she deserves your mercy, for it is because of yearning for you that she so unjustly suffers. Beware a lover's wrath; shun the nemesis which overtakes disdain. Many I know have repented of their stubbornness. In matters of love my experience is greater than yours. The gray head you see has observed many such struggles, but a temper as intractable and recalcitrant as yours I have never known." Then she addressed herself to Charicleia, who was present perforce, and had the effrontery to say to her, "Help me, daughter, to persuade this man—I don't know a suitable title for him —this brother of yours. You too will benefit from this affair. You will be no less loved and you will receive higher honor. You will become very rich and make a brilliant marriage. This is an enviable prospect even for people who enjoy prosperity, let alone for needy aliens."

With an ironic smile and a glitter in her eye Charicleia said, "It is devoutly to be hoped that the most excellent Arsace may never fall into such a state, and secondly, if she does, that she may find the fortitude to bear it. But since she is the victim of human frailty and has been overcome by her appetite, I too would counsel Theagenes not to refuse his compliance, if he may comply with safety. But let him not unwittingly bring both himself and the lady to harm if the matter come to light and the satrap come to learn of the unchaste deed." At these words Cybele leapt up and embraced Charicleia and bestowed kisses upon her. "Bravo, child," said she, "you have shown compassion for an unfortunate of your own sex and prudent forethought for the safety of your brother. But rest assured. Not even the sun, as they say, will get an inkling of it." "Enough for the present," said Theagenes, "give us time for reflection."

Cybele departed at once and then Charicleia said, "Theagenes, even the prosperity which fate vouchsafes us includes
misfortunes greater than the apparent felicity. But it is the
part of sensible people to turn even the inherent misfortunes to greatest profit. I do not know whether you are
minded to carry this matter through; nor would I abso-
lutely oppose if there were no other means to survival. But
if you consider the proposal absurd, as a good man would,
you must still pretend to comply. Nourish the barbarian's
expectations with promises; thwart sudden reprisal by deferring gratification; sweeten her with hope and mollify
her ardor with promises. Perhaps, by the will of the gods,
an interval of delay will beget some solution. But, dear
Theagenes, do not let calculation inveigle you to ugly behavior." Theagenes smiled and said, "Not even in so horrible situation have you got rid of the disease of jealousy
which is endemic to your sex. As for me, you must know
that I am incapable even of pretending, to speak shamefully becomes me as little as to do shamefully. In any case
there is one benefit in discouraging Arsace: she will stop
molesting us. If there is a price to pay, my fortune and my
reason have well prepared me to endure whatever may be-
fall." "Be careful you do not bring some great misfortune
upon us," said Charicleia, and then fell silent.

While the two were thus deliberating, Cybele put fresh
wings on Arsace's spirit. She said that prospects were now
favorable and that Theagenes had shown himself receptive.
She then returned to her own room and left matters alone
that evening. During the night she encouraged Charicleia
(who shared her bed from the beginning) to second her
efforts, and in the morning she again asked Theagenes what
he had decided. He roundly refused and declared that nothing was to be expected from him. Sadly she returned to
Arsace and reported Theagenes' stubbornness. Arsace ordered the crone to be thrown out on her head and then ran

into her room and lay on the bed in a tantrum. Cybele had just left the women's apartments, depressed and tearful, when her son Achaemenes saw her. "Nothing out of the way has happened, mother, nothing bad?" he asked. "Has some bad news distressed our mistress? Are the dispatches from the army unfavorable? Is our master Oroondates being hard-pressed by the Ethiopians in the war?" As he was running on with similar queries his mother said, "You are talking nonsense," and tried to hurry off. But he followed her obstinately and took hold of her hands and caressed her and begged her to tell her own son what was distressing her so.

She took him by the hand to a remote corner of the garden and said, "To no one else would I say a word of my own and my mistress' trouble. But she is in a very critical state and I am in actual danger for my life, for I know that Arsace's mad fury will fall on me. I must therefore speak. Perhaps you can devise some help for her who travailed with you and brought you to the light of day and nursed you with these breasts. Our mistress is in love with the young man who is in our house. It is no tolerable or ordinary passion but wholly incurable; my efforts and hers to remedy it have proved an empty disappointment. That is the meaning of the many kindnesses and the various courtesies which have been showered upon the foreigners. But that silly, insolent and stubborn fellow has rejected our proposals. She will not survive it, I know, and she will put me to death for mocking her and deceiving her with promises. That is the situation, my son. If you have any way of helping me, do what you can; if not, mourn for your mother as dead." "And what will my reward be, mother?" said Achaemenes. "There is no time for me to be coquettish with you and use periphrases and circumlocutions to promise my help when you are in such agony and peril." "Ask anything you like," said Cybele.

"Arsace has already made you chief cup-bearer out of regard for me. If you have any higher distinction in mind,
just speak. You will receive wealth beyond reckoning if you
prove the savior of that unfortunate woman." "I surmised
as much long ago, mother," said Achaemenes, "but I kept
my knowledge to myself and waited to see what would happen. It is neither high office nor wealth that I claim; if
Arsace will give me the girl who is called Theagenes' sister
in marriage, all of her desires shall be satisfied. I am in love
with the girl, mother, desperately. From her own experience your mistress knows the quality and intensity of such
a love, and it is but right that she help a fellow sufferer,
especially one who promises to put her own affair on a
sound footing." "Have no misgivings," said Cybele, "my
mistress will indubitably recompense her benefactor and
savior. In any case, we should probably be able to persuade
the girl ourselves. But tell me how you propose to help?"
"I'll not say a word," said he, "before your mistress binds
herself to fulfill her promise upon oath. And don't you
make overtures to the girl, for I find that she has a proud
and haughty spirit. You may spoil the affair for me." "It
shall be as you say," said Cybele, and ran to Arsace's chamber. There she fell at her knees and said, "Cheer up, everything is now in good order. Only have my son Achaemenes
called." "Let him be called," said Arsace, "but do not deceive me again."

Achaemenes came in and after the old woman had explained the situation Arsace swore that he should have
Theagenes' sister to wife. Then Achaemenes said, "Mistress,
Theagenes is your slave and must give over putting on
airs against his own mistress." "How can you say that?"
she asked, and he recounted the whole story: Theagenes
had been captured and had become a regular prisoner of war;
Mitranes had sent him to Oroondates to be sent on to the
Great King; Achaemenes himself had received him in charge

but had lost him in a bold ambuscade of the Bessaeans and Thyamis from which he himself had barely escaped. Finally, he exhibited to Arsace Mitranes' letter to Oroondates, which he had taken care to bring, and suggested that if she required further evidence she might have the testimony of Thyamis. At this Arsace began to breathe again. Without a moment's delay she left her room and repaired to the throne room where she was accustomed to grant audiences and ordered Theagenes to be brought in. When he came in she pointed to Achaemenes, who was standing nearby, and asked whether he knew him. When Theagenes said he did she next asked, "You were his prisoner and he was bringing you here, was he not?" When Theagenes affirmed this also she said, "Know then that you are my slave. You will conduct yourself as is appropriate for a slave and obey my nod regardless of your own will. Your sister I shall give in marriage to Achaemenes here who occupies a high position in my household; I do this for his mother's sake and in recognition of his own good will to me. I shall postpone the marriage only until a day is fixed and preparations made for a lavish feast." Theagenes was shattered by these words. He resolved, however, not to make a frontal attack but rather to feint, as in dealing with a wild beast. "Mistress," he said, "I thank heaven that we have at least this good fortune, now that we are fallen from our originally high estate, of being slaves to none other than you, who have shown us such gentleness and charity when you thought we were mere aliens with no tie to you. As for my sister, she was not taken captive and hence is not a slave. Of her own choice, however, she wishes to serve you and to accept whatever place you assign her. Do whatever you judge is right." "Let him be enrolled among the servants of the royal table," said Arsace. "Achaemenes shall instruct him in the duties of cup-bearer so that he may have adequate training for ministering to the King."

Both then withdrew. Theagenes was depressed and preoccupied with thinking of what was to be done, but Achaemenes laughed sarcastically and gibed at Theagenes: "You
who were just now so proud and disdainful, who would not
bend your neck as if you were the only man free, who refused to bow your head in obeisance, you will bend it
quickly enough now or my knuckles will teach it manners."
Arsace dismissed the others, except only Cybele. "Now
Cybele," said she, "every excuse has vanished Go to that
proud man and tell him that if he obeys and conforms
to my wishes he shall obtain his freedom and lead a life of
ease and abundance. But if he persists in his contrariness
he shall feel the fury of a disdained lover and an angry
mistress. He shall do the menial work of the newest and
vilest slave and be subjected to every form of torment."
Cybele went to report what Arsace had said, and of her
own accord added whatever arguments she thought would
help sway him. Theagenes asked for a brief delay and when
he was alone with Charicleia said, "We are done for, Charicleia. Every cable, as the saying goes, is broken; every anchor of hope is wholly lost. We no longer even have the
title of freemen to console us in our misfortune, but again
we are slaves. (Here he explained why that was.) We are
exposed to barbarian insults and must either submit to the
caprices of our masters or be numbered with the damned.
But even this might be endured. Most grievous of all is
that Arsace has promised to give you in marriage to Achaemenes, Cybele's son. But this shall never be, or if it shall,
I will never see it as long as I live and have a sword and an
arm to wield it. What must we do? What expedient can
we contrive to evade these abominable unions—mine with
Arsace, yours with Achaemenes?" "This is one," said
Charicleia to him. "If you will consent to the one union
you will prevent the other." "Watch your words," said he.
"The fate that persecutes us cannot have such power as to

pollute me, who has never touched Charicleia, with illicit commerce with another woman. But I think that I have found an effective remedy; necessity is the mother of invention." Then he went to Cybele and said, "Tell your mistress that I wish to meet her privately and alone."

The old woman thought she had succeeded and that Theagenes had succumbed. She so informed Arsace, was told to bring the young man to her after supper, and did so. She bade the attendants of the princess to keep silence and not to disturb those in the chamber, and then she brought Theagenes in. It being night, all the rest of the apartment was in darkness and permitted secrecy; only the chamber was lighted by a lamp. As soon as Arsace entered Cybele made to withdraw, but Theagenes stopped her, saying, "Let Cybele remain for the present, mistress; I know that she keeps your secrets faithfully." Then he took hold of Arsace's hands and went on, "Mistress, it was not out of willful resistance to you that I deferred submission to your orders, but only because I wished to procure complete security. Now that fortune has happily shown that I am your slave, I am much readier to obey your pleasure. Grant me but one of the many great favors you have promised. Break off the marriage of Charicleia with Achaemenes. To say nothing of other considerations, it is not right for one who vaunts such high birth to be mated with a home-born slave. Otherwise I swear by the Sun, the fairest of the gods, and by the other deities, I shall never yield to your will. And if any violence is brought to bear upon Charicleia you will first see me put an end to myself." "Be assured," said Arsace, "that I do not wish to refuse you any favor, for I am ready to give myself to you. But I am bound by a previous oath to give Achaemenes your sister." "Excellent mistress," said he, "do give him my sister, if I have one; but my betrothed, my bride, my all but wife you will not wish to give him I am sure—nor, if

you wish to, shall you do so." "What is this you say?" said
she. "The truth," he answered. "Charicleia is not my sister
but my bride, as I have said. You are therefore absolved of
your oath. If you wish further proof, celebrate my marriage with her whenever you like." Arsace was stung with
jealousy when she heard that Charicleia was not a sister but
a bride; nevertheless she said, "So shall it be; we shall console Achaemenes with another match." "So shall it be on
my part also; now this is settled, I yield." So saying, Theagenes stepped forward to kiss her hands. But she stooped
forward and presented her lips and kissed his. And so Theagenes departed, having been kissed without himself kissing.

He then found opportunity to tell Charicleia all, and it
was not without jealousy that she heard certain details.
He also explained the purpose of his disingenuous promise and the advantages that this single stroke would bring:
"Marriage with Achaemenes is broken off, and an excuse
is afforded for deferring Arsace's amorous insistence. But
the principal advantage is that Achaemenes will be furious
at being disappointed of the marriage he expected and indignant because I have supplanted him in Arsace's favor;
he will therefore probably throw everything into confusion. Not a detail will escape him, for I took care to have
his mother present at our interview, and she will tell him
all. I wished to have her inform Achaemenes of these matters and also to witness that my interview with Arsace
went no further than words. Consciousness of innocence
is doubtless sufficient basis for hope in the good will of the
gods; but it is also well to convince mortals also that our
day-to-day lives are open to view." Theagenes then added
further considerations. It was to be fully expected that
Achaemenes would now lay some plot against Arsace: "In
general the ruled is opposed to the ruler, and this man
whose lot is slavery sees that he has been wronged and that
oaths sworn to him have been violated, and he knows that

others have been preferred before him. He is fully aware
of Arsace's abominable and lawless behavior and has no
need to invent calumnies, as many aggrieved persons have
frequently ventured to do. The truth itself supplies a ready
means of vengeance to his hand."

On the next day Achaemenes brought Theagenes to
serve at table, in accordance with Arsace's orders. She had
sent him a rich Persian robe which he now wore, and he
was also adorned, not altogether against his will, with
golden bangles and a necklace set with precious stones.
Achaemenes offered to teach him and show him how the
wine was to be poured, but Theagenes went up to a tripod
on which cups were arranged, took up one of the most valuable, and said, "I need no teachers; my native wit will
suffice for the service of my mistress without making such a
bustle over a simple matter. You, my fine friend, have
been compelled to study such matters; as for me, my in-
stincts and the circumstances will suggest what I ought to
do." So saying, he poured a delicious cup for Arsace and
carried it to her on his finger tips, walking with measured
pace. The potion roused her excitement to higher transports. As she sipped she kept her gaze fixed on Theagenes
and drew larger draughts of love than of wine. She purposely failed to drain the cup but left a few drops to toast
Theagenes. Achaemenes rankled with a wound of a different sort: he was filled with fury and jealousy. Even
Arsace noticed that he was glowering and whispering to
the other attendants. When the drinking was finished Theagenes said, "Mistress, this is my first request: bid that I
wear this robe only when I serve you." Arsace gave her
consent, and Theagenes changed to his ordinary dress and
departed.

Achaemenes went out with him, reproaching Theagenes
for his forwardness. The mistress would overlook his youthful bumptiousness at first because he was a foreigner and

inexperienced, but if he persisted in his bravado he would
rue it. It was as a friend, said Achaemenes, that he was
giving this advice, and particularly because there would
soon be a family relationship between them, for Arsace
had promised that he would be husband to Theagenes'
sister. Achaemenes went on in this strain and Theagenes
walked along with his head lowered, as if he was not listening. Presently they met Cybele, who was on her way to
put Arsace to bed for the midday siesta. She noticed that
her son was downcast and asked the reason. "It is this foreign boy," he said. "He has been ranked ahead of me. He
arrived only a few hours ago and now he has been made
cup-bearer. Us veteran masters of the board and chief cup-
bearers he has snubbed; he himself took the position nearest
the royal person and handed her the cup. He has thrust us
out of our dignity and left us only the empty title. The
fact that he is so signally honored and is admitted to intimacy because of our ill-advised silence and co-operation
might be passed over, though it is really intolerable. But it
might have been done without insulting us, her devoted
ministers who have rendered her good service. But of this
we can talk another time. For the present, mother, it is
my promised bride, sweetest Charicleia, that I wish to see.
Sight of her may soothe the gnawing at my heart."

"What bride, my child?" said Cybele. "You seem indignant at trifling injuries, and know nothing at all of great
ones. You will not marry Charicleia." "What is that?"
shouted Achaemenes. "Am I not worthy to marry another
slave? Why, mother?" "It is our fault," said Cybele, "the
fault of our excessive compliance and loyalty to Arsace.
We have valued her caprice above our own safety, we have
reckoned her appetite higher than our own survival, we
have done everything to satisfy her whims, and as soon as
this gallant and dainty lover enters her chamber he has
only to show himself to persuade her to violate her solemn

pledges to you and to betroth Charicleia to himself. Now
he insists that she is not his sister but his betrothed." "Did
she really promise her to him, mother?" "She did indeed,
poor boy," answered Cybele. "I was present and heard it.
The wedding will be sumptuously celebrated in a few days.
She promised to find you another wife." At this Achaemenes heaved a deep sigh and rubbed his hands. "I will
make this a bitter wedding for them all," he said. "Help me
only by putting the wedding off for the time that I shall
need, and if anyone asks for me say that I have had a fall
in the country and am unwell. So the fine gallant calls his
sister his bride—as if it were not plain that he is only trying
to keep her from me. Even if he embraces her, even if he
kisses her, as he commonly does, even if he sleeps with her,
is that sure proof that she is not his sister? It shall be my
business to vindicate the gods and their violated oaths."

So he said. He was goaded by anger and jealousy and
love and disappointment—emotions capable of setting anyone in turmoil, let alone a barbarian. The first notion that
occurred to him he seized upon without reflection or deliberation, and he was dominated by his first impulse. When
evening came on he was able to take from the royal stables
an Armenian horse reserved for the satrap's use in festive
processions, and he rode off to great Thebes. There Oroondates was mobilizing forces and material of every description in preparation for an expedition against the Ethiopians.

8

THE KING OF THE ETHIOPIANS had circumvented Oroondates by a stratagem. By taking Philae, a place which was much fought over and which frequently changed hands, he had made himself master of one of the two prizes of the war and so had reduced the satrap to great straits; now Oroondates was obliged to organize an expedition hurriedly and to improvise its supply. Philae is situated on the Nile, a little above the lesser cataracts, at a distance of some hundred furlongs from Syene and Elephantine. It was once occupied and settled by Egyptian refugees, and its possession was thereafter disputed by the Ethiopians and the Egyptians. The Ethiopians claimed that their territory extended as far as the cataracts, and the Egyptians maintained that the settlement of Philae by these exiles had constituted a military occupation. It had been taken and retaken several times by both parties, and at this period had been held by a garrison of Egyptians and Persians. The king of the Ethiopians had sent an embassy to Oroondates to demand the return of the city and also of the emerald mines. (He had made the same demand previously, as has been mentioned above, but without success.) His ambassadors he had enjoined to precede him by a few days, and he himself had followed with forces he pretended to have mustered for a different war; the true object of his expedition he revealed to no one. When he reckoned that his ambassadors had passed Philae and had lulled its inhabitants and garrison by pretending that their mission was to discuss peace and friendship, he himself had appeared and had driven the garrison out. After a resistance of two or three days the city was forced to submit to his numerical superiority and his siege engines. Once in possession of the city, he had injured none of its inhabitants.

While Oroondates, who was apprised of these events by fugitives, was in a state of confusion, he was worse confounded by the unexpected and unannounced arrival of Achaemenes. Oroondates at once asked whether any misfortune had overtaken Arsace or other members of his household, and Achaemenes replied that a misfortune had indeed occurred but that he wished to speak of it in private. When they were alone he told him the whole story—how Theagenes had been taken captive by Mitranes and sent to Oroondates to be sent on as a present to the Great King if he saw fit, for the young man was a fine ornament for the royal court and table; how Theagenes had been abducted and Mitranes killed by the Bessaeans; and how Theagenes had then reached Memphis. Here he included the episode of Thyamis. Finally, he told of Arsace's passion for Theagenes, Theagenes' installation in the palace, the attentions showered upon him, his services and his cup-bearing. Perhaps no transgression had as yet been committed, he added, because of the young man's obstinate resistance; but there was reason to fear that the young foreigner might yield to compulsion or to the effects of time unless he were speedily removed from Memphis, and Arsace's erotic enterprise cut short. It was for this reason that he had left secretly and

had hurried to bring his information; his good will to his
master would not suffer him to conceal a matter which concerned his master's interest. When he had aroused Oroondates' anger by this story and filled him with indignation
and a desire for revenge, he further inflamed his passion
by expatiating on Charicleia. He extolled her (as she deserved) and spoke of her beauty as divine: such loveliness
had never before been seen and never could be again.
"Compared to her," he said, "all your concubines are nothing, not alone those in Memphis, but those you carry in
your train." In this strain Achaemenes continued, hoping
that even if Oroondates consorted with Charicleia for a
while, he himself could later ask for her hand in marriage
as a reward for his information.

Now the satrap was set wholly on fire, entangled at once
in the nets of anger and lust. Without delay he summoned
Bagoas, one of his trusted eunuchs, and sent him to Memphis
with fifty horsemen to bring Theagenes and Charicleia to
him at once, whenever he should find them. He also gave
Bagoas letters to deliver. One to Arsace read as follows:
"Oroondates to Arsace: Send me Theagenes and Charicleia,
captives, siblings, slaves of the king, to be dispatched to
him. Send them willingly, for even if you are unwilling
they will be taken and Achaemenes will be believed." To
Euphrates, his chief eunuch at Memphis, he wrote as follows:
"For your negligence in respect to my household you will
render an account. For the present deliver the Greek
captives to Bagoas to bring to me, whether Arsace be willing or unwilling. Deliver them in any case, or know that
the bearer has orders to bring you in chains, to be flayed
alive." Bagoas and his men set out to execute these orders,
which bore the satrap's seal so that the people in Memphis
should surrender the young pair promptly. Oroondates now
marched to war against the Ethiopians. He ordered Achae-

menes to follow him, having given secret instructions that he was to be watched until his denunciations should be confirmed.

During these same days certain other events took place in Memphis. Soon after Achaemenes had secretly left, Thyamis was invested with the full prerogatives of the priesthood and was hence regarded as a chief personage in the city. He performed the funeral rites for Calasiris and rendered his father the customary observances for the stipulated period. As soon as the priestly law permitted him to hold communication with the outer world, he took pains to inquire for Theagenes and Charicleia. After research and inquiry he learned that they were residing in the satrap's palace and immediately repaired to Arsace to ask for them. He had a special relationship with the young foreigners, he said, and moreover his father on his deathbed had enjoined him to defend and protect them. He thanked her for having so charitably entertained the young people, though they were foreigners and Greeks, during the intervening days when access to the temple was interdicted to the profane, but now he thought it right to resume the care of the charges entrusted to him.

"I wonder," replied Arsace, "that after you acknowledge my goodness and charity you should then condemn me as uncharitable, as if I could not or would not take care of the strangers and show them due regard." "Not so," replied Thyamis. "I know they would enjoy greater affluence here than with me, if they should wish to remain. But they are of an illustrious race, have experienced various tribulations, and are now wanderers; their supreme desire is to recover their family and their homeland. The task of helping them my father bequeathed to me; and I have my own reasons, furthermore, for befriending these foreigners." "It is well," said Arsace to him, "that instead of petitioning you invoke a legal claim. Of legality the preponderance is on my side, to the degree that ownership confers a stronger claim than benevolence." Thyamis expressed his surprise: "You own them? How?" "By the rules of war," she answered, "captives are slaves."

Thyamis realized that it was to the affair of Mitranes that she alluded, and so he said, "But Arsace, it is not war now but peace, and whereas war enslaves it is the nature of peace to set free; the one is a tyrant's caprice, the other a kingly principle. Peace and war are not distinguished by words but more truly by the intentions of those who use the words. By adding the notion of justice you would appear to be giving a better definition. As for the concepts of honor and profit there can be no question: how can it be either honorable or profitable for you to retain these young foreigners in whom you appear to show so ardent an interest?"

At these words Arsace no longer restrained herself but behaved as all lovers generally do: When they think their love is a secret they are bashful, but when they are discovered they lose all shame; concealment makes them timid, discovery audacious. So Arsace's conscience arraigned her soul; suspecting that Thyamis suspected her, she threw aside all respect for the priest and the priestly dignity and spurned all feminine modesty. "For what you did to Mitranes," said she, "you will not get off lightly. The time will come when Oroondates will exact retribution from those who slaughtered him and his men. The foreigners I shall not give up. For the moment they are my slaves, and presently they will be sent to my brother, the Great King, according to the law of the Persians. Rant about justice and honor and profit; your definitions are futile, for the powerful have no need of them, but can identify them with their own will. Leave my palace at once of your own will, or else you will be removed despite yourself." As Thyamis walked out he invoked the gods

to witness and said no more than that this would come to
no good end; his purpose was to make full revelation to
the people of Memphis and invite their aid. "Of your
prophecy I take no account," said Arsace. "The only
prophecy which love regards is success." With that she retired to her chamber, and with Cybele, whom she summoned, consulted upon her present situation.

When Achaemenes was nowhere to be seen Arsace conceived a suspicion that he had made off, and whenever she
asked Cybele about him, Cybele invented various incon-
sistent excuses, all calculated to make her believe anything
rather than that he had gone to Oroondates. But in the
end she was no longer convincing, and Achaemenes' long
absence made Arsace suspicious. On this occasion she said,
"What shall I do, Cybele? What remedy is there for my
state? Love does not relax but grows more intense; the
young man serves as fuel to spread the flame. But he is
stubborn and intractable. In the beginning he seemed more
humane than now, for then he soothed me by deceptive
promises. Now he rejects me unequivocally and categor-
ically. He may know that Achaemenes has done what I
suspect, and the knowledge may trouble him and make
him fearful of overt action. It is Achaemenes who vexes
me most of all. Can he have gone to inform Oroondates?
Will he convince him or at least arouse his suspicions? If
only I could see Oroondates! He could not resist a single
caress or tear of Arsace. The magic of femininity and
glances of intimacy exercise great power for winning men
over. More than terrible would it be if Oroondates should
be convinced before I see him and if I be overtaken by
condemnation and perhaps even punishment when I have
not even had my way with Theagenes. Therefore, Cybele,
move heaven and earth, try every device. You see that my
fate is on the knife's edge, on the very brink. You realize
too that if I am lost I will not spare others—how could

I?—and you will be the first to pay for your son's activities; how you can be ignorant of them I cannot conceive."

"Of my son's and of my own loyalty to you," said
Cybele, "your apprehensions, mistress, are unfounded, as
the facts will prove. But when you are yourself so indolent
and easygoing in the pursuit of your love, do not place
the blame on others who are not at fault. You are flatter-
ing the youth like a slave when you should command him
like a mistress. In the beginning this may have been correct, for his spirit seemed naïve and docile. But when he
rebels against his lover, assume the role of mistress; let
scourges and torments force him to your will. It is in the
nature of young men to be arrogant when courted, complaisant when curbed. And so this young man will yield to
punishment what he disdained to flattery." "What you
say may be right," said Arsace, "but, ye gods, how could
my eyes endure to see that body tortured or even chastised?" "Again you go soft," said Cybele. "Would it not
be better for him to be brought to a saner choice by a
few tortures and for you to gratify your desires after a
little uneasiness? You need not even distress your eyes with
the proceedings. Turn him over to Euphrates and say he
is to be punished for some offense, and spare yourself
the spectacle: ears are less susceptible to distress than eyes.
When a change of heart is perceptible we can say he has
been sufficiently punished and release him."

Arsace consented, for love rejected does not spare the
beloved and failure provokes vengeance. And so she summoned the eunuch and gave him his instructions. The eunuch rankled with the jealousy of his kind, and he had
moreover been long embittered against Theagenes because of the things he saw and suspected. He threw Theagenes into iron fetters at once, tormented him with hunger
and stripes, and locked him in a gloomy dungeon. When

Theagenes, feigning ignorance, asked why he was so treated,
the eunuch did not answer. Every day he increased Theagenes' torments beyond Arsace's wishes and orders. Following orders, he allowed none but Cybele to visit him.
Cybele came frequently and secretly brought him food,
on the pretense that she pitied him because of their former
acquaintance; in reality she came to discover his mood and
whether the torments had softened him up to the point
of yielding. But he showed greater fortitude and resisted
his trials more manfully. His body was worn down, but
the chastity of his spirit gathered strength. He gloried in
his lot, and despite the affliction visited upon him, he
exulted in the welcome opportunity it afforded him of
demonstrating his affection and loyalty to Charicleia. He
counted it the greatest blessing if she too should know
his feelings, and he repeatedly called upon her as his life,
his light, his soul.

When Cybele perceived this she instructed Euphrates
to intensify the torment, thus countermanding the orders
of Arsace, who had wished Theagenes to be only moder-
ately chastised and subjected to duress, not to death. When
she perceived that even after the new orders no progress
was being made and that her attempts failed of obtaining
the results she hoped for, she realized the danger she was
running. On the one hand, Oroondates would not long
defer his vengeance after he received Achaemenes' information, and on the other, Arsace might do away with
her in her impatience at being deluded by Cybele's promises of assistance. She therefore determined to confront
her difficulty boldly and to commit a heinous crime which
would either assure Arsace's success and deliver herself
from the expected danger at Arsace's hands, or else remove
all proofs of the intrigue by the death of all concerned in
it. She came then to Arsace and said, "Mistress, we labor
in vain. So far from yielding, that stubborn fellow grows

more audacious. Charicleia is always on his lips, and he
soothes himself by calling upon her as by a balm. Let us
fling out our reserve anchor, as the saying goes, and rid
ourselves of this embarrassment. When he learns that she
is no more, he will doubtless dismiss his yearning for her
and conform to our wishes."

Arsace snatched at this suggestion, which gave play to
her long jealousy and fury. "Excellent," said she. "I shall
at once give orders to have the pest removed." "But who
will obey them?" asked Cybele. "Your authority is paramount, but the laws forbid you to execute anyone without
trial by Persian judges. It will be troublesome and dis-
tasteful for you to invent charges and accusations against
the girl, and even so it is not certain that we shall win
credence. But I am prepared to do and endure anything
for your sake, and if you like I will manage the affair with
poison and put your adversary out of the way with a magic
philter." Arsace approved and ordered Cybele to proceed.
She started at once and found Charicleia dissolved in tears
and lamentations, and in her grief speculating how she
could rid herself of life. Though Cybele had at first tried
to conceal Theagenes' lot from her and had invented a
variety of excuses for his not appearing and not paying
her his customary visits, Charicleia now knew what his
situation was. "Unhappy girl," said Cybele, "will you not
stop troubling yourself and exhausting yourself in vain?
Look, Theagenes is free and will come to see you this
evening. The mistress was annoyed with him for a while
for some negligence in his service, and ordered him in-
carcerated. But today she promised to release him, in honor
of a traditional festival which she is going to celebrate, and
also at my entreaties. Rise up, then, and refresh yourself
this once by taking a little nourishment with me." "But
how can I believe you?" said Charicleia. "You have deceived me so often that I have lost confidence." "I swear

to you by all the gods," said Cybele, "that all your troubles
will this day be resolved and that you will be released from
every anxiety. Only do not do away with yourself by
continuing to starve yourself; do taste a bit of the meal
which is just now being served." Though with difficulty,
Charicleia was persuaded. Experience still taught her to
expect some deceit, but she partly trusted the oath and was
eager to credit the agreeable news. What the soul desires it
is wont to believe. And so they took their places and dined.
When the dainty waitress brought the cups of mixed wine
Cybele motioned to her to serve Charicleia first, and after-
wards she herself took a cup and drank it. The old woman
had not yet drained the cup when she appeared to be
seized with dizziness. She emptied what remained of the
drink on the floor, glared furiously at the servant, and
then fell in the throes of spasms and sharp convulsions.

Confusion seized all present, including Charicleia, who
tried to raise the woman. The poison worked more quickly
than an arrow steeped in deadly venom. It was potent
enough to destroy a young and vigorous body; the vital
organs of an old and worn-out one it seized more quickly
than one can tell. The old woman's eyes were inflamed, her
limbs, when the spasms ceased, were paralyzed, and a dark
tinge spread over her skin. But the soul of that vile creature was more malignant, I think, than the poison. Even
in death Cybele did not renounce her treachery. By signs
and broken words she pointed to Charicleia as author of
the plot, and as soon as the beldam breathed her last
Charicleia was bound and brought before Arsace. Arsace
asked whether it was she that had prepared the potion, and
threatened stripes and torture if she refused to speak the
truth. Singular was the spectacle which Charicleia then
afforded the onlookers. Her spirit was not downcast; she
bore herself proudly and seemed to regard the procedure
as a jest and a mockery. In the consciousness of her inno-

cence she scorned the calumny, but was very willing to
die if Theagenes was no more. To her it was a gain that
others would perpetrate the unholy act which she had
contemplated committing upon herself. And so she said,
"Virtuous princess, if Theagenes is alive I declare myself
innocent of this murder. But if he has fallen victim to your
holy intrigues you have no need to examine me. She who
poisoned the excellent nurse who educated you to such
fair practices you hold in your power: kill her without
delay. Such would be the desire of Theagenes, who lawfully despised your lawless intrigues."

Stung to fury by Charicleia's words, Arsace ordered her
to be soundly cuffed and then said, "Take this wretch in
her fetters and show her her precious lover who is in the
same state, as he deserves. Then load her with chains and
deliver her to Euphrates. He shall keep her guarded till tomorrow, when she will be condemned to death by sentence
of the Persian magistrates." While Charicleia was being
led away, the young girl who had served Cybele the wine
(she was one of the two Ionians whom Arsace had given
the young pair in the beginning for their personal service),
whether out of compassion for Charicleia, with whom she
had grown familiar, or whether by divine inspiration, burst
into tears and groans and cried out, "Ah, the poor innocent
thing!" Those present wondered at her exclamation and
pressed her to explain her meaning. She then confessed that
she had given Cybele the drug. She had received it from
Cybele to give to Charicleia, but had either been confounded by the enormity of the deed or confused by
Cybele's nodded direction to serve Charicleia first, and so
had interchanged the cups and handed the old woman the
one which contained the drug. The girl was immediately
taken before Arsace, everyone regarding it a godsend for
Charicleia to be absolved of the charge. Even the barbarian
heart is moved to pity noble character and bearing. The

servant repeated her statement, but Arsace merely remarked, "She too seems to be an accomplice." She ordered
the girl to be bound and to await trial in prison. Then she
sent to summon the Persian grandees who have authority
to consult on the common welfare, to pass judgment, and
to fix penalties.

In the morning these officials arrived and took their
places, and Arsace made her indictment. She gave a complete account of the poisoning, shedding tears all the while
for her dear nurse and for the loss of her precious and devoted servant. She called upon the judges to witness the
ingratitude of the foreign woman whom she had so kindly
received and entertained. Her accusation was sharp and
bitter. Charicleia offered no defense at all. She again confessed to the charge, declared that she had administered
the poison, and added that she would gladly have killed
Arsace also if she had not been prevented. She attacked
Arsace copiously and directly, and did all she could to
provoke the sentence of the judges. During the night she
had imparted her intentions to Theagenes in the prison
and had learned his in turn, and they had agreed that she
must voluntarily accept any death that might be inflicted
and be delivered from a wretched existence, endless wandering, and implacable fortune. Then they said what they
thought were their last farewells. The jewels which had
been exposed with her and which she was always careful
to carry secretly with her she tied around her waist, under
her dress; these were to serve for her obsequies. And now
she avowed every accusation that was made and invented
others that were not made.

The judges, accordingly, rendered their decision
promptly, and it wanted but little for her to be condemned
to the most savage of Persian punishments. But affected,
doubtless, by the youth of the victim and her irresistible
beauty, they sentenced her to be burned alive. The execu-

tioners immediately laid hands on her and led her a short
distance outside the walls. A herald preceded, calling out
at intervals that she was being taken to the pyre on a
charge of poisoning. A great multitude from the city
followed, some attracted by the cortege, others, who had
heard the news which had quickly spread through the city,
to witness the spectacle. Arsace, too, witnessed the proceedings from the walls; for her it would have been terrible not
to gloat over the spectacle of Charicleia's punishment. The
executioners built up an enormous pyre, and when it was
in full blaze began to draw Charicleia towards it. She asked
them to wait a moment, promising that she would herself
willingly mount the pyre, and raised her hands to heaven
in the direction of the sun's rays, and cried out, "Sun,
Earth, divinities celestial and infernal, ye who observe the
impious and chastise them, you are witnesses that I am innocent of the crime imputed to me and that I willingly
accept death because of the intolerable assaults of fortune.
Receive me kindly, but visit speedy punishment upon the
accursed, impious, and adulterous Arsace who has done
this deed to deprive me of my spouse." At these words
there was a general outcry that the sentence should be
deferred to a second trial. Some were preparing to hinder
the execution, others had moved forward to do so; but
Charicleia anticipated them by mounting to the center of
the pyre.

There she stood for a long while, untouched, the flames
flowing around rather than approaching her; then she
moved about, but the flames retreated whenever she advanced. Their bright illumination only made her resplendent beauty shine more brilliantly and more sharply. Encircled in flame she was like a bride on a fiery nuptial couch.
She bounded from one part of the pyre to another, herself
marveling at the event, for she was eager for death. But
it availed naught, for the fire always retreated, as if it

shunned her approach. The executioners redoubled their efforts, spurred on by Arsace's menacing gestures. They brought wood and heaped up river reeds and roused the flames with all manner of tinder. As their efforts proved futile the populace was more and more excited and thought the intervention was divine. "The woman is pure, the woman is innocent!" they exclaimed, and advanced to drive the executioners from the pyre. Thyamis had been apprised of the event by the great clamor and had hurried to the scene; he himself now led the movement and encouraged the people to intervene. Though they were eager to remove Charicleia they did not dare come near, and so urged the girl to jump down off the pyre: one who had endured the flames need not fear if she wished to leave them. Encouraged by these gestures and words, and believing too that the intervention on her behalf was divine, Charicleia resolved not to prove ingrate to the divine by rejecting its benefits and so jumped from the pyre. Moved by joy and surprise the whole populace shouted out as with a single voice and acclaimed the greatness of the gods.

Arsace could not contain her rage. She leapt from the walls and ran out at a postern gate with a retinue of guards and Persian grandees. She laid hands on Charicleia, and gazing sternly upon the people, said: "Are you not ashamed of attempting to deliver from punishment a vile woman, a poisoner, a confessed murderess caught in the act? Are you not aware that in helping this impious woman you are opposing the laws of the Persians and the King himself and the satraps and grandees and judges? Doubtless because she was not burned you have been deceived into pitying her and ascribe the deed to the gods; but have you not enough sense to realize that this fact proves she is a poisoner? So great is her sorcery that she can repel even the force of fire. Come, if you will, to the public assembly which will be held for you tomorrow. You will

see that she confesses the crime herself and is also convicted
by her accomplices whom I have been keeping under
guard." With that she seized her by the neck and dragged
her off, ordering the guards to disperse the crowd. The
people were indignant and looked about for means of
resistance, but they yielded, some induced to suspect that
Charicleia was a witch, others deterred by Arsace and the
forces at her disposal.

Charicleia was again delivered to Euphrates, again loaded
with even heavier chains, and again imprisoned to await
her second trial and punishment. The one great advantage
she found in her dreadful situation was in being with Theagenes and telling him her experiences. To satisfy her vengeance Arsace had conceived the cruel jest of imprisoning
the young people in the same dungeon so that they might
see one another in chains and torments: she knew well
enough that the sufferings of his beloved pain the lover
more than his own. But in this case, on the contrary, it
was a solace for them to be together, and they reckoned
it a gain to be tried by the same tribulations: if one was
less severely punished than the other he considered that he
was outdone in demonstrating proof of his love. Now they
could converse with and comfort one another and encourage each other to bear nobly and with fortitude the afflictions that befell them and their struggles on behalf of
chastity and fidelity.

Till late into the night, then, they conversed with one
another, and, as was natural for lovers who never expected
to meet after that night, they filled themselves with joy of
one another. Finally, they came to examine the miracle of
the pyre. Theagenes attributed it to the benevolence of the
gods who abhorred Arsace's unjust calumny and showed
compassion for her guiltless victim. But Charicleia seemed
equivocal. "My extraordinary preservation," said she, "does
certainly suggest divine and providential intervention; but

the incessant misfortunes which dog us and the variety
of torments which afflict us are signs of the unrelenting
hostility of a persecuting deity—unless some divinity were
demonstrating his miraculous powers by casting us into
extreme peril in order to save us when our condition seems
desperate."

As she spoke in this vein Theagenes adjured her not to
blaspheme and admonished her to show greater piety and
to persevere in her habit of restraint. Suddenly she cried
out, "Heaven be propitious! What a dream or maybe vision
has troubled my spirit! I saw it last night and did not
understand its meaning, but only now has it come to my
mind. The dream was expressed in verse, and it was the
divine Calasiris who uttered it. Whether it came upon me
as I was unconscious in sleep or whether I actually saw
him face to face I do not know. But this is what he said:
'If thou bear Pantarbe fear not the force of fire; easy it is
for destiny to accomplish the unexpected.' " Theagenes
too was seized with a prophetic agitation and leapt up, so
far as his chains permitted, and burst out, "Be ye kindly,
ye deities! I, too, can show forth poetic recollections of
an oracle from the same seer. Calasiris or some deity in
Calasiris' form visited me and seemed to say the following:
'To the land of the Ethiopians will you go, in the company of a maiden; tomorrow will you be delivered from
Arsace's prison.' The meaning of this oracle I can divine.
The 'land of the Ethiopians' means the nether world; 'in
the company of a maiden' signifies that I shall be with
Persephone; and 'delivered' means separation from the
body. And you, do you find anything contradictory in
what your verses say? The name Pantarbe signifies 'fearing
all things'; the oracle merely advises you not to be afraid
of fire."

"Darling Theagenes," said Chariclea, "long familiarity
with misfortune always leads you to the worst interpreta-

tions and conjectures; man naturally turns his mind in accordance with events. To me the prophecies seem to foretell much happier things than you think. The girl is very likely myself; what is prophesied is that you will escape Arsace's chains and go with me to my own country of Ethiopia. How, we do not know and cannot imagine, but to the gods all things are possible, and they will take care for the fulfillment of their oracle. Already, by the will of the gods, the prophecy which relates to me is, as you know, fulfilled. Beyond all expectation I am alive and with you. I did not then know that I carried the source of my safety about with me, but now I think I understand. I have always been careful to keep about me the tokens which were exposed with me, but particularly so when I was going to my trial, for I thought I would die. I tied them about my waist underneath my clothing, so that if I survived I could procure the necessities of life, and if I perished they would serve to adorn my funeral. These are costly necklaces and precious gems, Theagenes, from India and Ethiopia, but among them is a ring given by my father to my mother for their betrothal. In the circlet is set the stone called Pantarbe, inscribed with sacred characters and endowed with mystic virtues. Hence, I conjecture, it derives the power to repel fire and bestow upon those who wear it immunity even in the midst of flames. It is this which, by the will of the gods, preserved me. My basis for this conjecture—nay, knowledge—is the instruction of the divine Calasiris, who often explained that this property was described in the embroidery on the ribbon which was exposed with me and which is now wrapped about my waist." "The explanation is plausible, and indeed confirmed by the event," said Theagenes, "but what Pantarbe will deliver us from the dangers which confront us tomorrow? The stone does not promise immortality, alas, even though it is an antidote to fire, and that devilish Arsace is doubtless now devising some new and unheard-of kind of punishment. We can only wish that she may condemn us to the same death at the same hour; I would not count it death, but release from all our troubles." "Take heart," said Charicleia, "we shall have another Pantarbe if we trust the oracles of the gods. Our salvation will then be sweeter, and our sufferings, if such there must be, holier." Such were their sorrowful reflections, and each agonized over the other more than over himself. They laid their final injunctions upon one another and swore by all the gods and their present fortunes that they would be faithful unto death. And so they passed the night.

Bagoas and his fifty horsemen arrived at Memphis at night, when everyone was fast asleep. They quietly roused the sentinels at the gates, explained their identity, were recognized, and proceeded quickly and noiselessly to the satrap's residence. There Bagoas posted his troop around the house, to be ready to support him if he encountered resistance, and himself entered by a secret postern gate whose light bars he pried open. He announced himself to the porter and ordered him to keep silent, and then hastened to Euphrates, guided by his knowledge of the place and the faint light of the moon. He found him in bed, woke him, and when Euphrates called out, somewhat confused, "Who's there?" he said, "I am Bagoas; make no noise but order a light." Euphrates ordered a boy who slept near his room to light a lamp and not to awake the others. The boy brought a torch, placed it in the stand, and departed. "What is this?" said Euphrates. "What new calamity does your sudden and unexpected arrival portend?" "There is no need of words," said Bagoas, "take this letter and read. But first acknowledge this seal. You see that is Oroondates'. Execute his orders faithfully; darkness and speed will help you act secretly. Whether it is expedient

first to inform Arsace of the orders you yourself must decide."

Euphrates accepted the letters and read them both. "For
Arsace," he said, "this will be a fresh blow. She is even
now in a critical state. Yesterday she was attacked by a
fever, as by a divine stroke; burning spasms have been
running over her constantly, and there is little hope that
she can survive. But not even if she were well would I
give her these letters, for she would sooner die and destroy
us too than agree to surrender those young people. But you
must know that you have come in the nick of time; take
these foreigners and do whatever you can to help them.
They deserve your pity, for they are miserable and unfortunate. At Arsace's orders I have subjected them against
my will to a thousand torments, but they seem to be well
born, and as my experience and their conduct show, very
sensible." So saying, he led Bagoas to the dungeon. When
Bagoas saw the young people, even though they were in
chains and ravaged by their torments, he was struck by
their noble stature and their beauty. They for their part
thought all was over and that Bagoas had come at that
unseasonable hour to take them to their death. For a
moment they were agitated but quickly recovered, and
their cheerful and open countenances showed those present that they were indifferent or indeed pleased. When
Euphrates and his party approached and prepared to un-
fasten the chains from the wooden beam to which they
were attached, Theagenes cried out, "Bravo, Arsace! The
abominable creature imagines that she will conceal her
lawless deeds in the darkness of night, but the eye of justice is piercing and will shed light on the most secret
crimes. Do you carry out your orders. Whether it be fire
or water or the sword that is decreed for us, do us the
grace of giving us both the same death." Charicleia too

joined in this request. Even the eunuchs, who understood a little of what was said, wept as they led them out in chains.

When they were outside the residence Euphrates stayed behind. Bagoas and his men relieved the young people of their chains, leaving only enough to prevent escape, mounted each of them on a horse, placed them in the center of the troop, and galloped off towards Thebes. All that night they traveled without a stop and did not relax until the third hour of the day following. Then the heat of Egypt's summer sun was insupportable and they were weighed down too with want of sleep; they observed, furthermore, that Charicleia was unused to such strenuous riding. They therefore resolved to call a halt, breathe their horses, and give the girl a rest. At that place the banks of the Nile form a sort of promontory upon which the direct current of the river is broken. The water bends into a semicircle and then flows on in a straight line. The bend forms, as it were, a gulf of dry land which is well watered and lush. There is rich grassland and very abundant fodder for cattle. Peach trees, sycamores, and other species native to the Nile overarch the place and afford shade. Here Bagoas and his company bivouacked, using the trees for tents. He himself took food and invited Theagenes and Charicleia to share his lunch. At first they refused, on the grounds that eating was useless for people soon to die. He assured them that such was not the case, and explained that he was taking them not to death but to Oroondates.

The intense heat of midday was now abated, for the sun was no longer directly overhead but emitted its rays from a westerly angle. As Bagoas was preparing to resume the journey, a horseman came dashing up. He was panting and his horse was in a lather and barely able to stand. He said something to Bagoas privately, and then rested. Bagoas

remained sunk in thought for a moment, apparently re-
flecting on the tidings he had received. "Strangers," he
said, "take heart. Your enemy has paid her debt. Arsace
has hanged herself. As soon as she heard that you had left
with me she preferred a voluntary to an inflicted death.
She could never have escaped the vengeance of Oroondates
and the King, but would either have been killed or dis-
graced for the rest of her life. This is what Euphrates tells
me through the messenger who has just now come. Take
heart, then, and be of good cheer. I know that you have
committed no wrong, and she who wronged you, you are
now rid of." So Bagoas said, to win them over, and though
he pronounced his Greek badly and committed solecisms,
he spoke with genuine satisfaction. He admitted Arsace's
licentious and tyrannical way of life, and wished to encourage and comfort the young people. He thought, furthermore, that he would win Oroondates' high applause
for preserving a young man who would throw all the
satrap's other attendants into the shade and a maiden of
unrivaled beauty to be his wife after Arsace. Theagenes
and Charicleia, too, rejoiced at the news. They acknowledged the power of the gods and their justice, and thought
that no difficulties they might encounter could make them
suffer, now that that loathsome woman was dead. So sweet
is it even to perish, if one's enemies also perish.

Towards evening a refreshing breeze sprang up and invited the travelers to resume their journey. That evening
and all night till the following morning they pressed on
towards Thebes in the hope of finding Oroondates there.
But this hope was disappointed. En route a courier from
the army met them and reported that the satrap had set
out from Thebes and that he had himself been charged to
muster every soldier and every man under arms, even those
on garrison duty, and to proceed at full speed to Syene.
Everything was in confusion, and it was feared that the

city might be taken before the satrap arrived, for the
Ethiopian forces had pressed forward before their inten-
tions were known. Instead of proceeding to Thebes, then,
Bagoas turned towards Syene.

Arrived near his goal, he fell into an Ethiopian ambuscade. This was a numerous band of young and well-
armed soldiers who had been sent ahead as scouts to secure the safety of the main body of their army. Night,
unfamiliar terrain, and the remoteness of their friends
had discouraged their further progress, and they had concealed themselves in bushes by the river and kept watch
to secure their own safety and surprise any enemy force.
At break of day they saw Bagoas and his company pass.
They allowed him to proceed a little, to make sure that
there were no others following, and then, despising his
small force, they sallied forth from the marsh and pursued
him with a shout. Bagoas and his horsemen were astonished at the unexpected shout. From the complexion of
the newcomers they recognized that they were Ethiopians,
and from their number that resistance was useless. The
scouts were light-armed and numbered a thousand men.
The Persians did not wait for a nearer view, but took to
flight, moderating their speed at first in order not to seem
openly to be running away. The Ethiopians pursued, sending ahead the two hundred Troglodytes they had with
them. The Troglodytes are a nomad people who live in
Ethiopia on the borders of Arabia. They are naturally
swift runners, and practice the art from childhood. They
have no training whatever in heavy arms, but use slings
to attack from a distance. Either their speed disconcerts
the enemy, or, if they find themselves worsted, they run
away. No one ever tries to pursue them, for they are known
to be as swift as the wind and to hide in rocky caves with
small openings which are difficult to find. Though on foot,
these Troglodytes overtook the Persian horsemen and

succeeded in wounding some of them with their slings.
When the Persians faced about, the Troglodytes did not
receive their attack but scurried off towards their friends
whom they had left far behind. Seeing them turn about
and despising their small numbers, the Persians made bold
to attack. They beat off those that were nearest, and then
resumed their flight, spurring their horses on and making
the best speed they could. The main body dashed past a
bend of the Nile and were hidden from their enemy's view
by a promontory of the bank. But Bagoas was made
prisoner. His horse had stumbled and fallen upon him; one
of his legs was broken, so that he could not move.

Also taken were Theagenes and Chariclea. They refused to desert Bagoas, who had shown them marks of
good will and from whom they had hoped for further
kindness; they had dismounted to assist him, though they
could have got away. But they had another reason for sub-
mitting. Theagenes told Chariclea that this was the fulfillment of the dream and that these were the Ethiopians to
whose country it was fated for them to be carried as prisoners of war. It was better, he said, to surrender and deliver themselves to an uncertain fate than to incur certain
danger with Oroondates.

Chariclea perceived that fate was leading her by the
hand and was hopeful of a better future. She considered
her assailants as friends rather than enemies. But to Theagenes she imparted none of her thoughts and only gave
him to understand that she consented to his advice. Upon
their approach the Ethiopians recognized from his appearance that Bagoas was a eunuch and incapable of resistance; but they were impressed by the beauty and nobility of the unarmed prisoners and asked who they were.
They employed as an interpreter an Egyptian who spoke
Persian, supposing that either or both the languages would
be understood. Scouts and spies charged with procuring in-

telligence of what is done and said have learned by experience to take with them persons who speak and understand the language of the country. His long sojourn in Egypt had given Theagenes a smattering of Egyptian, and he answered that Bagoas was an important functionary of the Persian satrap and that he and Charicleia were Greeks. They had been carried as captives by the Persians, and were now surrendering to the Ethiopians, with hopes of better fortune. The Ethiopians decided to spare their lives and carry them to their king as their first and finest capture. Bagoas they reckoned the satrap's greatest treasure; in the Persian court eunuchs are regarded as the king's eyes and ears, for having no children or kinsmen to deflect their fidelity they are wholly attached to the master who trusts them. The young people they thought would be a fine present for the Ethiopian king, who would employ them in the service of his court. They carried them off mounted upon horses, Bagoas because he was wounded, and the young people because their chains made rapid movement impossible.

Here was a prologue to a drama and an induction for the action to come. Foreigners in chains who a little before were contemplating immediate execution were now being not led but rather escorted, and though they were prisoners, their captors would soon be their subjects. Such was their present situation.

9

SYENE WAS NOW ENTIRELY BLOCKADED; the Ethiopians had surrounded it as with a net. Oroondates had been informed of their approach only after they had passed the cataracts and were nearing the city. He had occupied it immediately before their arrival, had barred the gates, strengthened the walls with weapons, armor, and siege equipment, and was awaiting developments. When the Ethiopian King Hydaspes had received intelligence that the Persians were on the march to Syene he had given chase in order to attack them before they reached the city, and when he found he was too late he besieged the city and deployed his forces around it. Then he remained inactive, the mere spectacle of his army being irresistible. The plains of Syene were choked with countless quantities of men, arms, and animals.

It was here that the scouts who brought the captives found him. He was delighted at the sight of the young people, and without his knowledge his prescient soul was immediately attracted to them as if they belonged to him. The coming of prisoners in chains he accepted as a joyful symbol. "Well done!" he cried. "The gods give us our enemies in chains as our first booty. Let these our first captives, the first offerings of the war, be preserved for our victory sacrifices, as the ancestral usage of the Ethiopians requires; let them be kept as offerings to our own gods." He rewarded the scouts with gifts and sent them and their captives to the baggage train. He assigned a detachment who understood their language to guard the captives and enjoined them to show them every care, supply their needs generously, and in particular to keep them pure of any pollution, as being hallowed for sacrifice. He ordered that their iron chains be replaced with gold, for where other peoples use iron for ordinary needs the Ethiopians use gold. The king's orders were carried out. When their former chains were removed they thought they would be free, but their hopes were dashed when these were replaced with gold. Theagenes laughed and said, "A splendid transformation! Fortune is very charitable to us. We exchange iron for gold; our rich bonds make us more valuable prisoners." Charicleia too smiled, and tried to reassure Theagenes by recalling the predictions of the gods and lulling him with happier hopes.

Hydaspes now attacked Syene. He had hoped to seize the city and its walls at the first assault, but was beaten back by the defenders, who fought valiantly and insulted him with mockery and curses. Exasperated at their determination to resist at all and at their not willingly surrendering at his first attempt, he resolved not to wear the enemy down by blockades nor to attempt an attack in which some might be taken but many escape, but rather to destroy the city quickly and utterly by a gigantic and irresistible operation. This was his plan of attack. He divided the city wall into sectors and assigned to each sector of ten cubits ten men who were ordered to dig a wide and deep trench. As they dug others carried the earth out and still others heaped it up to make a wall as high as that of the besieged

city. The besieged did not hinder or resist the circumvalla-
tion. They could make no sally, for the besiegers were
too numerous, and they saw that the distance was too
great for their missiles. Hydaspes had taken thought to
make the distance between the walls sufficient to protect
his men from projectiles. This part of the work was dispatched with incredible speed, for a myriad hands hurried
it along. Hydaspes immediately began another similar
work. Part of the circle, about fifty feet wide, he left level,
without ditch or wall. From each extremity of the trench
he extended a long mound down to the Nile, each mound
rising higher and higher as it approached the river. The
effect was of two long walls, with level ground fifty feet
wide between them, covering the distance between Syene
and the Nile. When the mounds joined the banks of the
river he cut an opening for the water, which poured into
the canal formed by the mounds. As the water rushed
from the higher to the lower level and from the great width
of the Nile to the narrower passage and dashed against its
artificial banks, a great and indescribable roar could be
heard at the opening, and the rushing noise was audible at
a great distance.

When the people in Syene heard and saw these things
they realized their danger. The purpose of the circumvalla-
tion was to flood them. The surrounding trench and the
approaching waters shut them off from escape, and it was
equally dangerous to remain. They therefore made what
preparations they could to save themselves. First they
caulked the crevices between the boards in the gates with
tar and pitch. Then they reinforced the foundation of the
wall with earth, stone, or wood, every man bringing whatever came to hand. No one was idle: children, women, old
men, all lent a hand. Mortal peril makes no distinction of
age or sex. The robust and those capable of bearing arms
were assigned to dig a mine from the city to reach the

enemy's trench. This work was carried out in the manner following. Near the wall they sank a shaft five cubits deep, and when it had reached a depth lower than the foundations of the wall they dug horizontally, by torchlight, in the direction of the enemy's trench. The earth they excavated they passed in order from the first man to the second and so on, and carried it to a part of the city long occupied by gardens, where they heaped it onto a hill. Their purpose was to direct the flow of the waters, if they should come, into a void, but their calamity had anticipated their prudence. The Nile, rolling through the canal, fell into the circular trench, and its overflow made a lake of the interval between the two walls. Syene was now an island, surrounded by water in the midst of the land and beaten against by the waves of the Nile. In the beginning and for one day the wall held out. But the pressure of the water increased as its level rose. It penetrated the fissures of the black and slimy earth, which had cracked with the summer heat, and seeped down and flooded the foundations of the wall. The structure yielded to the pressure, and wherever there was a gap the wall settled and leaned over and its swaying portended collapse. The battlements swung in the air, and their defenders were swept off as by a tempest at sea.

Toward evening a section of the wall with its towers collapsed. The portion thus fallen was still higher than the water level by some five cubits, and so did not yet admit the flood; but the breach made the threat of inundation imminent. Now the mingled shrieks of those in the city could be heard even by the enemy. They raised their hands to heaven and, as their sole remaining hope, called upon the gods to save them. They also implored Oroondates to come to terms with Hydaspes. Though unwilling, he was ready to comply, having become the slave of fortune, but he was blockaded by the water and had no means of send-

ing an emissary to the enemy. Necessity taught him an expedient. He wrote down what he wished to say and attached his letter to a stone. A sling served as his ambassador
and a projectile carried his petition across the water. But
the attempt failed; the distance was too great for the mis-
sile, and it fell into the water. Again he shot the same message and again he failed. All the archers and slingers vied
with one another to reach the mark, the prize for the contest being life itself, but the experience of all was the same.
Finally, they stretched their hands out to the enemy, who
were standing on their mounds and viewing the townspeople's anguish like a theatrical show. With pitiful gestures
they expressed the intention of the missives as best they
could. Now they stretched out their upturned hands to
signify that they were suppliants, now they twisted them
behind their backs as if chained, to acknowledge slavery.
Hydaspes understood that they were pleading for survival,
and was ready to accord it: a fallen enemy arouses charity
in noble hearts. But for the moment he could do nothing,
and resolved to obtain more specific information concerning the enemy's intentions. He had prepared a fleet of river
craft, which he had brought from the Nile by the canal
and had moored at the circular trench. Of these he chose
ten that were newly built and on them embarked archers
and heavily armed soldiers. He gave them instructions on
what they were to say and sent them to the Persians. These
men crossed over on the alert, ready to defend themselves
if the men on the walls should make any unexpected move.
Novel indeed was the spectacle: a boat crossed from one
wall to another, a sailor voyaged over the mainland, a vessel moved over the tilth. War is always productive of in-
novations, but on this occasion its marvels were prodigious.
It commingled marines and men fighting from walls, it
armed infantry against a naval force.

The townspeople were already quaking in terror of the

dangers which surrounded them, and when they saw the boats and their armed contingents and observed that they were making for the breach in the wall, they supposed that even those who had come to save them had hostile intentions. In a critical situation every move arouses suspicion and fear. Men in despair count every minute that death is put off as a precious gain, and so they hurled their stones and shot their arrows from the wall. Their missiles were not meant to wound but merely to prevent the advance of the boats. The Ethiopians returned the volley, and since they took better aim, not understanding the purpose of the Persians, they struck two or more. Some of these were so surprised by the sharp and unexpected action that they tumbled from the walls head over heels and crashed into the water outside. The Persians desired only to keep their adversaries off, but the Ethiopians were furiously defending themselves, and a general battle would have flared out had not an elderly and respected citizen of Syene admonished the men on the wall. "Madmen," said he, "your calamities have made you crazy. These people we have been begging and imploring to come to our help and we had despaired of their coming; shall we now drive them away? If they come as friends, with proposals of peace, they will be our saviors; if their intentions are hostile we can defeat them easily even if they land. What will it profit us to annihilate these men when our city is encircled by water and surrounded by a cloud of enemies by land? Let us rather receive them and learn what it is they wish." All approved of this speech, and the satrap, too, accepted it. They abandoned the breach, and posted themselves on the wall at either side of it with arms grounded.

When the rampart was cleared of men and the people waved white flags to signify that the way was open, the Ethiopians approached, and from their boats as from a stage addressed the besieged who constituted their audience:

"Persians and men of Syene here present, Hydaspes, who
rules over East and West Ethiopia and now over you, knows
how to subdue his enemies and is by nature inclined to pity
his suppliants. The former he regards the part of manliness,
the latter of charity, the one the function of a soldier, the
other the expression of his own temper. Your survival or
the reverse is now in his power, but since you throw yourselves on his compassion he releases you from the manifest
and certain danger which your war has brought upon you.
The conditions of your deliverance he does not himself de-
fine, but leaves the choice to you. He does not exploit victory like a tyrant, but governs the fortunes of men without
offense to the gods." To this the men of Syene replied that
they delivered themselves, their children, and their wives
to him to use as he would, and that they surrendered their
city (if they should survive) which was now tottering to
destruction unless some device of the gods or of Hydaspes
himself should bring speedy salvation. Oroondates for his
part said that he renounced the cause and prize of the war;
he would cede the city of Philae and the emerald mines.
He requested that no constraint be put upon himself or
his soldiers to surrender. If Hydaspes wished to manifest
complete clemency he would permit them, on condition
that they caused no injury and offered no resistance, to retire to Elephantine. To himself it was indifferent whether
he perished at once or obtained an illusion of survival, for
he would be punished by the Persian king for surrendering
his army. The latter would indeed be the worse lot, for now
he would undergo a simple and regular kind of death,
whereas the Persians would devise cruel and exquisite tortures. After this declaration Oroondates further requested
that two Persians be received into the Ethiopian boats,
alleging that they would proceed to Elephantine; if that
city should be disposed to surrender he would not hesitate
to do likewise.

When the emissaries had received these proposals they took the two Persians on board and returned to report to Hydaspes. Hydaspes smiled at Oroondates' silly pretensions. The man was negotiating on terms of equality as if his hopes of survival or death depended on himself and not on another. "But it would be foolish," he added, "to destroy so many for the stupidity of one." He authorized Oroondates' emissaries to proceed to Elephantine, caring little whether the people there were plotting insurrection. One part of his own men he ordered to block the breach they had dug in the Nile bank, and another to dig an opening in the wall of the canal. When the influx from the river was stopped and the stagnant water flowed out, the land around Syene would be left dry and practicable for foot soldiers. The men so assigned began their task but deferred its completion to the day following, for evening and darkness followed close upon the issuance of the order.

The people inside the city did not relax their own efforts to help themselves, and did not despair though salvation seemed beyond hope. Some kept digging at the underground corridor, which they now supposed was nearing the enemy's mound; they had estimated its distance from the wall and used a rope of that length to measure their mine. Others repaired the breach in the wall by torchlight. Construction was easy, for in the collapse the stones had rolled inward. Even when they thought all was secure for the present there was a new alarm. In the middle of the night the section of the mound where the Ethiopians had been excavating the previous day suddenly gave way. Possibly the earth underneath was loosely heaped and not sufficiently compact to prevent infiltration and so gave way under its load; or perhaps the void created by the Persians' mine sapped the earth above; or perhaps the increasing pressure of water widened the narrow breach and poured through its new path in great force and reached a great depth; or perhaps it was a divine intervention. In any case there was a thundering crash, and its reverberations terrified all who heard it. Ignorant of the cause, Ethiopians and Syenites alike thought that the larger part of the city wall had collapsed. The Ethiopians, having nothing to fear, remained quiet in their bivouacs: they would find out what had happened in the morning. But the people in the city ran to every part of their wall, and when they found their own sector undamaged each group supposed that the trouble was in another part. The approach of daylight dissipated all doubts and terrors; they could see the breach in the mound and the retreat of the waters. Now the Ethiopians dammed the breach in the Nile through which the water had entered the canal. They erected a barrier of planks supported by thick wooden piles and packed it with earth and fascines. Many thousands worked simultaneously, some on the banks and some bringing materials in boats. The waters had retreated, but neither side could proceed to the other, for the earth was covered with deep slime. Even where the ground was apparently dry the surface coating was thin and the deep mud beneath was treacherous to horse and man alike.

In this way two or three days passed. Syenites and Ethiopians alike showed their peaceful intentions, the former by opening the gates, the latter by laying down their arms. The situation was that of a truce, but without intercourse between the parties. No sentries were posted by either side. Even more, the people in the city devoted themselves to festivity. The festival of the Nile, the greatest among the Egyptians, happened to fall at this time. It is celebrated at the time of the summer solstice, when the river begins to rise. The Egyptians observe it with greater zeal than any other festival, for they make of the Nile a god, and indeed the greatest of deities. They solemnly declare that the river is an equal rival to heaven, for without clouds and without rainfall it waters their fields with its annual inundation. So the common crowd holds. Their reasons for deifying the river are the following. They consider that the particular cause of human life is the conjunction of the moist and the dry, and they think that other elements are subordinate to and appear only in connection with these. The moist element is the Nile, and their own country represents the dry. Such is the laity's manner of speaking, but the initiates call the land Isis and the Nile Osiris, substituting names for objects. The goddess yearns for the god when he is absent and rejoices when he is present; when he disappears she again falls into grief and expresses her hatred for the enemy Typhon. Egyptians versed in natural science and theology are, I imagine, loath to unveil to the view of the profane the mysteries so shrouded. To them they communicate these under the form of a myth, but they reserve a clearer exposition for the true initiates, within the sanctuary illuminated by the torch of true reality. So much I may be permitted to say without offense to religion; on the profounder mysteries let reverential silence be preserved.

I return now to events in Syene, where the townsmen were celebrating the festival of the Nile with sacrifices and ceremonies. Though their bodies were fatigued and their situation critical, their souls were not forgetful of religious obligations, which they discharged as circumstances permitted. Oroondates waited for dead of night, when the Syenites had finished their feasting and were fast asleep, and led his army out. He had secretly passed word to the Persians of the hour and the gate for their departure. Each group leader had received orders to abandon horses and pack animals to avoid the difficulty of mustering them and the discovery which would result from the noise of the operation. They were to take only their arms and provide themselves with a beam or plank. When they were assem-

bled at the gate designated they proceeded to lay their
timbers across the mud. The timber brought by each squad
was laid end to end with the last, those in the rear passing
the planks up to those in front. The whole body then
crossed easily and rapidly, as over a bridge. When they
reached dry land they found the Ethiopians sleeping securely without having taken precautions to post sentinels.
Unperceived by the Ethiopians, Oroondates led his army
to Elephantine on the double quick, and without stopping
to draw breath. He penetrated into the city without hindrance, for the two Persians who had been sent ahead from
Syene had watched for his arrival, as they had been bidden
to do, night after night, and when the watchword was
given they immediately opened the gates.

When day dawned the Syenites became aware of the
flight: at first individuals were surprised not to see the
Persians who had been billeted upon them, then they compared notes with their neighbors, and finally they saw the
bridge. Again they were plunged into agony. For this second injury they were liable to charges far graver than the
first, for they would appear to have abused the clemency
of Hydaspes and to have connived at the escape of the
Persians. They therefore resolved to march out of the city
in a body, deliver themselves to the Ethiopians, and endeavor to move their pity by attesting their innocence
upon oath. People of every age assembled, took suppliant
branches in their hands, lighted tapers and torches, placed
the images of the gods, carried by priests, in the van to
serve as a herald's badge, and crossed over the bridge towards the Ethiopians. While they were still at a distance
they kneeled down in the posture of suppliants and at a
set signal uttered pitiful wails and cries of lamentation and
begged for mercy. To make their supplication more pitiful,
they threw their newborn infants on the ground and let
them wallow where they would, in order to mollify the

wrath of the Ethiopians by the show of unsuspecting innocence. The children had no understanding of what was going on and, to avoid the frightening cries and gestures,
turned from their parents and nurses in the direction of
the enemy. Some were creeping and others toddling with
uncertain steps and wailing all the while. They made a
moving scene, as if fortune had improvised a new mode of
arousing pity.

When Hydaspes saw this he thought the Syenites were
continuing their former petition and intensifying it because they wished to surrender. He sent to ask them what
they wanted and why the Persians had not come with
them. They then told all—the flight of the Persians, their
own guiltlessness, their traditional festival, their absorp-
tion in their devotions to the gods, and the deep sleep following the feasting which had permitted the Persians to
elude them; even if they had been aware of their intentions, men unarmed would scarcely have been able to prevent armed men from getting away. At these tidings Hydaspes suspected that Oroondates was preparing some mischief or trap for him, as was indeed the case. He summoned
the priests by themselves, prostrated himself before the
idols they carried to inspire greater respect, and inquired
whether they were able to give him further information
concerning the Persians. He asked whither they had gone,
whom they counted on to support them, and whom they
were going to attack. The priests declared that they knew
nothing, but conjectured that Oroondates had gone to
Elephantine, where the greater part of his forces was assembled and particularly his armored cavalry, in which he
placed his highest trust. So the priests responded, and they
begged him to enter Syene as though it were his own and
to lay his resentment aside.

For the moment Hydaspes did not think it wise to enter
the city himself. He sent two phalanxes of hoplites to see

if any ambush had been laid, and if there were none to
occupy the city as a garrison. The Syenites he dismissed
with promises of generous treatment. His army he then
put in battle array, to receive any attack of the Persians
or to pursue them if their advance was delayed. These dispositions had not yet been completed when scouts arrived
to report that the Persians were advancing in battle order.
Oroondates had long before given orders for his entire army
to assemble at Elephantine, but on the unexpected advance
of the Ethiopians had himself been compelled to dash to
Syene with a small contingent. There he had been blockaded by earthworks, had begged his safety from Hydaspes,
and received it upon parole. But he proved perfidious. He
had prepared the two Persians to cross over with the Ethiopians on the pretext that he was sending them to Elephantine to inquire on what terms that city would submit to
Hydaspes, but in reality to see whether those in Elephantine were willing and prepared to fight if he should be able
to reach them from Syene. His treacherous intent he now
put into execution. His army at Elephantine he found well
prepared, and without postponing his advance an instant,
marched against his adversaries in the expectation of taking
them by surprise.

Now he appeared in battle array, fascinating every eye
with his gorgeous Persian pomp; the whole plain glittered
with arms of silver and gold. The newly risen sun sent its
rays full in the face of the Persians, and they reflected an
indescribable brilliance to a great distance, as if the shining
armor was shedding a splendor rivaling that of the true
Medes and Persians. The hoplites in the van were followed
by archers in the rear so that the latter, unencumbered by
heavy armor, might shoot their arrows under the protection of the former. The Egyptians, Libyans, and all the
foreign contingents were ranged on the left. These too
were supported by javelin throwers and slingers, who were

assigned to make sallies and to attack the advancing enemy from the flanks. Oroondates himself held the center. He was mounted on a splendid scythe-bearing chariot, with a phalanx of guards on either side. Before him was only the troop of armored cavalry; it was his great confidence in these that emboldened him to venture battle. This phalanx was always the Persians' strongest force, and was posted in the van as an impenetrable wall.

The fashion of their armament is the following. The men are selected for physical ruggedness. Each man wears a helmet cleverly fashioned in one piece to fit closely over his face like a mask. It is solid down to the neck except for eyeholes to see through. The right hand carries a spear of uncommon length; the left is unencumbered, to manage the reins. A scimitar hangs at his side. Not his breast alone but his whole body is sheathed in armor. The armor is fashioned of a number of separate plates of iron or bronze a span square fitting over each other at each of the four sides and hooked or sewn together beneath, the upper lapping over the lower, and the side of each over the edge of the plate next in order. The effect is a shirt of mail which fits easily over the whole body and each limb separately, without hindering or straining movement. The armor is fitted with sleeves and extends from the neck to the knees; only the inside of the hams are uncovered, to facilitate riding. This mail coat deflects any stroke and prevents any wound. The greaves reach from the feet to the knee, where they are attached to the coat. The horse is as well protected as his rider. Greaves cover his legs, and a frontal fitted with a spike protects his whole head. From his back a sheet of iron mail hangs down either flank, loose enough not to impede his movements but at the same time affording him full protection. When the horse is so accoutered and, as it were, molten in his armor, his rider mounts him; because of his weight the rider cannot leap up, but is lifted by others.

When the time for battle comes, the rider loosens his reins, fixes his spurs, and charges his adversaries, looking like an iron man or a solidly wrought statue in motion. His spear extends directly forward much further than the ordinary spear. It is supported by a loop at the horse's neck and its butt is fixed by a noose to its croup. So attached it yields to no shock, but assists the hand of the rider, who merely directs the stroke. Propelled with such great force, the spear penetrates deeply and pierces everything it encounters; frequently it transfixes two opponents at a single stroke.

Such was the satrap's cavalry, and such the disposition of his forces. He marched directly forward, always keeping the river at his rear, using its waters as a wall to prevent encirclement by the far more numerous forces of the Ethiopians. Hydaspes also advanced. To the Medes and Persians on the right wing he opposed the trained warriors of Meroe, who were expert in close combat. The Troglodytes and those who lived near the cinnamon country, who were light-armed, nimble, and excellent archers, he assigned to harry the slingers and javelin throwers on the enemy's left. Being informed that the vaunted armored cavalry held the Persian center, he himself opposed them with his tower-bearing elephants. In front he posted the Blemmyes and Seres, heavy armed men, whom he carefully instructed in what they were to do when the action began.

Standards were raised on both sides. The Persians sounded the signal for battle with trumpets, the Ethiopians with timbrels and tambourines. Oroondates put his phalanxes into motion with a shout. Hydaspes, however, ordered his men to advance more slowly and to change their pace gradually; by this means the elephants would not be left unprotected, and the space over which the enemy had to charge would be lengthened. When they were within range and the Blemmyes saw that the armored cavalry was ready to charge, they proceeded to execute Hydaspes' orders. Leaving the Seres behind as a cover and defense for the elephants they dashed out ahead of their lines at top speed toward the armored cavalry. The Persians thought it was sheer madness for so small a group to charge a force so much larger and so perfectly equipped. Thinking such foolhardiness was a godsend to them and would enable them to sweep the enemy away at the first encounter, they charged the more furiously. But when the Blemmyes were within reach and all but impaled on the spears, they crouched down, supporting themselves on one knee, and avoiding the horses' hoofs they thrust their heads and backs under the horses' bellies. This unexpected maneuver worked great carnage. With their swords they sliced at the horses' bellies as they passed. Pain made the horses disregard the reins and throw their riders. Not a few were thrown, and lay like logs on the ground, where the Blemmyes dispatched them by piercing their hams. When he loses his guide a Persian armored cavalryman is incapable of movement. Those whose horses were unwounded rode on against the Seres, who, at their approach, dodged behind the elephants as if they were a bulwark or fortress. Here the cavalry were virtually annihilated. At the sudden uncovering of these strange animals, so huge and so terrifying, some of the horses turned tail and others piled together in confusion, so that the phalanx was quickly disorganized. The towers on the elephants each had a crew of six archers, two each on the front and sides with only the rear unmanned. These men shot continuously and with sure aim, as from a fortress. So thick were the arrows that to the Persians they seemed a cloud. The Ethiopians made their adversaries' eyes their special target, as if this was no war on equal terms but an exhibition of skill. So faultless was their aim that many of their victims dashed disorderly through the host with arrows sticking out of their eyes like a pair of flutes. Some

of the horses were unable to check their momentum, and
their riders were involuntarily carried up to the elephants.
Here they were either trampled and crushed to death by
the elephants, or attacked by the Seres and Blemmyes, who
made sallies from the protection of the elephants. Some they
succeeded in wounding, others they pulled from their
horses and threw to the ground. The few who escaped
had accomplished nothing and had not injured the elephants. On going to battle those animals wear iron armor,
and in any case have a natural immunity; their thick and
complete covering of scaly skin resists the point of any
spear.

The survivors now turned to a general rout. Most dis-
graceful was the flight of Oroondates, who left his chariot
and fled on a Nisaean horse. The Egyptians and Libyans on
the left wing were unaware of his departure and carried
on the battle with great gallantry. They received more
wounds than they inflicted, yet stood steadfast and resolute.
The men of the cinnamon country who were opposed to
them pressed upon them fearfully and embarrassed them
by their tactics. When charged, they fled to a great distance and shot their arrows backwards even while they
were flying, and when the Persians retreated they attacked
from the flanks, some using sling shots and some shooting
little arrows steeped in the venom of serpents, which caused
immediate and painful death. The archery of the cinnamon
people was more like a game than a serious enterprise. On
their heads they placed a round band, in which they stuck
their arrows in a circle, the feathered ends toward the head
and the points sticking out like so many rays. In battle
they plucked arrows from this band as from a quiver. They
attacked their adversaries, twisting and contorting themselves with abandoned satyr-like leaps and vaults, completely nude except for their crown of arrows. These arrows require no iron for their heads. The cinnamon people

take the dorsal bone of a serpent, about a cubit long, and straighten it, file it down, and sharpen its point to make a natural arrow. That is why our word "arrow" sounds like our word for "bone." For some time the Egyptians stood firm and protected themselves against the arrows with interlocking shields. They are long-suffering by nature and are prodigal of their lives not so much for profit as for glory, and perhaps also for fear of punishment as deserters. But now they learned that the armored cavalry, which they regarded as their strongest force and best hope, had been destroyed, that the satrap had levanted, and that the vaunted Mede and Persian hoplites had performed no brilliant exploits, but had inflicted only some little injury on the troops of Meroe, receiving much worse at their hands, and had followed the others in flight. On this intelligence the Egyptians too gave ground and fled in disorder.

Hydaspes watched the brilliant victory from the vantage of a tower. He sent runners to direct his pursuing men to refrain from slaughter. They were to take as many as they could alive and bring them to him; he was especially desirous of capturing Oroondates. And so it was. The Ethiopians extended their lines on the left, and then reduced their depth and deployed them in length on either side. Then they brought the wings up to encircle the Persians, leaving their enemies no opening for escape except the Nile. Many were thrust into the stream by the horses and scythe-bearing chariots and routed mob. They now saw that the mistaken stratagem of the satrap was unexpectedly turned against themselves. In fear of being surrounded he had originally kept the Nile at his rear, but he had failed to realize that by so doing he was blocking his own retreat. He himself was then taken captive, just at the moment that Achaemenes was plotting to take advantage of the tumult to kill him. He had informed Oroondates of what was going on in Memphis and now regretted his charges

against Arsace because the witnesses who might bear him
out were dead. But the wound Achaemenes inflicted was
not fatal, and he himself was immediately punished for it.
An Ethiopian recognized the satrap and wished to keep
him alive as he had been ordered to do. He was indignant
at seeing a treacherous attempt being made upon one who
had escaped the enemy by a friend who had apparently
been watching for an opportunity to repay a grudge. And
so he shot Achaemenes dead on the spot.

The Ethiopian brought captive Oroondates in gasping
and covered with blood, and when Hydaspes saw him he
had his experts stanch the flow with their incantations. He
was determined to save his life if possible, and spoke words
of encouragement to him. "My dear sir," said he, "it is my
intention to save you. It is a noble thing to surpass an
enemy in valor when he stands before you in battle, but
nobler to show generosity when he has fallen. But why did
you show me such perfidy?" "To you," Oroondates replied,
"I have been faithless, but I have been faithful to my
master." "Now that you have fallen, what punishment do
you think appropriate for you?" Hydaspes asked, and
Oroondates replied, "Such punishment as my own king
would inflict if he found one of your generals keeping
faith." "If he is truly a king, and not a tyrant," said Hydaspes, "he would praise him and send him away with
presents; by praising strangers he would rouse his own
people to emulate their fidelity. But, my good sir, in assert-
ing your fidelity you inculpate your own folly in so rashly
attacking an army of so many thousands." "It was no
folly on my part," said Oroondates. "I understand the
temper of my king; he is more severe in reprehending
cowardice than generous in recognizing valor. I resolved
to confront danger boldly and to achieve some great and
astonishing exploit, for the fortunes of war do admit of
such miracles; if I failed and yet survived, I would have

room for defense, for I could maintain that I had done all that in me lay."

After these exchanges Hydaspes praised Oroondates and sent him to Syene, with orders for the physicians to bestow every care upon him. He himself then entered the city with the elite of his army. All the populace, without distinction of age, went out to meet him; they pelted the army with nosegays and Nile lilies and chanted songs of triumph for Hydaspes. Mounted on an elephant as on a triumphal chariot he entered the city and went directly to the temples to offer thanksgiving to the gods. He asked the priests to show him the noteworthy sights of the city, and in particular inquired about the origin of the festival of the Nile. They showed him the pits which served to measure the rise of the Nile. Like those at Memphis these were built of regular blocks of polished stone, marked with degrees at intervals of a cubit. The river water entered the pit from underground, and the inhabitants were able to measure the rise and fall of the river according as the indices on the stone were covered or laid bare. They also showed him sundials whose upright prong cast no shadow at noon. At Syene the sun's rays fall in a straight perpendicular at the summer solstice and illuminate the whole dial, so that the pointer can cast no shadow. For the same reason the pits are illuminated down to the very bottom. These things Hydaspes did not find very remarkable, for the same phenomena occur at Meroe in Ethiopia. Their festival they praised in reverent terms and they extolled the Nile. They called it Horus, the life-giver of all Egypt, the savior of Upper Egypt, and father and creator of Lower Egypt, for every year it brings new soil (*nea ilus*), whence its name is derived. It marks out the seasons of the year—summer by its rise, autumn by its fall, spring by the flowers which grow upon it and by the breeding of the crocodiles. The

Nile, indeed, symbolizes the year, as its name proves; the numerical value of the letters which compose it amounts to 365, which is the number of the days of the year. They also spoke of the particular flora and fauna of the Nile and extolled the river in many other ways. "But these high praises," said Hydaspes, "belong not to Egypt but to Ethiopia. This river, or god as you call it, and all that it contains is sent here by Ethiopia, which should therefore justly receive your adoration as the mother of your gods." "We do indeed adore it," said the priests, "both on other accounts and because it has vouchsafed us a savior and god in your person."

Hydaspes recommended that they abstain from blasphemous adulation and retired to a tent, where he spent the rest of the day in refreshing himself. He invited the Ethiopian notables and the priests of Syene to a banquet and gave permission to the others to celebrate. The Syenites furnished the army with quantities of beef, mutton, goat, and pork and with abundant wine, partly by gift and partly by sale. The next day Hydaspes sat upon a high throne and distributed to his soldiers, according as he judged the merit of each, pack animals, horses, and other booty which had been taken in the city or on the battlefield. When Oroondates' captor appeared Hydaspes said to him, "Ask whatever you like." "I need ask nothing, your majesty," the man replied. "If such be your pleasure I am content with what I took from Oroondates when, following your orders, I saved his life." With that he displayed the satrap's sheath, which was set with jewels. This was an exceedingly valuable object, worth many talents, and the bystanders shouted out that it was too precious a treasure for a private soldier and worthy only of a king. But Hydaspes smiled and said, "What could be more kingly than for my magnanimity to transcend this man's greed? Moreover the rules of war per-

mit a victor to plunder his prisoner. Let him then receive
from me what he might easily have hidden and kept without my knowledge."

After this the captors of Theagenes and Charicleia came
up and said, "Your majesty, our booty is not gold or precious stones, things common among the Ethiopians and
stored in heaps in your palace. We bring you a girl and a
young man, brother and sister, Greeks by origin. Their
stature and beauty surpass all mankind, next after yourself, and we think we ought not to be unrewarded by your
munificence." "Thank you for bringing them to mind,"
said Hydaspes. "In the excitement and confusion I had but
a cursory view of them. Let someone bring them, and have
the other captives come too." They were brought forthwith; a runner was dispatched to the baggage train outside
the walls, and he ordered their guards to bring them to the
king at once. The two captives asked one of the guards who
was half-Greek where he was taking them and were told
that King Hydaspes was reviewing the prisoners.

At mention of Hydaspes the young people cried out
with one voice, "Ye savior gods!" Up to that moment they
were uncertain whether he was still reigning. Theagenes
whispered to Charicleia, "Darling, you will surely tell the
king who we are. Time and again you have told me that
Hydaspes was your father." "Sweetheart," said Charicleia,
"affairs of weight require weighty preparations. Where the
deity has involved the beginning in an intricate skein, the
denouement requires long unraveling. Nor is it expedient
to uncover in a brief moment matters that have been coated
by layers of time, especially when the principal personage
of the plot, upon whom the entire entanglement and discovery depends—I mean my mother Persinna—is not here
present. But, thank heaven, I hear that she is alive." "But
what if we should first be sacrificed?" interrupted Theagenes. "What if we are given away as a present, like slaves,

and can never get to Ethiopia?" "Nothing is less likely,"
said Charicleia. "You have often heard the guards say that
we are being fattened as victims to be sacrificed to the
gods at Meroe. There is no danger that we shall be given
away or that we shall be killed beforehand. We have been
solemnly consecrated to the gods, and men with religious
scruples would never transgress such a vow. If in our jubila-
tion we blurt out our whole story, with none present able
to confirm and corroborate it, we might unwittingly exacerbate our audience and excite Hydaspes' righteous indignation. He might regard it as an insulting mockery for
captives condemned to slavery to contrive the incredible
fiction of pretending that they are children of the king."
"But the tokens which I know that you have saved and
carry with you," said Theagenes, "will prove that there
is no fiction or deceit." "Tokens," said Charicleia, "are
tokens only to those who recognize them or exposed them
with me. To those who do not or cannot recognize them
they are merely treasures and jewels, which might, indeed,
attach a suspicion of thievery or brigandage to those who
carry them. Even if Hydaspes should recognize them, how
could he believe that it was Persinna who gave them to me,
that they were a gift from mother to daughter? The only
infallible token of recognition, Theagenes, is a mother's
instinct. From the first contact the maternal instinct con-
ceives a tenderness for its offspring and is moved by an inexpressible affinity. Let us not deprive ourselves of the one
token which will give credit to all the rest."

This conversation brought them near the king. Bagoas,
too, had been led into his presence. When Hydaspes saw
them standing near, he started from his seat and said, "Ye
gods, be merciful!" Then he sat down, wrapped in thought.
The dignitaries who surrounded him asked what the matter
was. "I dreamt that just such a girl was born to me and
that she suddenly grew to womanhood," said he. "I paid

no attention to the dream, but the striking resemblance recalled it to me." His courtiers remarked that imagination often presaged and boded forthcoming events. Passing over his vision for the present, he asked who they were and whence they came. Charicleia remained silent, and Theagenes said that they were Greek brother and sister. "Well done, Greece!" said he. "It produces fine and noble specimens and has supplied us with appropriately symbolic victims for our thanksgiving sacrifices." Then he smiled and said to his companions, "But why was not a son, too, born to me in my dream if this youth is the girl's brother and, as you say, we must look upon dreams as presages of the future?" Then he addressed himself to Charicleia, speaking in Greek (the gymnosophists and the kings of Ethiopia study the language): "Why are you silent, girl?" said he. "Why do you not answer my question?" "At the altars of the gods for whom we are kept as victims," said she, "you will know me and my begetters." "And where on earth are they?" said he to her. "They are here," she replied, "and will surely be present at my sacrifice." Again Hydaspes smiled. "The dream-born daughter of mine is surely herself dreaming," said he, "when she imagines that her parents will be transported from Greece to the middle of Meroe. Take them away and tend them well so that they shall make our sacrifice decorative. But who is that standing near, with the air of a eunuch?" "He is indeed a eunuch," said one of the attendants. "His name is Bagoas and he is highly valued by Oroondates." "Let him follow along," said the king, "not as a sacrifice but as a guardian of one of the victims, the girl. Her beauty necessitates very great care to assure her remaining pure until the time of sacrifice. Eunuchs are naturally a jealous breed and suitable for barring others from pleasures which they are themselves denied."

Having said this he passed the other captives in review

and decided their lot. Those whom fortune had originally
made slaves he gave away as gifts; the well born he gave
their liberty. Ten young men and as many maidens in the
prime of youth and of outstanding beauty he selected to
serve the same purpose as Theagenes and Charicleia, and
he gave orders that those should accompany them. After
he had attended to all other individual requests he turned
to Oroondates, who had been carried in on a litter. "Now
I have attained the objectives of the war," said he. "Philae
and the emerald mines, which were the cause of hostility,
I have made my own. I am not afflicted with the common
disease and will not convert my success to ambition, nor
expand my realm by conquests. I am content with the
boundaries by which nature originally separated Egypt
from Ethiopia—the cataracts. Now that I have obtained
that for which I marched forth, I revere justice and retire
again. Do you, if you recover, continue as satrap, and send
this word to the Persian king: 'Your brother Hydaspes has
proved victorious, but has been minded to release what is
yours to you. He welcomes—if you are willing to give it—
your friendship, the fairest boon of mortal men; but if you
renew hostilities he will not be backward.' As for the
Syenites, I remit their fixed tribute for ten years, and bid
you do likewise."

Upon these words cries of approval were raised by citi-
zenry and soldiers alike, and the applause resounded for a
great distance. Oroondates stretched out his two arms,
crossed the right over the left, bowed low and did obeisance; this is a gesture which the Persians are accustomed
to employ to no one except their own king. "I do not
think I am transgressing my ancestral usage," said he to
the bystanders, "if I acknowledge as king him who bestowed my satrapy upon me, or that I am violating the law
in paying obeisance to the most law-abiding of all men,
who charitably gave me life when it was his right to kill

me, and who made me satrap when he might justly have made me slave. In return for these benefits I pledge profound peace and eternal friendship between Ethiopians and Persians, if I recover, and for the Syenites I shall do as I am bidden. But if I do not live, may the gods grant Hydaspes and the house of Hydaspes and all his line requital for his benefactions to me."

10

FOR THE EVENTS that took place at Syene the above account must suffice. From the brink of terrible danger the city was restored to happiness by the clemency of a single individual. Hydaspes sent the main part of his army ahead, and himself marched towards Ethiopia, escorted for a good distance by all the Syenites and all the Persians, who called blessings down upon him. At first he proceeded along the banks of the Nile or the country adjacent to the river, but when he reached the cataracts he sacrificed to the Nile and to the deities of the frontier and then turned his march inland. At Philae he gave his army a respite of two days, again sent the greater part of his forces, including the captives, forward, and himself remained long enough to repair the walls of the city and establish a garrison in it. Before he set out he sent ahead two selected riders who were to change horses at every city and village and so speed the glad tidings of victory to Meroe.

To the sages called gymnosophists, who are assessors and advisers to the king in affairs of moment, he wrote the following: "King Hydaspes to the sacred synod: I give you tidings of victory over the Persians. I do not vaunt success,

for I deprecate the mutability of fortune, but write to
render homage to your prophecy which has on this occasion
as always proven true. I invite you and enjoin you to be
present at the customary place so that your presence may
render our thanksgiving sacrifices for victory more august
in the eyes of the Ethiopian people." To his wife Persinna
he wrote as follows: "Know that we are victorious and,
what concerns you more nearly, safe and sound. Prepare
magnificent processions and thanksgiving sacrifices. Invite the sages, to whom I also have sent instructions, to
hasten with you to the field outside the city which is dedicated to our ancestral gods—Sun, Moon, and Dionysos."

When these letters were delivered Persinna said, "This,
then, was the dream I saw last night. I imagined I was
pregnant and in labor and brought forth a daughter who
was straightway ripe for marriage. The travail of my
dream doubtless symbolizes the agonies of war, and the
daughter victory. But go into the city and fill it with this
joyful news." The runners did as they were bidden. Their
heads crowned with Nile lotus, and waving branches of
palm in their hands, they rode through the principal streets
of the city publishing the news of the victory by their
very appearance. Meroe was at once filled with gladness.
Night and day there were dancing and sacrifices to the
gods in every family, every quarter, and every tribe, and
the temples were decorated with garlands. It was not so
much for the victory that they rejoiced as for the safety of
Hydaspes who, by his justice, benevolence, and affability to
his subjects, had inspired his people with filial love.

Persinna had sent to the field before the city herds of
horses, sheep, antelopes, gryphons, and various other species of animals. There were enough to supply a hecatomb
of each species for sacrifice and to furnish a feast for the
people. Then she went to the gymnosophists, who lived in
the temple of Pan. She delivered to them the letter of

Hydaspes and supported the king's invitation by request-
ing that they gratify her also by honoring the festival with
their presence. They asked her to wait a little, and entered
the sanctuary to offer prayer as was their custom and to
ask the gods what course to follow. After a short interval
they returned; the remainder of the synod kept silence,
and only Sisimithres, their president, spoke. "Persinna,"
said he, "we shall come, for the gods permit it. But the
deity foretells that the sacrifice will be attended by disturbance and tumult which, however, will be turned to
delight in the end. Some member of your body or some
limb of the state has been lost, and fate will then reveal
that for which you seek." "Even the most fearsome situation will take a turn for the better if you are present,"
said Persinna. "When I learn that Hydaspes is coming I
shall inform you." "There is no need to inform us," said
Sisimithres. "He will arrive tomorrow morning, and you
will presently receive a letter to that effect."

And so it was. When Persinna returned and was approaching the palace a horseman handed her a letter from
the king announcing that he would arrive on the morrow.
Heralds at once spread the news. Only men were permitted
to go out to welcome the king; women were forbidden to
do so. Since the sacrifices were to be performed to Sun and
Moon, the purest and most resplendent of deities, it was
forbidden for women to mingle in the crowd lest the rites
be affected by even an involuntary pollution. The only
woman permitted to be present was the priestess of the
Moon, and this was Persinna. Law and custom dictated
that the king should be priest of the Sun and the queen
priestess of the Moon. Charicleia, of course, was also to be
present at the ceremonies—not, however, as a spectator
but as a sacrificial victim to the Moon. The movement
that seized the city was irresistible. The people did not
wait for the day announced but crossed the river Asta-

borra in the evening, some by the bridge and others on
boats. These are made of reeds and are to be found in
abundance at many points on the bank to afford a quick
crossing for those who live at a distance from the bridge.
They are very speedy because of the lightness of their material and can carry a load of only two or three persons.
The reeds are split down the middle, and each half makes
a boat.

Meroe, the metropolis of Ethiopia, is situated on a tri-
angular island surrounded by three navigable rivers—the
Nile, the Astaborra, and the Asasoba. The Nile flows down
upon the island from above and divides to either side of
the island. The other two pass the island on either side and
then join in a single stream with the Nile, to which they
surrender their names. The island is very large and might
be taken for a continent; its length is 3000 furlongs, its
width 1000. It supports very large animals, among them
the elephant, and its fertile soil also produces trees beyond
the common size. Gigantic palm trees bear enormous and
succulent dates. The stalks of wheat and barley are tall
enough to hide a man mounted on a horse or even a camel.
The island multiplies what is sown 300-fold. The growth
of the reed is as I have indicated above.

All night, then, the people crossed the river at one
point or another, and they went out to welcome Hydaspes
and to extol him as a god. These had gone a considerable
way, but the gymnosophists waited to meet him only a
little in front of the field. They shook hands and then embraced and kissed him. After them Persinna waited, in
the forebuilding within the temple precinct. There they
prostrated themselves to the gods and offered prayers of
thanksgiving for victory and safety. Then they left the
sacred precinct, and addressed themselves to the public
sacrifice. They took their seats in a pavilion which had
been erected on the field. This was fashioned of four freshly

cut canes, which were fixed to serve as pillars at four
corners of a square. The tops of the canes were bent to
meet together and form a vault, which was roofed over
with palm branches and other material. Near this was another pavilion, raised on a platform, in which were placed
images of the native gods and heroes, Memnon, Perseus,
and Andromeda, whom the rulers of Ethiopia regard as
the founders of their race. On a lower platform, under
their deities, as it were, sat the gymnosophists. Surrounding these a phalanx of hoplites was posted in a circle. Their
shields were fixed upright and touched one another, to keep
the multitude off and provide a clear space within which
the ceremonial could be performed without disturbance.
Hydaspes addressed the people briefly, reporting the victory
and the benefits it brought to their country, and then
ordered the sacred ministers to begin their rites. Three
altars were raised to a great height, two in one part, joined
to one another, to the Sun and the Moon, and the third,
alone and in another part, to Dionysos. Upon this last they
immolated animals of various species, because, as I suppose,
Dionysos is a universal deity, gracious to all and to be
appeased with a variety of offerings. On the other altars
they sacrificed four white horses to the Sun, appropriately
devoting the speediest of animals to the speediest of divinities, and to the Moon a yoke of oxen, appropriately conse-
crating to the deity who is nearest the earth the animals
who help work the earth.

While these activities were still in progress indistinct
and tumultuous shouts arose such as might be expected
from a vast and promiscuous multitude. "Let our ancestral
rites be performed," the spectators cried; "let the sacrifice
prescribed for the safety of our nation be performed, let
the first fruits of the war be offered to our gods." Hydaspes
understood that it was a human sacrifice they desired, an
offering which it was customary to make only of captives

taken in a war against an alien enemy. He waved his hand and signified by a gesture that their demand would soon be satisfied and ordered the captives who had long ago been designated for the purpose to be brought forward. These, including Theagenes and Charicleia, were led in, now freed of their chains and wearing garlands. The rest, as was natural enough, were downcast, though Theagenes was less sad than the others; but Charicleia's face was shining and she smiled. She looked fixedly at Persinna, so that the queen was moved at the sight of her. "Ah, husband," she said with a deep sigh, "what a girl you have chosen for the sacrifice! I think I have never seen such beauty. How noble is her look! How proudly she bears her fortune! What a pity to perish in the bloom of life! If my own little girl, my sole offspring who was so miserably lost, had chanced to survive she would be about the same age. Would, my husband, that it were somehow possible to save this girl. It would give me great solace to have her serve me. Perhaps the poor girl is Greek; her face is not Egyptian." "She is Greek," said Hydaspes to her, "and presently she will say who her parents are. Show them she cannot; how could she?—though she did promise she would. But to deliver her from the sacrifice is impossible. I would like to, for I, too, am strangely moved and have compassion for the girl. But you know that the law prescribes that a male be offered and sacrificed to the Sun and a female to the Moon. She was the first captive brought to me and was designated for the present sacrifice, and the people could never understand why she should be exempted. Only one thing can save her—if when she undergoes trial by fire, as you know she must, she is proven to have lost her chastity by having co-habited with a man. The law enjoins that the victim offered to the goddess must be pure, and that offered to the Sun also; concerning the sacrifices offered to Dionysos it is indifferent. But consider whether it would be proper for a woman who was proven to have had sexual relations to be received into your house." "Let her be proven unchaste," said Persinna, "provided only she be saved. Captivity, war, long wandering away from her native land would excuse a slip, and especially in a girl whose beauty must have exposed her chastity to constant attack."

She was still speaking, and trying to hide her tears from the bystanders, when Hydaspes ordered the brazier to be brought. The ministers then collected a number of boys below the age of puberty (only such could touch the brazier with impunity), and these brought it from the temple and placed it in the midst of the assembly. Then each of the captives was ordered to step up on it. The brazier was fitted with a grill of golden bars which possessed such virtue that any impure or perjured person who touched it was immediately burned, while others could tread upon it with impunity. Most of those who stepped on the grill had their soles burned at once, some being unable to endure the first slight contact with it. These were destined for Dionysos and the other gods. Only two or three of the young women did the brazier prove to be virgin.

Theagenes in his turn ascended the brazier and was proven chaste. All admired his stature and beauty, and wondered that so handsome a man, in the prime of youth, should have had no experience of Aphrodite. As he was being destined for sacrifice to the Sun he said softly to Charicleia, "The Ethiopians understand how to reward pure living; slaughter and immolation is the prize of chastity. But, my darling, why do you not declare yourself? What occasion are you waiting for? Until the knife is at your throat? Speak, I beg you, and reveal your identity. Perhaps you can save me, too; if you are recognized you can intercede for me. If not, you at least will certainly escape the danger, and if I know that you have, I shall be content to die." "My cue is near," said Charicleia, "our fate now

hangs in the balance." Without waiting for the order of
the guards she took out of the scrip which she carried the
sacred robe of Delphi, woven with gold thread and embroidered with rays. She loosened her hair and like a
woman inspired ran forward and leapt upon the brazier.
There she stood for a long while, without hurt. Her beauty
shone forth more resplendent than ever; mounted upon the
brazier she was observed by every eye, and her impressive
vestment made her seem more like the statue of a goddess
than a mortal woman. All were struck with astonishment
and admiration. Inarticulate cries of wonder ran through
the crowd. They admired her superhuman beauty but were
more astonished that such a bloom of loveliness had been
preserved untouched: her chastity was a finer adornment
than her ornaments. Yet were they distressed that she had
been found suitable for sacrifice, and despite their religious
sentiments would have been delighted to see her saved by
some *deus ex machina*. Most distressed of all was Persinna,
who could not refrain from speaking to her husband:
"How luckless and hapless is this girl! How untimely her
just pride in her chastity! For all her praiseworthy virtue
her recompense is death. But husband, can nothing be
done?" "It is in vain that you importune me," said he, "in
vain you pity the girl; she cannot be saved. So surpassing
a character as hers seems to have been destined for the
gods from the beginning."

Then he turned to address the gymnosophists and said:
"Sages, everything is ready; why do you not begin the
rites?" "Watch your speech!" said Sisimithres, speaking in
Greek, so that the multitude might not understand. "We
have been sufficiently polluted by what we have seen and
heard up to this point. We shall retire into the temple; we
regard human sacrifices as impious, and do not believe that
the deity welcomes them. We could wish that sacrifices of
other living creatures were also forbidden, for in our judg-

ment prayers and incense are sufficient. Do you remain;
a king is sometimes obliged to comply when the impulses
of the crowd are ill considered. Carry out this unhallowed
sacrifice which the ancestral usages of Ethiopian custom
make inevitable. But afterward you will require purifica-
tion—but perhaps you will not require it. I cannot think
that this sacrifice will be consummated. I am led to this
belief by certain divine tokens and particularly by the
luminous splendor which envelops the strangers. This signifies that some deity is protecting them."

When he had said this he arose, along with his colleagues,
and made ready to retire. But Charicleia sprang from the
brazier, ran up to Sisimithres, and fell at his knees. The
attendants thought she meant to beg respite from death
and tried to restrain her, but she said, "Sages, wait but a
moment. I have a case to plead before the king and queen,
and I understand that you alone have jurisdiction in such
a suit. You must be the arbiters in this contest for my life.
You shall learn that it is neither possible nor just for me to
be immolated to the gods." They accommodated themselves readily to her petition and said, "Your majesty, you
hear the challenge and allegation of this foreign woman?"
Hydaspes smiled and said, "What suit can lie between me
and this woman? What pretext or what equity can she
invoke?" Said Sisimithres, "That, her own declarations will
show." "Would it not seem an indignity rather than a
lawsuit for a king to enter into litigation with a slave?"
"Justice shows no respect to persons," Sisimithres answered
him. "In judgment he alone is king whose arguments are
superior." "But it is only in suit with natives," said
Hydaspes, "not with foreigners, that the law permits you
to sit in judgment upon a king." "In the eyes of the wise,"
said Sisimithres, "judgment acquires validity not merely
by appearances, but also by conduct." "It is clear," said
Hydaspes, "that she can have nothing serious to say. As

is common for persons in danger of death, she will invent
some empty tale to gain time. Nevertheless, let her speak,
since Sisimithres so desires."

Charicleia was sanguine in the expectation of deliverance
from imminent peril, but when she heard the name of
Sisimithres she was overjoyed. He was the man who had
taken her up when she was first exposed and had handed
her over to Charicles ten years before, when he was sent
as ambassador to Oroondates at Catadupa on the business
of the emerald mines. Then he was merely one of many
gymnosophists; now he had been designated their president.
His face Charicleia did not recall, for she was a young
child, only seven years old, when they were separated. But
she did recognize his name, and it filled her with joy, for
she expected that she would have an advocate and helper
in effecting her recognition. Stretching her hands out to
heaven she cried out in a clear and audible voice, "O
Sun, founder of my line, and ye other gods and heroes who
were leaders of my race, be ye my witnesses that I utter no
falsehood. Support me in the judgment which lies before
me. Of the available arguments I begin with the first. Is
it natives or foreigners, your majesties, that the law prescribes for sacrifice?" "Foreigners," said the king. "Then
must you seek other victims," said she, "for you will find
that I am native born."

The king was surprised and declared she was romancing,
but she said, "You wonder at lesser things, but there are
greater to come. Not only am I a native, but of royal
blood and very closely related to the king." This speech
aroused Hydaspes' contempt as being mere folly, but
Charicleia continued, "Cease, father, treating your daughter with disdain." Now the king not only showed his contempt but was angry at what she said, considering it pure
insult and mockery. "Sisimithres and you others," he said,
"you see how my patience is tried? The girl is downright

crazy. She is trying to put her death off with the most brazen lies. In her desperation she introduces herself as my daughter, like a *deus ex machina*. You know I was never so fortunate as to have children. There was one, but I heard of its death at the moment I heard of its birth. Take her away, someone, before she thinks up another delay for the sacrifice." "No one shall take me away," cried Charicleia, "until the judges so order. You are a party to this suit, not the judge. The law may enjoin that aliens be killed; but neither the law nor nature, father, permits the killing of your own children. And though you deny it the gods will this day prove that you are my father. Every suit and every case at law, your majesty, recognized two principal kinds of proof, written affidavits and the oral testimony of witnesses. I shall advance both kinds to prove that I am your daughter. As witness I cite not the first comer but my judge himself; a defendant can acquire no greater credit than when the judge himself has knowledge of his claims. As affidavit I produce the narrative of my fortunes—and yours."

So saying she brought forth the ribbon which had been exposed with her and which she wore around her waist, unrolled it, and handed it to Persinna. As soon as she saw it Persinna became speechless and numb. For a long time she stared alternately at the writing on the ribbon and at the girl. She trembled and quivered and flowed with perspiration. She was rejoiced at the discovery, but at a loss how to confront this unexpected and incredible event. She feared these developments might provoke Hydaspes' suspicion, his incredulity, perhaps his anger, and then punishment. Hydaspes observed her confusion and the agony she was in, and said, "My wife, what is this? Why does this writing so trouble you?" "My king," she said, "my master, my husband, there is nothing for me to say. Take it and read. The ribbon will tell you all." She handed him the ribbon, and then relapsed into anxious silence. Hydaspes received the ribbon and bade the gymnosophists come near and read it with him. As he read the writing he himself was filled with amazement, but Sisimithres was even more astonished. His expression revealed a kaleidoscope of emotions; he looked eagerly at the ribbon and then fixed his gaze on Charicleia. Finally, when Hydaspes had reached the account of the exposure and its reason, he said, "That a girl was born to me I know, and at the time I was informed that she had died. Now I learn, and Persinna herself asserts, that she was exposed. Who took her up, preserved her, brought her up? Who brought her to Egypt where she was made prisoner? How do I know that this is the same girl? The exposed child may have perished and another have come upon the tokens and exploited her opportunity. Perhaps some deity is making sport of us. He has taken on the appearance of this girl and is amusing himself with our eagerness for posterity. He will make a supposititious and illegitimate child my successor and veil the truth with this ribbon as with a cloud."

Hereupon Sisimithres said, "For your first question there is a ready answer. I am the man who took the exposed infant up and secretly reared it and brought it to Egypt when you sent me there on an embassy. You know that I am not allowed to lie. I recognize the ribbon which, as you see, is embossed with Ethiopian characters, which resolve all doubt of its origin. You yourself can best recognize Persinna's own handiwork. But there were other tokens exposed with the child. I gave them to the Greek who received her from me. He was to all appearances a gentleman." "I have those too," said Charicleia, and displayed the jewels. When Persinna saw these she was even more agitated; when Hydaspes asked her what the matter was and if she had any further means of proof, she answered that she had but that examination of them had best be

made indoors. Again Hydaspes seemed perplexed, and
Charicleia said, "These tokens are my mother's, but this ring
is your own." She showed him the Pantarbe, and Hydaspes
recognized it as the present he had given Persinna at their
betrothal. "My dear," he said, "the tokens are mine; but
that you who make use of them are mine and not some
stranger who has acquired them I am not yet certain. Aside
from other considerations, your complexion is totally unlike an Ethiopian's."

Here Sisimithres intervened: "The child I took up was
white, and the interval of time corresponds to the age of
this girl. It is about seventeen years since the exposure. I
recall the look of her eyes, moreover; indeed I recognize
the character of her over-all appearance and her superlative
beauty, which correspond to what she was then." "All of
this is very fine, Sisimithres," Hydaspes said to him, "but
you speak as an ardent advocate rather than as a judge. But
when you clear up one trouble, take care that you do not
raise another more serious difficulty which is in fact in-
soluble. This affects my consort: how could we two, both
Ethiopians, produce a white child?" Sisimithres glanced up
at him from under his brows and smiled ironically. "I do
not know what has come over you," he said, "that you
should deny your true character and reproach me with
partisanship. I do not regard partisanship as culpable, for
I consider the advocate of justice the truest to judge. And
why should you look upon me as the girl's advocate more
than yours? With the help of the gods I am proving that
you are a father. This daughter I preserved for you when
she was in swaddling clothes; should I abandon her now
that she has survived to adulthood? But of me think what
you will; I offer no apology. We direct our lives not to
please others; we strive for what is fair and good, and our
ambition is to satisfy our own standards. As to the difficulty concerning the girl's complexion, the ribbon here

provides a clear solution. In it Persinna avows that she conceived a certain impression of the likeness of Andromeda from viewing her picture when she consorted with you. If you wish to convince yourself further, the original is available; examine the Andromeda; the picture will show an unmistakable resemblance to the girl."

Servants were sent to fetch the picture, and they set it up beside Charicleia. The striking accuracy of the likeness filled everyone with joy, and there was general and tumultuous applause. Those who had some comprehension of what had been said and done informed their neighbors. Even Hydaspes could no longer doubt, and mingled surprise and delight held him speechless. "One point still remains," said Sisimithres. "The issue concerns royalty and the legitimacy of the succession, and, above all, it concerns truth itself. There was a black birthmark etched out above the elbow. Bare your arm, girl; there is nothing indecent in uncovering it to prove your family and kin." Charicleia at once bared her left arm, and there could be seen a black circle etched on the ivory of her skin.

Now Persinna could no longer contain herself. She sprang from her throne and ran up to Charicleia and embraced her and tearfully clung to her. Her transports of joy were expressed in a kind of moaning: the manifestations of excess of happiness are often like those of grief. It wanted but little for both to fall fainting. When Hydaspes saw his wife in tears he pitied her and his spirit was moved to compassion, but he kept his eyes glued on the spectacle as if they were horn or iron and fought off anguish and tears. His spirit was tossed between the waves of paternal emotion and manly fortitude; strife between these impulses agitated his mind, he was drawn irresistibly to one and then the other, but finally he succumbed to overpowering instinct and not only believed that he was a father but demonstrated a father's emotions. Persinna and her daughter had sunk to the ground in a close embrace. Hydaspes raised them up and openly embraced his daughter and consecrated his paternity with a libation of tears.

Nevertheless, he was not wholly distracted from his obligations. For a moment he stood looking down upon his people. They were moved by similar emotions and shed tears of delight and compassion at the spectacle fortune had staged. They raised an awesome cry to the very heavens and paid no heed to the heralds who were enjoining silence, though they did not clearly signify the meaning of the disturbance. The king raised his hand and gestured for silence and stilled the tumult of his people.

"All ye here present," said he, "the gods have made me a father, as you have seen and heard, beyond all expectation. This girl is identified as my daughter by many proofs. But so great is my love for you and for my country that I am ready to disregard the perpetuation of my race and the dear title of father, both aspirations which she can fulfill, and to sacrifice her to the gods for your sake. I see that you weep and manifest a natural human emotion; I see that you pity the girl's youth and the frustration of my own hope for an heir. But it is nevertheless necessary, even if it happens that you do not desire it, that I obey our ancestral law and prefer the public welfare to my private interests. Can it be pleasing to the gods to give and take away at the same time? That is what happened when she was born, and now happens again when she is found. I know not what to say, and I leave it to you to decide whether the gods now find acceptable the sacrifice of the girl whom they exiled from her native land to the ends of the earth and whom they then brought back and miraculously delivered into my hands as a prisoner of war. When she was my enemy I did not slay her and when she became a captive I did not harm her; but now she is proven to be my daughter I shall not hesitate to sacrifice her if such is your pleasure. I will not yield to the emotion that might be pardonable in another father; I will not importune you nor implore your permission to suspend the law in this case and to subordinate it to instinct and the affections which nature inspires on the argument that the deity may be appeased by other means. Because your sympathy is obvious and because you ache with my pains as if they were your own, it is all the more my duty to place your interests above my own. I must disregard the loss of my sole heir, I must disregard the distress of poor Persinna here, who is made a new mother and childless at the same time. Dry your tears then, and cease pitying me in vain; let us get on with the sacrifice. And you, my daughter—that name I yearned for I now utter for the first time and the last— in vain your beauty, in vain have you recovered your parents. Your own country you find more cruel than foreign lands, unhappy girl! Abroad you were preserved alive, at home you are destroyed. Do not melt my spirit with plaints; now if ever is the time to show your virile spirit, your royal temper. Follow your father; I cannot clothe you in a marriage robe, I cannot lead you to the bridal canopy. It is for sacrifice that I adorn you, and the torches I light are not for marriage but for immolation. Your incomparable beauty I offer as a sacrifice. Pardon, ye gods, my words if, overcome by emotion, I have uttered impiety—a man who greets his child and simultaneously proves its slayer."

So saying he laid hands upon Charicleia, making a show of leading her to the altars and their fires. But his heart was smouldering with a hotter fire, and he prayed for the failure of his captious speech to the people. The Ethiopian multitude was deeply stirred by what he said and would not suffer Charicleia to be led a step farther. A great clamor suddenly arose. "Save the girl!" they shouted, "save the blood royal, save her whom the gods have saved!

We shall be content; our law has been satisfied. We have
acknowledged you our king; do you acknowledge yourself a father. The gods will look kindly on this seeming
transgression. A greater transgression would we commit
by opposing their will. Let no one slay whom they would
preserve. You are father to your people; be no less father
to your own household." A thousand exclamations of
this sort were uttered, and finally the people showed their
resistance would go beyond words. They stood in front
of Hydaspes and opposed him, and they demanded that
the deity be appeased through other sacrifices. Willingly
and gladly did Hydaspes suffer defeat, voluntarily he submitted to the violence he prayed for. When he saw that
the people long continued to indulge in shouted felicitations
to one another and were actually skipping about in their joy
he permitted them to continue their manifestations of pleasure and waited for them to subside to silence of their own
accord.

Hydaspes himself approached Charicleia and said, "Darling, the tokens indicate that you are my daughter, and
wise Sisimithres has testified to the fact. The benevolence
of the gods is proven. But who is the man who was captured with you, the man who has been kept for the triumphal offerings to the gods and is now standing by the
altars ready to be sacrificed? How did you come to call
him brother when you both were first brought to me at
Syene? Surely he too cannot be found to be our son;
Persinna gave birth only once, and you were her only
child." Charicleia hung her head and blushed. "I lied about
his being my brother; need compelled me to fabricate.
Who he is he himself can best tell you. A man can speak
more boldly than a woman and can explain matters without shame." Hydaspes did not grasp the import of her
words, and said, "Pardon me, child, if I embarrassed your
maidenly modesty by my indiscreet inquiries concerning

the young man. But go and rest in the pavilion with your mother. Let her take her joy of you, greater than her travail when she bore you. Give her pleasure by your presence and comfort her with the story of your adventures. I must take care of the sacrifices and try to find a worthy victim to immolate with the young man in your place."

Chariclea almost shrieked aloud, so harrowing was the mention of Theagenes' slaughter. With difficulty could she hold fast to the ultimate advantage and master her frenzied feelings to serve the need of cautiously attaining her goal. "Master," she said, "perhaps it is not necessary for you to find another girl, once the people have remitted the sacrifice of a female in my person. But if anyone insists that victims of each sex must be sacrificed, you should seek not only a girl but also another young man. If you do not, then do not seek another girl either but sacrifice me." "Hush!" said he, and asked her why she said such a thing. "Because," said she, "it is fated that I must live with this man if he lives and die with him if he dies."

Hydaspes still did not grasp the situation and said, "I admire your charity, my daughter. Here is a foreigner, a Greek, a contemporary, a fellow captive, with whom you have contracted a familiarity during your exile. It is humane of you to pity him and try to save him. But it is impossible for him to be exempted from the sacrifice. It would be altogether sacrilegious for our ancestral rite of thanksgiving sacrifices to be entirely abandoned. Nor would the people tolerate it; it was only with the gods' help that they were moved to yield in your case." "Your Majesty," said Chariclea, "—father perhaps I may not call you—if my body has been saved by the benevolence of the gods, that same benevolence must save my soul. So closely have they interwoven his fate and mine that they know he is my soul. But if the fates be found unwilling, and the sacrifice must inevitably be adorned by the slaughter of the foreigner, do grant me this one favor: bid that the sacrifice be performed by my hand. I shall receive the sword as a precious treasure and demonstrate my fortitude in the sight of all the Ethiopians."

At these words Hydaspes was confounded. "I do not understand this sudden reversal. Just before you were trying to defend the stranger and now you ask to slaughter him as if he were your enemy. For a girl of your position and age I can see nothing dignified or glorious in such an act. Even if there were, you could not do the deed, for according to traditional law it is reserved solely to the priests of the Sun and Moon. For this service it is further required that the priest of the Sun have a wife and the priestess of the Moon a husband, so that your virginity alone would preclude your unaccountable request." "As for that," Charicleia stooped and whispered into Persinna's ear, "there is no obstacle; there is someone who is ready to give me the title of wife if you but give your consent." "We shall give our consent," said Persinna with a smile, "and we will marry you at once, heaven willing, if we find someone who is worthy of you and of ourselves." "Then," said Charicleia, raising her voice, "you need search no longer; he is already found."

She was on the point of speaking more openly, for the imminent danger for Theagenes was before her very eyes and compelled her to cast maidenly reserve aside and take a bold stand. But Hydaspes now lost patience and cried, "Ye gods! How you do seem to mingle evil with good! The unhoped-for bliss you have bestowed upon me you mar; you present me with a daughter I never expected, but she is evidently mad. Surely her mind must be touched when her speech is so incoherent. She calls a man her brother when he is not, and when she is asked who the stranger is she says she does not know. Again she is eager to save this unknown man, as if he were a friend; and when she learns that this is impossible she begs to kill him with her own hand as if he were her worst enemy. When we tell her that this is forbidden, such sacrifice being reserved for a wedded woman, she declares that she has a husband, but who he is she does not say. How could she, when the ordeal of the brazier proves that she is unmarried? Surely it cannot be that the Ethiopians' infallible test of chastity has falsified only in her case, and by dismissing her from the fire unscathed has favored her with a spurious reputation for chastity. Would it exempt one who called the same persons friends and enemies simultaneously and invented imaginary brothers and husbands? Do you go into the pavilion, dear wife, and try to restore this girl to her sober senses. Either she is being made delirious by the god who is visiting this spot for the sacrifices, or the excessive joy of her unhoped-for good fortune has distracted her mind. I myself shall order someone to search for and find the victim we owe to the gods in her stead. In the interval I shall give audience to the ambassadors from various nations and receive the gifts they have brought to celebrate our triumph."

So saying he mounted an elevated throne near the pavilion and ordered the ambassadors to be introduced and whatever gifts they might have brought to be presented. The Lord High Chamberlain, Hermonias, asked whether they should all be brought in together, or separately according to the nationalities. Hydaspes said they should be brought in separately and in proper order, so that each might receive the honor which was his due. "In that case, Your Majesty," said Hermonias, "the first to be introduced is Meroebos, your brother's son; he has just arrived and is outside the enclosure waiting to be announced." "You stupid simpleton," cried Hydaspes, "why did you not inform me at once? He is not an ambassador, as you well know, but a king, and at that the son of my own brother who has so recently died. It was I who put him on his father's throne, and I regard him as a son." "I was aware of this, my lord," said Hermonias, "but I considered that the duty of a Lord Chamberlain required him beyond all others to preserve a proper time and season. Forgive me; you were conversing with the royal ladies and I was loath to interrupt that pleasure." "Well then, let him come in now," said the king, and Hermonias hustled off and immediately returned with the striking visitor.

Meroebos was a magnificent young man. He had just passed adolescence and was now seventeen years old. In stature he surpassed almost all present, and he was escorted by a brilliant suite of guards. The Ethiopian troops showed their admiration and respect, and broke their circle to make a passage for him. Hydaspes himself did not remain in his seat but rose to meet him. He embraced him with fatherly affection and gave him a seat next to himself. Then he took his right hand and said, "You have come in good time, my boy. You will participate in the triumphal festivities and also offer sacrifices for marriage. The gods and heroes who are the ancestors of our line have found a daughter for me and, as it seems, a bride for you. The details you will hear another time; for the present, if you wish to attend any business for the nation you rule, speak up." At mention of a bride Meroebos was so pleased and at the same time so embarrassed that a blush showed purple even on his black skin; it was as if soot were tinted with a ruddy flame. After a moment of silence he said, "The other ambassadors, father, have brought you each the choicest products of his own country as friendly tokens to crown your renowned victory. As for me, I think it appropriate that your prowess in war and your illustrious gallantry be complimented by a gift of similar quality. I bring you a champion no less invincible in bloody war than unrivaled in wrestling, boxing, and racing." So saying, he motioned for the man to come forward.

The champion came forward and did obeisance to Hydaspes. So huge was the man, so titanic his stature, that even stooping to kiss the king's knee he was on a level with the party seated on the raised platform. Without waiting for orders he stripped, and standing nude challenged all comers to a contest with or without weapons. The herald made repeated proclamations of the challenge, but no one came forward. Then King Hydaspes turned to him and said, "You shall receive a prize commensurate with your prowess," and with that ordered an enormous old elephant to be presented to him. The beast was brought, the champion received it with great pleasure, and the people burst into a shout of laughter. They were delighted at the pleasantry of the king, and consoled themselves for their discomfiture with his derision of the giant's braggadocio.

Next the ambassadors of the Seres were brought forward. These brought silken skeins and webs produced by insects of their country. Some were dyed purple, others were a brilliant white. Their gifts were accepted, and they then petitioned the king for the release of some of their compatriots who had been condemned to imprisonment, and the king granted their request. The ambassadors of Arabia Felix then came in, and filled the place with the fragrance of aromatic herbs, cassia, cinnamon, and other perfumes in which their country abounds, each of the value of many talents. After them ambassadors from the Troglodytes appeared. These brought the gold dust which their ants collect and a team of gryphons guided by golden reins. Next came the embassy of the Blemmyes, bringing bows and sharp arrows made of serpents' bones and arranged in the form of a crown. "Here are our gifts to you, your Majesty," they said. "They fall short of the others in value, but they have proved their worth against the Persians by the river, as you yourself observed." "They are more valuable," said Hydaspes, "than gifts of great price, for it is to them that I owe the other things that are now brought me." At the same time he encouraged them to make any proposals they wished. They requested a reduction in their tribute, and he remitted it to them altogether for ten years.

Almost all the ambassadors had now been received in audience. Each received presents equal to those they had brought, and to many the king presented gifts even more valuable. Finally the envoys of the Auxomites appeared. These were not tributary but friends and allies of the king. To mark their pleasure at his success they too brought presents, and among other things a marvelous animal of extraordinary appearance. His size was about that of a camel; his skin, like that of a leopard, was decorated with spots in a floral pattern. His hindquarters and belly were low and like a lion's; the shoulders, forefeet and chest were of a height out of all proportion to the other members. The neck was slender, and tapered from the large body to a swanlike throat. The head was shaped like a camel's and was almost twice as large as that of a Libyan ostrich. The eyes were brightly outlined and rolled terribly. His heaving walk was unlike the pace of any land or sea animal. He did not move his legs alternately, one after the other, but first put forward his two right legs by themselves, and then the two left, as if they were yoked together. Thus first one side of the animal was raised, and then the other. Yet so docile was his movement and so gentle his disposition that the keeper could lead him by a light cord looped around his neck, and he obeyed the keeper's guidance as if the cord were an irresistible chain. The appearance of this creature astonished the entire multitude, and extemporizing a name for it from the dominant traits of his body they called it camelopard.

But the camelopard occasioned a great disturbance in the assembly. This is what happened. Near the altar of

the Moon there stood a yoke of bulls, and near that of
the Sun a team of four white horses prepared for sacrifice.
At the sudden sight of this strange, unfamiliar, and monstrous creature they were agitated as by some phantom.
Filled with terror one of the bulls (apparently the other
had not seen the creature) and two of the horses broke
their bonds and galloped wildly away. They were unable
to break through the circle of soldiers, whose joined shields
made a tight wall, but they dashed wildly about the space
within and in their mad whirling struck and overturned
everything that came in their way, whether vessels or victims. The incident provoked mingled cries. Those in the
animals' path shrieked in fear, and others howled with glee
at the spectacle of people being knocked over and trodden
upon. At the sounds even Persinna and Charicleia could
no longer remain quiet in their pavilion, but pulled the
hangings aside and so became spectators of what followed.

Theagenes, whether stirred by his native manliness of
spirit or affected by some divine impulse, when he noticed
that the guards posted about him had scattered in the
tumult, suddenly rose upright. He had been crouching on
his knee by the altar, awaiting imminent slaughter. He
seized a piece of kindling that lay near the altar, grasped
one of the horses that had not run away, leapt upon its
back, and using its mane for a bridle, his heel for a spur,
and the kindling for a whip, he galloped in pursuit of the
runaway bull. At first the audience supposed that Theagenes' action was an attempt to escape, and every man
called to his neighbor not to let him pass the barrier of
the soldiers; but as the action proceeded they learned that
his motive was not cowardice or dread of being sacrificed.
As soon as Theagenes caught up with the bull he rode
close behind it for a while, nudging it and urging it on
to greater speed. He followed it close in all its twistings
and turnings, and he deftly dodged whenever the bull

turned to charge him. When he had got it used to his presence and movements, he galloped side by side with it so that the flesh of the animals touched and the horse's breath and sweat mingled with the bull's. The pace of the animals was so equalized that spectators at a distance might fancy that their heads belonged to the same creature. Theagenes was extolled to the skies for having welded the novel team into a hippotaur.

Whereas the multitude was filled with admiration the sight filled Charicleia with fear and trepidation. She did not understand the object of Theagenes' maneuver, was afraid he might tumble, and agonized over his imagined injury as if it were her own death. Persinna perceived her agitation and said, "My child, what ails you? You seem to be anticipating the stranger's danger for him. I, too, am distressed and I pity his youth. I pray that he may escape his peril and be preserved for the sacrifice, so that our obligations to the gods should not be altogether unfulfilled and neglected." "It is absurd," said Charicleia, "to pray that he may not die in order that he may die. But if it is possible, mother, save this man; do this for my sake." Persinna did not understand the true reason of this request, but suspected that it had something to do with love. "It is impossible to save him," said she. "But what is your connection with this man for whom you are so anxious? Do not hesitate to speak out to your own mother. Even if there is some youthful stirring which is indecorous for a maiden, a mother's instinct understands how to forgive her own daughter and a sympathetic woman how to veil the frailty of her own sex." Charicleia burst into a flood of tears and said, "Here is a misfortune in addition to all my others. Even intelligent people find my words unintelligible, and when I speak of my own calamities my words are not heard. I am forced to proceed to a naked and unvarnished accusation against myself."

After this declaration she was on the point of revealing the truth when she was again interrupted by a resounding shout which arose from the multitude. Theagenes had spurred his horse on to its best speed and when he had got a little ahead, so that the chest of his horse was level with the bull's head, he leaped from the horse, which he let run loose, and threw himself on the bull's neck. He put his head between the bull's horns, placed his arms around them like a crown, and laced his fingers together over the bull's forehead. The rest of his body he let hang on the bull's right shoulder, and being carried without touching the ground was little shaken despite the bull's bounding and cavorting. When he felt that the bull was panting with his weight and relaxing its muscles from their high tension, just as he passed the place where Hydaspes was sitting, he shifted his position to the front, entangled his legs with the bull's, and by kicking him continually, hindered his movement. The impetuosity of his onset thus thwarted and his energy worn by Theagenes' vigorous blows, the bull stumbled, fell head first, and rolled over on his shoulders and back. For a while he remained supine, his horns fixed in the ground and his rooted head immovable, while his legs thrashed about in vain, churning the air and proclaiming his defeat. Theagenes placed himself over the bull, but used only his left hand to hold him down; his right he held up to the sky and waved repeatedly. To Hydaspes and the rest of the crowd he turned a happy face, and his smile invited them to join in his pleasure. The bellowing of the bull trumpeted Theagenes' victory, and the shouting crowd re-echoed the blast. There were no articulate words of praise but with mouths gaping they uttered one continuous roar of admiration which rose to the skies as a single and uniform sound. At Hydaspes' bidding servants ran forward, some to bring Theagenes and stand him before the king, others to throw a noose

over the bull's horns. They led him back to the altar,
weak and dispirited, and again tied him up, along with
the horse which they had recovered.

Hydaspes was now preparing to speak with Theagenes
and deal with him. The people had felt a sympathy for the
young man from the moment he appeared and were now
delighted with him. They were greatly impressed with his
exhibition of strength but even more greatly annoyed by
the arrogance of Meroebos' Ethiopian champion, and so
they all shouted as one man, "Let him be matched with
Meroebos' man!" "Let the man who received the elephant
fight the man who took the bull!" they kept shouting. At
their incessant insistence Hydaspes consented. The Ethiopian was brought forward. He glared fiercely about him
and swaggered forward, deliberately throwing out his chest
and slapping his elbows. When he came near the royal pavilion Hydaspes looked at Theagenes and said to him in
Greek, "Stranger, you must fight with this man; the people
demand it." "Their will be done," answered Theagenes.
"What kind of contest shall it be?" "Wrestling," said
Hydaspes. Theagenes said, "Why not with swords and
armor? Whether I succeed or fail I might thus move
Charicleia. She still persists in keeping silence about me,
and seems determined to forget me entirely." "Why you
wish to involve the name of Charicleia in this you may
know best. But you must wrestle and not fight with
swords. It is not lawful for spilled blood to be seen before
the time of the sacrifice." Theagenes understood that
Hydaspes was afraid he might be killed before the sacrifice.
"You do well to keep me for the gods," he said, "they will
have care of me."

So saying he took up dust and poured it over his shoulders and arms, which were dripping with sweat from chas-
ing the bull, and shook off the dust that did not stick.
Then he put his arms straight forward, planted his feet

firmly astride, bent his knees a little, rounded his shoulders
and back, leaned his neck slightly forward, tensed all the
muscles of his body, and stood ready to receive the painful
holds of his adversary. The Ethiopian looked at him with
a sneer and indicated his contempt for his adversary by
sarcastic gestures. Suddenly he rushed forward and struck
Theagenes' neck with his arm as with a crowbar; as the
smack rang out the braggart again preened himself and
laughed exultantly. Theagenes had been brought up in
the gymnasium; from his youth up he had been carefully
trained in the refinements of Hermes' art. He decided to
give ground at first and try out his adversary's strength;
instead of advancing directly against such monstrous mas-
siveness and savage fierceness he would get the better of
brute force by suppleness and skill. He therefore staggered
back from the blow a little and, feigning greater pain than
he felt, exposed the other side of his neck to a blow. The
Ethiopian struck again, and Theagenes yielded to the blow
and pretended to be almost falling on his face. Now the
Ethiopian despised his adversary and was certain of victory. He rushed forward unguardedly, brandishing his
arm for the third blow, when Theagenes suddenly darted
under his guard and dodged to avoid the blow. With his
right Theagenes thrust hard at his adversary's left arm
and, as he was already off balance by reason of having
missed his hard blow with his right, threw him to the
ground. Then he seized his armpits, got upon his back and
with difficulty spanned his stout belly. By kicking vigorously and incessantly at his feet and ankles he forced him
to rise on his knees. Then he straddled over him, pressed
him in the groin with his legs, forced apart the wrists on
which he was supporting himself, twined his arms about
his temples and forced his head back, and so compelled him
to collapse flat, with his belly on the ground.

At this a single long shout, louder than before, was

raised by the crowd. Even the king could not contain himself but sprang from his throne and cried, "Ah, cruel
necessity! What a man does the law compel us to sacrifice!"
At the same time he called Theagenes to him and said,
"Young man, it remains for you to be crowned for the
sacrifice, as custom ordains. You deserve a crown too for
your glorious but unprofitable and ephemeral victory.
Even though I would, I cannot save you from your doom,
but whatever I can do for you I will. If you know of
anything that can give you satisfaction while you are yet
alive, ask for it." So saying he placed upon Theagenes a
crown of gold set with precious stones, and was unable
to dissemble his tears. "Well then," said Theagenes, "I do
make a request, and I beg you to grant it in accordance
with your promise. If it is wholly impossible to avoid the
sacrifice, order that it be carried out by your newly discovered daughter."

This request gave Hydaspes a twinge, and his mind
turned to the similar request made by Charicleia, but in
the press of business he did not think the occasion opportune for thorough inquiry. "Stranger," said he, "I bade
you ask and promised to grant anything possible. But this
the law forbids. She who performs the sacrifice must be a
married woman, not a maid." "But she does have a husband," said Theagenes to him. "This is the delirious bab-
bling of a man about to die," said Hydaspes. "The ordeal
by fire demonstrated that the girl has had no experience of
marriage or of cohabiting with a man. If you are referring
to Meroebos as her husband—how you heard of that I do
not know—he is not yet her husband; he is only her fiancé,
and at my designation." "You may add that he will never
be her husband," said Theagenes, "if I know anything of
Charicleia's mind. And you must believe me, for a victim's
prophecy is inspired." At this Meroebos interposed, "Not
while he is alive, my good sir; it is only when the victims

have been slaughtered and dissected that their entrails reveal the future to the prophets. You are right, father; the stranger talks folly, like a man about to die. Bid someone take him to the altar then, if you will, and when you have attended to anything that remains to be done, begin the ceremony." Theagenes was then led away to the place indicated.

When Theagenes was victorious Charicleia breathed again and conceived better hopes, but now that he was being led away she was again plunged into grief. Persinna tried hard to comfort her, and said, "Perhaps the young man can be saved if you would only tell me the rest of your story plainly and clearly." Pressed by necessity and seeing that the occasion admitted of no delay Charicleia prepared to recount the essentials of her story.

Now Hydaspes inquired of the Lord High Chamberlain whether any embassies remained to be heard. "Only those from Syene, your Majesty," said Hermonias. "They arrived just a short time ago and bring a letter and presents from Oroondates." Hydaspes said, "Let them come in," and they entered and delivered their letter. Hydaspes opened it and read as follows: "To Hydaspes, the merciful and blessed king of the Ethiopians, from Oroondates, viceroy of the Great King: After conquering me in battle you have conquered me still more in magnanimity by voluntarily restoring a whole satrapy to me. I shall not be surprised, therefore, if now you consent to a slight request. A girl who was being brought to me from Memphis was involved in the hazards of war, and I learn from those who were with her and escaped that she was sent to Ethiopia by your orders. I ask that she be released and bestowed upon me as a gift. I myself am eager to see the girl, but am more concerned to restore her to her father. He has roamed over a great part of the world in search of his daughter, and at Elephantine was taken prisoner by the garrison during the war. I saw him when I was reviewing the survivors, and he begged to be sent to your clemency. He is in your presence now with the ambassadors. His manners are sufficient indication of his good birth, and his appearance commands respect. Send him back rejoicing, your majesty; send back one who is not only called but is in fact a father."

When the king had read the letter he asked, "Who of those present is seeking his daughter?" When an old man was pointed out, he said to him, "Stranger, all that Oroondates asks I am ready to do. I ordered only ten young women to be brought as captives. Of these one has been recognized and is surely not your daughter; the others you may examine, and if you recognize your own you may take her." The old man stooped down and kissed the king's feet. The girls were brought, but when he examined them the old man did not find the one he sought and again was plunged in sorrow. "It is none of these, your Majesty," he said. "You have my good will," said Hydaspes; "blame fortune if you cannot find her you seek. You can satisfy yourself by looking around that no other captives were brought besides these and that she is not somewhere about the camp." The old man struck his forehead and burst into tears. Then he raised his eyes and surveyed the crowd in a circle. Suddenly he sprang forward in a frenzy, advanced to the altar, twisted the skirt of the cloak he was wearing into a noose, and threw it over the neck of Theagenes. Then he dragged him off, shouting in a loud voice, "I have you, my enemy, I have you, detestable and execrable villain!" The guards interposed and tried to pull him away by force, but he held fast as if he were glued to him and succeeded in bringing him before Hydaspes and his synod. "Your majesty," he cried, "this is the man who stole my daughter away, this is the man who desolated my house and made it childless. He ravished my soul from the very altar of Apollo, and now he sits at the altars of the gods like some saint." All were thrown into a commotion by these events. Some understood what the old man said; to the others what they saw was astonishing enough.

Hydaspes bade him speak his meaning more clearly, and the old man, who was none other than Charicles, set forth in brief summary so much of his story as was not prejudicial to himself. The true account of Charicleia's birth he concealed, fearing lest he should come into conflict with her true parents if it should prove that she had died in her flight. "I had a daughter, your Majesty," said he. "Only if you saw her could you believe that I speak truthfully of her sagacity and her beauty. She was a virgin and priestess of Artemis in Delphi. This monster, a Thessalian who had come to my city Delphi as a leader of a religious delegation to perform some ancestral rite, secretly abducted the girl from the very shrine of Apollo. This sacrilege may rightly be regarded as affecting you also, for Apollo is your own ancestral deity, being identical with the Sun, and it is his temple the villain has profaned. His accomplice in this impious outrage was a false prophet from Memphis. I hastened to Thessaly to demand him of his fellow citizens of Oeta, but could not find him, though the Thessalians were willing to give him up to execution if he should be found, as a man accursed. I conjectured that they might have taken refuge in Memphis, Calasiris' country, and so went there. Calasiris I found had died, as he deserved, but from his son Thyamis I learned all about my daughter, and among other things that she had been sent to Oroondates at Syene. I missed Oroondates at Syene—I went there too —and was overtaken by the war at Elephantine. I now come here as your suppliant, as is set forth in the letter. The thief you hold. Search for my daughter; you will render a service to a man who has endured much and will find satisfaction in honoring the request of the satrap who has interceded for me." He fell silent and then began sobbing.

Hydaspes turned to Theagenes. "What will you say to this?" said he. "The charges are all true," said he. "To this man I am a thief, a robber, a violent man, an embezzler; but to you I am a benefactor." "Then give back what is another's," said Hydaspes. "You have been consecrated to the gods; suffer a glorious death as a sacrificial victim, not a felon's death as punishment." "Not he who commits the injury but he who holds its object must return it," said Theagenes. "You are the man. Return Charicleia then, unless the old man denies that it is she." None could suppress his emotion, all were stupefied. Sisimithres had long understood the meaning of what was said and done but he had held his peace, waiting for clarity to increase and truth to assert itself. Now he ran forward, embraced Charicles, and said, "She whom you regarded as your daughter, whom you once received from my hands, is safe. She has been recognized by her true parents, whom you know."

Charicleia now rushed out of the pavilion. Disregarding the reserve appropriate to her sex and age she dashed up to Charicles like a bacchant possessed and fell at his knees. "O my father," cried she, "no less revered than my begetters, punish me as you like; I have been impious and a parricide. It does not matter that some god has brought this about and that all has been effected by divine providence."

In another part Persinna embraced Hydaspes and said to him, "It is all true, husband, do not doubt it. That young Greek is really our daughter's fiancé. She has just told me the whole story, though it was hard for her." The people, on the other hand, cried out their blessings and danced for joy. Every age and condition thrilled with delight at what had come about. Most of what had been said they did not understand, but they conjectured the truth from what had taken place with Charicleia. Perhaps the divine impulse which staged these dramatic events brought the people to an understanding of them. Dissonances most diverse it had reduced to harmony, joy and grief were intertwined, laugh-

ter and tears commingled, darkest gloom transformed into
festivity; they that wept laughed and they that lamented
rejoiced, persons not sought were found and those expected
to be found were lost, and finally, the slaughters anticipated were transmuted into pious ceremonies.

Hydaspes asked Sisimithres, "What, great sage, is to be
done? To deny gods their sacrifice is impiety, but to slaughter those vouchsafed us by the gods is sacrilege. We must
consider what must be done." Sisimithres responded not in
Greek, but in Ethiopic, so that all might understand. "Your
Majesty," he said, "even the most intelligent of men, it
seems, have their wits clouded by excessive joy. You ought
long ago to have perceived that the gods did not favor the
sacrifice you prepared for them. Blessed Chariclea they
declared to be your daughter from the very altar. Her
foster father they brought here from the middle of Greece,
like a *deus ex machina*. The horses and bulls they filled with
panic and confusion at the very altar, indicating that even
victims which are regarded as most perfect must be rejected.
Now as the crown of their benefactions and as the culmina-
tion of their drama they reveal that the young stranger is
the betrothed of the maiden. Let us take cognizance of
these miraculous manifestations and let us be collaborators
in their divine will. Let us have recourse to holier offerings;
let us abolish human sacrifice forever."

These words Sisimithres pronounced in a clear voice, in
the hearing of all. Hydaspes took Chariclea and Theagenes
by the hand, and himself, too, spoke in the native tongue.
"All you here present," said he, "since these things have
come about by the will of the gods, to oppose them would
be impious. Therefore, in the presence of the gods who
have woven this web and of yourselves who have shown
yourselves amenable to their decrees, I declare this pair
united by the laws of marriage and authorize them to live
in procreative wedlock. And now, if you will, let our reso-

lution be confirmed by sacrifice and let us turn to our sacred duties."

These words the host acclaimed with a shout, and they clapped their hands as if the marriage were already being consummated. Hydaspes approached the altar, and as he was about to begin the ceremony he said, "Lord Sun and Lady Moon, since it is by your will that Theagenes and Charicleia have been declared man and wife, they may now lawfully becomes your priests." So saying he took off his own miter and Persinna's, the symbol of the priesthood, and put his on Theagenes and Persinna's on Charicleia. Upon this, Charicles recalled the oracle he had received in Delphi and found that the divine prophecy was confirmed by events. The oracle had said of the young people that upon departing from Delphi

> They will come to the dark land of the sun;
> There they will obtain the prize of their virtuous lives,
> A white crown upon dusky temples.

Crowned with white miters and invested with the priesthood the young pair performed their propitious sacrifice. Then, accompanied by lighted torches, with the music of flutes and pipes, Theagenes with Hydaspes rode on one chariot drawn by horses, Sisimithres with Charicles in another, and Charicleia with Persinna on a chariot drawn by white oxen. With felicitations, applause, and dances they were escorted to Meroe, where the more august marriage ceremonies would be celebrated with greater brilliance.

This is the end of the Ethiopica, the story of Theagenes and Charicleia. Its author is a Phoenician of Emesa, of the race of the Sun—the son of Theodosius, Heliodorus.